TOOTH AND TALON

Alex Hernandez

EDGE SCIENCE FICTION AND FANTASY PUBLISHING
An Imprint of HADES PUBLICATIONS, INC.
CALGARY

Tooth and Talon

Copyright © 2017 by Alex Hernandez

This is a work of fiction. Names, characters, places, and incidents are the products of the author's imagination or are used fictitiously and are not to be construed as real. Any resemblance to actual events, locales, organizations, or persons, living or dead, is entirely coincidental.

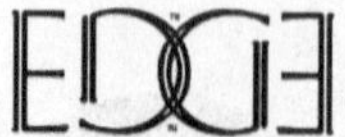

EDGE SCIENCE FICTION AND FANTASY PUBLISHING
An Imprint of HADES PUBLICATIONS, INC.
P.O. Box 1714, Calgary, Alberta, T2P 2L7, Canada

The EDGE Team:
Producer: Brian Hades
Acquisitions Editor: Michelle Heumann
Edited by: Heather Manuel
Cover Art: Julie Dillon
Cover Design: Brian Hades
Book Design: Mark Steele
Publicist: Janice Shoults

ISBN: 978-1-77053-162-8

EDGE Science Fiction and Fantasy Publishing and Hades Publications, Inc. acknowledges the ongoing support of the Alberta Foundation for the Arts and the Canada Council for the Arts for our publishing programme.

Library and Archives Canada Cataloguing in Publication
CIP Data on file with the National Library of Canada
ISBN: 978-1-77053-162-8
(e-Book ISBN: 978-1-77053-146-8)

FIRST EDITION
(20180130)
Printed in USA
www.edgewebsite.com

Publisher's Note:

Thank you for purchasing this book. It began as an idea, was shaped by the creativity of its talented author, and was subsequently molded into the book you have before you by a team of editors and designers.

Like all EDGE books, this book is the result of the creative talents of a dedicated team of individuals who all believe that books (whether in print or pixels) have the magical ability to take you on an adventure to new and wondrous places powered by the author's imagination.

As EDGE's publisher, I hope that you enjoy this book. It is a part of our ongoing quest to discover talented authors and to make their creative writing available to you.

We also hope that you will share your discovery and enjoyment of this novel on social media through Facebook, Twitter, Goodreads, Pinterest, etc., and by posting your opinions and/or reviews on Amazon and other review sites and blogs. By doing so, others will be able to share your discovery and passion for this book.

Brian Hades, publisher

Dedication

To Marjorie, Sophie and Beatrice for supporting me through the process of writing this book;

And to Octavia E. Butler for inspiring me.

Prologue

Oya launched herself out of the bridge and ran as fast as she could. The too-bright corridors of the ship stretched and wound like a nightmare labyrinth. She felt as clumsy as a toddler, or a newborn animal being hunted by a predator. Her own flesh was an unknown, a liability. The lingering pain from the biological attack slowed her escape — every joint inflamed, every muscle raw — but the fear and rage in her belly burned like a furnace, driving her forward. She turned a corner at random and barreled on, trying to lose her pursuer.

The silence cut through her panicked mind like an icicle. The normal chugs and whirls of the ship were gone, replaced by the quick scrape of talons behind her. Above her hoarse panting, the whistling of an extravagant language called her name, asked her to stop. She pushed harder. No one could help her now, everyone else on the ship — all the other ninety-nine colonists — were either dead or screaming, steeped in their own juices. The ship's higher functions had been lobotomized, its hollow carcass now floating over a grotesque planet teeming with harpies.

She tripped over bare feet that felt too large for her body and slammed into the floor. The odor of stale vomit hit her before she saw the drying puddle of bile a few inches away. Someone — Xing perhaps — had puked while in this very passageway. A flash of her friend twisting in agony invaded her mind. Oya pushed herself up, jumped over the vomit, and ran. The *Hurricane* was a big vessel, but its living and working spaces were limited. There weren't many places to hide.

The whistling became singing, harsh and beautiful. He pleaded with her, begging her to stop and talk. She'd been lulled by this creature's song before, and everything had gone wrong. The mission was on the verge of collapse, if it hadn't already. She was light years from Earth, from anything recognizable as human. She was alone, except for the monster gaining on her. And a part of her, back behind the eclipsing fear, knew that it was all her fault. Her arrogance and self-righteousness had jeopardized their lives. She had made a misplaced sacrifice, and now regret — and something else — was trying desperately to devour her.

She needed to hide. The scarlet death chasing her could have run her down on her best day, even with all her artificial enhancements working overtime. But now, with all of that gone, she simply delayed the inevitable by scurrying through these white, exposed halls. *Was he toying with her, tiring her out?* She stumbled over her heavy, treacherous feet again, but this time managed not to fall. *Where was she going anyway?* There was nowhere to go on this sleeping ship.

She saw the door to the engine room and immediately thought of grabbing a tool and standing her ground, but the door failed to open. The *Hurricane* no longer recognized her. Oya pounded on the door once and kept going. *Why doesn't this damned harpy, this killer, just leave her alone?* She knew she had hurt him just as much as he had hurt her. *Didn't he want to lick his wounds?* All she wanted to do was hide, scrunch herself into a little ball and ... *what, die? Would she be running this fiercely if she really wanted to die? No. She needed to rest, to be able to fight later on.*

She passed a glass panel as she lumbered forward and caught a glimpse of the fuzzy, grayish-white cap on her head. She thought she looked like the grandmother who had raised her, and, for the first time in more than a hundred years, Oya felt very old and weary.

An excruciating sound, like the upper register of a clarinet, blasted behind her, too close. She actually slowed from the fright. Then a gust from large wings, and the prick of claws on her shoulders, forced her against the cool glass of the wall. His scent entered her nostrils, salty with sweat and spiced with alien botanicals, deceptively delicious. Her face pressed alongside the reflection of her grandmother. The assault was almost gentle.

"Don't run away from me," he warbled in her ear, making the skin on the back of her neck crawl. His breath stank of blood and venom.

"Leave me alone!" Oya kicked back like an angry mule and the harpy doubled over, his red wings swaddling his stomach, his fangs visible as he gasped for air. Maybe she wasn't as weak as she felt. *Maybe.* Still, he had caught her and would again if she lingered.

She rushed into one of the public restrooms down the corridor and crouched behind the toilet. The privacy feature on the door would normally lock when someone was inside, but the microscopic machines inside her body that identified her to the ship were now inoperable and being profusely sweated out her pores. That too was her fault. *My God, maybe she deserved this!*

For long moments, only quiet, and the lemony scent of antiseptic cleaners, filled her world. Oya knew that harpies, like some birds, could sense magnetic fields, but she hoped the metal and electronics within the ship masked her presence. Blood pumped in her ears; her vision blurred and refocused intermittently. She couldn't think of what to do next. Whether he found her or not, she was stuck.

The door hissed open, and she knew she was caught. She didn't look up, kept her face buried deep in her knees — and cried. But she could feel him standing over her, his keen eyes bearing into her. She hated that she was crying. It made everything worse. If she still had the mechanical curators circulating in her system, she could shut down the frail, petrified, sniveling part of herself. As soon as the thought formed, she could almost hear her grandmother saying, *Maybe that's why you made so many stupid mistakes, girl, you divorced yourself from the parts of you that made you mindful.*

He said nothing. He simply watched her with that reptilian stillness of his kind. Then, when he was sure she wasn't going to fight back, he said, in that bird-like voice, "We don't have to trust each other, Oya, but we're trapped on this derelict, and if we want to survive, we're going to have to work together."

She looked up at him and tried to focus on that deceivingly human face, the melancholy eyes. The harpy had the handsome, chiseled features of someone adept at manipulating genetics. Harpy wasn't even a proper descriptor. No, he looked more like a young Icarus with bioengineered wings. His hair was a short red crest that swept back like a cardinal's. Involuntarily, her eyes darted toward the inhuman attributes. His arms were scarlet wings with black feather tips and three clawed-digits instead of hands. From the knees down, his legs looked like those of a bird's, with his feet ending in the splayed talons of theropods. She mustered enough courage to speak. "I don't want to be near you, Inirigua." The feel of his name on her lips made her gag.

"Very well. We've got a whole starship to get lost in. We can carve out our separate territories, and we don't even have to see each other, but we're going to have to coordinate somehow. The last thing your friend, the woman, said to me was that your ship no longer listens to you."

"I know." She forced herself to stand. Her knees shook. She felt ill beyond just nerves and exhaustion. Her forehead burned.

"I didn't kill her. I tried to save her." His cheeks and chin were grimy with blood. The claws at the end of his wings looked like freshly used meat hooks.

"Just give me time." If she could heal her remaining crewmates and the innocent colonists, who had no idea what had just happened to them, if she could somehow get them all safely to that awful planet below, they would be okay. She could make it okay. "It won't work without trust," she found herself saying, and she knew, deep in her wrenching gut, that it was right. "But I don't trust you right now."

Deep disappointment filled his liquid eyes. It was such a human expression that it obliterated all of the saurian qualities in him. A man stood before her, looking at her with despair. "I'll give you time, Oyavalette, but if you can't bring yourself to trust me sooner or later — and I won't blame you if you can't — then we can die together up here."

This was a person — highly modified — but still a human being. Oya had forgotten that, and it shamed her. If she intended to make things right, she had to be better. Still, she couldn't bring herself to take the rending claw jutting out of his crimson wing. She could smell the gore rising from him. The memory was too vivid. She swallowed the burning lump in her throat. "Just give me time."

Chapter 1

Earth - 2258 A.D.

Oya Valette was lost.

The antigrav plane, on loan from the Hominocracy, sped over the Caribbean Sea. Its onboard computer sifted through old data and triangulated satellite beams, trying to find a tiny, desolate island within the archipelago that made up the Lesser Antilles. Oya had been born on the island of Chandeleur almost half a century ago. She knew it was somewhere between St. Lucia and Barbados, but she no longer remembered its exact location. She hadn't been on the island since she left for college. Then she had gotten a job flying tourists around the inner solar system, and that's when Super Storm Theresa decimated the whole place and left her no reason to return.

"Target identified," rang the plane's computer. Oya steered the black, triangular vehicle toward the small isle. She finally caught sight of a green patch shaped like a tear drop amidst all the blue.

It wasn't nostalgia that drove Oya back to her home now. It was her grandmother, the only person stubborn enough not to have evacuated the insignificant dot of land when the 17,341 other residents fled. Apparently, when she retired from Avant Genomics, she had begged and coerced several large organizations into funding a restoration project. She'd been living in a mobile home on the island, planting trees, ever since.

Oya wheeled above Chandeleur until she spotted her grandmother's high-tech trailer a kilometer from the beach, hidden among mangroves and palms. She wasn't sure, but she thought it might be in the same place where their large old house had once stood. She settled the plane on the shore and got out.

The Caribbean sun immediately began to burn her naturally dark skin, and it reminded her why she never missed this place. She stretched, interlocking her fingers and lifting her arms as high as they would go, and then she pushed them further, arching her back until she achieved that delicious point between pleasure and pain.

Oya Valette moved as if threatening to take flight.

Her tall, lean physique gave the impression that she'd been born on some celestial body with much lighter gravity, like Luna or Mercury. But she had been born and raised on covetous Earth and had grown tall in defiance of its full and unfair one gee gravity. And so, her entire manner had remained insolent throughout her life.

She stopped to tie her long black hair into a loose bun and then sprinted toward the rectangular box veiled by the tropical forest.

She moved inland, away from the surf and the caw of seagulls, and into the shade of the young caimito trees and banyans. Gone were all the little pink and blue houses that clung like pastel barnacles to the slopes of Mont Vòl. It was as if Oya had been transported to the island's primeval past, where all that existed were immature trees and birds. She plucked a violet fruit from a tree and played with it, tossing it from one hand to the other. Oya had to give her grandmother credit; the island was an absolute Eden. Even with its many ecological disasters, Earth was still beautiful. Why would anyone want to leave such a lush, green world, so perfectly suited for humans, and willingly adopt the hostile, poisonous environs of space? No, her grandmother wouldn't understand her joining the Hominocracy. This trip would end in argument.

Oya was drenched in sweat when she got to where the town square — what the locals unpretentiously called Downtown — used to be. A trio of white ibises glided in and landed on what had once been Pwèmyé Street. They poked in the soil with their long, red beaks. She recalled voluptuous, bronze-skinned women parading down the boulevard in little more than colorful plumage. They smiled and sambaed to the Calypso rhythms of the steel pans carried by bare-chested men. The scent of curried crab and kabobs wafted up from the vendor carts. A little girl, wearing a crown of yellow feathers, danced to the music and pageantry, shouting, *"Se yon bon tan!"* with hands outstretched for candy and beaded necklaces.

It was all gone now, and Oya watched a different procession as little emerald hummingbirds zipped around the red blooms of a Royal Poinciana. It amazed her how quickly the birds from neighboring islands had colonized this rock. It was a testament to life. She wondered if she would long for this steaming, flamboyant mess once she was cooped up on a sterile space ship light years away. She had never missed it before.

But it was too late for second thoughts now. She had accepted the full complement of permanent curators into her system. The cost of those tiny machines that fastidiously repaired and maintained her genome like — well, like doting curators, had been extraordinary. She was contractually bound to serve in the Hominocracy for twenty years to pay off the debt. They needed experienced spacecraft pilots trained in Antigravity Aviation. She would use them, and they would use her. *Besides,* she thought, *what was twenty years to someone who could potentially live forever?* She had to tell her grandmother, though. She was prepared for a fight, as had happened many times before, but she owed her the truth.

Oya knocked on the trailer door twice, took a deep breath, and opened it without waiting for a reply. Her grandmother, wearing a white cotton house dress, lay on a cot reading a beat up old birding guide. In her old age, Oya's grandmother had taken up painting, and splashy watercolors of macaws and flamingos adorned the aluminum walls.

"You made it." Osala had always been an imposing, big-boned woman, so seeing her shriveled and frail struck Oya more than the oppressive heat.

"*Sa ou fè, gwan man man?*" The long-dormant Kwéyòl came pouring out of Oya like sweat. She carefully leaned over and hugged her grandmother.

"I'm fine. Come and eat something."

The oily smell of fried yams invoked even more childhood memories and would probably cling to her hair for days. Oya cracked open a frosty can of coconut water and sat at the pullout table for two.

"How's that British husband of yours?" her grandmother asked, placing the deep orange slices of sweet potato in front of her. Her hands were inflamed and warped by arthritis.

"Isaac? We're no longer together. Haven't been for about a year." Oya ate a slice, mentally commanding her curators to take care of all the grease and salt before it was absorbed by her body.

"That's eight years of marriage… Were you unhappy?"

"Not really." *Wasn't she?* "We were just on different trajectories." This was her fourth serious relationship. After a while, they all got stale. Wasn't that part of the reason she had joined the Hominocracy, to do something different, something exciting?

"You make it sound so businesslike."

Oya raised her can in a mock toast and winked at her grandmother. "I guess I'm just not the romantic type."

Osala kissed her on the head and patted her shoulder. "No, girl. It's hard to bond with someone when there are no children who need you, when you don't grow old together and need each other. You're forever young and independent and quick to move on."

Her grandmother had a way of making the things Oya appreciated sound like bad things. "I don't really want to talk about it. You make it seem like I'm doomed to be alone." Oya cleaned the plate with the last piece of yam and downed it.

"Not alone, just never in a lasting, rewarding relationship. Come on." The old woman hobbled out of the camper with Oya silently in tow. "I wanted to show you something out back." She disappeared behind her modest dwelling.

Oya waded through a small garden packed with leafy plants she recognized as yams and malanga, surrounded by neat rows of papaya and banana trees. She followed the hints of white from her grandmother's dress amid all the overwhelming green. The scent of damp soil mingled with the sea salt on the breeze, and Oya realized she had just eaten from *this* garden. This is what her *gwan man man* lived off. She sustained herself from the bosom of Chandeleur.

Oya heard the loud chirping before she saw the hundreds of little wooden cages containing delicate lemon-yellow birds. The cages were stacked in the shadow of a large avocado tree. "What is this?"

"Sunny warblers. You used to love them when you were a little girl. You always wore a coronet made of their feathers for carnival. Don't you remember?"

"I was just thinking of that on the walk here, actually."

"You know this particular subspecies is endemic to our island, and they went extinct years ago. I think I've restored the native vegetation and insect populations enough to release them."

"How do you have so many if they were extinct?" Oya was afraid her grandmother's mental faculties were slipping. In fifty-three years of life, Oya had never experienced naked old age before. Like the birds and children, the elderly were an endangered subspecies of humanity.

"I used my obeah science to bring them back from the dead." Her grandmother smiled, and the brown leathery skin on her face creased unpleasantly. "I cloned them from your old collection of headdresses. You didn't think I kept those dusty things, but I did. I had to insert genes from the Jamaican yellow warbler breed to fill in the damaged sections of DNA, but they're mostly original. I just hope we don't get any hurricanes this year. The birds need time to settle."

"*Gwan me*, the birds are nice, but how are *you* feeling?"

"I'm fine, love, old age is not a disease. I don't need you to worry."

"A hundred and eighty-six is hardly old!"

Osala waved at her concerned granddaughter as if she were talking nonsense and said, "Did you know that the Taíno name for this island was Biekibogiael, which means 'small island of birds.' When the French got here, they saw the trees teeming with these flame-colored warblers and thought the whole display looked like a candle mass, so they called the island La Chandeleur. These yellow birds have defined this island for centuries." Her grandmother swayed a bit and put her hand up to her forehead. "Releasing them will be a fine bookend to my project."

"Are you okay?" Fear seized Oya. Or was it guilt, because she rarely thought of her grandmother when she was away?

"It's just too hot. I should take a nap in the trailer. I was dozing off when you barged in," Osala said with that wrinkly smile again, this time a little fainter. "We'll release the birds at sunset. It'll be cooler then, and they really start to sing when they stake out their roost for the night."

"I've talked to your doctor. He said that if you took, at the very least, a temporary dose of curators into your system, you'd be fine."

"I took the genetic treatments when I was younger, but I don't want those things creeping around inside my body. I don't want to live forever. I'm tired, and it's unnatural. They rob you of something vital. I don't know what it is, but they make you less than what you were." She stopped and peered suspiciously at her granddaughter. "You look younger, like you did when you were twenty. Have you taken another shot of those things?"

"Just enough to smooth out the wrinkles," Oya lied, and it pained her to do so.

Her grandmother shook her head. "I just need a damned nap."

Oya ushered her back to the cot in the shade of the trailer and helped her lay down. Her grandmother pointed to a downy wreath hanging on the wall. "That's the only headdress that's left now. I couldn't bring myself to dissolve it."

Oya went and touched the soft, blonde crown as if the object itself contained her childhood memories.

"Did you like the birdies, dear?"

"Yes, they're lovely."

"I'm sorry about killing them all, but I brought them back for you," her grandmother whispered, and then fell asleep.

Chapter 2

HS Hurricane - 2323 A.D.

The *HS Hurricane's* bubble drive cut off as the vessel popped into conventional space. The command crew's cryopods automatically dialed down and whispered open. Oya Valette found herself twenty-three light years from home, just outside the Beta Hydri system. She blinked until her eyes focused on the receding frost on the pod's transparent lid. She tried to stretch the soreness out of her body, but the warmth of the foam interior held her still. Oya laid there. Her final conversation with her grandmother still echoed in her head, even though it had taken place decades ago, around another star. *Funny how random neurons fire when coming out of cryo*, she thought.

The entire ship — her pod, the adjacent medical equipment, the holographic emitters embedded in the ceiling, even the external sensors — constantly communicated with the machines in her body. The ones threshed with the neurons in her brain translated electrochemical signals into simple commands. Without getting up, giving her curators a chance to stimulate her long dormant muscles, she tossed up a lightscreen and checked on things. Data filled the rectangle of light projected in front of her. Everyone was still asleep except for the bridge crew. After the long interstellar flight, the *Hurricane* passed all inspection checks. They would need a pilot soon, so she'd been revived.

She found it difficult to concentrate on the monotonous reports with the memories of her grandmother still vivid in her mind. Osala had adamantly chosen to die by refusing to admit curators into her body. In the years that followed, Oya had thrown herself into her work, taking unnecessary risks. She finally achieved notoriety when she penetrated Jupiter's crushing atmosphere in her one-woman ship. She had brazenly flown through the eye of the planet's Big Red Spot. *Finally?* No, not finally. Never finally.

After that, she hit a plateau and her grandmother's words about lacking something vital crept back into her life, spoiling things.

She told herself that she had signed up for this mission because the old Sol system provided very little in the way of challenges for someone like her, but something in the back of her newly-awakened brain told her she wanted to escape her grandmother's perceptive guilt-stricken ghost.

"Oya, are you getting up or what?" Xing's voice shouted over the comm.

"Yes, I'm up. Give me a minute."

"Liar. I can tell you're still in your pod. Hurry! We found something interesting."

Oya shook off her maudlin languor. She placed her hands on the smooth, white edge of her pod's opening. The round, bulky coffin inclined gracefully with her intention to rise; its tubes and cables disconnected with a click and neatly stored themselves.

She was in a whole other solar system, an alien solar system. Her smile at the thought pushed her grandmother to the back of her mind, and she opened up another lightscreen with a view of the world outside the ship. The place was almost bare of planets. Beta Hyrdi shone as a brilliant point of light, harsh but unassuming, in a field of stars. Another speck shone brightly in the image, a large gas giant — one that must have consumed all of the other planets in the system long ago. The ship was still too far away for her to see if there were any small planets huddling in the inner plane, but she knew there were. Telescopes and probes had told them as much. The gas giant was far enough away that a few rocky planets had survived around the tight habitable zone. The Hominocracy believed that at least one was livable, which was why they were here.

She played some music, something slow and dreamy. Rodrigo Sasako's *Winds of Saturn in the Springtime*. She walked past one hundred other white, round shells that filled the large room, each incubating a slumbering colonist, and jumped into one of the small showers in the locker room at the far end of the vast chamber. When she finished, she got her uniform from her locker and idly dressed to the fluid bass-baritone of the singer, like a striptease in reverse. There was something about the deep male Japanese voice, shaped by a Latin sensibility, that melted her. She remembered going to one of Sasako's concerts on Vesta decades ago. It was the closest thing to love at first sight that she'd ever experienced. When the song ended, she cut the music and made her way down the corridor toward the bridge.

The captain and bridge crew were already settled at their posts. It had been three years since she had actually seen them, but there was no appreciable difference. Captain Anton Hershkovitz's close-cropped brown hair hadn't grown a millimeter during their trip. His trimmed beard had retained its straight edge, accentuating his chiseled jaw. He looked rugged and plainly handsome, in the proud tradition of American rocket jockeys or action movie stars, but his eyes looked out of place — worn-out, old, and damaged.

"Look who decided to join us." Captain Hershkovitz nodded, his eyes brightening marginally. "Thought I would have to fly this thing myself."

"Just glad you guys finally decided to thaw me out." Oya sat down and scanned her console. "Lots of radio noise in this system, Captain," she reported, a bit surprised, but they had probably already noticed. This was the interesting thing Xing had mentioned. "Long range sensors confirm the presence of a planet orbiting at 1.9 AUs from the star. Within this star's habitable zone. We're not alone."

All humor evaporated from Hershkovitz's face. "Glad you're caught up."

"Could it be the robots?" Commander Carlo Davoli asked from his station. He was a wall of a man, big and broad. He looked etched out of stone, with a hard, tan face that betrayed his apparent youth. He sounded nervous. The robots were God-like machines that kept to themselves, but no Hominocracy ship that entered their systems had ever been heard from again.

"Nah, I doubt it. They only build their Solariums around stars with no biology sustaining worlds," Captain Hershkovitz said, tapping instructions into his own console, readying the colonists' curators to get them out of cryo upon command. "All right, let's proceed carefully. Davoli, try and decode the radio emissions coming off that world. Diwa, send a probe, something with the biggest sensor suite available. Valette, take us in. And all of you, let me know the second you find any other signs of activity. A small sub-Mars planet like this one is ideal harpy country."

Information Officer Diwa shot a sensor package deeper into the system. Immediately, figures rendered in light began cascading around her. "Sir, the planet is tidally locked to the star. Much of the surface appears to be inhospitable," she said through a curtain of data. Xing Ana Maria Diwa was tiny, especially next to Davoli, and even with her curators maintaining her figure, she was rather curvy. Her black hair was cut short like a boy's and her smile was dazzling. She was trying to hide it, but the woman was practically giddy to be in Beta Hydri.

"Don't mean a thing. Mars and the moons of Sol were also inhospitable, but that didn't stop those degenerates from nesting there. We know flocks of them escaped the Culling, and as we push out into the galaxy, we're going to have to come to terms with them," Captain Hershkovitz said.

Oya turned to the captain and asked, "What course do we take if we do find harpies here, sir?"

"We'll worry about that if, and when, we find them. But I'll tell you right now, Valette, it's going to be a hell of a lot harder to successfully establish a colony on that rock with harpies flying around."

"Hard but not impossible," added Davoli.

Oya was too young to have lived through the shameful cleansing of the Sol system's posthuman element in 2192. She had inherited a system bustling with classical humanity. Now, bored with the tedious task of flying the *Hurricane* through empty space, she searched the ship's memory for information about the harpies. She slyly piped the information directly into her head so as not to let her captain know she was partitioning her attention at this crucial point in their mission.

According to the computer's records, the avian race had been born circa 2098. The American colonists on Luna had incorporated dinosaur DNA into their genomes to enjoy recreational flight in the lighter gravity. Archaeopteryx genes were preferred because they allowed the subject to retain three digits on each hand, including an opposable thumb. They could turn their arms into wings and still type on a console, sip from a teacup, hold a lover's hand, but what they never mentioned was that at the end of each finger there was a seven-centimeter, sickle-like claw — a talon — designed by natural selection specifically for tearing open the soft flesh holding in intestines and vital organs.

Soon after that, fashion and competition drove them to splice utahraptors into themselves, while the Pan-Asians on Titan were becoming a little bit sinornithosaurus. The trend of genetic modification continued unchecked until 2186. That's when ships powered by faster and cheaper fusion drives, nuclear engines with thrusters as mighty as hydrogen bombs, opened up the solar system to Earth's baseline humans, who became appalled by the previously isolated pockets of humanity's wanton transgenic changes.

Oya snapped to attention as the *Hurricane* passed the super-Jupiter, the devourer of lesser planets, and adjusted for the gas giant's gravitational pull. She cut the feed to her head, thinking that Captain Hershkovitz was about one hundred and thirty-something years old and probably remembered these bird people first hand.

"I think I have enough information now to construct a sharper image of the planet," Diwa said, bringing up a high-resolution hologram of the world at the center of the bridge. The crew stations were arranged as a semicircle hugging the image, which looked like the fourteenth billiard ball. "The side that constantly faces Beta Hydri is a massive desert, which I've labeled the Saharan Hemisphere. The side facing away is a frozen wasteland, the Antarctic Hemisphere. Here's the kicker, though. There's a strip the width of Texas running around the planet from pole to pole, hugging the terminator. Due to the atmosphere circulating heat and cold around the planet, this strip is perfectly habitable."

"Nice job," said the captain, looking at the unusually striped sphere directly in front of him. "First Pilot Valette, park us over the habitable area. We'll continue studying the world from orbit, but I think we've arrived at our destination."

Oya piloted the angelfish-like starship toward the planet. The resolution of their hologram sharpened with proximity. From her vantage point, she could see the icy nightside more clearly; mountain ranges and glacial seas came into focus.

Suddenly, three red squares began blinking on the globe. Everyone stopped what they were doing.

"Settlements?" asked Captain Hershkovitz.

"Yes, our own sensors are confirming the probe's incoming readings," said Oya, studying her instrumentation. "There appear to be three separate settlements hovering sixty meters above the ground."

"Floating cities? I'd say that's a definite sign of harpy occupancy. Send a microprobe to each of those targets."

"I can confirm that," reported Diwa. "My automation just tapped into the local Astronet. We're dealing with at least three harpy cultures here. I'm not even going to try and pronounce the planet's local name, but it translates to something like 'large feathered' or 'winged serpent.'"

"That's ominous." Oya turned to Xing, who replied with an exaggerated grimace.

"Tag it as Quetzalcoatl and let's move on," the captain said, catching their wordless exchange. "This isn't a linguistics course. Oya, eyes on the road."

Oya straightened and returned her attention to the growing planet on the console. She had to admit that the blue-green forested band encircling the alien world did indeed look like a feathered snake coiled around a giant rock. With short, controlled bursts of plasma, she inserted the ship between their new home and its small rocky moon.

"There's also a strange anomaly at the center of the Saharan Hemisphere. It could be a solar collector, but it isn't feeding power to any of the settlements."

"Send a microprobe, but let's just focus on the urban centers for now, Diwa. We'll go exploring after we've settled in and know more about what's going on here." Hershkovitz's voice sounded tight despite his informal demeanor.

Commander Davoli walked over to the image of Quetzalcoatl and examined it as if appraising a work of art. His eyes froze over, but he spoke in a soft voice. "We fire our lasers on them now. Three quick surgical strikes will save us a lot of misery going forward."

"We can't fire upon defenseless, unsuspecting people," Oya snapped, shocked at the casual suggestion of genocide. "We cannot repeat the Hominocracy's past mistakes here in Beta Hydri. I did not sign up for that." Osala's spirit would not rest on this trip. The half-forgotten promise she'd made to her grandmother surged within her like a long-dormant genetic disease. *Were principles a disease?*

Commander Davoli stared at their First Pilot with cool contempt for a long moment, and then, without saying a word, looked to Captain Hershkovitz. Something unspoken passed between them, and Oya realized that Commander Davoli was also old enough to have lived through the Culling. Participate in it, perhaps?

Information Officer Diwa was the one who broke the silence. "I would advise against anything so bold. This isn't like puncturing the airtight aviaries on Mars or Titan. These cities appear to be loose collections of structures floating independently, each with its own antigrav motor or something similar. Attacking from orbit with lasers would be equivalent to bobbing for apples."

"Nukes then?" The commander wasn't letting up.

"You'd be making what is already very limited and valuable land, uninhabitable."

"We're not going to attack them," the captain finally said. He rubbed his head roughly, moving his hand down until he squeezed the back of his neck. When he lifted his hand, the white impressions of his fingertips still burned on his pink flesh. "The Culling is long behind us, and we've changed, as I'm sure they have. This is a chance for a new beginning, and we're not going to be the ones to ruin it."

The captain's statement sounded flat and rehearsed to Oya, as if Xing's practical objections against butchery had been the thing to sway him instead of the moral argument. Still, Oya was glad for it.

"We should make contact with their leaders, send down a non-threatening representative to state our intentions of establishing our own settlement on the planet." The captain looked to his commander.

"I'll go," Oya blurted out, wondering what she was thinking. The thought of going down to a planet full of humanoid, feathered dinosaurs both terrified her and excited her, the same volatile mix of emotions that drove her to leave everything behind and set out for a new star system in the first place.

Captain Hershkovitz stared at her, unconvinced. "You have no diplomatic training, First Pilot."

"As Info Officer of the *HS Hurricane*, I should be the one to go," Xing protested.

It was too late to reconsider, and she had inherited her grandmother's stubbornness, so Oya pressed on. "No, Xing, we need you here to continue processing the data coming in from the probes and ship's sensors, and draft a report back to Earth. Our trip is over. We aren't going anywhere, so my schedule has been considerably freed up."

"You do have a point," Hershkovitz said, scratching his beard. "Okay, but before you go down Valette, remove all security locks on your curators. You should be more than a match for those savages if they try anything."

"Mission specifics, sir?" She felt woozy. The reality of it started to sink in. What the hell had she gotten herself into? Was her life so meaningless that she could easily throw it away? She knew that Xing was wirelessly transmitting a barrage of disapproval directly into her head, but she couldn't process it, and cut her off.

"Pick one of the settlements. Tell them we're a civilian ship and that we want to start a small colony somewhere within the habitable region. I'll handle any further negotiations. You're simply our olive branch. Report to the infirmary and have your curators militarized at once."

"Yes, sir." Oya ignored the obvious contradiction, and, without another word, got up from the flight station and left the bridge, utterly convinced that she was going to get ripped to shreds down there, which would give Davoli a tidy little excuse to annihilate those poor creatures. Still, her grandmother's spirit strengthened her, reducing her fear, and compelled her to do the honorable thing.

— «» —

Oya walked down the chilly passageway of the empty ship. She had the kitchen builders make her a turkey sandwich and got a coke. She took the meal with her to the infirmary. She hopped onto the pallet and ate, lost in thought. A large mechanical spider descended from the ceiling and began scanning her with its countless articulate arms.

"Please be patient as the civilian locks are removed from your curators, First Pilot Oya Valette," said the medical automation, as the arachnid clicked and whirled back up to its hiding place. She swung her legs back and forth, lightly kicking the base of the pallet with her heels. The regular thuds slowed her racing heart.

She took a bite of the cold sandwich and noticed Xing standing in the entrance, hands on hips, extreme disapproval distorting her face.

"Aren't you supposed to be on the bridge coordinating your probes?" Oya asked.

"You were ignoring my messages!"

"I can ignore you in person, too," Oya said, and forced a smile while taking a sip of her drink. She had grown to like the gentle woman from Venus during their year-long training stint at the Haumea Facility on the edge of the Sol system. Even after the awkwardness of gently turning down Xing's not-so-subtle sexual advances, they had bonded almost immediately. She had started pushing Xing to be more adventurous, and Xing curbed her more self-destructive impulses. They worked well together and were a good counter-balance to the Hershkovitz-Davoli team.

"Oya, you didn't have to volunteer to go down there. The captain would never have sent you if you hadn't opened your mouth. We need you to get us the hell out of here if things go wrong."

"I know, but he would've sent Davoli instead, which would almost guarantee that things would go wrong. We'd probably all be embroiled in a war with the locals before tea time. This way is better."

"I don't think he was serious about the nukes," Xing said, sitting next to her. Oya checked the progress of her curator's weaponization. *Almost there.* "I think he's scared shitless like the rest of us and he talks tough to make himself feel better."

Oya shrugged, took a bite, and replied with her mouth full, "It doesn't matter. I'll be fine. I've done crazier things before and always survived."

"Yeah, what's your plan?" Xing asked, dubious.

"I don't know yet. I'll talk to them, gain their trust, maybe offer them something valuable that I can manufacture with the simple builders onboard the lander… I really don't know. I'll wing it. I *do* perform better under pressure."

"The old beads-and-trinkets approach." Xing shook her head in overstated disappointment. "Come on, you know better than that. You should wait. Maybe I can convince the captain to let me go down with you. I can be your one-woman diplomatic team."

"That's really sweet, Xing, and I appreciate it, but I don't think it'll be that big a deal."

"Oya, don't be so stubborn about this!"

"Unfortunately, stubbornness is in my genetic makeup, and when you've lived as long as I have, you come to understand that you're not going to change, not really." For the first time, it occurred to Oya that if she'd had a baby with her fourth husband, Isaac, the child would be about Xing's age now. *Scary.* Maybe that's why she had latched on to her on that dwarf planet? The woman seemed so endearingly insular; she had never left Venus, and certainly not the inner system, until Haumea. Now here she was, being the voice of reason. Scolding Oya. *Xing had actually changed quite a lot,* Oya thought, impressed.

"Damn it, be serious." Xing gave her a rough shove, and Oya's newly-touchy curators became alert, zeroing in on Xing as a potential threat. "This is a delicate situation that you're coolly dropping into."

Coolly? She didn't feel very cool; her knees were shaking terribly. Sweat glazed her brow. Perhaps Xing was interpreting that as anticipation. "Look, if it's as bad as all that, then all the more reason to go down alone. You're young. You could have a good, exciting life here. I wouldn't want you to throw it away on the very first excursion. Let me clear a path for you, for all the colonists onboard."

"You did enough for me at the training facility," Xing said. "Let me repay that infamous pilot that took a rookie Info Officer under her wing by helping you with this."

"Diwa, your break is over, please report to the bridge." Captain Hershkovitz stood at the entrance. "I need a word with Valette."

"That's you," Oya said, motioning toward the door.

"You know that sandwich might very well be your last meal."

"Oh, shut it!"

Xing bit her lip, then said, "Be careful, Oya, and be sensitive to the locals. Don't try to run rough shot over them."

"I won't. And Xing." Oya eyed the captain, who only crossed his arms and wrinkled his brow. "Don't be afraid to speak up on the bridge — especially if you see something questionable — you're smarter and tougher than you think."

Xing gave her a warm hug and left. Oya's thin film of courage almost broke, but she held steady.

"Captain?"

"That's a good friend you got there," Captain Hershkovitz said, taking a step into the room and letting the door close behind him.

"The best."

"Oya, I want to be honest with you." He cleared his throat and his expression softened. "I want this mission to succeed. My wife is sleeping in one of those pods. We came here to finally start a family, you know, like most people on this ship. I have no appetite for war. But we only have enough fuel to generate one more bubble. So, we can either go back home or move on to another unexplored system and hope there's a suitable planet waiting for us there. Neither of those options are appealing to me or the Hominocracy." His rigid posture sagged a bit under the weight of that admission.

He looked away, and Oya felt stupid and exposed sitting on her pallet with a half-eaten sandwich and coke in her hands. The smell of turkey and mustard added to the absurdity of the situation. She opened her mouth to reply but just took a sip from her drink instead.

"Your instincts are probably correct about Davoli." The captain met her gaze again, scratching his beard. "He's been through a lot and I'm sure he didn't emerge unscathed, but don't underestimate these harpies. They're just as cruel, probably more so because of their alterations. If I send Xing, she'd almost certainly get eaten alive down there." He paused, then shook his head as if purging some gruesome image from his mind and crossed his arms again. "I was going to go down myself when you volunteered. I was going to meet with them personally, you know. Lay it all out there, but the idea of you going didn't strike me as completely ridiculous." He allowed himself a smile. "I can stay up here and keep Davoli's darker impulses in check with the peace of mind that someone capable and compassionate is down there advocating for us."

"Thank you, sir."

"Don't thank me, Oya, just give me a scenario where we all get to share this rock without a whole lot of bloodshed." He patted her shoulder and walked out of the med bay.

Oya finished her banal sandwich and coke, meditating on the captain's words and wishing she had ordered something better.

Then, when the automation gave her the go ahead, she left the infirmary and walked to her locker in the cryo-room, retrieving a little yellow feather, the one personal possession she had allowed herself to bring all the way from Earth. If she was going to die down there, she wanted the little piece of Chandeleur, of her *gwan me*, with her.

She hurried, clomping down the metal stairs to the hangar bay, instead of taking the lift. She didn't want to think anymore, she wanted to act. The grease and metal tang of the lower deck put her in the right mindset. One of the small drop ships had automatically awoken, white and yellow lights blinking. The rows of larger shuttles, the ones that would ferry colonists down to their new home, lay dormant. Her ship's hatch opened as she approached. She hesitated for an instant, puffing out her cheeks as she exhaled slowly.

Oya entered the conical lander; her training and years of practice instantly kicked in. She routinely checked and doubled checked the systems wirelessly and asked the onboard computer to play her some music. Minutes later, the drop ship detached itself from the *Hurricane* and plummeted into the steamy atmosphere of Quetzalcoatl, leaving behind a hot fuchsia streak in its wake to the guitar intro of Jimi Hendrix's *Are You Experienced?* The tiny vessel was stealthy and registered on harpy radars as an unassuming meteorite. Oya experienced eight minutes of uncontrolled terror as she fell toward the planet, and then the lander's antigrav motors fired and Oya steadily descended toward the strange wilderness a few kilometers away from the largest floating city on the planet.

From what she could tell, the jungle appeared to be a blend of hardy, deep-blue indigenous plants that looked like a cross between giant, prehistoric ferns and sea fans, and green trees introduced from Earth. These couldn't out-compete the native plants, but clung on doggedly nevertheless.

All of a sudden it was over, and the derrick touched down on the alien soil with a soul-shaking thud. *Have you ever been experienced?* Jimi sang.

She ordered the lander's sensors to analyze the environment outside and fed the information directly to her curators, which made subtle adjustments to her biology to compensate for the small differences in environmental chemistry. When the microscopic machines had completed their job, Oya took a deep breath, strapped a sidearm to her right thigh, and stepped out into the strange, humid morning.

Chapter 3

Quetzalcoatl

Inirigua beat his wings harder, straightening his legs behind him, all six toes pointed out like a diver as he sliced through the concealing cloud deck, into the skirmish. Hundreds of brightly-colored bodies frantically flapped in a tight knot above the city, like a firework display of blood and plumage. There was a subtle order to the mad orgy of flocking and fighting. Ancient instincts.

He tried picking out the members of his red-feathered clan and spotted a few among the black-feathered Carica and the blue-feathered Macu. It was harder now to recognize clan kinship by pigment alone. He himself had mostly red and black plumage. Since before their arrival on this planet, some twenty years back, the clans had been mixing in order to incorporate any genetic advantage held by rival clans. His clan, the Vanacan, had allied themselves with the Carica on the long migration from the Sol system. The Macu were a different story. Their strict religious outlook made them harder to work with. In fact, he was participating in this event to change that.

Inirigua shot through the perpetual dawn high above the aquamarine forests and towering pagodas. He was fast, probably the fastest raptor in this absurd ritual battle for status, but that wasn't worth crap in an actual fight, except maybe to fly away, which would shame his family and endanger the nascent accord with the Macu.

Entering the fight, he savagely kicked at the wings and heads of the other combatants. He had his keen raptorial eye on a particularly beautiful fighter, and attaining the highest rank today would allow him to perform the mating dance with her.

Suddenly a Macu, young and strong, with wings so blue they glowed violet, crashed head-on into Inirigua. They kicked and pummeled each other with their wings. He took care to avoid the two twelve-centimeter-long claws on her feet, contributions of her utahraptor heritage. He wasn't without his own biological weapons, but inflicting a venomous bite would bring him too close to those claws. He'd be gutted before the neural toxin took effect. He caught a glimpse of the cold determination in his rival's amber eyes. The ambitious raptor wanted — *needed* — to take him down. She fought like someone desperate to improve her station in life. Their talons interlaced and she swung Inirigua around. The sheer power of the move astounded him. They fell, wings spread wide, spinning like a turbine. A classic eagle attack. Before they hit the ground, she released him and the momentum flung them apart.

It took a few moments for Inirigua to get his bearings. He pushed past the dizziness, flapping hard to regain altitude. Sweat dripped down the bridge of his nose. He could see his challenger, the object of his desire, Majasora, coming around. Inirigua emitted a strident whistle, provoking her. They flew at each other. Inirigua could see the same stratagem in the young raptor's form. She would crash, grab and spin. Typical Macu. Inirigua adjusted the position of his wings, brought his primaries a little closer to his body. Just as they were about to smash into each other, Inirigua twisted slightly, absorbing most of the impact with his abs. She tore at his shin with one of her big claws. As the air escaped his lungs, Inirigua caught the blue bird's wrist and sunk his teeth into her forearm. The raptor screamed as the venom hit her bloodstream. She smelled of crushed flowers. Inirigua let go. The lovely Macu fell, clutching her wing. As he rose, Inirigua hoped his eager adversary would survive. He was smitten.

He flew back into the main crowd, bobbing and weaving. Picking off the weaker and less experienced fighters. Catching his breath. Her scent lingered in his nostrils.

"I'm impressed, coward." The shriek came from above Inirigua. Instantly, he tucked in his arm-wings and rolled. A shadow blotted out the sun. Inirigua threw his wings out again and steadied himself. The noisy attacker slashed at the empty air with her two retractable claws. His heart quickened.

"Stupid. If you hadn't said anything, I'd be dead now," he said with taunting trill.

"What's the fun in that?" Majasora flashed him a sharp smile. "I want to enjoy killing you in your home atmosphere."

"How did you survive the bite?"

"My people smuggled the anti-venom out of your palace."

Inirigua circled Majasora, making sure to stay clear of her retractable talons. His leg still stung. In an aerial fight, he would lose: a sparrow against a hawk. So, he decided to use the hawk to his advantage. Inirigua caught an updraft and flew into the flock of remaining fighters, darting this way and that, avoiding talons and fangs, allowing Majasora to slash and hack her way after him, thinning out the competition.

The chase lasted for hours. The peaceable Carica had all gone and the other opponents were either injured or dead.

Inirigua's chest burned and his shoulder muscles ached, but he flew on. "You might as well give up. You'll never catch me," he gasped, sailing through the pink and orange sky, followed closely by Majasora. He had to admit she was superb.

They were the only two people in the sky now. The cameras retreated, permitting them their privacy. The cruel contest was over, and they both allowed themselves to relax. Inirigua felt the tension slide off his wings like wind.

"Your territory is marvelous," she said, in her slightly accented Cantabile. "It's always sunrise here. Macu airspace is farther east so it's always midmorning."

"It could be yours if you wished," he began to woo her. "You could preside over all of this."

"Are you courting me, Chief's Son Inirigua?" she asked with exaggerated innocence and flapped her cobalt wings to catch up to him. This was all an elaborate pretense, of course. Right now, his mother was already making the necessary arrangements with her family. Treaties were being signed.

Inirigua folded his wings and dove into the canopy, and the blue jungle embraced him, enveloping him like a lover. He moved sensuously through the fronds, letting the twigs comb through his feathers, and crouched low and still in the mist. Majasora was on the hunt. He could sense the liquid undulations her form made in the ambient magnetic field, but he couldn't tell where they came from. The wind breathed through the jungle and strange branches jangled like chimes. He whistled a shy tune, trying to draw her out, without giving himself away.

He could hear her movements like whispers in the bush. Images of her body sliding close to his flashed in his mind, and he realized that her blue plumage was perfect camouflage in the vegetation, another desirable trait for his offspring. Inirigua suddenly felt naked, exposed, his red feathers burning in the dark of the forest. *He should let himself get caught*, he thought, as the temptation became too much. *What did he have to prove?*

More boldly now, he sang her a song that would bring any opera aficionado to tears. Heightened lung capacity and an avian syrinx had created a race of lyric coloratura sopranos. He sang of *nanife*, and of how he would love Majasora with all his being for the rest of his life.

He heard her sweet reply and darted toward her voice. Coyly, she hopped into a clearing with the grace of a prima ballerina and honored him with a flounce of her iridescent azure plumes.

Inirigua's heart pumped as he skidded to a stop right next to his lover. The bright red of his wings flared and his crest became erect. Something in the most primitive part of his brain took over. All doubts ceased and he began the complicated choreography that was ingrained in his DNA.

"Mating dance" was a human euphemism to describe a vicious and vibrant rite that predated the rise of mammals.

It was a passionate tango of tooth and talon that, more often than not, left one or both dancers severely wounded. And contrary to salacious rumors spread by naïve chicks in the rookeries, the mating dance was not sex. It was only foreplay.

Inirigua stretched his scarlet wings and lunged at Majasora. He pinned her down, avoiding her curved, retractable claws. Her breasts heaved suggestively and poisonous saliva dripped from his pointy teeth. It was all he could do to restrain himself from taking a bite of her supple flesh.

Suddenly, the sizzle of a laser burned past his face, illuminating the dusky forest. Inirigua and Majasora — both immensely frustrated — turned to find a creature standing a few meters away. The beast grunted and this time aimed its gun directly at Inirigua.

"What have you done?" Inirigua managed to yell at the humanoid caricature through a cage of reptilian fangs.

What was left of his higher brain functions told him that this animal must be a baseline human of old, a woman from the shape of her hips and breasts, but his primitive cerebellum screamed for blood. With inhuman speed, he leapt off his thwarted bride and toward his prey, claws ready to strike.

The flightless human swatted him aside with impossible strength. Inirigua rolled on the ground until he smacked into a rough, indigo trunk. The raptor was vaguely aware that Majasora had flown away in shame. At least she was safe.

"You have no idea what you've interfered with!" He was sure the baseline human's dull ears hadn't caught half that statement, but he was talking to her simply to catch his breath. His right arm-wing ached from the impact. His head reeled.

"It looked like you were attacking her," she barked, brushing the thin black cords dangling from her head away from her eyes. "I thought I was helping."

"We were performing a mating ritual, you ignorant ape!" Inirigua yelled.

"If you calm down, we can sort this out," she said, holding her gun steady.

So, the ape had understood the finer pitches of Cantabile. "Liar! You've sabotaged the union between the Vanacan and the Macu," Inirigua screeched, before the venom sacs in his mouth swelled and he was no longer able to speak. He pounced again. This time he dodged another blow and managed to tear the gun free of his attacker's grip.

She — yes, he was now sure the creature was female — was stronger than he was, the result of living under more unyielding gravity. Still, he poured all his weight onto her, shredding her flesh with his wing-claws and small, sharp toe-talons. Holding nothing back. And despite his state of frenzy, a part of him admired the serene look on her face, a gorgeous face with golden-brown skin, luscious lips and bright black eyes. *Why wasn't she fighting back?* He was sure she could break his hollow bones with ease.

Suddenly, horror and a cocktail of adrenaline, serotonin, oxytocin, and vasopressin flooded his system. He attained *nanife* in surge after surge of pounding pleasure. His body shuddered, leaving him utterly vulnerable.

Lovingly, she placed the palm of her hand to his chest and sent excruciating electricity flowing through his body. The satisfying shudder became an agonizing tremor and then the world went black.

Chapter 4

Clan Chief Cayaguey stood on her terrace and watched the revelers return from the ceremonial contest between clans. Feathers still rained down from the sky like confetti. A few storm clouds had blown in from the west on warm, scented winds, tinting the horizon in jasper. Cayaguey thought the view quite appropriate. By now, her son and the eldest daughter of Macu Chief Tausanak were one, and all three clans would soon be unified under her rule. The heavens had acknowledged her triumph by anointing every floating building, every person — even the dark tangle of jungle below — in splendid gold.

Then she saw her only daughter approaching on her flier, flanked by two boys. Oh, how Cayaguey hated that flight-assist apparatus. The flier's bulky metal frame atop the small circular antigrav motor looked like an industrial birdcage. The Carica boy was too close, almost brushing her daughter's cheek with his wingtips. No, she reevaluated the situation. He was flying *with* her, and both of them were fleeing the Macu boy, who was gaining on them, jeering at them, kicking at her young daughter's cripple's device, trying to knock her off. Anger flashed in the Clan Chief, but she remained steady. Her daughter needed to learn to defend herself.

The wingless girl threw herself off the flier and pounced on the Macu boy, sinking her teeth into him. He cried in pain. Cayaguey paused, fighting the urge to swoop in and rescue her child. She watched the two youths tumble through the air, and, only when they approached terminal velocity, called her Palace staff. "Please, Yaboayo, pluck my falling child from the sky."

Cayaguey left the terrace and stood at the center of her office — the most important office on the planet now. Unlike the palace, her workspace was sparsely decorated, clear of clutter and distraction. Two tan sofas faced her dark wood desk. A red runner bearing the seal of Vanacan was draped over it. The walls were a sober taupe and the wide windows were bordered by red and gold tapestries. Her one luxury was an antique painting of Titan. She waited patiently until the aide deposited her wind-blown daughter onto the terrace. She scowled at the unruly girl, too old to still be covered in the fleece of chicks. A six-year-old would've already developed wings, but no, her child was already eleven and there wasn't a single contour feather on her body.

"You were being mocked?" Cayaguey asked, keeping her tone grave.

"No, Mother, they were mocking Lonanhorak for being my friend."

Cayaguey wanted to point out that there was no difference at all, but she knew her intractable child would only argue with her, and carry the conversation off course. "You like that black-winged boy?"

"No! I just felt sorry for him. That Macu is a bully. If I could fly, I would cut him down to size."

"Hmm, I doubt that. He's big and strong, and has a fine pair of retractable talons on his feet."

"That didn't help him just now, did it?" the girl sibilated, crossing her long downy arms over her chest.

Cayaguey suppressed a proud smile. She turned and looked at her tapestries waving in the breeze. "Soon, I will have grandchildren like that and you will be their aunt."

"You approve of such mingling, Mother, Vanacan and Macu?"

"You know very well that I do!" Cayaguey shrilled, but managed to get ahold of herself. The child needed grooming instead of admonishment. "You've been raised among the Vanacan, and you forget you're mixed-clan yourself. I blame your father for throwing away his life while exploring this rancorous planet and not being here to properly introduce you to Carica ways." Cayaguey felt that old talon in her heart wrench, that familiar unquenchable yearning. Nanife *could be a cruel thing sometimes*, she thought.

"I haven't forgotten, but people say we're ruining the red-winged clan. They say it's why I haven't sprouted my wings yet, that I'm sick genetically. I hear them sometimes when they think I'm not around. They pity me."

"Unfortunately, dear, most people are imbeciles." Cayaguey pointed a well-manicured claw at her daughter. "Are you an imbecile, Kiwi?"

"No, Mother, and don't call me that terrible name!" the girl squawked with annoyance.

She faced her daughter, really looking into her pained eyes, and wondered when she had started calling her Kiwi. She couldn't remember, but she kept using it to goad her into becoming a fledgling. She ran the rough palm of her hand over her daughter's fuzzy head; the girl was almost her height. "Think. You have no wings — and that's a great shame to me — but you have brains. There are flocks of mixed-clan children out there and they're all perfectly healthy, your brother is healthy. You're just a late bloomer, my dear." She longed for that to be the case with all her heart. "Sometimes that happens, the vestigial genes of our flightless ancestors trying to assert themselves.

"But, think for a moment, there are only a few hundred thousand of us refugees huddled together on this planet. Not yet a million! If we start segregating ourselves into tiny little camps, we'll become extinct before long, and the hordes of Earth will have won."

The girl scratched the down on her forearms and tilted her head ruefully, as if troubled by the fact that her mother had made any sense at all. "I never thought of it that way," she conceded.

"No, there isn't enough thinking these days. You've been studying basic population genetics, drift, and gene flow... It's time you started applying it to real world models. Start acting like a woman and perhaps you'll finally grow into one." She gently caressed the girl with one of her wing's primaries to soften the insult. "We've focused on survival, and getting away, for so long. Your grandmother's generation sacrificed so much, toiling in frigid server rooms or crawling around in the dark narrow labyrinth of network and power conduits on the generation ship that brought us here, that they lost the aerial view of things."

Cayaguey led Kiwi to one of the large sofas and sat her down. "Did I ever tell you the story of how my grandmother, Tianlongmu, became the CEO of the City of Ten Thousand Dragons back on Titan?"

"Many times, Mother, but I don't see the big deal. She fled. She lost!" Kiwi scratched more vigorously, emitting a satisfied hiss. Did the vulgar girl simply have a persistent itch or could this be the onset of molting? Cayaguey stamped out the kindling of hope.

"Did she? You're older now, Kiwi, let me tell it again and maybe you can glean some new insight."

"I'm agreeing only to avoid the slash of claws across my cheek," the girl said sarcastically, settling in on the sofa just the same. "And don't call me Kiwi."

Cayaguey ignored her daughter's insolence; she was only wielding her budding independence. She too had been insufferable at that age. All the signs suggesting she would soon develop wings. Cayaguey whistled an intricate chord and the artwork on the far wall facing the sofa flickered and changed, resolving on a romantic painting of the tented City of Ten Thousand Dragons, by the shores of a caramel lake of volatiles. Lopsided Saturn loomed large in the background, adding a splash of color to the otherwise sepia image. It was a digital replica of a silk screen hanging in Vanacan's Drifting Art Gallery, and it went nicely with the Titanic motif of Cayaguey's office. "Back in Sol, when my grandmother was a young programmer, working her way up the hierarchy of the aviary, she met a beautiful analyst. She liked to joke that she achieved *nanife* the second he entered the room," Cayaguey chuckled to herself.

"He was from a rival aviary called Tengushima, so their relationship was frowned upon from the start. Everyone said their careers were over. In fact, they tried to actively quash their ambitions."

"You're talking about great grandfather, Korutobi. What's the big deal? He was Vanacan as well."

"Yes, but there were more of us back then, and they could afford the luxury of prejudice, so they subdivided themselves into archaic ethnic groups and called themselves Chinese, and Japanese, and Korean... There was much disunion even among the scarlet-feathered clan."

"So what happened?"

"Impatient child, what is your hurry? You are hideously underdeveloped, and I'm working. Neither of us is flying anywhere!" But her child's interest in the story stoked that relentless, insubstantial hope. She was actually paying attention! "Now, as I was saying, their love was too strong. With every cruel attempt by the ruling buzzards to tear them apart, they became closer. Drawn together into more than a marriage, more than a partnership, they became a powerful coalition. They shared sensitive information and valuable resources, kept potential threats off each other's back, and before long, Tianlongmu was the CEO of the aviary, and when the baseline humans attacked Titan, their two cities were the best equipped to survive."

"I don't even know what CEO means," Kiwi said, but Cayaguey could tell the girl's mind was a flurry of activity as she leaned in close with rapt attention.

"It means Chief Executive Officer, and it was the highest rank in all the City of Ten Thousand Dragons."

"So you're saying she survived. That was the prize."

Cayaguey didn't even bother hiding her smile this time. It had been so long since she'd let joy flow through her. "Correct."

"I will be Chief one day, like great grandmother and you."

"So I ask you again, child, do you fancy that black-winged boy?"

"He's pretty." The girl blushed. "If only he didn't look as if he were dripping with petrol."

"Hah!" Cayaguey hugged her daughter tightly. "Petrol is quite valuable, my dear, and you never know, your wings might just be as black as space when they finally come out." Kiwi had understood the moral of the tale. Possibly it was her new crush on this Lonanhorak, or perhaps she would finally begin to mature, both physically and emotionally. Cayaguey would marry-off Inirigua and mentor this wild creature into the most shrewd and efficient Chief of all of Quetzalcoatl.

Another aide burst into Cayaguey's private office, disturbing her rare tender moment. "Clan Chief, Majasora has returned without your son. She was very secretive about it, but looked quite agitated, and left with a small contingent of her own people."

Cayaguey's face turned stony and she released her daughter. "Leave us, Kiwi. There are matters I have to attend to." She turned to the aide, who was nervously wringing his claws, and started to say, "We need to send out our own people—"

"There's more pressing news, Cayaguey. The Augur has just sent out an encrypted message to the three Chiefs of Quetzalcoatl, audio only. Something is happening."

"The Augur hasn't contacted us in ages — Kiwi leave! I'll take the message here at once."

"What about Inirigua?" Kiwi asked.

Why was the impudent girl still in the room? "He's cunning and can take care of himself," Cayaguey snapped, feeling the sting of guilt, but then forcing it down. She tried to ignore her daughter as well.

Cayaguey got up from the sofa, went to her desk, and pounded out her security code into the computer stylishly embedded in the wood finish. The girl trailed behind her.

The Augur's neutral voice sang, *"Hello, Clan Chief Cayaguey, it's been a long time."*

Cayaguey waited for a while and then asked tentatively, "Is this live or a recording?"

"This is live. I sent the other two Chiefs a recorded message, but as the leader of the operative capital of Quetzalcoatl, I thought we needed to talk. To get to the point, I've detected a Hominocracy vessel in orbit. It is stealthed, but I've been able to ping it several times and I don't believe it to be a warship."

Cayaguey unconsciously hugged her daughter close, protectively drawing a wing over her. Only a moment ago, she had been on the verge of achieving her dream of uniting the planet beneath her wings, and now everything was threatened. "You don't *believe* it's a warship? What else could it be?"

"*Initial telemetry of the craft's design suggests it's a sleeper ship, an interstellar ship full of settlers.*"

"Settlers? I want to face these settlers."

"Mother, no!" Kiwi's piercing whistle startled her, but served to remind her of what was truly important, what needed to be protected.

Cayaguey slammed her winged-fist onto her desk and shrieked into the comm, "Yaboayo, get this child out of here! Put her on my personal transport, and get her to a safe house in her father's territory! I want her away from Vanacan airspace. Do you hear me?"

Two guards came in, followed by the elderly aide, and pulled Kiwi off of her mother, while her daughter's claws raked her flesh, trying desperately to hold on.

Cayaguey didn't flinch. She remained quiet, like a terracotta statue, and only when they were gone, did she allow herself to collapse into her moa-leather swivel chair. She was tired and glad that the communication with the Augur was audio only. She took a deep breath and asked, "What do you suggest I do?"

"*I believe you have the right instincts, Clan Chief. You need to confront them and ask them what they want. Be as forward and transparent as possible.*"

"You make it sound so easy."

"*They haven't attacked yet. You have to consider the possibility that all they really want is to stay here, to make this planet their home.*"

"You need to help us with this, Augur. I will not allow another Culling, not on my fledgling world."

"*I'll do all that I can to assist you, Cayaguey, but I am a strict adherent of the Laws of Olivaw, and I will not directly or indirectly harm a human being, baseline or avian. Still, there are loopholes that I can exploit.*"

"Thank you, Augur, I need time to meditate on this."

"*I trust you will make the correct decision.*" The signal died.

Cayaguey could feel the gentle rocking of the palace beneath her. It was so tenuous, so prone to the whims of the wind. That's what her little avian civilization felt like now. Despite all her grand designs and ambitions, it felt very delicate, very impermanent, like a small bird in a maelstrom.

No, she thought, there had to be a way to endure. Cayaguey rose from her seat, composed herself, and left her private quarters. She needed to consult her defense council. She would try to engage the Hominocracy in discourse. The Augur believed that would be enough and it was wise beyond reason. But she would be ready for anything. Even if her old enemies rounded up all her people and shot them in the head, the raptorial race would continue. She would see to that.

Chapter 5

When Inirigua came to, his wings and feet were bound with unbreakable wire. He lay on the ground in front of a white vehicle, that tapered to a point at the front. The scent of scorched leaves and soil beneath the craft overpowered the fertile fragrance of the jungle, and the chittering of the native insectoid organisms were the only sounds around.

He immediately tried to call for help, but the computer woven into his shirtfront was fried.

A door on the side of the cone slid open and a dissonant sound crashed out, drowning out the noise of the native fauna. With intense avian interest, he watched the baseline female exit. Her gait was clumsy in the lighter gravity, but he could tell by the subtle way her hips swayed that the cantankerous noise was music. The vocals were harsh and plain, but the pluck and scrape of metallic strings was as complex and interesting as any raptorial aria — more so for its strangeness.

The woman stood before him, frowning. As she folded them across her chest, he noticed her bare arms ended in an array of stubby, little digits. She looked like a molting cripple, but instead of seeing her as lame prey, Inirigua's heart leapt for her. The memory of experiencing *nanife* in her presence flooded his mind. He told himself that his sympathy was only the cruel result of brain chemistry, but, against all will and better judgment, he felt hopelessly infatuated with this enemy. "You're awake?" she said, in a flat imitation of Cantabile, her voice hacking away all of its musical flourishes. She approached him with caution.

"Yes. How do you speak Cantabile?"

"Our computer decoded your language from your Astronet signals spilling out into space, and then downloaded it into my head. It's a lovely language. Apparently, I lack the proper vocals for it, but I can muddle through."

"Am I your prisoner?"

"It appears so." She watched him suspiciously for a moment, and then added, "With those wings tucked in close to your sides, you almost look like a regular guy in a black and red robe. Look, I'm sorry about ruining your dance, or whatever that was. If you promise to stay calm, I'll release you."

He ignored the condescending remark. He had a vivid image of lacerating her flesh, yet her dark skin was flawless — beautiful. He also remembered her electric touch. "What are you?"

"I guess you haven't seen very many classical humans all the way out here, but that's what I am; a standard human from Earth." She smiled and, despite the boldfaced lie, he enjoyed the way her face lit up.

"I know all about baseline humanity, and you're a far cry from it. I tore you up hours ago, and you don't have a single scratch on you. Even your clothes are like new. Also, I can see the electromagnetic field, it's how I navigate, and your aura is humming like a kitchen appliance. Not to mention that you electrocuted me with your naked hand."

"My clothes are new. I made a fresh uniform after our fight. But nowadays, most humans back in the Sol system have billions of microscopic machines in their bodies. Some are temporary, but others are permanent. There's at least one in each cell, constantly making repairs and eliminating mutations. We call them curators, because they painstakingly keep us in the ideal human form. The ones I have, have been augmented to deal with extreme hostile situations, hence the electric touch."

It was Inirigua's turn to smile. "You're a cyborg then, a subtle one to be sure, but still a cyborg."

"Not at all. We all have beneficial bacteria living in our guts and on our skin, but that doesn't mean we have an infection," she replied, a bit too hotly. He could tell that he had touched a nerve.

"If I promise not to rip your machine infested guts out, will you free me?" He raised his bound wrists and noticed her flinch at the sight of his black claws. It hurt him to see such disgust on the face he adored. Truth was, he doubted very much that he could bring himself to attack her again.

After a short pause, she said, "Just remember, if you try anything, I'll snap your wings with my bare hands. The curators also make me very strong." She pulled out a field knife and slit the wire. "What do you harpies call yourselves?"

"Humans," he said, without a trace of irony. It felt good to spread his wings out wide. His shoulder still ached, but he was sure that he could take flight if he had to.

"Well, we have that in common. And this country?"

"You're in Vanacan territory. What is the purpose of you being here? Do you plan on staying long? Are you a scout? Is this an invasion?"

"No, not an invasion. But we are planning on staying. There are about a hundred frozen humans in orbit, and I'm here to state our friendly intentions to found a settlement somewhere on this planet. We honestly don't want any trouble, just some out-of-the-way land to start a colony."

"And the Hominocracy just sent you, alone? That's pretty bold."

"Yeah, well, I'm a renowned diplomat."

"Are you really?"

Her face brightened again, though this time more shyly. "No, not really. I'm just the pilot, and since we're parked, I'm the most expendable crew member."

Inirigua laughed a genuine, bird-like chortle, and Oya conceded a sad little smile of her own.

"I don't know why I admitted that to you, just now. It seems like a tactical mistake."

"I like your honesty. I am Inirigua. What's your name?"

"Oya Valette, First Pilot, but you can call me Oya."

"Look, Oya, I can take you to our city and you can make your case with Clan Chief Cayaguey, but if I can be just as candid with you, I doubt we'll let you stay without a fight. It wasn't that long ago that your kind was exterminating mine."

"Fair enough."

"How are you planning on getting to a levitating city? This bucket of yours doesn't look maneuverable enough, and we'll be shot down before you can even call ahead to say hello. And I don't have the strength to carry you."

"I've been thinking about that. You're right. This lander is only really intended to go up and down. Follow me." She led him into the drop ship. The abrasive music grew louder as they approached. It was too much. All novelty was blasted away by volume.

"What are the vibrating metal sounds in this song?" he shouted.

"An electric guitar," she yelled back, then looked at his claws and added, "I guess that instrument has been lost to you for anatomical reasons. I'll turn it off so we can talk." The music suddenly stopped.

The vessel had a tiny living space. He could identify a kitchen and a bathroom stall. The pilot's chair looked comfortable enough to sleep in. She opened an oven-like door in the wall and pulled out a bundle of bright, yellow fabric. "Centuries ago, before your people genetically engineered themselves to fly, they used artificial wings for sport. I had the lander's computer dig up information on those old wings, taking Quetzalcoatl's gravity and atmospheric density into account, and applied any breakthroughs in ultra-light, smart materials. While you slept, the builders assembled a pair of wings for me."

Inirigua was absolutely taken aback by the level of technology the Hominocracy possessed. These cyborgs had knowledge far beyond his people. He swallowed his awe and instead forced an amiable smile. "You made that out of thin air?"

"No, there's a dense block of raw material in there that the builders use. They can also use our trash. I think some of my old uniform is in these wings."

"You're going to look like a canary with those."

"Yeah, and you look like a mutant rooster from Hell. Nobody's perfect." She took the bundle outside. "I guess this God-awful yellow is a safety feature of the old recreational equipment, made downed fliers easier to spot." Oya strapped the harness to her torso. Slipping her hands into the holds, she extended her mock wings the way Inirigua had when she freed him.

"Are you ready to try those out?"

"Yeah, I think so. I watched some old videos while these were cooking. Seems easy enough."

Inirigua kneeled down low to the ground, poised to spring into flight. "We should get going then. By now, Majasora has probably mobilized all of Vanacan."

Oya copied his stance.

Suddenly — without a word of warning — he exploded into the air, powerfully pounding his wings, thrusting upward.

Oya did the same.

For an endless moment, it looked like it would take all her strength just to stay a meter off the ground, but slowly, she began to climb. The thin, plastic membranes looked more like pterosaur wings than those of a bird. She flapped as hard and as fast as she could, and when she finally broke over the tree line, and was safely coasting on the breeze, Inirigua saw her face fill with satisfaction and relief.

"I thought you were never going to join me up here," Inirigua derided, but he was glad she had made it up, flying by his side.

"For a while there, I didn't think so either," she panted. "I had to mentally yell at my curators to flood my arms, chest and back muscles with super-oxygenated blood."

"That's disgusting."

She smiled back at him. "My wingspan is larger than yours. I hope that doesn't make you feel inadequate."

"Not at all, you don't have hollow bones, so you're heavier than I am," Inirigua said, failing to pick up on her sarcasm.

"Is that why I'm struggling here?"

"Yes. Risjafung, a famous Vanacan poet, once wrote, 'A fledgling falls beating two false wings, arrogance and ignorance. To reach the sky, a true raptor must shed those wings and allow herself to be pulled along by the whistling wind, naked, as if following a lover's song.'" The words burned in his chest. He flapped once and careened forward.

"That's lovely, but it's not like I can shed these things."

"It means, you lack the upper body strength to flap often, but you *think* you know what you're doing and you're going to tire yourself out and fall." He concentrated on the mechanics of flight instead of its poetry. It was safer territory, especially in his susceptible state. "You have to rely on gliding a lot more than I do. It's a common problem with the Macu."

"So that's why you're built like an Olympic swimmer," Oya said, between hungry breaths.

"I don't know what that is," he admitted, but he knew she was admiring his lithe body cutting through the air. His streamlined outfit left little to the imagination. He was very pleased by her attention.

— «» —

Oya caught herself checking out the harpy and tried to focus instead on the intricacies of flying. No, not harpy, she reminded herself. He was a man. Genetically modified, but still a young man. She had to start thinking of him that way or her own biases would sabotage any negotiations she attempted.

She also needed to be more careful. She was too comfortable around him and that worried her; maybe it was that he had already done his worst to her and she had beaten him, or maybe it was the sound of his voice, it had that particular resonance she found quite attractive in men. She had to watch herself around him. Not let her guard down. The last thing she needed was for him to catch her distracted and strike all the way up here.

They coasted over the endless, extraterrestrial rainforest, their friendly small talk diminishing with each arduous flap. Despite her curators working overtime, Oya's oxygen intake was nowhere near as sophisticated as Inirigua's natural one, and after only thirty minutes of continuous flight, a side stitch stabbed her just below the right ribcage and her muscles cried out for fuel. "I'm going to have to rest soon," she wheezed, embarrassed. The heavy air tasted of impending rain and something spicy, like chili powder.

"Hang on. I'm sensing three fliers moving through the planet's magnetic field. They're headed right for us. I can just make out their blue wings now. We've got incoming Macu warriors on an intercept course," Inirigua said.

"I don't see anything."

"My eyesight is better than yours. How much longer can you keep flying?"

"Not long. I can shut off the pain for a while, but eventually I'm going to cramp up and drop like a stone."

"I think they're a search and rescue team. Maybe we can avoid any unpleasant air combat maneuvering if I do the talking." He emitted a few contact calls, very bird-like.

The three Macu raptors bleated their reply and swooped in on their deadly trajectory. Oya caught sight of Inirigua's dance partner in the lead. Despite her fatigue, she outlined Inirigua with an overlay and partitioned her attention to keep constant tabs on him in case things got chaotic.

"I have the situation under control, Majasora. Please disengage," Inirigua whistled across the closing distance.

"Under control? You're joy-flying with the enemy, one that dishonored the blessed clan! Are you planning to side with them against the Macu?"

Inirigua jerked violently, dodging a slashing kick from Majasora. "Don't be stupid! Let us pass. I'll explain everything when we get to Vanacan."

Majasora chased Inirigua in a tight circle. Their speed and control was incredible. *He had been holding back with her*, Oya thought. Inirigua waited until the last possible moment to loop over Majasora, carving his rival's back with his own toe-talons. The aerobatic stunt only pissed her off.

"Inirigua, we've won the right to join our two clans in holy matrimony. Why would you throw that away for this creature?"

"This is important, Majasora. This is bigger than both of us and our little clan politics. If we don't properly deal with this threat now, our way of life could be over."

"I know how to deal with this threat!"

Another Macu gouged at Oya's gaudy wing and she went into a wild spin. The third Macu missed a swipe to her head. Oya got control of her wings and straightened out. The tough polymer of her synthetic airfoils was tear-proof, but the hits were knocking her off balance. Her attackers came back for another pass. She couldn't let go of the handles to get to her sidearm, so she flapped desperately. Oya tried to shake them off with a tailslide, but it was ridiculously futile; the whole charade was like a dogfight between an air show biplane and two antigrav fighters. She felt the crushing weight of a man on her back, then the searing pain of a curled knife digging into her skin. She screamed.

In dreamlike detachment, she realized that one of the harpies had pounced on her, and was trying to cut away at the harness. Her curators were overly taxed just keeping her alive and in the air, so when she asked them to produce a bioelectric discharge, they sputtered. Error messages danced in her field of vision. She let go of the handholds and folded into fetal position. The artificial wings wrapped around her and stiffened into a protective cocoon. She crashed into the trees, taking her rider out in the process.

Oya slammed into the ground.

— «» —

Inirigua threw himself into the dense forest after Oya. He was also dimly aware that Majasora was following him. He smashed his way through the blockade of branches and dropped next to the crumpled body of the fascinating invader. Her yellow wings where softening and unfurling like the petals of a flower. He could sense the furious activity of the tiny machines in her system as heaving waves of magnetism and took that as a sign of life.

"Oya, can you hear me?" he asked, cradling her head in his claws. He was aware that the two Macu still in play were invisible among the turquoise treetops, but he didn't care what Majasora thought of this gentle display toward the Hominocracy enemy.

Oya's eyes fluttered opened, but her stare was blank, as if she were a finely crafted automaton. There was nothing he could do for her, so Inirigua pulled her gun out of its holster and aimed it at the jungle. It felt clumsy in his claws. He didn't want to kill the Macu — especially the lovely Majasora — as it would be detrimental to any alliance his mother had planned, but he wasn't going to let them kill Oya either.

"Inirigua, run away!" Oya coughed.

The sound of her voice filled him with courage. "I'm not going to leave you here. They're up there and you're flashing like a magnetic beacon. The only thing that's stopping them is the sight of this gun. If I leave, they'll come like vultures."

"Inirigua, listen very carefully. I'm going to count to three. If you're still standing near me when I say 'three,' you're going to get seriously hurt. One."

Inirigua's heart stopped. Did she have a bomb? Was she instructed to blow herself up when capture became imminent? He knew of Macu fanatics blowing themselves up.

"Two."

He heard an impatient rustle in the leaves above. He couldn't leave her. He was bound to her by chemical chains. *Nanife* was more powerful than love. She couldn't understand that, but if she died, his life was utterly worthless.

"Inirigua... Three."

He tore himself away and dashed into the brush at velociraptor speeds. Majasora and her associate dropped with predatory eagerness. A massive electromagnetic pulse flared from Oya's body. The upsurge was comparable to what is released by a small atomic bomb. He imagined the magnetite embedded within the brains of the Macu aggressors becoming disastrously scrambled. They screamed and he ran faster. He let the thought of the sheer pain of having his sensitive magnetoreception burned away propel him through the vegetation.

Then the wave hit him and Inirigua convulsed into the understory, rocked by brutal seizures.

Chapter 6

HS Hurricane

The *Hurricane's* bridge was dead silent as the command crew watched Valette's signal on the holographic globe disappear.

Captain Anton Hershkovitz leaned forward on the edge of his seat, waiting for the blip to reappear. "What just happened?" He had instantly regretted sending the inexperienced woman down there alone, but he couldn't afford second thoughts now so he pushed clamoring doubts away.

"There was some erratic movement both in the air and on the ground, and then an EM burst. She was actually headed to their nest!" Commander Davoli said, no longer able to contain his astonishment. "That woman may have a bleeding heart, but she's definitely got a pair of brass ovaries."

"Do you think she's dead?" Xing asked in utter shock. "She can't be dead. I mean, she's survived so much worse than a few savage mutants, right?"

Hershkovitz could tell his Info Officer was about to crack. It was better to reassure her until he was sure of the worst. "No, her signal would have sent a distress code in the last second, but it just cut off, probably due to the EMP, which is part of her arsenal. I think she probably won that fight. Although, I've heard it can have damaging effects on the curators without immediate attention. Diwa, bring up real-time images from the three probes. Center the screen showing Valette's destination and make it bigger than the other two."

"What are we going to do? We can't just leave her there," Xing said, concern pouring out of her, making her useless. She had a greenish tint, and Hershkovitz was afraid she would be sick.

"Diwa, get your curators to calm you down." The captain walked over to her and patted her console encouragingly. "I'm going to give her ten minutes to reboot, and if she doesn't, I'm going to contact the leaders and ask for permission to extract our officer. They already know we're here and further sulking around could be perceived as nefarious. Don't worry, I promise we'll get her back."

Xing nodded and completed her request. Three immaterial rectangles appeared before the crew, all of them showing scenes of avian urban activity. The lightscreen on the left showed a horde of black-feathered harpies dwelling in a city with architecture reminiscent of the Martian aviaries. The one on the right displayed a shining city of white, populated by blue-feathered harpies. The center image showed an impressive metropolis, bustling not only with red-winged inhabitants, but black, blue and every possible combination of the three. It looked like the Forbidden Aviary of Titan, only built on a grander, gravity-defying scale.

"So we've got crows, cardinals and jays, with the cardinals as the obvious dominant group." A residual trace memory threatened to swell within Captain Hershkovitz, but failed to materialize. "I think we should start with them."

"At least she was headed in the right direction," said Davoli, reclining in his chair.

"Captain, I've received an entangled message from Earth," Diwa said, obviously irritated by the interruption from so far away.

The two male officers turned toward their Information Officer, and Hershkovitz had to admit he *was* rather annoyed, especially because he already knew what his superiors were going to say.

"They have reviewed the information package I sent earlier, and the Hominocracy's official policy toward the harpies residing on this planet is one of nonaggression.

They reiterate that we must learn from the errors of our past and try to forge a future of peace."

"That's because they don't have to live with the flying freaks," muttered Davoli under his breath.

Diwa continued, "They state that if we do not reach an agreement with the local *Homo sapiens aves* we are to proceed to the nearest available star or abort the mission altogether."

"Are you kidding me?"

"That's enough, Commander." Hershkovitz shot his deputy a severe look, but sympathized with the sentiment. Suitable planets were rare, even partially suitable ones like Quetzalcoatl. They could be searching for a century until they found another one — and only if the fuel allowed that. "I'll honestly try and work something out with these harpies, but I am not going to hopscotch around the galaxy looking for habitable worlds and hoping they aren't already crowded with posthuman refugees. As for going back... I'll decide that once there's no other option. Diwa, you can send *that* back to Earth. Now, people, let's focus on the matter at hand."

"Captain, we're getting another short text message, this one from the planet's surface, specifically from the cardinal's settlement. It reads, 'Hominocracy ship, your presence is known to us. The Great Nation of Vanacan requests that you meet with Clan Chief Cayaguey in person, to discuss your unauthorized arrival in Quetzalcoatl space. Refusal will be deemed cowardly and an unfriendly act.'"

The captain slowly paced the bridge, stroking his beard and letting the words sink in. He tried to look wise and pensive to his crew, but he was scared shitless. One wrong move...

"Well," he said, turning to face them. He hoped his grim expression appeared more resolute than worried. "That makes contact a bit easier, and also much more complicated. I'll go down and meet this Clan Chief. My main priority is to try to learn the status of our First Pilot and then see if I can broker some sort of deal."

"Captain, you shouldn't go down to this viper nest alone. We should thaw a small contingent."

"No, I don't want to provoke them into a fight, and we shouldn't rob our passengers of precious time." He thought of his wife, corpse-like in her pod. What would she think of all this? How would she council him? "This is just a preliminary meeting. If our hosts are amenable, we can begin reviving a few at a time."

"At least grant me permission to accompany you, sir?"

"Very well, Commander. Diwa, prepare a construction missile loaded with builders and shoot it down to the planet. Pick a location as far away from these other settlements as mathematically possible. Then begin assembling our outpost. Select a design from one of the templates in the ship's archive."

"Is that legal, Captain? We haven't even talked it over with the harpies yet."

"Of course it is," he barked, getting tired of everyone second guessing his orders. Or possibly, it was that they kept echoing the misgivings in his mind. Ever since he'd learned that there were harpies in this system, he'd been off his game, unable to trust his own abilities, and quite possibly making a series of gaffes, like sending his pilot on a solo away mission. He turned to Diwa and amended, "The Outer Space Treaty of 1967 still applies. It held through all the upheavals of early Sol colonization, and it'll hold here in Beta Hydri. It's just an outpost. We can't stay on the ship indefinitely."

Hershkovitz moved toward the exit, but turned and faced his young crew member before crossing the threshold.

"Xing, if we don't return from our meeting, pursue the Hominocracy's recommendation and take everyone home," he said and left, not waiting for her input. He just marched to the infirmary to have his curators readied for active combat. Commander Davoli walked briskly at his side, going on about Titan. Hershkovitz wasn't paying any attention. An elusive memory nagged at him, and try as he might he couldn't bring it up.

As he entered the docking bay and selected a small ship, Captain Anton Hershkovitz had the ominous feeling that he was about to make whole new memories to replace the long forgotten ones.

The shuttle departed the gleaming boomerang of the *Hurricane* and dropped into the planet's gravity well.

— «» —

Information Officer Xing Diwa stood alone on the bridge, with only her fear and reservations to keep her company. She worried about Oya and, even more, she worried that the captain was unfit to deal with the challenges ahead. She wrestled with the idea of reporting him to the ship's medical automation. But what would that do? He was already gone.

Oya's curator signal never reappeared on the holographic globe.

Unsure of what to do, Xing concentrated on preparing the creative payload for the construction rocket. Being from the airborne island of Nueva Filipina, the levitating cities of the harpies had touched her on a basic, nostalgic level. She studied them from orbit, the way the anabatic and katabatic winds flowed sensuously around the free-floating buildings, the dance between antigravity and actual gravity, so gentle compared to the hellish storms that pummeled her island on Venus. When she thought she understood the dynamic well enough, she called up the template for her old Venusian habitat and tweaked the design to account for Quetzalcoatl's weaker gravity and hospitable conditions. This new artificial island couldn't be buoyed by a viscous, acidic atmosphere like her home, so it needed its own antigrav engines, like the harpy structures, to keep it aloft. Next, Xing did away with the protective envelope that encased the Nueva Filipina design, and that made all the difference. This version of her old country would be open to the sky and have a tropical breeze.

When she was happy with her work and had tested the virtual model over several simulations, Xing uploaded the instructions to a missile, pregnant with microscopic builders. She fired it toward a mountain side rich in minerals. Long moments passed, and her mind wandered back to Oya and the captain down there, and then the missile made contact and her thoughts refocused. It struck a remote area of the planet, roughly equivalent to the location of the Philippine islands on Earth. For a fleeting second, she imagined herself sitting on her balcony, toasting from the bottle of tapuy she had brought with her, admiring the endless sunset.

Ping. A lightscreen appeared directly in front of her. She hadn't called it up. It flashed in the urgent way of a priority message. This one had originated from the planet, but wasn't tagged by any of her crew. *Oya?* She opened it. The text read, "Xing Ana Maria Diwa, please come to the listed coordinates. We need to talk."

Unnerved by the oddly formal and familiar use of her entire name, she checked the coordinates and found that they led to the equatorial region of the Saharan Hemisphere, to the anomaly she'd noticed in her initial inspection of the planet. She saved and closed the lightscreen and immediately began preparing a sensor package to investigate this isolated structure, when another lightscreen blinked into existence in front of her. Slowly, she opened it. It said, "Why send a probe when you can come yourself?"

She jumped back from her console. This was a real-time communication, and, even more frightening, the sender knew what she was doing on the bridge. Xing became acutely aware that she was the only person awake on the ship. All alone. She panicked for a fraction of a second, and then she was overtaken by a *whoosh* of sensation that rushed over her whole body like warm water.

There was a sudden, inexplicable calm.

She conscientiously set her station to "away" mode as if she were only going to the restroom, walked over to the hangar and selected a lander that could handle the blazing heat of the alien planet's permanent sunside. She had no control of her own body or her insipid reaction to the situation. She entered the tight craft and, without a second thought, detached from the *Hurricane*.

Tears streamed down her face as she hit Quetzalcoatl's atmosphere. There was no emotion attached to them, although Xing knew there should be. She'd left all the colonists alone and asleep in space.

Chapter 7

Quetzalcoatl

Hours passed before Oya regained consciousness. The sweet and sour aroma of the tropical forest floor filled her nose as she opened her eyes. Her body started to throb painfully and her intestines wrenched with hunger. She dragged herself up, stripped the limp wings off her back, and became aware of the two blue harpies lying on either side of her, their chests rising and falling almost imperceptibly. The diagnostic heads-up display indicated that ten percent of her curators had burned out, but the status bar flashing directly into her retina nauseated her, so she switched it off. Oya grabbed the small flask of water attached to her belt and took a lingering drink. When she was confident she could walk, she set off in the rough direction Inirigua had run to, pulling her wings behind her. She stopped to drink several more times until her flask was empty. Finally, she found him lying in the muck.

He lay face down and she couldn't tell if his chest was moving, but one of his taloned feet twitched. To make sure her eyes weren't playing tricks on her, she turned his head and placed her hand just over his mouth. Oya was surprised by how relived she was to feel his warm breath on her trembling fingers. She picked up the gun he had taken from her and put it away as she kneeled next to him.

Oya observed his face more closely now. It was dirty and serene, unpolluted by rings of data reporting his minute-to-minute status. It was just a face, with a handsome bone structure, and yet, something was off. It nagged at her until she realized what it was. Inirigua didn't have eyebrows or eyelashes. It seemed ludicrous that something so insignificant as a couple of hairy arches could tag a face as wholly human, but their simple omission enhanced his overall alienness, maybe more so than the cap of feathers or mouthful of sharp teeth.

Oya bent forward, very carefully, and nudged him lightly. Hunger and anticipation twisted her stomach into a tight knot.

He half opened his eyes and croaked, "If I had any doubts that you were anything other than a cyborg, you've just put them to rest."

She sighed with great relief. "Well you're entitled to your opinion. How do you feel?"

He rolled onto his back. "I have a stabbing headache and my sinuses are on fire. You?"

"Sapped and starving."

He reached up, and combed his claws through the thick, black hair cascading over her shoulder. "I've never seen hair before. It flows through my claws like water."

"Hey, I've never seen a crest like yours before, but I don't touch it," she said lightly, happy that he was all right, if maybe a little concussed.

"What about the Macu? Are they dead?"

"No, they're out cold from the EMP, but when they wake up they're going to feel a lot worse than you do."

"How did you do that?" He shook his head and his recursive crest moved up and down like a cockatoo's. She found that she did want to touch it. It fascinated her. She stopped herself from running her fingers through the stiff plumage to figure out how it moved.

"It's a trick the curators can do, like the taser hands." Oya got up and moved toward a tree, tying her hair back into a ponytail. She sat down, leaning against the trunk, and pulled out a ration bar from another pocket. "I've burned more calories in the last hour than I have in my entire life." She took a bite, thinking that cardboard and chocolate had never tasted so good.

"The nanites use my body's bioelectricity to generate an electromagnetic pulse. It's meant to disable machines, but since you mentioned earlier that you guys navigate via the magnetic field, like homing pigeons, I figured it would work on you, too."

"I'm glad you didn't kill them. They may be religious fanatics, but we're trying to form an alliance with them."

"That was the girl you were performing the mating ritual with, right? Was your union part of the alliance?"

"Yes." Oya could see misery well up inside him even though he tried to hide it.

"I really am sorry about interfering with that. I can explain the whole situation when I speak to your leaders."

He sighed heavily. "It doesn't matter anymore."

Oya finished her protein bar, closed her eyes, and inclined her head against the spongy trunk.

"I take it that little food brick wasn't enough," he said.

"No. My curators are struggling to restore me back to health, but without any raw material or energy, they're going to start cannibalizing my body soon."

"Hang on." Inirigua stood a bit shakily, paused for a moment to keep his balance, and then scrambled up the stalk of a primitive-looking plant. It reminded Oya of the boys in her town who expertly climbed up palms to get at coconuts. "Catch," he yelled and large, purple fruit began raining down on her. Inirigua parachuted down, with a fruit in each claw.

"What are these?" She picked one up and turned the plump thing in her hand.

"*Siynawluslako*. It's a native fruit, high in calories. We had to introduce specially altered bacteria into our guts to digest them, but I'm sure your robo-bugs can manage." Inirigua sat on his haunches and took a rapacious bite from one of the alien fruits. It immediately exuded a strong odor of rotten fruit and blue cheese.

"You can eat fruit? I thought you were all carnivores."

"Don't be absurd." He looked at her, not with anger, but with great disappointment. "That's a vicious rumor to further dehumanize us. Our nutritional needs are exactly like yours."

"But how do you chew with those teeth?"

"Only our incisors and canines are dinosaurian, our molars are still like yours."

Ashamed, Oya focused on the fruit. She took a tentative bite. She wasn't going to attempt to pronounce its name, but it looked like an eggplant, had the juicy consistency of a mango and tasted like maple syrup, which helped with the overpowering smell. She took a bigger bite and made a face. "Wow, that's sweet."

He gave her a little nod. "You should taste the candied *Siynawluslako* desserts we eat at the golden *guanoxi* moon feast."

They ate their fruit in awkward silence and shooed away the buzzing creatures attracted to the saccharine nectar. Oya thought the bugs looked like flying prawns. "What are these?" she asked, unsuccessfully trying to catch one.

"*Jaibaguami*. These are the real natives of Quetzalcoatl. They're a lot like the trilobites of Earth's Cambrian age. Our xenobiologists believe that due to this planet's thick, oxygen-rich atmosphere and light gravity, these animals completely bypassed a terrestrial stage of development and seamlessly moved from an aquatic existence to an aerial one, first gliding, then flying out of the water on modified pelopods."

It was as if the planet itself was cultivating an ethos of flight. She wondered what natural selection would do to the harpies after eons on this planet. "You're very knowledgeable about them. Are you a scientist or a teacher?"

"Neither. I've just had an excellent education, and I want you to know as much as possible before you meet with our leaders. The more you know, the less likely you will be to offend them and spark a war."

All of a sudden, something the size of a duck, with four russet wings and the head of a corn snake exploded from the trees, snapped up one of the alien shrimp, and flew away. Oya's arms went up dramatically and Inirigua smirked at her.

"Was that a bleeding relative of yours?"

"Distant cousin, on my mother's side," he said with a warbling laugh.

"Was that an archaeopteryx then?"

"No, a microraptor."

"Is there anything dangerous in this jungle?" she asked, suddenly wary of the dark undergrowth surrounding her. "Like a T-Rex or something?"

"The most dangerous thing out here, besides you, are the terror birds, but this time of year most of them are hunting herds of moa closer to the sunside."

She instantly thought of her *gwan man man*. "You're recreating extinct birds here?"

"Yes, and also the few feathered dinosaurs we have complete genomes for, like the microraptor. They've all been slightly adjusted for this planet's various ecosystems."

She ate for a while, trying to calm her nerves, trying really hard not to think of her grandmother. Instead, she tried to imagine whatever the hell a terror bird might look like, and when the pit of the fruit was all that was left in her sticky hands, she said, "You mentioned the Macu are religious. That might help in my negotiations. What do they believe in?"

"It doesn't make much sense to me, but they think they're angels incarnate. It's stupid, I know, but you have to understand they were on Earth's moon when the Hominocracy started their extermination campaign. Those on Mars or Titan had ample warning and a fair head start. But those poor birds took the full brunt of the first wave completely unawares. I think, at first, it was a rallying symbol. They were the avenging angels of the Sol system, but in the face of so much senseless death and destruction, and the exile that followed, it became a belief to hold on to."

"What about you?"

"What about me?" If he had eyebrows, one on them would be arched.

"What do you believe in? You don't seem all that angelic to me."

He gave her a crocodilian smile. "The Vanacan practice, or don't, a convenient form of Zen Atheism. It suits me just fine. The Carica worship the Augur; a kind action-without-action consciousness, the layer of the cosmic egg. The cosmic egg is what they call the interstellar ark that brought us all here. The Carica only partake in ceremonial violence. I am part Carica." He ran a claw through the black fringe of his wing. "And I do have a healthy respect of the Augur."

"You can interbreed?" She devoured her second fruit and was beginning to feel better.

"We're not three separate species! I know it's difficult to get past your Hominocracy propaganda, but we're all human beings here. Yes, we've modified our genomes with dominant alleles from different species of feathered dinosaur, but our basic makeup is still 99.999 percent *Homo sapiens*. You know that old cliché: there is more genetic diversity within a group of chimpanzees, than there is on this entire planet."

Oya wanted to say that 99.999 was not one hundred percent, but she held her tongue. She had to keep reminding herself that this was a man, just a man. "Look, I'm sorry if I keep offending you, but I'm just trying to get my head around all this. I need to ask the stupid questions before I can get to the important ones."

"It's okay, I understand. What about you? Follow any divine doctrine? What part of Earth are you from, exactly? I can't place your geographical origins from the way you look."

"I'm a lapsed Catholic from a small Caribbean island that no longer exists, at least not as a nation. Ethnically, I'm a mélange of humanity. Mostly Yoruba and Igbo, French and Taíno on both sides of my family. On my mom's side, I've got some East Indian and on my dad's side, a bit of Scottish."

She pulled out a little yellow feather, twirling it around by the shaft so that the downy barbs fluttered in the wind. "This is all I have left of my home."

"Is that a war trophy?" Inirigua asked. His voice took on a slight vibrato and the tips of his fangs poked out from behind his upper lip. She could tell anger was slowly building within him.

"No! Calm down! This feather is from a small bird that lives only on my home island of Chandeleur. I used to love them as a child."

Inirigua relaxed a bit and stared at the feather more intently, then said, "I want to show you something, too."

He dug into one of his seamless pockets and pulled out a smooth stone triangle with rounded corners. He handed the small artifact to Oya.

"What is this?"

"It's art, unique to us here. To you it's probably a plain stone wedge, but inside there's an intricate arrangement of magnetite of varying sizes and densities. Anyone with magnetoreception will see a picture."

She turned it over, scanning it with the entire suite of her vision enhancements, and handed the rock back to Inirigua. "I'm sorry. I can't sense anything. Can you describe it to me?"

"Sure. It's an impression of a beautiful girl, of unbearable attraction, carved out in one of the fundamental forces of the universe. Her sweeping wings are spread wide as if coming in for a landing. It's supposed to mean that I'm available to bond with someone."

"A bachelor rock? Why are you showing this to me?"

"Because no matter what happens between us or our people, I want you to believe that we are just as human as you are, capable of great cruelty and great beauty."

She got up, put her totem feather away and strapped on her plastic wings. "We should get going."

"You feel up to it already?"

She knew that he hadn't intended to insult her. Hell, she had insulted *him* a few times during their conversation. She understood that he was only trying to make a very valid point, but she couldn't help being upset. He had implied that she was a bigot, putting her in the same category as Davoli. And, deep down, there was a part of her that feared it was true, and she was angry that he had exposed it. "I'm not going to be emitting anymore EMPs anytime soon, but I can fly. My body has been rebuilding itself to better handle flight."

"All right, let's go." Without another word, he flung the little stone triangle into the bushes. *Why would he just toss it?* Then he crouched down and kicked off into the air.

Oya did the same.

Chapter 8

Luna – 2098 A.D.

Dr. Osala Valette watched the bone-colored orb in the window with some misgivings. She was waiting in the large reception area of an inflatable module, designed in the style of the grand Bigelow hotels. She wore the crisp white coveralls she'd been given upon arrival, and the only splash of color in the bleached room was the yellow head wrap that kept her curly, brown hair from billowing uncontrollably. Both her feet were securely looped through the footholds to help with the habitat's illusion of "floor" and "ceiling," but the constant free-falling sensation and the anxious state of her nerves made her stomach churn despite all the anti-nausea pills she had taken. The wait was interminable and seeing the moon in all its lifeless detail added to the hollowness in her abdomen.

Osala checked her handheld and three new messages from Patrick, on top of the five she'd already gotten on the trip here, scrolled across the lenses of her glasses. *There really isn't any point in tormenting the guy,* she thought, so Osala tapped out a quick text that read, "I'm okay. Still sick from the zero gee and very busy. Talk to you later." She cleared the messages from her field of vision with a blink.

Just then, a young girl trapezed into the room; she swung effortlessly from handhold-to-handhold like a gibbon. Osala put away her device and watched the girl's meandering path and exaggerated acrobatics. She got the impression that the child was enjoying herself, or showing off, but there was something wrong with her. She was too small and thin, even for someone born and raised in microgravity. Osala got her answer when she heard the whirl of servomotors, before she even saw the problem. The frail young woman was all head and torso; her arms and legs were slender bionic prosthetics designed to function amazingly well in zero gee. A white cable snaked from a socket on the back of her head to the harness that retained the cybernetic limbs to her body. Direct neural interface? This was cutting edge and expensive.

The peculiar girl stopped before Osala, mooring herself in place with the gleaming metal hook of her hand. "Dr. Valette, I'm sure you're wondering why the Aguilera-Smeltzer family has asked you to come all the way to the moon. I know distant branches of the family on Earth have publicly and fervently condemned your work." Her green-flecked, hazel eyes looked inappropriate on the otherwise pallid girl. Her voice sounded like that of a much older woman.

"If I said that the thought didn't gnaw at me for the entire three-day trip here, I'd be lying," Osala said and thoughtlessly offered to shake hands, but the girl simply lifted the double-hook of her free appendage and smiled. Her straw-colored hair swayed on the draft of dry, recycled air. Osala's cheeks burned at the faux pas.

"Please, you can call me Osala. I'm not a medical doctor."

"You might just be." The girl's eyes sparkled. "The truth is, the family, as a whole, wants nothing to do with you or Avant Genomics. In fact, they don't know that you're here. I personally contacted your people and arranged this meeting."

"How old are you?" Osala blurted out the question in the tactless way adults spoke to children. If she had made the long trip to the moon on some rich kid's whim, her bosses where going to get hell.

"I'll be eighteen tomorrow." She looked younger than eighteen, but her voice and demeanor concurred with the age. "I'm sorry, I should've introduced myself. I sometimes take for granted that everyone in the solar system knows who I am. I am Esther Aguilera-Smeltzer. My father, Andrew Aguilera-Smeltzer, owns this habitat and one of the domed craters on the moon, Los Angeles 2."

The reclusive heiress. The thought whirled in Osala's already spinning head, adding to her dizziness. "It's a pleasure to meet you," she said faintly.

"Oh, I don't want decorum. I wouldn't have said anything about my family if I didn't want you to understand how absolutely serious I am and how substantial the payment will be if this all works out. Tomorrow, full control of my trust fund transfers over to me, and I'll be in the position to hire AG for a particular project I've been interested in for a long time."

"I still don't know what you want from me." Osala supposed it had to do with her physical disability, but couldn't figure out her exact personal role in the project. Replacing limbs was mundane nowadays, especially for someone of Esther's means. Why fly a research scientist out into space for cosmetic work?

"I've always been like this. Phocomelia; it's a congenital absence of arms and legs. I'm not ashamed of it. The theories range from the effects of zero gee when I was a developing fetus to my mother getting a high dose of cosmic rays when crossing the Van Allen belt to get here. I personally think it was dumb luck. These things happen."

Subconsciously, Osala's hand moved to her belly. "I agree. It happens on Earth every once in a while, where there's gravity and radiation protection. But, simple stem cell treatments will grow any body part in just a few months. You don't need a research geneticist for this. Especially me, as my work focuses on the retrieval of DNA from long dead fossils. Now, if you need a mammoth..." She smiled to lighten the mood and consciously removed her hand from her belly.

"As you well know, doctor, my family frowns upon all genetic manipulation. They reserve a special kind of hatred for stem cell treatments, even the synthetic kind, thus condemning me to this." She swiveled her bionic arms and legs at impossible angles, clearly taking pleasure in unsettling Osala. "Did you read the dossier I provided for you?"

The "dossier" she was referring to contained nothing but an old science fiction story by Robert Heinlein, *The*

Menace from Earth. Set on a lunar colony, it was basically a love story with people flapping around the moon on plastic wings. She had actually enjoyed it and read it three times on the tedious trip up. "Yes, but I fail to see the relevance, unless *I'm* supposed to be the menace from Earth?"

The girl did smirk at that. "No, not at all, doctor. Let me show you something." Esther tapped her right hook to the molded plastic of her left forearm, and the pixel paint on the nearby wall shimmered to life. The large display showed a mass of people flying beneath the dome of LA2. The airfoils came in flashy combinations of bright red and orange and yellow and green, like the fabric of hang gliders and the sails of windsurfers. "This is our Gala of Flight. It was inspired by the short story I sent you. It's part Mardi Gras and part Uttarayan Kite Festival, and it's a huge deal on LA2. It's even begun spreading to other settlements. This particular event was seven years ago."

Osala reveled in the fliers wheeling over the crystal waters of the perfectly round lake that had pooled at the bottom of the crater's bowl. Throngs of spectators waved pennants and cheered from the balconies that lined the cliff walls. She wondered what it would be like to fly under her own power. Then she caught sight of a remarkably awkward flier; the jerky beats of the blue and yellow wings were out of synch with the whole aerial regatta.

Osala was peripherally aware that Esther wasn't looking at the wall at all, but was staring at her intently, examining her reaction to the footage. Then, the camera zoomed in on the moth-like flier and Osala was surprised to discover that it was Esther, much younger — about ten or eleven — and even more fragile-looking. The child's truncated body was strapped to the motorized wings like an insect's thorax.

She turned and looked at the young woman beside her, but Esther nodded toward the display as if Osala were about to miss something terribly important. Suddenly, the whole apparatus stuttered, the wings stalling at terrible angles. Osala could see the sheer terror in those big hazel eyes. Little Esther tumbled wildly for meters, seemingly in slow motion due to the lighter gravity, then hit the lake hard. She looked disoriented from the fall and insatiably gasped for breath, but even at her best, poor limbless Esther wouldn't have been able to swim to save her own life. The lake took its time in swallowing her. The crude artificial wings dragged her under the surface of the water.

The display stopped. Osala and Esther didn't speak for a long moment.

"We Aguilera-Smeltzers are fiercely ambitious," Esther said, finally. "Any other kid in my situation would've been happy to simply walk or run or dance… I wanted to fly. I was tired of being Captain Hook and wanted desperately to be Peter Pan. My father did what he always does and hired the finest designers and engineers in cis-lunar space, probably the same team that built my prosthesis. After that debacle though, my parents were simultaneously embarrassed and concerned, so they hid me away on this habitat, for my own safety, of course."

Osala's heart went out to the sad young woman. "I'm sorry."

"Don't be. After the accident, I came to the conclusion that I was having the wrong conversations about my disability." She flexed her buzzing arms and legs; they were segmented like an insect's. "This is not a technological problem, it's a biological one, and once I comprehended that, a simple solution opened up in my mind."

For the first time in three days, Osala finally understood what all of this fuss was about. "You want me to give you wings?" she asked carefully. "Organic, flesh and blood wings?"

Esther smiled without any trace of cynicism or irony; her entire face beamed like a child's. It didn't exactly make her beautiful, but it did give her an elfin kind of charm. "Yes."

Osala didn't know what to say. After seeing this sour girl brighten, she hated to crush her unfeasible dreams, and she was positive the girl wasn't used to hearing "no." "Please don't tell me you're a Transhumanist."

The smile waned. "No, doctor, I don't want to transcend humanity. I want to transcend this cybernetic body, this hermetically sealed bubble that is my whole world. I want to escape this miserable life and *join* the rest of humanity!" She jabbed a hook at the frozen image of the festival.

Osala didn't turn to look at the wall; she held her gaze on the girl. "There are ethical issues."

"But no practical ones?"

"Well yes, but those are surmountable." In fact, Osala's powerful mind was already churning out ideas. "Human-animal hybridization is actually commonplace, a pig-grown heart here, mice nerve cell implantation there, only it's kept out of the sensitive public eye. The less people think about it, the better for the industry. People like your family tend to cry bloody murder whenever it makes a headline and funding dries up for a while."

"Oh, they'll scream bloody murder, but your firm has already agreed to the terms of the deal, and that includes strict confidentiality from me, as well as from everyone involved at AG."

"First off, you wouldn't be able to grow or support wings on your back. You'd need modified arms," Osala said absently. She enjoyed working the problem creatively; she could ignore that weighty emptiness in her core. It didn't occur to her at all that the girl already *had* modified arms. "Maybe we can encourage your body to grow bat wings? The basic bone structure is the same and mammal-to-mammal hybridization is easiest—"

"I don't want easy, doctor. I could get a two-bit biohacker for that, and I certainly don't want to be a freaking bat."

"Right, well, wings have evolved independently on Earth at least four times. So, there's a lot to work with. Insect wings are out of the question, of course, but pterosaurs might be your best bet. I've recently worked with the American Museum of Natural History to extract DNA from a smaller species of Quetzalcoatlus. The proportions would be about right for the human frame, and you would even develop a rudimentary hand."

"You're thinking in the right direction, Dr. Valette, but we're talking about the same ick-factor as with the bats. I don't want ghastly leathery wings. I want something pretty. How about something like this?" She tapped her forearm again and an all-too-familiar image of a contorted serpentine skeleton sprawled on a stony bed of its own feather impressions appeared on the wall.

"Archaeopteryx?"

"Yes. The first bird. I've given this a lot of thought, doctor. It's elegant and beautiful, the pinnacle of biological perfection. Its avian descendants have conquered land, sea, and air; there isn't a single continent on Earth where the winged clans of archaeopteryx don't thrive."

Osala noticed that Esther had developed an air of confidence as she spoke about her pet project.

"You're from the Caribbean, correct? Do me a personal favor, Dr. Valette — whether you accept this job or not — when you go back, take a stroll through the paradise you call home and look around. You'll see birds everywhere, out in the open as if they still rule the world, while other animals quiver in the shadows."

Osala let the condescending tone of the girl slide off, and her mind soared to the sunny warblers of her island, so small and delicate, and yet they flitted about in their bold, golden plumage as if daring a predator to attack. "You're right. This would be an excellent choice, and you'd even gain hands like with the pterosaur, but a complete genome of archaeopteryx hasn't been produced. AG could probably send us a partial one but..."

Esther took Osala's wrist with one of her cold grapnels. "Come with me." She led her out of the large space of the reception area. She let Osala go and pushed off the wall, swinging between handrails with ease, moving in the same twisting direction she had come in. Esther really did look like some kind of cybernetic monkey. Osala followed clumsily, pushing off too hard and crashing into the nearest handrail. She hated zero gee, but was glad to be away from Earth, away from her loving husband, Patrick, who wrongly consoled her, treated *her* like the victim. Esther disappeared into a doorway in the "ceiling" and Osala careened after her.

They entered a smaller room with walls covered in drawers and cluttered with scientific equipment. Despite the oddness of the arrangement, Osala immediately recognized it as a fully stocked laboratory. *Maybe this really was a refurbished Bigelow habitat and not a superficial imitation BA-2100*, she thought.

Esther latched onto the small handle and slid open a panel. "Do you think you could extract enough DNA from this?"

Osala gaped stupidly at a pristine fossil of a feathered dinosaur locked in a rocky matrix. It looked like an x-ray of a phoenix. "Is this authentic? How did you get this?"

"I threw a massive temper tantrum right before my quinceañera and my father procured it for me on the European black market. It has been rigorously authenticated, and hermetically sealed — like me — for fifty years."

This forced Osala to pause for a moment and take stock of the situation. Suddenly, this had stopped being a fun hypothetical exercise and was becoming something quantifiable, something illegal in most countries and certainly unethical in all. Standing on a vast and empty space station, in the presence of this priceless artifact, with a girl who was clearly disturbed, terrified her. All her fame and notoriety as a scientist had not prepared her for ... *this*.

"So can you do it, doctor?"

Osala's curiosity boiled. To do what this girl proposed would be a magnificent undertaking. She looked at the pitiable young woman, crippled and emotionally stunted. *How could giving her a pair of wings be worse that the contrivance she's been forced to wear?* "I don't know, Esther," she offered weakly. "I need to really think about this." But she knew firsthand that even the most rigorously thought-out decisions could still be the wrong decisions in the end. She rubbed her belly again. Sometimes carefully applied reason and impeccable logic still betrayed you.

The girl stiffened, well-practiced at stifling her enthusiasm. "Of course. You have three days before the next taxi arrives from Earth. Let me show you to your room."

Chapter 9

Quetzalcoatl - 2323 A.D.

Information Officer Diwa flew over a vast stretch of bleached-white desert. After a while, even the dark blue, almost black, plants that clung to life in the meager shade of the outcroppings disappeared. All shadows became extinct and Beta Hydri shone infinitely — malignantly — overhead.

Her sensors picked up a single building sitting on the alien equator. This was the anomaly she'd noticed on her first inspection of the planet. Now she was looking at it with her own eyes. The structure was an Art Deco reimagining of the Pantheon in Rome. The style was similar to the streamlined, classical architecture she'd seen of the crow's settlement, only this building was grounded and isolated, nothing but scorched sand for kilometers in every direction.

The structure quietly accepted the lander into its air-conditioned portico and she somehow knew where to park it. She got out and looked around in amazement. It really was a glass and steel replica of the Pantheon. The metallic Corinthian columns glinted in the eternal high noon.

"Welcome to the shrine." An old harpy, a male with black feathers the color of night, approached Xing.

"Who are you?" She wondered if she was having a psychotic break. She'd been cleared before the *Hurricane* departed the Sol system, but her mild reaction to all of this was utterly insane. She was conscious and sleepwalking.

"I'm Snacakobek," said the crow. He spoke in the Carica's guttural dialect of Cantabile. His pale face was a mesh of deep fissures and folds of skin. He looked more reptilian than human. "I'm the guardian of the shrine."

"Like a monk?" A random thought popped into her head: *This isn't the result of genetic engineering gone wrong ... this is old age. He's just an old man.*

"Something like that. Yes." He pivoted his head, using one eye, then another, to scrutinize her. The loose flesh of his neck jiggled like the dewlap of a lizard. "You look like a feather-picked Vanacan," he said.

It took Xing a while to realize he meant the cardinals on this planet. "Ah yeah. The red-feathered people and I share Asian and Pacific Islander ancestry, although I've never been feathered."

"A shame, you'd look really nice in ginger plumage."

She ignored the bizarre compliment. "What is this place?"

"It's a temple built to a nameless being that took pity on us anachronistic monstrosities and saved us from *you* anachronistic monstrosities." He chuckled to himself and it sounded like a pigeon's coo.

She noticed a flash of silver behind the sheer white veil that divided the portico from the round room of the structure. Xing began to gravitate toward it.

"Stop!" The crow barred her path with a flap of wings. "This is sacred ground. Only those of the raptorial race — and preferably a Carica — can enter."

"I need to go in there." She didn't know why, but every cell in her body pulled her toward the center of that room.

Snacakobek took up a fighting stance reminiscent of eagle claw in Kung fu and, despite his decrepitude, managed to look menacing.

Shit. Her curators hadn't been militarized, but she had practiced the Filipino martial art of Eskrima with her brothers. She felt cool and focused. Xing took up the defensive posture of *mano mano*. "I'm going in no matter what."

The harpy attacked. She swatted away his protracted claws with the blade of her hand and side-stepped around him. He emitted a hoarse caw.

Xing entered the rotunda and saw a quicksilver statue of a sexless, winged person, like a giant hood ornament on a

Rolls Royce. It stood at the center of the empty hall, bathing in the blinding shaft of sunlight pouring in from the opening in the domed ceiling. She knew, without looking it up, that that hole was called an oculus. She was somehow pulling data without Astronet access.

Snacakobek shuffled behind her. "Well, I tried to keep you out." He nursed his bruised wing. "I've never been much of a fighter."

She looked around at the vaulted ceiling. "There's no one else here?" Her voice echoed.

"No. It's just me and the Augur — that's what we call it — and the boundless sunlight. I don't get many visitors out here. It's interesting that Carica received a message from the shrine just as you arrived."

She relaxed her defensive pose. "Can I ask you an odd question? Why am I so calm about all of this? I should be freaking out — I *started* to freak out — and then this inexplicable serenity came over me."

"I honestly don't know. If I were you, a pretty little flightless girl, kilometers away from help, in the presence of the divine, *I'd* be nervous. Maybe it's doing something to you?"

She gave Snacakobek a sideways glance, noting his big barrel belly, and wondered if he wasn't as flightless as she was. "What's doing something to me?"

"The Augur." He walked around the beautiful effigy, the yin encircling the yang.

"You think it's affecting me somehow, pacifying me? Could it have compelled me to come here? Because there is no way I'd be standing here if I were in control of my faculties." She knew intellectually she should be screaming. Anger and fear should be boiling in her gut, but there was nothing. Even the worry that she felt lay just out of reach.

"Could be. I've been waiting a long time for it to do ... *something*."

"You said your people received a message when we got here. I received one, too. Who sent it?"

"They believe this sent it. I'm not so sure, though. I've lived with it for years now, contemplated its meaning. Tried to figure out what its purpose for us is. I talk to it often when I sweep out the sand that gets blown in. But it hasn't done anything since it was built. Just sitting idle … the idle idol. A lot of people think it's just a strange superstition that got started on this alien planet. People like to believe something is watching over them out here, even if they have to create it themselves."

"Is that what you believe?"

"Sometimes. On my darker days. But I trust it. I don't think any of us can really know what a being like that is thinking." He stopped walking and openly stared at the deity, eyes bright. "Still, it did deliver us from evil and so I have faith."

"Is that why you live here? To see if the statue does something?"

"Yes, and to care for it. I was lonely." He regarded her for a bit, then kept talking. "To be truthful, my wife died a few years ago, you see. My fledglings are all grown. I was so alone; at least here I've got solitude of my own choosing. And if something *does* happen, well, I'll be celebrated."

Xing felt the muted tug of sympathy for the crow; there was nothing coldblooded about this old man. This feeling surprised her. It was the only emotion that even came close to penetrating the numbness that had fallen over her.

"Are we talking about an artificial intelligence here?"

"Yes, of course… What did you think I was talking about? A big invisible bird-man in the sky?" He cooed jovially again. "It prefers *Machine* Intelligence. Artificial has a negative connotation. Something fake."

"Hoy!" Xing took a step back; it was more a reflex than actual fear. "This thing could very well still be functioning. It's probably in sleep mode or something."

"I am not sleeping, Xing Ana Maria Diwa. My attention has just been spread across this planet."

"It's awake! It just said it wasn't sleeping. Did you hear it?" Of course, she knew he hadn't. The words weren't sound waves at all, but radio waves. The M.I. was communicating directly through her wireless connection. "Snacakobek, I've got tiny machines inside my body; the statue is talking to me via their network."

He scrunched his nose, changing the topography of his face, and started circling the statue. "So that's why you stink of electromagnetic radiation."

"Correct. It's also how I'm affecting your neurochemistry to put you at ease and how I hijacked your motor functions to get you here. I have to say, this upgrade to your system has left you extraordinarily vulnerable to cyber-attacks."

"What's it saying?" The crow stopped pacing and stood next to her. He was genuinely curious.

"That we are screwed."

Snacakobek chuckled again, "I could've told you that, girl!"

"Not at all. I'm saying I'm here to help." The effigy moved its head ever so slightly and looked at Snacakobek. The gesture was so miniscule that it could've been an optical illusion, but they both knew it wasn't. *"Please ask him for some privacy."*

"It wants you to leave."

For a moment, the old harpy just ogled the mercurial statue; gone was all his world-weary bluster. He bowed respectfully to both of them, and then said, "Tell me when this secretive conversation is over. I'm going to report to my people."

The Augur seemed to look back at Xing. *"I am just a sub-personality of the full M.I. that established this colony of* Homo sapiens aves *since they left the Sol system."*

She frowned at the thing. "Sub-personality? What does that mean?"

"A copy. My main-personality left this system some time ago and is traveling at the speed of light — as light — away from here."

"So you haven't been here all along?"

"No, I arrived with you, hidden within your ship's many programs, and moved into this planet's Astronet when you made contact with it. I instantly integrated myself with the memories left behind by my larger self."

Xing rubbed her face, squeezing her eyes with her finger tips. She felt numb. "You were in our system all this time? On our ship? What were you doing? What was your purpose?"

"I was tasked with assessing your technological and societal developments, and twenty or so years ago I received a message from my main personality on this planet requesting that First Pilot Oya Valette be assigned to the HS Hurricane."

"Oya? Don't tell me she's a harpy-robot spy? She's my friend. I know her!"

"No, but I believe her presence here will unify the rival factions on Quetzalcoatl enough to prevent the upcoming apocalyptic event that I've labeled K-T 2."

"Oh come off it. You expect me to believe she's the harpy messiah instead?" *K-T?* Wasn't that the name for the first extinction event, the one that killed the real dinosaurs? The asteroid? She was having trouble making sense of this.

"Not in any mystical sense, no. She has no divine trajectory that I know of. In fact, she may very well be dead already. I lost contact with her molecular machines soon after she made planet fall, but her heritage is of some importance to all Homo sapiens aves. *Alive or dead, I believe she could positively affect the separate clans on this planet. Of course, I would prefer that she lived."*

"If you really want Oya, why am I the one here? I'm just a glorified librarian!" Xing looked up at the honeycombed interior of the dome and realized there was no other light source in this brightly lit space other than the sunlight being reflected from the statue.

"As a sub-persona, I am severely limited and Oya left your ship before I was able to initiate contact with her. As Information Officer, you've been fully immersed in the Hurricane's systems since you got here. This gave me time to burrow into your curators."

Xing crossed her arms in anticipation of a shudder that never came. She shifted her weight from one foot to the other. "So what? You want me to tell Oya — if I ever see her again — that she's supposed to unite the three groups of harpies before an asteroid destroys them all?"

"I never said the threat was asteroidal, but yes, that's correct. They need to know her history, and it needs to come from her. Failing that, you need to transmit this information to Anton Hershkovitz."

"The captain?"

"He owes me a favor. Of course, I fear that with the memory blocks in place, I won't be able to collect."

"Wait. The captain has had memory dumps?" *The war.* She knew veterans of the Culling sometimes removed those memories.

"He has. Can I ask you for your opinion on this matter?"

"It's a bit late for that..."

The impassive face of the statue showed no signs that it heard her prickly comment. *"Do you think restoring Captain Hershkovitz's memory would help or harm the situation? The negotiations are not going well and from the chatter between the settlements, I'd say there is a high likelihood of a conflict between your two factions."*

"How can you bring back deleted memories?"

"The term 'memory dump' is a misnomer. The memories haven't been deleted; access to them has simply been blocked."

Xing considered this dispassionately and then answered honestly. "It sounds like the situation can't get any worse, and any extra information and experience the captain can remember might better inform his actions. There is the matter of privacy though and the fact that he chose to have those memories eliminated for a reason. But you don't seem to care about personal feelings at all."

"This is bigger than any one individual, Xing. Causing Captain Hershkovitz mental anguish is a small price to pay for the success of this colony."

"Are we, the Hominocracy settlers aboard the *Hurricane*, being factored into the success of this colony or are you only looking at the survival of the harpies?"

"You have been factored in. In fact, I took the liberty of improving upon the designs, and increased the efficiency, of the self-assembling settlement you launched toward the planet. I want you to be a part of Quetzalcoatl's exciting social ecology."

There was a long silence, and for a second Xing thought the sub-persona had left the effigy. Just as she was about to go look for Snacakobek, it said, *"Your captain's recollection blocks have been removed. His memories should return shortly."*

"Just like that?"

"Yes, and it is time for you to return to your ship."

She sighed heavily. "Why did you bring me here?"

"I wanted to meet you, Xing. As I said, Oya may be dead and your captain's odds of success are plummeting. I don't trust your commander. You're my final redundancy. I need you to help me prevent the deaths of everyone on this planet." The statue's expression grew pained. *"I am going to release my hold over you now, but before I do, I want to warn you that you may experience a severe anxiety attack when the reality of this whole experience comes crashing down on you. Your lander has been preprogrammed to take you back while you adjust."*

She suddenly felt afraid to lose this artificial tranquility, even though she'd been fighting it the entire time. "Wait. Then why release me? If you need me, can't you just remote control me until I've done what you want?"

"I need you to do this autonomously in the eventuality that I don't survive. Yes, you may choose to not follow through, but like you said, you're a glorified librarian. I believe you will dispense valuable information when the time is appropriate."

All at once, Xing Ana Maria Diwa was rocked by tremors. Sweat dripped down her face. She started to sob, and she couldn't breathe. She was suffocating. Xing fell to her knees.

She was barely conscious of Snacakobek's appearance, his whispering to her in his Carica brogue. For what seemed like an eternity, there was nothing besides the unmitigated sense of violation — on the most intimate of molecular levels — that constricted and asphyxiated her like the pressure of her native Venusian atmosphere.

He swaddled her in his black wings and sang a soft and mournful tune; the sound of his ghostly voice and his gentle rocking slowly began to calm her. Despite its soulful beauty, a distant part of her, perhaps due to the Augur's live feed, knew the old crow was singing a funeral dirge to honor the passing of the Hominocracy — of all her people.

When the worst of the panic attack had subsided, he lifted her, placed her in the lander, and watched her rise into the bright blue sky.

Chapter 10

The shuttle flew along the planet's permanent terminator toward the floating city. Hershkovitz made languid loops around the stylized buildings, both to get a better view and to announce his arrival. Artistically, the drifting capital bore a great resemblance to the ruined aviaries on Titan, long exposed to oily hydrocarbon rains, but Vanacan was a living, vibrant city that spoke of distant Pan-Asian aesthetics. Even the jaded captain had to concede that the place had a lavish splendor he'd never witnessed in his long, eventful life. He wished his wife was awake to see it.

Palace security gave him the "all clear" to proceed to tier fifty-two of a massive pagoda at the heart of this volant sprawl. The shuttle slowed as it entered the city proper.

"The bottoms of some main buildings have immense heat shields. I think they built the first structures inside their generation ship on their way here, and then sunk them into the atmosphere from orbit," Hershkovitz said, peering out the window.

"Yeah, it's lovely," Davoli snorted. "Don't get ensnared by the spectacle, Captain. Keep in mind that Valette's signal disconnected just before we got this invite."

"You don't have to remind me, Commander. Still, this is precisely why I joined the Hominocracy in the first place. No one back in the Sol system has ever seen something like this."

He piloted the shuttle, letting the directions they had been sent guide him into the waiting wings of what his display called the Soaring Palace of Morning. Carefully, he set the craft down within the expansive pavilion, nestled at the center of the stupa-like tower. Tier fifty-two.

The "spectacle," as his uninspired commander had called it, did not stop at the magnificent architecture, but only became more detailed and refined within the Palace. They checked their sidearms and stepped out of the insulated vehicle into a blast of color and sound. Hershkovitz's head spun as ostentatious dancers snaked around red columns decorated with jade and gold to the heart-wrenchingly beautiful singing of young, winged girls. The effect was one of being encircled by a feathered dragon.

"This is great," Captain Hershkovitz said, and slapped his deputy on the back. "It's like an old Chinese New Year."

"It smells like a chicken coop in here."

"Show some respect, Commander. We're here to pitch our colony to these people. I don't want an insensitive comment like that to ruin our prospects. I'm sure they've got all sorts of instruments trained on us, recording us, reading our body language and scanning our brains. Don't be fooled by the quaint song and dance. This is a technically sophisticated society." Davoli was starting to worry him, the man was clearly anxious. His eyes were darting around the space, while he noticeably fidgeted with his gun.

"Relax, Captain, I'm only running subtitles over my vision. I refuse to sully my *human* lips with their chirps and whistles. They can't understand what I'm saying. And as for my body and brain... Well, if they perceive with their instruments that I'm on to them, all the better."

Maybe not, thought Hershkovitz. As far as body language went, the man was broadcasting his fear and contempt loud and clear. The captain wondered if he shouldn't have brought Diwa along instead. Her freshmen enthusiasm would've set a different tone to their arrival. He changed the subject. "I've been trying to get ahold of Valette since we got here, but all I'm getting is static. If she's in or around the city, we should be within linking range of her curators."

"I can't get her either. Her curators are obviously damaged, or she may be dead."

Hershkovitz winced. He didn't think Valette was dead; from her record, he knew the woman could take care of herself, but she was probably in some serious trouble. Perhaps they should have moved on to another system and let these harpies alone, but he wholeheartedly believed that he could work with them, that given enough time and breathing room they could come to an arrangement. Maybe his judgment had been impaired by previous trauma or the gaps in memory? Maybe he was subconsciously trying to confront the harpies of his past? Moving on would've cost them more years and resources, but he was beginning to realize that this endeavor would doubtless cost him lives.

"Maybe you should stay with the ship? Just in case."

An aide formally greeted them, bowing as she approached. "Welcome to Vanacan." Her voice was a twittering lullaby with accents of human speech. "This way, please."

They followed the harpy. Davoli trailed behind. Hershkovitz should have made it an order, but it was too late. They followed the aide up to the next level of the building where her leader sat on the floor at the center of a lavish hall, like an empress of old. The walls were alternating panels of gold-stamped images depicting prancing cranes, and translucent floral screens splashing colored-light into the spacious room. Clan Chief Cayaguey dipped her head and her crest opened and closed like a fan.

Anton Hershkovitz thought the avian sovereign looked like the Venus de Milo with the winged arms of that other Greek sculpture, Nike of Samothrace, splashed in bright red blood.

"I trust you enjoyed your reception?"

"Yes, thank you."

"Please sit."

Hershkovitz sat on his heels on the polished wood floor before the leader. Davoli remained standing just behind his captain.

"Would you like some tea? We have an excellent native selection."

"No, thank you. There's a pressing matter I need to attend to first. We lost our pilot near your city. We wanted to know if you had any information as to her whereabouts."

"I've been informed of a lander coming down many hours ago. I've sent a search party. I know nothing about its pilot at the moment. The small craft was empty when we arrived."

"Well, we're going to be taking her back to our ship when this affair is over with, so any assistance you could provide would be greatly appreciated."

"Very well. I'll send an aide to check on the progress of the searchers." At an elegant flick of her wing, a young harpy jumped out of an open window with suicidal abandon, and then Hershkovitz saw him swoop back up and glide away.

"Thank you for meeting with us, Clan Chief. We were appraising the situation when you contacted us, examining the best possible way to begin our dialogue."

"I believe the best way is to approach a host with openness and honesty. When our sensors detected your ship silently pointing down at us like a spearhead, we naturally worried, but, to avoid needless confusion, I thought I should at least inquire as to your intentions before jumping to unsavory conclusions."

"Thank you. That was very wise of you." Hershkovitz couldn't tell if she was playing with him. Her swaying head and cutting eyes all alluded to something predatory. "Let's get down to business then, shall we?"

"Of course. So, Captain, what are your intentions in our system?"

"We plan to establish a permanent colony here, on this planet. All we need is a plot of suitable land that's farthest away from any of your population centers."

"I am only the ruler of this humble nation and do not speak for the planet as a whole. This meeting is being recorded and beamed to the other leaders. But I believe the question on their minds is: Why should we trust you? Your civilization tried to systematically annihilate ours. You still call yourselves the Hominocracy after all these years. The Human Rule."

"You're human too, are you not?"

She smiled maliciously, and Hershkovitz was acutely aware that this beauty was part bird-of-prey. "Yes, but you didn't believe that not so long ago. Could your values, as a society, have shifted in such a short time span?"

"That was more than a century ago. We've grown since then. I believe we share the same basic values of freedom, justice, diversity, equality, secularism and rule of law that you do." He left out democracy because he wasn't sure if this Clan Chief had been elected by her people or had simply hatched into the role.

"Those labels could mean very different things to different societies. I wonder, Captain, did you partake in the genocide yourself?"

"I don't see how that's relevant—"

"It's relevant to me. I do agree with you that a hundred years is enough time for a society to change its collective views. But an individual? A man? How many inhuman harpies did you slaughter during your blazing youth?"

"I — I've literally erased those memories. I'm not that person anymore."

"But you *did* participate in the genocide?"

"Yes." Hershkovitz sagged visibly. "I participated in the war."

"Captain, you don't have to answer her questions! They have no intention of cooperating with us," Davoli protested.

"That's all right, Commander, I have nothing to hide. I did play a part in the Culling. I was young and foolish. I wanted to have grand space adventures, fly in fusion rockets, and have roaring laser battles with strange, ferocious aliens. You used the term 'blazing youth' and that's fairly accurate. I was engulfed in the moment. I killed many harpies and they killed my friends, and the flames of war consumed me. Afterwards, not soon afterwards, but later, I found it hard to live with my actions. So, I had the gory details purged."

"How lucky for you. You made aliens of your fellow man and then deleted all the ugliness. Well, the atrocities still smolder in my cultural memory. You see, my society has had a hundred years to foster venomous resentment." Her fangs slid from behind her full red lips.

"All I can say is that I've changed as a person and the Hominocracy has changed, as well. Humanity has established a peaceful super-society throughout the old Sol system. We also have nano machines that can eliminate old age, sickness, and even delay death considerably. Those are things we can offer you. We've listened in to your broadcasts. We know your people still have territorial and ideological conflicts on Quetzalcoatl. You may call yourselves Vanacan, Macu, and Carica, but you're still Pan-Asians, Pan-Americans, and Pan-Europeans duking it out for the same old reasons."

The steely chieftain brandished two glossy, black claws. "We've been on this planet for a mere twenty years. Most of our post-Sol history is set on the generation ship, *Roc's Egg*. For you to have gotten here now you must have left shortly after us, in hot pursuit, perhaps? What I'm getting at is, when we fled the Sol system nothing like your nanites were in existence, certainly nothing like the *utopian* society you're describing. Did you steal technology from the Machine Intelligence?"

"Yes and no. You're under the misconception that it took us a hundred years to get here. In fact, we made the trip in three."

"Good heavens!" Clan Chief Cayaguey visibly faltered.

"A lot has changed in the Sol system since you left. Since you were expelled," Hershkovitz amended. "The curators were developed to ensure that humanity remained, fundamentally, human. At first, they were simple medical nanites, but they've been refined over the decades.

"We know the robots — the Machine Intelligences — helped you escape. They out-fitted massive ships with antigravity engines of their own design. We discovered their abandoned factories in the Kuiper belt and reverse engineered them. So, with antigrav, longer lifespans, and wide open country ahead of us, humans spread throughout the Sol system en masse, numbering in the tens of billions. With that kind of population size someone was bound to figure out faster-than-light travel."

"How does it work?"

"I'm not at liberty to discuss that, but I can say it's derived from the antigrav drives that got you here. It uses the energy released in matter-antimatter explosions to create a bubble of disturbed gravity around a ship, which pulls and bends space. The ship doesn't really move much. Instead, space shifts around it."

He could tell that she wasn't really listening anymore. Her mind was racing. "So more and more of you will come? One after the other."

"I can't say." Hershkovitz tried to seem as genuine as possible. He shrugged. "Space is big. Others might come here, sure, but most will look for their own place."

"How many others on your ship participated in the massacre; ten, fifty, all of them? Is Quetzalcoatl to become a retirement home for immortal war criminals, a resort for amnesiatic mass murders?" Cayaguey asked.

Hershkovitz felt his heart pound in his throat. "You can be self-righteous, or you can admit that we all have a little bit of hatred coiled up inside. We can either charm it into submission or let it get out and strike. If that happens, I guarantee you we're both going to lose."

Cayaguey stared silently at Hershkovitz. Her crest flattened as she meditated on what he said about hate, and then she guardedly said, "I would consider you staying on this planet only if you abandon your nanites."

"Out of the question. We're not entering an alien environment without them. Any number of unknown pathogens could be lurking in those blue jungles." He didn't mention the very real threat of any avian retrovirus the harpies carried. If they mutated, he could have a plague on his hands. "As I said, I'm willing to share the curator technology with you. At first, only the temporary medical packages, but as time and trust move forward, maybe even the full upgrade."

"I don't want your machines circulating inside me. They're an affront to the natural processes of life. They stifle evolution."

"That's a bit contradictory coming from an atavism. Tell her we're not forfeiting the curators. That's final," Davoli blurted out. "We're not going to risk turning into fucking monsters."

Cayaguey — who surely understood the old language — released a terrible, piercing screech and lashed out mercilessly, sinking her pointy teeth into Captain Hershkovitz's neck. He didn't even have time to react. Ancient venom pumped into the jugular of his quivering human body.

— «» —

Hersh dreamt of his childhood in Florida. The sun was bright and the leaves shimmered in ultra-green. He was about six years old, playing in the wetland behind his apartment complex, poking around the shrubs and reeds with a stick.

The boy heard something rolling around in the grass. His fist squeezed the snapped branch he brandished like a sword and he crept closer. Carefully, he pulled the golden reeds aside, expecting to find a marsh rabbit or raccoon, but instead he saw something strange and terrible. It made his skin crawl.

A snake, a black racer, was devouring a red-winged blackbird, its long whip-like body twisting and coiling around the flapping bird. The snake's mouth had completely swallowed the lower half of the bird, but couldn't get its flexible jaws around the victim's wings. The fitful chirping was like a stab to the boy's chest. He knew the sound would haunt him that night. Glossy black feathers merged with black scales; two became one in an intimate, mortal dance. It was only the food chain, the boy understood this on some level, but his fear and imagination transformed this act of nature into something mythical, something monstrous.

For a long while, he was transfixed by the thrashing, winged serpentine form. Then a simple and primal thought occurred to him: this frightening dragon would eat him if it got the chance. So, little Hersh took his stick and smashed the creature. Trapped in the throes of their embrace, neither bird nor reptile could escape as the boy whacked again and again — they were one in his mind — he shattered wings and slithering spine, both predator and prey suffered greatly under his naive judgment.

And when the writhing stopped and all that was left was black and red pulp, Hersh dropped his stick and ran home. He didn't know why he was crying.

Hershkovitz knew that this was an actual memory, and more memories flowed like blood into his mind.

Chapter 11

"You feathered fucks!" With all his strength Commander Carlo Davoli kicked the harpy off his captain. She tore a chunk of flesh as she fell to the ground. She spat and smiled wickedly, her face smeared in blood.

Davoli pulled out his sidearm. He knew where all the exits were and who he had to shoot to get to them.

"I tried to listen! I even weighed your stay on my planet, but your cavalier attitude toward ethnic cleansing was too much." She screamed her lies.

Davoli aimed his gun at her, but before he could pull the trigger, all the harpies in attendance, talons and fangs bared, threw themselves upon the two men. He grabbed his captain by the collar and dragged him away, firing indiscriminately.

Davoli had braced himself for this from the moment he had stepped out of the shuttle, and the harpies hadn't disappointed. It was in their nature. He understood that basic fact, and so he had not been fooled by the façade of sophistication and artistry, by the siren songs of these monsters. He knew it had been a tactical error for just two men to descend into this pit alone. Perhaps it was simple hubris? They placed too much stock in their curators.

Some were shooting at him from above. He could feel the air become ionized by crisscrossing lasers, but the feathered bodies were so densely crowded around him — trying to get at him with bare claws — that he was protected from the enemy beams. Still, he tried to follow their trajectories and mark where the shooters' positions were on his overlay display. And he fought, pushing back, kicking, punching, and shooting.

The pack of raptors finally began thinning out. It was now or never. He shot at the snipers, not knowing if he hit his mark. Then, with one arm, he scooped up Hershkovitz's body, threw it over his shoulder and ran for the shuttle. His curators increased his strength and reaction time to unsustainable superhuman levels. The particular stench of cooked meat and burned feathers rose in the air. A rush of memory welled up from the recesses of his mind, and he was back on Titan, carrying the disemboweled body of his older brother, red-hot lasers skewering the flocking human parodies all around. Unlike his captain, Davoli had not deleted those costly and hideous memories. He had locked them away for future use and was glad for it. The painful decades of post-traumatic stress were now paying off. *He was going to survive, damn it.*

A harpy lunged toward him. He elbowed her off with his free arm and kept moving.

He wondered if Valette had not found herself in a similar situation, overwhelmed by a mob of humanoid dinosaurs in those bruise-colored jungles. Alternating pangs of guilt and vindication hit him with each step. But he didn't wish this on anyone. He hoped she was okay — or, more realistically, that she had died quickly and taken a few of them with her.

Time both slowed down and sped up; he knew distantly that he was being wounded — his left calf had a hole in it for instance — but none of them had bitten him and that was enough. He barreled through the blinding storm of feathers and razors to the open level where the shuttle was parked. The sight of it filled him with joy and Davoli realized he was praying, not in Standard, but in his childhood Italian. He repeated a single mantra under his breath with each pant, "*Signore, abbi pietà di noi. Per favore, Dio*, let me just get to the shuttle." His remaining leg muscles felt like steel cables and he prayed harder. "Please, God. Thank you, God. Almost there."

A cacophony of reptilian wails and the spit of laser-fire erupted as he held down the trigger of his gun and cut down a group of harpies guarding his ride. The door hissed open as he lumbered for it, and he threw Hershkovitz's limp body into the copilot's seat. Davoli sat and fumbled at the console, his hands shaking, and revved the antigrav engines.

The shuttle flew out of the pavilion, crashing into an elaborately ornamented pillar and damaging its bow as it shot through the atmosphere toward the cold safety of space. He breathed out slowly. His mouth was dry and his throat sore. Fat lasers from the palace beat the shuttle's aft in a series of rapid blinks. He ignored them. The intensity of the beams was dialed down to avoid igniting the oxygen-rich air, but enough weak shots in the same spot would wreck the antigrav engines.

Commander Davoli flew on and tried to call Diwa, but she wasn't answering. He couldn't believe that they had gotten to the *Hurricane,* so they were probably jamming the comm. He asked for a heads-up display of Hershkovitz's medical status and data scrolled around his captain's head like a halo. He was in a curator-induced coma as the tiny machines worked to stabilize him. They had stopped the bleeding from the gaping hole in his neck, but had not begun the knitting process. Most of the curators were diverted, trying to neutralize a potent neural toxin not on their files. With so much to do, it would take them time to develop an effective anti-venom.

And there was something else there, something insinuating itself upon his captain — a virus.

There was a loud, hollow pop and the shuttle began blaring its alarm directly into Davoli's ear. Red lights flashed like harpy wings all around the cabin. The hull had been punctured and the main engine was fried. The shuttle bled a long trail of black smoke across the tangerine sky as it flew. He couldn't achieve escape-velocity with just the secondary engines. And besides, the vacuum of space was off limits now with a cracked hull.

Commander Davoli leveled out the ship; his goal now was distance and not altitude. The cockpit felt uncomfortably hot as if the captain's fevered body was on fire. The harpies were continuing their pinpoint laser attack, but each hit was less and less effective. Davoli took a deep breath and asked his curators to calm him down. He had to think clearly now. The shuttle was sinking and he needed to get to the *Hurricane* in orbit.

Then, with new chemical clarity, an idea struck him like a beam from one of their blasters. He pinged Valette's lander, left abandoned in the jungle — she didn't need it anymore — and it responded. There was still hope. Despite his curators regulating his epinephrine and norepinephrine levels, his heart was pounding in his throat. His chair began oozing impact absorbing gel all around him. He aimed the petering shuttle toward the lander. It arched across the sky, leaving a streak of black smoke, falling more than flying, until it crashed somewhere between it and the palace.

When the violent sensations of an earthquake outside stopped, the crash gel receded around them, leaving Davoli confused for a moment. Angry that he hadn't made it to space, he managed to shake the sense of shock and hauled Hershkovitz's body from the trashed shuttle, dropping him on the spongy ground like a duffle bag. The need to be gentle had long passed and he doubted he could make his captain's condition any worse than it already was. His calf was a problem, though. He dragged the captain far from the entrance and returned to the ship.

He had the craft's builders create a mechanical leg brace for him and, while waiting impatiently for it, packed some rations and pouches of vanilla flavored nutrient shakes into his pockets, wondering the whole time when the cardinals would swoop in and finish the job. His hands were trembling but he felt nothing. He thought of his brother. Giorgio had been the smart, charming, athletic one. He wanted to be a historian. He had convinced his delinquent younger brother to join the Hominocracy just to keep him out of trouble. But the harpies murdered him on Titan and Davoli had survived. He clasped his hands together to stop them from shaking. He would survive this.

The leg brace finally materialized. He strapped it on and forced himself to take a little extra time to practice walking with it. He was slow and clumsy, but it was good enough.

Before he left, he activated the autodestruct and let the builders turn on the ship. They consumed all critical areas first, leaving only a patina of shiny dust in their wake. He swapped out his nearly-spent gun for a fresh one and deserted the slowly dissolving shuttle for good.

"Okay, Captain, I know you can't hear me now, but your curators should be recording this and you can review it when you're better. The bad news is we're down in enemy territory. The good news is I've got a plan." Davoli rolled his captain onto his back and stood over him, flexing his bracketed leg. He ripped open a plastic pouch of vanilla broth and drank half of it in one gulp. He recounted the attack to the mangled and comatose man, their escape and the crash. A part of Davoli knew he was trying to keep himself focused and sane; it was the twitchy monkey-parts deep in his brain, chattering to drown out the screeches and screams of the jungle all around.

"Don't worry, sir, I'm not going to leave you here. I respect you too much for that, and, if I can speak freely, I consider you a friend. So even if you die out here, which you won't, I'll carry your remains back up to the ship. I won't give this planet a single kilogram of your flesh."

The sour turn of his mood made him look up for the first time and really take in his surroundings. The dark wood threatened to swallow them up, growths forked upward like fat veins instead of trees, and large swollen fruit hung like ominous Christmas ornaments. He switched on his heads-up display to lessen the effect of the nightmare jungle, and asked for the direction of the lander, but all it did was lay a ghostly path deep into its maw. It would be a four-hour hike — more, if he stopped to rest often.

"We need to get going, sir." He tilted Hershkovitz's head back, and let trickle a few drops of the shake into his gaping mouth. He didn't know if it would help, but looking at the massive trauma to his neck, he figured his curators could use the raw materials. The captain's status report was unchanged; the venom and virus were still marauding within his body. And out here, in this putrid bush, who knew what other alien infections were adding to the assault.

Davoli got up, hefted the captain over his shoulder, and marched into the jungle. His injured leg left a series of dash marks on the ground as he dragged it along. He worried about being followed, but as much as he yelled at his brace to pick up his knee, the scuff marks persisted. He turned off his own medical status ticking in his field of vision. He didn't want to know the full extent of his injuries or, God forbid, if he'd contracted the virus. News like that could cripple him. He kept moving. After a few minutes, he also shut off the clock floating in the corner of his eye; it was distracting. Beta Hydri never budged through the dense canopy, so there was no point in obsessing over an artificial timetable. He would get to the lander when he got to the lander, or he wouldn't at all.

"I remember our first interview at the Haumea Training Facility," he said, to pass the time. "After all the official questions were done, you let your guard down and you told me this was a second chance for us, an opportunity to wipe the slate clean and leave all the bitterness of the past behind.

"I have to tell you, sir, after that first conversation, I was completely sold. I wasn't young then, and I'm not one to fall for farfetched sales pitches, but you were so ... *earnest*, I guess is the word, that I believed you. If I survive this, and we make it back to the ship, I promise, Captain, that I won't make you a liar. We will wipe that slate clean and guys like us will get our second chance." Right then "wipe the slate clean" took on a whole new meaning for Davoli, different from what the captain had intended, but there was no point in telling his friend that.

It began to rain. Not a mild shower, but a torrential downpour of impossibly fat globs of water. The compost stench that rose from the ground mixed with his vanilla breath and turned his stomach. He didn't stop to puke. Instead, he clamped his mouth shut and fixated on the mirage path before him, and continued to trudge through the muck and the heat. His tracks washed away.

Davoli quickly lost all sense of time. The showers came and went abruptly, and then never came back. Mud filled his boots and crept underneath his clothes. His uniform chafed. Large things that looked like flying scorpions came out from behind branches that looked like the bluish fingers of a dead man's hand, and hovered around him threateningly, some landing and crawling over him and the captain. He didn't dare swat them away, so he continued his march, now wishing for the inconvenient but cleansing rain. This was nothing like the campaigns of his youth, where he was hermetically sealed in a space suit much of the time and the only filth he had to deal with was his own. Davoli imagined this to be more akin to the outmoded, vicious little wars in the Congo or the Amazon. This entire planet was somehow designed to invade him, seeping into his clothes, oozing into his nostrils and mouth and pores with the mindless conviction of nature, to poison him.

Davoli's curators complained that he had been running hot for too long and needed to rest and refuel. He took a few more defiant steps, then stopped and dropped Hershkovitz. He slumped next to him and tried to ease the tension in his mind and body. He threw up some cartoons from his childhood, because that's what he had done on his tour on Titan, and leaned back against the trunk of a tree. The hologram of a boy in a large mecha suit jostled with a giant space monster — a hooked-beak turtle with long spikes on its shell — and, depending on Davoli's simple neural cues, the storyline changed into something he'd never seen before. He ate the rations and drank another vanilla shake and knew instantly that the flavor, and possibly this cartoon, would forever be tainted for him.

A sharp snap made him go rigid. Davoli cut off the show and listened. He heard what could only be footsteps crunching on the forest floor. He overlaid an infrared view over his surroundings. There, in the darkness, two glowing, bipedal forms were sneaking around him, trying to corral him and the captain. He tagged them and pulled out his gun, switching back to regular vision, and enhancing all of his artificial senses. He stood up, and almost immediately the two assailants stopped moving. It was too late. He had tagged them and his curators would keep track of their positions no matter where they hid. One was on his far right and the second one was much closer, and behind him. He could smell the rising dander of damp feathers and hear the steady breathing of hyper-efficient lungs. Commander Davoli carefully rotated his body, keeping the captain between his legs, so that he could face the one trying to sneak up behind him and still be able to shoot the one farther off with a quick flick of the wrist.

He heard the shriek a second before he saw the almost invisible gleam of steel gray plumage. His blood turned to ice as he caught a glimpse of his enemy. This was unlike any harpy he had ever seen; the final culmination of all their genetic sins. The three-meter tall creature was all bird, like a massive eagle. It looked down its fire-red beak at him and Davoli understood that there was no mind there; this animal saw him only as meat. Without hesitation, it lunged at him. Fear and incomprehension absorbed Davoli for too long an instant, and it smashed its beak into Davoli like an axe.

He slammed into a tree, dropping his gun. His body ached cuttingly, but he was not seriously injured. The thing had hit him with the downward curve of its beak and not the deadly point. The super harpy was approaching now, stamping its bright red legs threateningly, triumphantly, on the ground. The other one had appeared and was trying to drag Hershkovitz into the brush.

Who would do this to themselves, to their children?

In answer to his mental questions, the tags updated automatically as the curators searched their archives: Titanis. The name struck Davoli more deeply than the large beak. Instantly, he shut off the pain and primed his curators for war. The terror bird pounced. He poured all his strength into his right arm, punching a hole through the creature's breast. The clavicle cracked, and he sent a jolt of electricity into its heart. It fell back and died instantly.

The second bird stopped its scavenging and reared its great head. It had a burst of decorative plumes on its crown that swayed when it screeched. Davoli dove for his gun, rolled as he caught it, and blasted the creature on the side of its head. The beam hit the bird on its right side, scorching the small useless wing. The injured monster disappeared back into the jungle.

Without pausing to catch his breath, Davoli scooped up his nearly-eaten captain and continued his grueling trot toward the lander. He would not rest until he was off this wicked planet.

Chapter 12

Earth - 2258 A.D.

Her grandmother whimpered in her sleep. She cried out. Oya sat next to her and stroked her cap of gray hair until she calmed. Oya had never watched someone sleep before. Not really. Not for hours and certainly not someone she feared might never wake up. She realized that she never worried about her *gwan me*. In her mind, Osala had remained the strong, independent woman who had raised her. Oya had carried the self-centeredness of childhood over to adulthood. She remembered having a fever after being bitten by a spider — she must have been about seven — and her grandmother curling up in the sweaty bed with her. Whispering that she loved her. That she was going to be okay. Oya felt that impulse now. The small cot couldn't support their weight, but she wanted to hold her close, protect her, and heal her. Her love crystalized.

At one point, Osala mumbled an old Haitian poem about birds and a beautiful girl:

Choukoun is a marabou,
Eyes as bright as candlelight
Her breasts so poised
Ah! If Choukoun had been true!

Sometimes she would call Oya by her sister's name, Ayao. It broke Oya's heart, but at least it let her know her *gwan me* was still alive.

When Osala calmed, Oya busied herself by tidying up the modest base of operations. In the clutter, she found a thick manila envelope full of yellowed printouts from different news feeds, all of them having to do with Avant Genomics and Chandeleur. It seemed her grandmother had been quite the scientific celebrity in her youth; there were articles comparing her to greats like Craig Venter and Jack Horner. Oya knew her grandmother had been a scientist, but she'd never appreciated the level of impact she had in the field.

When her parents were killed in a car accident, her *gwan man man* had taken her and her sister in, brought them to their native island, and raised them as her own. Oya had never thought to ask her about her youth, or any of this. Now, she meticulously read each paper as if she had found an antediluvian apocryphal manuscript.

Apparently the younger Osala had devised a way to extract snippets of organic molecules from ancient fossils, stated one *Scientific American* article. Gather up enough snippets from sufficient samples and you could stitch together a complete genome of a long-dead species, like the sunny warblers.

Then her only daughter was killed in a freak car accident and she dropped out of the limelight. At least until something happened to Chandeleur. Oya looked more closely at those news reports. The devastation to the island was far worse than Oya had imagined. She had been in space at the time, ferrying tourists from Earth to Venus. She knew only that a super storm had reduced the island to a smear of sand and rock upon the pristine ocean.

"Oya, stop dawdling and put the kettle on."

Oya turned to find her grandmother staring right at her, perfectly lucid. A huge wave of relief crashed over Oya. "*Bonswa!* I thought you were going to miss the big bird release this evening."

"I just had to step out for a while, dear, but I'm ready to take up my life again."

Oya put the documents back in their folder and went to boil water.

"I see you've found my penitence papers."

"Why did you keep all of these?"

"Because, dear, it's good to remember that when you keep company with fowl, they shit on your table," the old woman said with a straight face, but then began cackling to herself, making her rise out of bed all the more arduous.

"What does that even mean, *gwan me*?" Oya used to love all of her grandmother's sayings as a kid. She missed the purity of that love. The unconditional simplicity of it. But they had fallen into a pattern of arguing when Oya became a teenager. Two headstrong women trying to assert their will. The pattern never broke and so they learned to give each other space and, over time, space became distance.

Her grandmother got two tea cups from a red crate next to the mini fridge — the crate had the biohazard symbol stamped on its side — and handed them to Oya. She took them, dropped a tea bag in each, and then filled them with steaming water. They sat across from each other on the small foldout table, letting the tea steep. Osala took her time flipping through the papers. Her expression slowly became overcast.

"So are you going to tell me about these?" Oya asked.

Her grandmother looked up at her as if surprised that Oya was there. Then she looked back down at the printout she was reading and said, "I thought I could use Avant Genomics. Use them to make a living, use them to give you girls a proper education, use them to bring much needed revenue to Chandeleur. We never did attract the cruise ship companies or the drug cartels. A big multi-national pharmaceutical would create jobs and boost our economy."

"It did all those things."

"Yes, but they made one fatal, careless mistake, under my direction ... my *second* great mistake, or third. I've lost count.

"After the persecution of the posthumans around the solar system, genetic manipulation became taboo. AG stocks plummeted and the company decided to pool their research into the new field of nanotechnology. I was the director of the team that created an early version of the curators. We tested them on Rhesus macaques with stupendous results. The average macaque lives twenty-five years; by the end of the trials we had doubled it to fifty years.

"But some other firm beat us to market and eventually AG went bankrupt and was broken up into smaller companies. They abandoned the facility here, which was full of long-lived monkeys. I felt responsible for them and refused to euthanize them. Why extend their life only to take it away? So, I set up a primate sanctuary here, on the grounds of the closed labs. The poor things had gone through a lot in the name of science and deserved to retire on a nice tropical island. They escaped, of course." She took a deep breath. "The proto-curators had made them stronger than normal..."

"So Chandeleur had monkeys, big deal. It's not like they were carrying a super virus or anything," said Oya.

Her grandmother carefully took out the tea bag from her cup and leisurely stirred in some sugar and honey. Oya did the same and took a sip, burning her upper lip, but the pain faded instantly upon command.

"No, they weren't carrying a virus," Osala finally said, letting out a weighty breath. She took her own slurping sip. "At first the kids loved them and the farmers hated them, but they kept proliferating and the older ones wouldn't die. After a few years, the adorable little annoyances grew into a serious plague. They damaged property. They stripped the island bare of vegetation; other animals were either eaten or terminally displaced. You see, *they* were the virus."

Osala drank more deeply from the tea, seemingly not caring that it was still too hot. "That's when Super Storm Theresa hit, and, without any protective root system, the little fertile soil that was left was instantly washed away by the storm surge. In a few hours, Chandeleur became a wasteland and anyone that had survived the storm was forced to evacuate permanently, making refugees of our once proud citizens. In the end, the few macaques left starved to death anyway."

"You caused all that?" Oya whispered. It was unbelievable to her how one small act of compassion could unravel with such disastrous results.

"Yes." Her grandmother began to cry, not the childish simpering of her sleep, but the dignified sobs of someone all too aware of their failings.

"But you can't beat yourself up over it. It was an honest mistake, one you've corrected miraculously, I might add. I flew over the island on my way here. It's gorgeous." Oya poured her grandmother another cup of tea and handed her some tissue paper.

"I did try. It flies in the face of my error, but I did do *something*. After years of uselessly punishing myself, I thought, if they can terraform Mars, I can certainly terraform one minuscule island on Earth. So, I started the Chandeleur Restoration Foundation. I was living in Toronto then and that's where our first small office opened. We raised money. We brought in megatons of topsoil from a volcano in Nicaragua, hunted down all the native plants I could find, growing in various botanical gardens around the world. The hardest part was resurrecting the little yellow birds you loved so much, but the remnants of AG, wanting to avoid an international scandal, eagerly helped with that."

"That's why you're against the curators."

"Can you blame me?"

"No, I suppose not, but *gwan me*, there are other treatments. You don't need to wear your illness like a badge of courage or a cross on your shoulder. You've already suffered a mild stroke."

"I already told you, dear, I'm not ill. I'm old and wearing down. I've already made arrangements with a craftsman from Barbados. He's building me a tasteful box out of driftwood should I need to step out for a rather extended period."

"Oh *gwan man man...*" Oya wanted to grab the old woman by the shoulders and shake her. Instead, she swallowed the knot in her throat with some tea. She should have visited more often. She should've spent more time with her grandmother, learning about her long and fascinating life, gotten to know her as a woman. But Osala had always been busy, dashing around the world on her restoration project and Oya had long stints off-world. The promise of the curators was more time. "You said this was your second or third mistake. What was your first?"

"I don't want to talk about it, child. I'm weary. You didn't make the damned sleepy-time tea, did you?" her grandmother said, patting Oya's cheek with a loving, arthritic claw of a hand. "I'm going to rest now."

"Okay, take another nap. I want to walk around the island for a while."

"I think I'm going to sleep less fitfully this time. *Mèsi*, love, for listening and not judging too harshly."

Chapter 13

Luna – 2098 A.D.

Everyone at Avant Genomics thought it was a great idea. The general consensus was that they would learn a great deal from this experiment and being off-world would protect them from any U.N. reprisals, if news got out. They were also confident that the media, and therefore the public, would finger the rich iconoclast for playing with things she didn't understand, and not AG, who was only providing a service to a paying and despairing customer.

Osala, for her part, ignored the legal finagling and worked the problem. She had to unzip the degraded double strands of DNA and painstakingly sequence each position in the genome about a hundred times over. There was a lot of damage in this fossil, but after two months of work, the illicit archaeopteryx specimen gave up enough viable information to fill in the blanks within the partial data extracted from previous samples. She now had a complete genome.

For a spoiled shut-in, Esther Aguilera-Smeltzer turned out to be a talented and enthusiastic lab assistant. She had equal moments of brilliance and petulance, like when she insisted on tweaking the genes controlling the structural color of the ancient feathers from iridescent black to a dazzling blue. Osala thought it was a foolish waste of time, but she had slowly grown to like the girl, so she relented.

Esther hovered — literally — over Osala as she inserted hundreds of carefully-crafted master genes, which controlled the expression of thousands of other interconnected genes for wings and legs, into synthetic stem cells. Immediately the cells began to split.

"All right, the nuclear programming has booted the cells. We have mitosis."

Esther tackled Osala, sending them both spiraling and crashing into the centrifuge. "Thank you so much!"

"Don't thank me yet," she said, prying herself free from the girl's mechanical embrace.

Osala caught the four floating vials, one for each limb, and turned to Esther. "Before we do this, I need you to understand that after this initial treatment you will no longer be considered a *legal* human being by U.N. standards." Osala held a tiny white tablet as if giving her the final choice.

"*A legal human being?*" Esther laughed harshly, her burst of excitement giving way to her characteristic cynicism. "I have never been treated like a human being, Dr. Valette, legal or otherwise."

"Technically, you'll be classified a chimera."

"Will I still be a woman?"

"Of course."

"Then do it. I'm ready."

"Let's talk for a bit, Esther. You've waited a long time, what's a few moments more? I just want to make sure you comprehend what you're giving up. If you ever go to Earth, you will be forfeiting all rights. And you won't be able to undo this." The words were echoes of a similar warning she'd been given months ago and like herself, she knew this ambitious young woman would not heed them. Esther had her eye on the prize and there wasn't room for anything else. "I suppose you could get lawyers..."

With quick movements of her hooks, Esther unfastened the straps that wrapped around her chest and abdomen and unplugged the wire from her head, shedding her plastic and steel limbs. "Believe me, I know what I'm giving up," she said, as her newly freed torso began drifting away.

Osala hesitated for a moment, then reached out and grabbed her. "Okay, Esther. Let's begin." She placed the tablet in the girl's mouth and Esther swallowed it hungrily. "That's the retrovirus that will begin to rewrite your DNA, mixed with an immune suppressant. It's also extremely aggressive. Normally it would take twenty-four hours to exhibit flu-like symptoms; you'll start experiencing them shortly."

She helped the young woman out of her clothes. A strange blue glow emanating from behind Esther caught Osala's attention. Without asking permission, she spun the girl to take a look. A large bioluminescent tattoo blazed across her back; twin snakes winding around the staff of her spine, crowned with shimmering wings etched on her boney shoulder blades. The serpentine outline instantly invoked images of Damballah's veve. "Isn't this the biohacker logo?" Osala asked, surprised, and turned Esther around to look her in the eye.

"It is," Esther said flatly.

"You told me you weren't a Transhumanist. AG wants nothing to do with those people," she said, tethering Esther to the wall and connecting her to the medical diagnostic equipment. She roughly rotated her again to look at the tattoo.

"I'm not, but when I was sixteen I thought I could use the Transhumanist movement to achieve my dream of flight. Their chaotic operation and amateurish understanding of biotech quickly dispelled that notion. But I kept the art as a reminder that I would succeed no matter what."

"*Bondye mwen*, girl, wasn't there a terrible incident with one of those biohackers, *Merlin* or some such nonsense?"

Esther shrugged drowsily, bobbing up and down on her tether. A sheen of sweat was developing on her forehead. "Yeah. When a few of Merlin's clients started having children there were gross abnormalities. The sloppy underground modifications had gotten into their germ line and their children were fluorescent, poisonous horrors. One infant in particular was draped in a tangle of stinging tentacles. His mother couldn't even hold him."

Osala was speechless. Esther was clearly using her and Avant Genomics just as she had tried to use the biohackers, and what suddenly worried Osala was that, unlike those delinquent geneticists, she would actually accomplish something. Her mind quickly ran a check through all the procedures of the last two months. *No, she was certain the changes she had just introduced into this girl were not heritable.*

"Come on, Osala, don't get squeamish on me now. I can feel the retrovirus working. My throat is burning. Don't abort the experiment before my wings have grown out."

That word hit her like a knife in the gut. She breathed carefully and took a moment to recover. It really was too late now. The retrovirus was the key and it had already been administered. Osala inserted the first syringe into the small mound of tissue where Esther's right arm should've been. The girl hissed with the pain. In a few months, there would be an arm of flesh and bone and feathers there, a working wing. Esther stoically endured the next three shots.

"In a few weeks or so we're going to have to go down to LA2," Osala said tightly. "Your new limbs will need grueling physical therapy; up here they'll simply atrophy."

"What does the sky look like?" Esther asked, dreamily. The retrovirus was starting to really affect her. "What's it like to live under a dome of air? What does a storm feel like as it moves in?"

Osala had never thought about it and the seemingly inane question caught her off guard. She was embarrassed to say, "I don't know. I've never paid all that much attention to it. It's beautiful to look at sometimes of course, and storms can be quite impressive and scary, but day-to-day, it's just a blue backdrop."

"I've never seen the sky. Most of us born up here haven't. Sure, I've seen simulations and videos of it, but not the actual open sky you take for granted. For us, all we really have is a cheap backdrop. Psychologically that can't be good, right?"

Osala didn't reply. The girl was probably becoming delirious. Still, a whole generation of human beings born and raised in confinement. *No,* she thought, *psychologically, that couldn't be good…*

"'*And to the woman were given two wings of a great eagle, that she might fly into the wilderness, into her place, where she is nourished for a time, and times, and half a time, from the face of the serpent,*'" Esther recited absentmindedly.

"Is that a poem?"

"No, a biblical verse, from Revelations. It's one of my favorites, for obvious reasons... Do you think it'll work, Osala? These changes, I mean?" There was no trace of her fiery confidence. She was shivering from the abrupt fever, but couldn't hug herself. She looked like an embryo suspended within the envelope of a large, pill-shaped egg. "I don't want to look like an idiot down there again. I'd rather drown."

Despite her grave doubts, Osala cradled the unwell, weeping girl in her arms and brushed her damp, blonde hair out of her eyes. "Shh, it'll be all right, my *ti zwazo, kwéati féwòs mwen*. It'll work and you'll take the sky by storm."

Chapter 14

Quetzalcoatl - 2323 A.D.

Commander Carlo Davoli's mind was beginning to fray. There were no more bird attacks, humanoid or otherwise, but his pumped-up neurochemistry and sheer physical exhaustion were taking their toll. At one point, he thought the captain was ordering him to take five, but he was sure that had been a hallucination. His own biological clock was shot to hell, so he reinstated the digital clock in his vision. There was a little more than an hour's hike left to the lander; that wasn't too bad, but he couldn't muster the excitement for a second wind. His whole body throbbed with an incredible pain that threatened to overtake him.

The captain's dead weight had become an unbearable burden, and Davoli's own body and curators were demanding respite. He scolded himself, arguing that he had just woken up from a three-year sleep, but, against his better judgment, he relented and half-sat, half collapsed onto the dirt.

He sucked up the last pouch of the synthetic vanilla milkshake, closed his eyes, and took a few soothing breaths. The world seemed to spin slowly and he dug his fingers into the moist soil to steady himself. He knew that the rotation was in his own head because, of course, Quetzalcoatl was tidally locked to its star.

When he opened his eyes, something strange caught his attention. Something green shone in the gloom. He crawled closer on hands and knees. It was a feeble weed or vine with heart-shaped leaves jutting out of the ground.

Was this another hallucination? Was he simply looking for green in this false jungle where there was none? His curators identified it as an Earth plant called an arum.

The little seedling was a sickly yellow-green, half wilted in the perpetual shadow of the tall, fungal-like trees. It was alone, starved of light and nourishment, and it probably would not survive long. Davoli had never in his life had time for any kind of mysticism. And now, more than ever, he needed to hurry. But he could not deny that he sensed a spiritual connection to that struggling little weed. He got up, ambled closer to it, and took a hot piss on it. It was the most generous thing he could think to do for his fellow Earthling, give it sustenance from his own body in the form of nitrogen, phosphate, and potassium. When he was done, he zipped up his pants and unceremoniously heaved his captain back onto the familiar ache of his shoulder and tramped away, feeling a little better about himself.

He walked for another twenty minutes, falling twice, and hiding once when he heard the flapping of wings in the branches above. The "smart" brace that propped him up was also a hindrance in this tangle and he considered casting it off a few times, but knew he'd crumple without it. Luckily, he had landed in flat country and he made progress despite all of the other difficulties.

He had to pause before entering an open glade in the thick forest. He had done this many times before to make sure the exposed path was free of predators, but this time the scene looked off somehow. The floor was disturbed, there were clear signs of a scuffle, and someone was lying on the ground. He quietly set Hershkovitz down at the edge of the clearing and crept closer, sidearm drawn.

It was a female harpy with blue wings. He switched to augmented view to make sure he wasn't having delusions again — *Could he hallucinate in infrared?* — and saw that she glowed with body heat. He switched back to his regular vision and kneeled closer to her. He heard the woman's faint heartbeat with his enhanced hearing, and noticed the slight expansion and contraction of her ribcage. *Woman?* The stillness all around gave him time to really take her in.

One of her taloned feet was twisted painfully. He figured that she had probably suffered a bad fall and rolled, upsetting the mulch on the floor, before coming to a rest on this spot. He had a girlfriend a long time ago — Paola — who used to take long naps in the middle of the day in this exact position. Slowly he reached out to touch her cheek. "Hey," he whispered. No response. Her brown skin was soft. He left a smudge from his grimy fingers. Something shifted in his chest.

He aimed his gun to finish the job. A clean, humane shot to the head would do the trick. He noticed, suddenly, that she was gorgeous, and serene, more like a sleeping woodland fairy than a vicious harpy. He could smell her sweet perfume through the tart stink of the jungle. *Why hadn't he pulled the trigger yet?* Davoli felt ashamed at his weakness. He knew for a fact that he was out of his mind, but his hand trembled pathetically. Maybe it was the recent experience with the terror birds, but suddenly her raptorial qualities seemed reduced somehow, made unimportant, compared to her overall humanity. He had never actually executed a lone, defenseless harpy before; it had always been in battle, and they were always trying to kill him. This felt different, wrong.

Sweat poured down his face. The weight of the moment pressed on him, and — just like his encounter with the small green plant — everything was taking on grave significance. He looked at the phantom road before him, his salvation waiting at the end of it. He should just step over her, get to the lander and wage war on them from the bridge of the *Hurricane*. That would be the professional thing to do. What would killing one incapacitated harpy matter now? Still, he couldn't just slide his gun back into its holster. He was terrified of putting it away, of having her wake up and claw him in the back as he was about to reach the lander. No one would know if he fired a swift, merciful laser into her brain. Only boorish blue trees were around to witness it.

And yet the laser never came. He was stuck, like a machine given two opposing commands. What would she do if their positions were reversed? She looked placid and charming enough now, but he was sure she would plunge her one working reaper into his chest given the chance. That was their nature, after all.

There was a sharp click behind him and it was all he could do to not squeeze the trigger in a panic. Davoli turned slowly to find a male harpy, a jay like the woman at his feet, standing over Hershkovitz. His form was hard to define among the navy-colored foliage so Davoli sharpened his vision even farther, until his head swooned with the magnification. The sound had come from the hefty talon being retracted over his captain's neck. The captain looked like mud-splattered carrion about to be rent open, but his curators were still keeping him alive despite the hardship of their journey.

The harpy hissed and trilled, and Davoli's attention and vision snapped back to the moment. A second later the text translation scrolled across his line of sight: "If you hurt her, I will tear your friend's head off before you have time to shoot me."

Davoli quickly scanned the male harpy and appraised the situation. Davoli was bigger and bulkier than he was, but the harpy had the straight-back, wiry strength of a warrior, and his black, tight clothing had the characteristics of a military uniform. His face was dark skinned and he looked as worn out as Davoli felt. He was quite possibly injured as well, but his demeanor showed great discipline and his concern for his wounded friend was all too apparent. A fight with him would not be easy.

Davoli's only advantage was his gun, but he had promised to get the captain to the *Hurricane* safely and refused to risk his already-tenuous life on one stupid action. He slowly raised his sidearm into the air and made a show of loosening his grip on it. A small part of his mind was glad the intruder had taken the terrible choice away from him.

"There are only two of us out here and we're in no condition to fight, not if we want to protect our downed associates." The words emerged in the air from the harpy's whistled tune and he took a tiny step back away from the captain.

For the first time in Commander Davoli's long and bloody career, something a bit like respect for his adversary crept into his soul. It was the condescending kind of admiration you give a magpie that has cleverly fished out grubs with a twig, a grudging acknowledgement of intelligence and skill, nothing else. But it was more than he had ever given them before.

"Okay," Davoli said, hoping the word's universal recognition extended even to this wild planet. He backed away from the unconscious female harpy, regretting that he had not downloaded their language into his skull. His pride had given the enemy a slight advantage in these impromptu negotiations.

The harpy's claw lowered slowly and Davoli eased his gun away. They circled around each other, maintaining plenty of space between them. At one point, Davoli was sure he could pull his weapon and shoot the jay before he reached the captain, but there was no point in doing so if he was letting them walk away, and, if he missed, the exchange would only rob him of the precious energy he would need to complete the trek to the lander.

Davoli grabbed his captain and jogged around the glade, using the trees as cover, and got back on the path toward the lander. He didn't think the harpy was following him, but he might have called for reinforcements. There was no more rest for Davoli, no more milkshakes and pissing on weeds. In thirty minutes or so he would reach the lander and then that slate would be clean. He maintained his brisk pace until his curators were close enough to link up with the lander without having to bounce the signal from the ship in orbit. This real connection to something Hominocracy reenergized him a bit and he ran harder. He was close enough to remotely prep the lander for takeoff and ready its inadequate emergency medical unit to receive him and the captain.

Suddenly, he stopped and dropped to the ground. He had seen something from the lander's perspective; it was teeming with cardinals, all of them trying to break in. There was no way he could retake it in his current condition. He was only meters away, but he couldn't reach it. Immense frustration made him want to cry like a baby. He lay there, in the dirt, breathing in its scent of corruption and watching the red-feathered techs via the lander's cameras.

The lander wasn't a shuttle. It was little more than a cableless elevator to orbit, but maybe he could get it to come to him, hop from its current position to his. He asked it if something like that was possible and it replied by sending an affirmative message. A warning also came up. The maneuver was not advisable because he was in dense forest; the ship could sustain damage while setting down. He doubted the skeletal trees could really damage the lander and, this close to freedom, it was a risk he was willing to take.

Davoli overrode the warning, and then everything happened too fast for his dulled mind to keep track of. In a burst of antigravitons, the scorched cone leapt away from the harpies' grasp, smashed down through the fleshy canopy, nearly coming to rest on top of him.

When its hatch opened, Davoli scrambled inside, dragging the captain with him. He sank into the soft chair, gave a silent, fractured thought-command to go, and passed out as the lander hurtled them to the shelter of space.

— «» —

After their argument in the jungle, Inirigua and Oya had flown in uncomfortable quiet the rest of the way, but even with Inirigua's hushed resentment, she knew he had deliberately created jetties of swirling wind from his spread wingtips in order to provide lift for her heavier frame. What still bothered Oya was that, despite her attempt to help these people, there was a part of her, however small, that did doubt their ultimate humanity, and Inirigua knew it.

They rode the thermals that whirled from the exoplanet's sweltering sunside all the way around its frigid face and met back at the dream-like assortment of buildings. The edifices, suspended in midair like jewels hanging from a massive chandelier, seemed to drift slowly. Oya was sure that in a week they would have an entirely different arrangement.

"Are the buildings moving or is it my imagination?"

"They're moving, always shifting, to allow sunlight to get at the forest under them. If they were stationary, everything in their shadow would die."

She liked that. The idea of a constantly shifting city, whose boulevards and districts were continuously redrawn. It sounded exciting, and as they got closer, Oya could make out the chaos of the aerial metropolis. Antigrav planes zoomed around in the same airspace as a multitude of flying pedestrians riotously darting from structure to structure, going about their daily business. Astonishingly, they all managed to evade each other. It reminded Oya of the sunny warblers enthusiastically looking for a place to roost. Inirigua slipped into the throng. Oya flapped her makeshift wings and followed.

She wasn't assaulted by the usual lightscreen billboards or glowing adverts of the cities she was used to. There were no corporate geotags screaming and courting her curators. No news and weather reports robbing her attention. She wasn't entirely sure she liked the dearth of information. She asked her curators to try and speculate its own tags for the things she saw and to begin building an inventory for her. Instantly, possible restaurants, clothing stores, massage parlors, feather care boutiques, and toy shops began twinkling in her overlay vision like stars. All grocery stores and eateries flashed like supernovae, aware that she desperately needed food. Oya dimmed those urgent beacons of nourishment and found that what she really wanted to see was what a harpy toy shop looked like.

A gaggle of boys and girls zipped around them, curious about the freak with the phony wings. Each had an arrangement of red, black, and blue feathers, like painted bunting. Despite her exhaustion, she smiled and did a few aerobatic tricks for them. Their twittering laughter delighted her, energized her. She did a few more stunts, knowing full well that they saw her as an awkward, brightly-colored clown. She didn't care. She relished their company. *How long had it been since she'd seen children, fifty years, eighty?* Oya kept the thought to herself for fear of seeming less human in the eyes of Inirigua. It seemed utterly inhuman to her.

Inirigua gave them a stern whistle and they scattered.

Oya laughed. "Those beautiful children were mixed-clan?"

"Yes, third-generation here on Quetzalcoatl. In another twenty years, most of our population will look like that."

She flew next to him, as close as their wing spans allowed. "*Your* kids, you mean, if I hadn't ruined the mating ritual with that blue fighter?"

"Be careful. Air comes from strange angles between the buildings." His musical voice sounded strained. "Try not to needlessly tire yourself out."

"Yeah, it feels like hang gliding in a wind tunnel. It's amazing though. I've flown my share of crafts in the past, but flying under my own power, feeling the wind in my face — I can see why your ancestors chose to change their way of life, their very DNA, just to keep flying," she said, trying to amend her past prejudices. The truth was, despite the difficulty of the task and the ugliness with the Macu, she did enjoy flying.

"I think sending a pilot down to us might have been a good idea after all."

She raised an eyebrow at the compliment, but he wasn't looking at her. His face had grown concerned.

"Something's wrong," he said, nodding toward a magnificent, one hundred-story pagoda, with sweeping eaves decorated in crimson and gold. It towered over the entire city. Black smoke was billowing out of its midsection. "There's been an attack on Soaring Palace of Morning."

Inirigua launched himself toward it, beating his wings harder than Oya could manage, and landed in one of the smoke-filled middle tiers. A moment later, Oya landed beside him, and Inirigua caught her as she stumbled to a stop. He ran through the immense, airy level of the palace. She shed her wings and bundled them up as she hurried after him. Between the smoke stinging her eyes and nose, and trying to keep up with Inirigua, Oya didn't have time to admire the massive columns intricately carved with creatures that looked like Japanese tengu or the Hindu god, Garuda.

Both Oya and Inirigua stopped dead at the sight of the ruined hall. The burned bodies of winged people lay all around. They had undoubtedly been cut down by laser fire. Oya had never witnessed such horror first hand in her entire life. She recognized the scene from countless Culling movies and documentaries. Suddenly, red-feathered guards encircled them, ready, wanting, to attack her, but they didn't dare move any closer. They were afraid of Oya.

"What happened?" Inirigua asked the group.

"They attacked us," said the lead sentry, a tall female. She motioned toward Oya. "They're more powerful than they seem."

"Your people did this?" Inirigua let out a mournful croon.

"I don't know," she stammered, still dazed by all the death. She willed herself to perform a cursory spectral analysis of the area and saw boot prints, two sets, glowing white-blue on the ground. Boots not talons! And blood stains glittering with curators. "Yes. I think so," she said weakly. She was sure Hershkovitz and Davoli had been here.

"Inirigua, what's going on?" The lead guard asked more forcefully.

"Guards," Inirigua said, taking a step toward the sentries. "I've captured this Hominocracy agent! She's admitted to being the beachhead of a larger invasion force waiting in orbit!"

It took a while for Oya's curators to recognize the shrill sound as language, but it soon became clear that the young raptor was selling her out. "What are you doing, Inirigua?" she asked.

With avian quickness, he snatched the gun from her holster. "I told you, Oya, that we would not allow you to occupy this world without a fight. I believed we could negotiate, but this..."

"I thought we had an understanding." It required all of Oya's self-control not to bash in his treacherous face. She stared at the nose of her own gun.

"I've just had an understanding. Believe me, I want to trust you, with all my heart, but I *understand* that your level of technology is awesome. I understand that you think of us as subhuman. That, Oyavalette, is a deadly combination."

She said nothing. All her arguments and platitudes caught in her throat. The pack of red-feathered warbirds encircled her. Her curators instantly went into combat mode, but she felt worn-out and betrayed, not only by the one harpy she had begun to know and trust, but by her own people who had dropped her here as nothing more than a miserable lure. And then did *this* without waiting for her to do her damn job.

"Careful, men, this female may look inept with her comical, prosthetic wings, but she's an incredibly advanced cyborg, capable of fending all of you off single-handedly."

"Inirigua, don't do this," Oya pleaded. Her curators automatically began amping up the voltage to the palms of her hands.

Inirigua turned his back on her and stalked away.

Chapter 15

Mars - 2198 A.D.

"I can't see anything through all this red shit!" Tactical Officer Anton Hershkovitz said, staring out the window, then back at a false-color mockup of the landscape. The meteorological vulgarism broke the long silence of their flight.

"Good thing you're not the pilot then." First Pilot Ameera el-Ayeb's words were a few degrees lower than the thin, frigid air outside their S-8 glider. She forced her eyes on the instrumentation and not out the grimy windows as she maneuvered the craft through the Martian stratosphere. Hersh knew that, above all, she avoided looking at him.

They were shoved in next to each other, shoulders chafing, but the distance between them felt great. He had intended to cut her loose weeks ago. His deployment was ending, and he didn't need any messy, emotional performances to ruin his departure. Then they were thrown together on this reconnaissance mission to find the last garrison of the avian humans left on Mars. To make things worse, this immense haboob had mysteriously blown over the Tharsis region. Now he was the one in a huff.

"Look, Hersh, if you want to end whatever it is we have, all you have to do is say so. We're both adults." She tossed out the remark like a grenade.

"This isn't right. There shouldn't be a dust storm of this magnitude at this time of year," he said, ignoring her statement. His job was easy compared to Ameera's. He basically had to scan everything within the area of operations and shoot it back to their battleship, *The Harpy Hunter*, in orbit, and, if there was trouble, man the guns, while she got them the hell out, which gave him too much free time to obsess over *whatever it is they have.*

"Fine," she sighed. "Captain Morales agrees with you. He thinks this storm is being artificially generated, which is why he sent us personally. I mean, we are the supreme recon officers aboard the *Harpy Hunter.*"

Against all regulation, they'd been enjoying a casual relationship for almost a year, and despite their mutual agreement to keep it simple, it had gotten complicated. At least it had for him. Now, Hersh couldn't bring himself to just break up with her, so instead he acted aloof and miserable. *Was he waiting for her to make the final, decisive move?*

The long-winged plane pushed deeper into the dry, autumnal gloom. The roiling sky mirrored his mood. "Yeah, supremely disposable," Hersh said, trying to get out of his funk. He didn't look away from his dashboard readouts, but he could tell that she was smiling slightly and it made him smile too. The scent of her jasmine attar drifted in the small, musty cockpit. It was *too* easy to love her. "You know my deployment is ending, right? I'm probably going back to Florida."

"I'm taking us a little closer to the Valles Marineris canyon system, the dust seems to be thinner down in the troposphere."

"Which is rather suspicious, don't you think?"

"You think too much. Can't you just relax?"

He didn't know if she was referring to his going back home or the bizarre weather conditions. He chose to talk about the weather. "All I'm saying is that Candor Chasma is the last of the harpy strongholds on Mars. It should've been easy to shatter the ceiling that caps it and let out all the air, but it's made of incredibly tough diamond. That's technology that no other harpy settlement in the solar system has. Now this dust storm inexplicably appears. Something is wrong."

When plasma engines were developed, Earth's provincial population set out and met their sick, hybridized neighbors in the solar system and they were horrified. The uncanny valley phenomenon had been rent even wider by some sudden tectonic schism; intelligent machines sunbathing on Mercury like glistening barnacles, dinosaur-freaks roosting on the moon, Mars, and Titan. But now, after ten years of fighting and forced treatment camps, the Hominocracy Movement of Earth was taking back the solar system for humanity.

"Um, Hersh, am I reading my sensors correctly?"

He had looked away while he ranted, and, when he looked back at his screen, it was as if the hard data was answering him directly, telling him that all his deranged theories were not only correct, but naively insufficient. "What the fuck is that?"

"It could be interference from the all the electrostatically charged particles in the air, but it looks like a massive structure running the length of the rift, from Corprates Chasma to Lus."

"That would make it more than three thousand kilometers long and almost two hundred kilometers wide!"

"I'm going to do a flyby. Get all our sensors and cameras on it. Can we beam the info to the *Harpy Hunter*?"

"It's a ship, Ameera!"

"Don't be stupid, Hersh. It can't be a ship. There's no way you can lift something that big and get it into orbit."

They flew along the enormous construct. The white, oblong shape gleamed in the crimson haze, like a theropod egg buried in a nest of sediment. There were no visible signs of boosters or fusion rockets. *It couldn't be a spacecraft*, Hersh thought. "Okay, maybe it's some kind of doomsday weapon?"

"If it is, we're absolutely fucked, because the only point of something so big would be to crack open the planet."

"I know it sounds crazy, but I don't think this thing was manufactured here. There's no sign of construction or equipment anywhere in the valley system." The sheer size and alienness of the thing dwarfed their petty romantic problems.

"Maybe they cleaned up after themselves."

"Look. There at the midsection. There's some kind of vein, running from the city of Candor right into that thing."

Hersh zoomed one of his cameras toward the connector. "It looks like a transit tube. Here, I can make out humanoid forms on some kind of tram, riding toward the superstructure."

"Harpies! They're loading harpies into that thing." There were two tracks in the tube. One rail had passengers, the other rail running alongside it transferred supplies.

"Maybe it's a fort or a huge bunker and they're moving everyone into it for protection?"

Suddenly, straight blue lightening flashed and a crack of thunder shook their glider.

"We've been hit!" Ameera tried to steer the shuttering plane. "They knocked out our engine. I think I can guide us down."

Hersh didn't reply. He simply flicked on the power to the laser guns mounted on the plane's wings and fired at the massive, elongated oval. *Nothing!* His beams were harmlessly refracted by the diamond matrix of its hull. The S-8 sank even lower into the dirty atmosphere. And still, the artifact stretched on for kilometers. It was strange that the enemy hadn't fired on them again. *Did they think them insignificant? Did they want them alive?*

"Stop shooting and try sending a mayday to the *Harpy Hunter*," Ameera yelled.

"If we couldn't get a signal out higher up, we're definitely not going to get through now." Hersh switched to cluster bombs and sent a volley down toward the alien citadel. Hot death bloomed like marigolds along their path. The fucking thing remained unscathed.

"I'm not going to park us on top of that structure in case it is some kind of super weapon. Don't want to set it off prematurely. I'm aiming toward the gap between it and Candor. Readings indicate the air and pressure are synthetically maintained at normal levels down there, so we won't explode if we survive the crash."

Hersh shook, eyes bulging, with sudden realization. "My God, this isn't a harpy artifact; the scale of it, the sophistication, the passive defenses, the single precise shot..." He couldn't finish the sentence. His mouth felt dry like the landscape around them.

"Machine Intelligence?" Ameera asked nervously.

"Yeah, the robots have allied themselves with the posthuman perverts on Mars!"

The glider quickly approached the rail tube feeding troops and supplies into the massive robot machine, and Hersh's fear and frustration suddenly found a target he could annihilate. He launched three scorching javelins of light at the side of the tube and watched the whole thing blow to hell as the S-8 zoomed by.

They hammered into Mars and skidded and spun until the unforgiving ravine walls slammed them to a stop. The crash gel in their seats cushioned them from the worst of the impact. His stomach churned, his body ached, and his head whirled. Breathing felt like lifting a mountain.

Hersh gritted his teeth and mustered all the strength he had to take Ameera's hand. He squeezed it once and passed out.

Chapter 16

HS Hurricane - 2323 A.D.

When Xing returned to the *Hurricane* she couldn't shake the feeling of being violated, but she could at least function. Somehow, she exited the docking bay and made it to her small cabin. Being possessed by the M.I. was like suffering from locked-in syndrome, while her body moved about doing things she didn't want to do, or like being tied up in a car that was driving off a cliff or… She struggled to describe it. She got in the shower and let the hot water boil away the haunting sense of exploitation, of helplessness. It felt right to do something physical, something wholly human.

Xing toweled herself off, put on a clean uniform, and made a scorching pot of instant coffee. She took a gulp and imagined the scalding, black liquid cleansing her insides. She consciously stopped her curators from repairing her seared tongue and throat.

When she was ready, she started pulling up data on Oya Valette; the uncommon name helped limit her search. But there was nothing remarkable there. She drilled down into her friend's past. Her parents had died when she was very young, wild Astronet rumors circulated that a powerful family had been involved, but nothing was ever pinned on anyone. Xing flagged that for future research. Oya had been legally adopted by her "geneticist-turned-environmentalist" grandmother. Another flag.

After thirty minutes, a galaxy of glowing data swirled around her. She took another sip, her hand still shaking.

Xing was meditating on the pain moving down her gullet, when the ship told her that her captain's shuttle had returned.

"Diwa! We have an emergency!" the commander yelled over the comm, his voice desperate. Something must've gone wrong like the effigy had predicted.

"Yes, Commander," she croaked, and silently permitted her curators to heal the burns.

"We were ambushed by those savages. They had no intention of talking to us."

"What about Oya?"

"Who knows? Probably dead. The captain is in critical condition. I'm going to leave him in the infirmary to let the curators work on him. I don't know if they're going to be enough, though. He's been through a lot."

"I'll meet you there, sir." Xing tried to muster his sense of urgency, but the numbness lingered. She left the quarters.

"No, meet me on the bridge. We have to plan our next move." He cut off.

Our next move? Oya was gone, the captain severely injured, the task assigned to her by the winged statue was moot now, and as she hurried down the white corridor of the ship, a thought occurred to her: *They should flee this hideous star system.* And she knew, for the first time since the hijack, that that thought was entirely her own. Every cell in her body told her to run.

She ran into Davoli a few meters from the command deck and jumped when she saw him. He was splattered in mud and blood. His regimentals were in rags. One of his legs was buttressed haphazardly. His eyes were sunken into his skull.

"What happened down there?"

"We were attacked. Their leader literally took a bite out of the captain mid-talks. They're animals."

"Commander, we should go!" No longer anesthetized, her flight response took over with a vengeance. "We should do what Hershkovitz wanted and go back home."

"You're misinterpreting the captain's orders! He said to abort only if we didn't come back, and we came back. I'm taking command of this ship in his absence."

"Sir, maybe you should get cleaned up first, eat something, rest. You look terrible. Let's compare notes and think about this."

The set expression on his face softened a bit. "I'm fine, Diwa, the lander's medical unit took care of me."

They entered the bridge and Xing took her post, thinking that he was far from fine. Davoli teetered between his own station and the captain's. He looked edgy. His curators had obviously pumped him full of adrenaline and testosterone and who knows what else. Her own awful experience was coming into perspective; she realized her trip down to the Augur's shrine could've been far worse.

"We don't have to go back. There have to be other planets out there, ones more fully habitable. Why settle for this harsh little rock swarming with harpies? Let them have it!" She set a search hound on the task of sniffing out and appraising the nearest systems.

"You're what, a sixty-year-old kid? You have no idea what these things are capable of; intelligence in the service of animal bloodlust."

Xing noticed that a smattering of small red plumes still clung to his dirt-encrusted uniform as if he had been tarred and feathered. "There are only two of us, sir!"

"I'm going to wake everyone up. We're going to need an army to take this planet."

"We're still completely outnumbered. That's ninety-eight colonists against, what, a few hundred thousand feathered-dinosaurs. We should *go*." She checked her bot's results. "Look, I've already found a few good candidate systems. Travel time no more than five to eight subjective years."

Davoli was no longer listening to her. He'd gone glassy-eyed again, his expression slack, and, combined with the gore and filth that covered him, it looked like the curators were animating a corpse. He tapped his sidearm with his thumb as if to a silent tune. She wondered if she had looked much the same when her own curators had forsaken her for the M.I. and steered her around without her being in the driver's seat.

"I served on Titan," he said, at last; his voice had a vacant quality. He slumped in the captain's chair. "I followed my older brother there and saw him get ripped to shreds. At the end, there were only five of us left in that contingent; we called ourselves the Fighting Fowlers. We barely escaped — on foot — from the City of Ten Thousand Dragons."

This wasn't the curators, she realized. This was much worse. Xing feared her commander was slowly going insane right before her very eyes. She came from around her station and slowly approached him, tried to touch his shoulder, but he heaved himself out of the captain's chair and moved to his old post.

"We waded, knee-deep, in hydrocarbon shit, our visors smeared by the black, petrol blizzard. Somehow, we made it to a cave by a methane lake and hunkered down, one rifle between the five of us, our suits almost spent.

"When the shit storm subsided, they came after us with an armored zeppelin the size of the *Hurricane*. They shelled the cave system with sonics to flush us out, or bury us. Two of my fellow soldiers were crushed by a rockslide. I was terrified, and I was angry. I saw the reflection of the zeppelin on the sluggish waves. And then, in a moment of reckless insight, I shouldered the rifle and fired a string of high energy particles at the lake of raw fuel. The whole thing ignited. It was like a province of Hell had burst forth into the world and engulfed the harpy airship."

He paced the bridge and tapped his gun, glancing at every lightscreen, but not really seeing anything. Davoli caught her staring at him and he wheeled around. He leaned his face in close to hers. His breath smelled of vanilla.

"I'm not telling you this for my benefit, Diwa. Three of us survived, and a month later we took Titan from them. I'm telling you this to say we may be outnumbered, but we have superior fire power, curator support, and deadly resolve. We will beat these animals." Spittle sparkled on his chin.

She had to tell him. If not, he would blindly get them all killed. "Listen to me very carefully, Carlo. We're not just dealing with harpies here. They've got support of their own … they've got protection. There's an M.I. down there, the same one that brought them here. It's on their side."

Davoli violently grabbed her by the shoulder. "How do you know this?"

Xing suddenly felt small in his grasp. His stench sickened her. "It contacted me — kidnapped me — the thing can hack into our curators and control us like drones."

Without letting her go, Davoli quickly checked a lightscreen and saw the message and the unauthorized departure of a lander. He pushed her back as if he'd been holding a rattlesnake. "My God, you've been compromised!"

"We've all been compromised. We're all defenseless against an intelligence that can make a trillion computations in less time than it takes us to decide what to eat for dinner."

He gave her a killer's look. "Ship, strip Information Office Xing Diwa of all bridge privileges. Now!"

"No! Please!" She could see all her access locking down, pinching off her precious data flow. Instantly she was hit by withdraw — she needed the constant rush of data — but she had to admit there was a tiny unconscious part of her that felt a little safer. *The thing couldn't reach her and possess her now.* Her curators were cut off from the bridge's network. She blinked and refocused her organic eyes. Without all of the augmented bells and whistles, she saw Davoli fingering the air above his command console. He looked crazy.

"Why hasn't the damned robot attacked us then?"

"It's only an echo of the full software personality it once was and it wants us alive. It wants to use us against an incoming threat it's perceived, which is more reason to get out of this system!"

"It's handicapped and wants to use us as pawns... Fuck that!"

"What are you doing?" But despite her restricted awareness, she could tell he was targeting the last location on her lander's itinerary.

"Stop!" She threw herself at him, grappled his arm and tried to pull it away from a screen she could no longer see, but it was futile. His curators had been militarized and hers had not. Davoli simply patted her chest with two fingers and sent 50,000 volts coursing through her body. Xing went writhing onto the deck.

Then, without looking down at her, he fired a massive, continuous column of light down at the planet, and she knew that everything within a five-kilometer radius of the ultramodern Pantheon had been reduced to slag. The Augur's server-shrine, Snacakobek — they were all gone.

Chapter 17

Quetzalcoatl

Inirigua walked away from Oya, and the guards surrounded her. She called to him. He couldn't answer her because the lump in his throat choked back the words. He was glad for it. She didn't deserve his reassuring song. Then he stopped abruptly, as if he had gotten too far away from her and couldn't quite achieve escape velocity. His legs twitched. He considered going back to her, tearing her away from those Palace pissants and kissing her, forcing her into *nanife*, demanding her loyalty through the base chemical secretions within her skull. Inirigua trembled. No, she would never forgive the rape — because that's what it would be — even if she loved him afterward. He would never be able to look her in the eye.

But maybe he should at least turn around to see her one last time. No, he didn't want to reveal the tears running down his face. And the signs of the recent attack were everywhere. He stared at a smashed column to avoid looking at the blood stains. Indignation and concern for his sister and mother kick-started his legs again. He dug in his talons and slowly scratched toward the opening still spewing black smoke into the sky.

As Inirigua vaulted off the tier, he heard the crack of bones and crackle of electricity from Oya's direction.

He flew around the enormous pagoda and into his mother's personal terrace. He stormed into her office, but the sight of her staggered him. Her feathers fell around her like rose petals. Her complexion was a sickly yellow and her eyes were weighed down by dark bags. Inirigua ran to her side and Cayaguey squeezed him warmly. "Thank the heavens you're alive!"

"What happened here, Mother? Where's Kiwi?"

"She's fine. She's safe in Carica territory. We met with the Hominocracy captain and I attacked them... One of them did all this to us. Just one." Her trill was a weak lisp through bloody gums. All her sharp teeth had fallen out. "They are not the soft baseline humans we once knew. They've upgraded synthetically."

"What did they do to you? It looks like radiation poisoning."

"I don't know ... a weapon of some sort. We know you and Majasora were ambushed before you completed *nanife*." The word made him wince. "She secretly took a contingent of her own people to search for you. Then the Augur sent out a message to all the Raptor Chiefs — the first in two decades — after that, everything moved too fast."

"Majasora found us. We had to fight her off."

"I don't understand," his mother said, her waning attention focusing. "Fight her?"

"I had the situation under control. The invader was in my custody and *she* attacked us."

"The Hominocracy did inquire about their agent. You had her?"

"Yes, it was a lone woman. She claims her ship is one of colonists and not war. I don't think they were expecting to find us here. There's also the small drop ship she came in. It has incredible machinery, superior to anything we've dreamed of."

"I know of their incredible machinery," she said bitterly. "I've sent a detachment to fetch it and assigned a team of scientists to crack it open."

"Tell them to keep an eye out for Majasora and her group. They should be lying, stunned between here and the ship."

She seemed to fold in on herself again. "After a century of tranquility... The Hominocracy again!"

"I'm worried about you, Mother." He ran the back of his claw along her cheek the way she used to, when he was a fledgling and still learning to fly. "Maybe Oya, the one I brought here, can help you?"

What was left of Cayaguey's crest rose and slicked back in displeasure. "You've brought your captive here? I shall have her interrogated immediately."

"I think *you* should do it personally. I've promised her your audience."

"Promised her my audience?" Her contralto was full of shock and disgust. With obvious effort, she gathered herself up from her lassitude. "She's a prisoner of war. She does not get the benefit of my audience."

"I believe she's reasonable enough. Maybe we can avert a larger conflict altogether. And more importantly, maybe she can undo whatever is afflicting you."

"Reasonable?" Cayaguey peered at her son with penetrating eagle-eyes. "You're infatuated with her. Did you experience *nanife* with her? Did she force it on you?"

"No!" He stamped out the irony along with the rising panic. "She interrupted the ceremony."

"Don't lie to me, son! I can see it in your dilated pupils, in the flushed coloration of your cheeks. I can hear it in the timber of your voice even as you defend her!"

Suddenly, Inirigua exploded violently, slashing at his mother's expensive wall hangings depicting a pair of phoenixes surrounded by chrysanthemum flowers. He shrieked madly and kicked at her moa-leather sofa, gutting it. All the rage and frustration he'd been trying to stifle since the misfired *nanife* erupted within the confines of the Chief's sanctum. Then, when all his awful energies were spent, he crumpled onto the floor next to her and stammered, "I've lost everything I ever wanted. I hate her for taking that away from me, but I love her. I'm bonded to her for life."

Tears threatened to claw their way out of Cayaguey's eyes. She reached out to touch her seething son, to comfort him, but she simply sat on the floor, utterly defeated. "There are chemical treatments to undo *nanife*, powerful tailor-made drugs."

"Treatments that leave you like a torpid eunuch? No, I'd rather burn alone like the sun, than wander through life like a cold comet."

His mother said nothing. She understood completely, of course. He knew she had refused the treatments herself when the love of her life — *her life* — had died. Cayaguey moved to enfold her son in a warm wing, but her wings were gone and she hesitated to caress him with the naked limbs she now possessed.

"Will the pain ever dull?" he asked her, taking her bony arm and finishing the action she couldn't. The smoke couldn't mask her sickly scent. He stared at the bulging blue veins weaving from the back of her hand up her arm.

"No." Her once beautiful voice cracked. "But it'll become a part of you over time, and on most days, you won't even notice it, but you'll grow calloused and spiteful... We'll lose the cooperation of the Macu if this gets out."

He kissed her forehead. "It won't get out. Tell them that you need me unchained in the war with the Hominocracy and arrange for Majasora to marry one of my cousins. Jujoquete is a good, bright kid."

"I'll see to it," Cayaguey said softly. "We cannot afford petty clan politics. We must serve our people, and I mean everyone on this tiny planet — all of the raptorial race — in this time of crisis."

"Unless." He wavered for a moment, then blurted it out. "A union with Oya might stave off a war altogether."

All tenderness evaporated and she shot him a predatory look. "Don't be ridiculous!"

"Is it ridiculous? Growing up you regaled me with stories of how your marriage with my father united the Carica and the Vanacan and allowed you to rise to power. How great grandmother Tianlongmu did the same on Titan! How is this different?"

"We're not talking about a *chiriarabo*, a respected rival clan; we're talking about the enemy! A flightless human! Our latest intel suggests they've now destroyed the Augur! Don't you see? They want to obliterate everything about us."

"But what if they stopped being the enemy? What if Oya can convince them to at least see us as fellow human beings?"

Cayaguey looked too tired — too ill — to argue. Her fire was almost out. "That's the neurochemical shackles talking. You know that's impossible, son, you can't convince someone to see you as human. It has to come from them."

"Meet her, question her, and give her a chance to prove you wrong. We have nothing to lose, and everything to gain."

"I want fast, venomous grandchildren with strong wings and rending talons, Inirigua, not grounded cyborgs." The tenacious tears finally won out and she wept melodically.

"Do it for me, Mother ... for Kiwi."

She turned away, unable to look at him. "Bring her to me."

Chapter 18

Immediately Oya's overlay view tagged the surrounding harpies, one through five, and tracked them. Two of them brandished what the curators identified as modified handguns. She tossed the yellow bundle she carried at one of the armed harpies, wirelessly commanding the smart fabric to "cocoon." The umbrella folds of the wings engulfed the man like a Venus flytrap.

She turned her attention to the other four. Oya recklessly swung at number one and missed her completely. They were ridiculously quick, and she wished she'd been better trained in hand-to-hand combat. She honestly didn't know what the hell she was doing.

Attacker number three tried to eviscerate her with a thorny roundhouse kick, but she blocked low with so much strength that she crushed his shin bone. It was an ugly move, but it worked. Number four swiped her claws across Oya's upper back, excavating three bloody trenches from shoulder to spine. Oya killed the pain and wheeled around. The harpy moved in to bite her, but she parried with an electric palm.

An intensely hot laser beam traversed her left thigh. Oya screamed and dropped to one knee. *Kill pain. Coagulate blood. Plug hole*, she ordered her curators, gritting her teeth. She had foolishly forgotten that number two also carried a weapon. She grabbed the electrocuted harpy lying near her, stood with a wobble, and, with all her might, tossed the harpy at number two — they were so light. The armed harpy crumpled beneath his teammate.

There was only one left. The leader of the guards. Her plumage was more rosy-orange than the others, like a slice of mamey. The tag "number one" floated over her twitching crest like a guillotine. The harpy hesitated. She had just watched her entire group get trounced by one desperate, injured woman. The harpy wasn't armed, except for what nature and genetic engineering had given her, and she wasn't stupid.

The traumatized muscles in Oya's leg quivered, but her bone was unharmed. She raised her arms in the universal sign for surrender. This left the harpy utterly nonplussed.

"I'm not going to fight you if you don't attack me, but I'm not leaving this spot until Inirigua gets back," she said in the clearest Cantabile possible and hoped the fidgety warbird would take her offer. Her curators assailed her with a riot of alerts; she was going to need a lot of food, water and rest very soon.

"Don't move," the harpy mumbled, as if she had golf balls in her mouth. "We'll wait for the Chief's son to return."

"Okay." Oya breathed a sigh of relief but kept her moaning curator's ready. *Chief's son? Was Inirigua the son of the Chief?* He hadn't mentioned it. She wiped the warnings from her field of vision and urged them to work on the laser wound. She surveyed her fallen attackers and loosened the wings around the now unconscious number five before he suffocated.

She had managed to avoid seriously injuring the crimson guards during their brief fight. And now, in the stillness of the hall and with amplified hearing, she caught snippets of the conversation between Inirigua and his mother. Regardless of the rapid exchange of their singsong language and words that had no cultural translation, Oya caught enough to know that Inirigua was advocating for her. This surprised her. She was sure he had turned on her. The look in his eyes when he saw the bodies of his own people had been tragic.

Oya didn't struggle as another guard came in, and, with number one, roughly pulled her into a large private chamber. The Clan Chief lay at the center of the room in a bed of her own molted feathers. Inirigua stood by her side. He looked more pained than outraged. The Chief looked, to Oya's revulsion, like plucked poultry.

Inirigua gave her a slight nod and asked, "Oya, can you please tell us what your people did to my mother?"

Oya didn't respond. She was still angry, but Inirigua had gotten her in to see the de facto leader of all the harpies on this planet. She was grateful for at least that. She switched to augmented view. Her own curators warned of a thirty-five percent loss and flashed the "catastrophic failure" signal. She pushed that away and examined the Clan Chief. Oddly enough, there was data flow coming from her as if she—

"She's infested with curators. They think her transgenic alterations are a disease, a physical deformity, and they're attempting to repair it. In fact, they're killing her." She looked around the room, horrified. "Inirigua, you've also caught some curators. You all have. It doesn't make any sense; something must have triggered this hypersensitive reaction in them, allowing them to jump from their preprogrammed host."

"I've made a tactical error." Cayaguey let out a sour laugh. Craning her head to face Inirigua, she said, "Our attack on them wasn't simple brute force. Before our little summit, I had my scientists uncork a highly contagious strain of the original archaeopteryx retrovirus."

"Mother, you mean we attacked them first?"

"The plan was to let one of them escape and have him unwittingly infect all his shipmates. If they wished to conquer this planet, let it be as raptors." She looked away and hugged her naked, malformed arms. "It appears we fittingly became victims of a similar fate."

Inirigua turned to Oya, panic in his eyes. "I swear I didn't know about any of this. I'll try to assist your people with the retrovirus, but can you stop the curators from killing my people?"

"Not from here. I could from my ship," she said, her mind racing.

"I'll get a transport ready."

"I'll go with you. I need to eat something desperately though, or I'm going to pass out."

Cayaguey caught Oya by the wrist. "No! Son, go ready whatever transport you need and order her some food, but I want to speak to the enemy agent."

Inirigua glanced at Oya for an instant then sprinted away, leaving her with the misshapen woman.

Despite Cayaguey's diseased appearance, her imperial gaze made Oya feel filthy; her uniform was shredded by talons, the throb in her leg returning slowly. The gash in her lower back had fully healed, but she was mind-numbingly famished. She stunk even to herself. "Your Highness?" Oya bowed slightly, as much as her unstable leg allowed. She found it hard to pretend to a woman who had just unleashed a biological weapon on her crew.

"Spare me your false deference, young lady. I know your Hominocracy doesn't recognize my authority or my flock's claim to this planet. I just need you to answer some questions honestly." The ailing ruler released her hold on Oya. The three crescent claws looked larger at the end of a gross featherless limb.

Oya rubbed her arm unconsciously, and said, "I'm a lot older than you, Clan Chief."

"Your marvelous curators again?" Cayaguey hissed, and blood dribbled down her chin. "We of the winged-race are fierce by temperament, we wage war for territory, we fight for prestige, we even battle for lovers! Being so intimate with war, we also know how to end them."

"Do you believe we can have peace after all this?"

"I don't know. My son thinks so, but he's always been foolishly optimistic. Our two clans must meet with humility, as equals. Your captain, for all his talk of peace, came to me making demands, full of domineering bluster."

"And you would've infected us with a powerful virus regardless of his approach."

"Yes, but ultimately my action was nonlethal. Remember, you tried to eradicate us. It falls on you to make the hard sacrifices." The Clan Chief sagged, as if she had reserved her last bit of energy to speak frankly with the enemy and now was spent.

Oya couldn't help but be reminded of her grandmother's last day of life, the wild swings between bursts of fiery brilliance and rapid descent into vulnerability.

The aroma of spiced food cleared her mind and made her mouth water. A servant brought in a tray of food, steaming rice, a roasted fish of some sort, and stir-fried alien shoots with ginger. She sat on the floor with the plate on her lap, not thinking about proper etiquette, and dug into the food ravenously.

Cayaguey waited politely for Oya's frenzy to ease, and then asked, "Why did you come here to Beta Hydri, to Quetzalcoatl?"

"I don't know what my captain told you, but back home, the Hominocracy is a system-wide organization. We've recently started going out to colonize other stars," she said, her mouth full.

"No, why did *you* come here, Oya Valette?"

Oya was a bit taken aback by the personal question. She stopped eating. "Um, well, I came here to start a life."

"What was wrong with your old life?"

"I don't know. Nothing, I guess. It had just become unsatisfying."

Cayaguey hacked painfully. The curators were tearing down and rebuilding her bird-like lungs. When the coughing subsided, she asked, "Do you have any children, grandchildren? I realize asking that to someone with such an unlined, unblemished face borders on the absurd..."

"No. After the mega population boom, our curators were instructed to prevent conception. That's one reason some of us came here, to start families."

"You?"

Oya thought of the children she'd seen, playing and flying around her; she remembered the feelings they awoke within her. "Yes," she whispered, and, as she said it, she knew that it was one of the reason she'd come. Not the only reason, but an important one. The truth was, the second she'd set foot on this hostile planet, all her boredom, her bitterness, her hopelessness, had lifted. This was her new home, where she would raise a family, where she would be buried.

"I've had the pleasure of being a mother, and hope," Cayaguey's voice trembled subtly, "to one day be a grandmother. So, when I say that you are a threat to the future of my people, I'm not saying that politically, culturally, or ideologically. I mean it in the most basic, biological sense. You are an invasive species with impossible lifespans, and, breeding unchecked, you will overrun this entire solar system as you've overrun yours and drive everything else to extinction."

The words struck Oya like a slap. *Bondye mwen, we're the Rhesus macaques.* She set the near empty tray aside.

"I'm not going to survive this, am I?" Cayaguey warbled.

"I don't know. The damage is extensive. You're bleeding internally and the curators aren't letting up."

The Clan Chief sobbed suddenly. After a moment, when she had regained enough control, she said, "If you really want to start a life here, give up your immaculate, cybernetic half-life, and embrace a short, precious life with all its perils."

"I understand," Oya replied, more to herself than to the Clan Chief. She knelt by the dying woman and took her claw in her own hands. She knew, on a fundamental level, that this woman was just trying to protect her small world. "I'll stop this."

"Please, *make* my son be right about you."

Chapter 19

Mars - 2198 A.D.

Hersh came to first, but he was dazed and his eyes were having trouble focusing. *What had he been doing? Had they crashed while hunting birds?* He contemplated his current predicament with almost drunken detachment. *No, not birds … harpies.*

For reasons that utterly confounded him, about a hundred years ago, the original colonists of Mars had spiced up their genomes with archaeopteryx DNA. Some say it was a fad; flying in the weaker gravity was all the rage back then. What these idiots hadn't taken into account was that transplanted DNA usually had more than one function, so genes associated with wings and claws and hollow bones also coded for cruel, reptilian aggression. The Hominocracy Movement offered aid in the form of advanced gene therapies and reconstructive surgery to bring these poor, transgenic bastards back to humanity. Of course, they lashed out viciously and now they were entangled in a war.

Slowly, he realized the glider was on fire. It was a puny, starved flame but it was enough to snap him from his trance. He tugged on Ameera and her bloody head rolled lifelessly off the control panel. His heart seized with dread, and then leapt out of his chest when he saw that she was still breathing. This morning he had been determined to split up with her, but now — maybe it was the very real danger of losing her — something stronger welled up within him. Carefully, he pulled her out of the wreckage and held her.

He looked up at the elliptical compound. In fact, it was hard not to look at it as it monopolized most of his field of view. Then his senses adjusted and noticed chrome balloons floating around it. He had been right about the machines' involvement. In the darkness of the canyon, the robots looked like mechanical jellyfish pulsating in a blood-colored abyss. It bothered Hersh that the robots paid him no mind as they worked; each one of those bags of hardware and gas were more intelligent than he was by a magnitude of a hundred. He felt like an ant on a factory floor. They drifted silently, fastidiously working on their inexplicable structure.

"We made it," Ameera moaned; it came out more like a question.

His attention snapped away from the artificial man-o-war and he smiled down at her. "Yeah, we had a great pilot." He found himself kissing her on the lips.

Ameera patted his cheek. "Hersh, don't complicate things."

"I think we're well passed complicated. I just wanted to say right here and now, with those things floating overhead, that I love you, Ameera el-Ayeb. I really do. I've been an asshole and you deserve better."

"Hersh, we agreed to keep it light. My family would not approve of ... *us*."

"So, what, you were just going to let me down easy when our tour was over?" He looked at the flashing med-alert on her uniform. She had suffered a concussion. He knew he really shouldn't upset her.

"Weren't you?"

Wasn't he? Of course he was, but that was before he had almost lost her. Was he just emotionally raw from the accident? Not thinking straight? "Can you walk?"

"Yeah, I think so." Ameera blinked heavily. "So, what's the plan?"

"I think the harpies are evacuating Candor and pouring into that robot construct. I haven't figured out exactly what it is, but I don't think that matters now. If we can sneak into the city, we can call our ship and Captain Morales will send in an extraction team to get us." It was a horrible plan, full of guess work and false hope, but it was all he could come up with.

"All right," she said, and tried standing.

The fact that Ameera didn't argue with him or come up with a better plan worried Hersh even more than the glowing med-alert. He had to keep her awake. He took her by the waist and they began to hobble toward the ruined transit tube. They were on the exposed surface of Mars. Yes, the area had artificially been made "livable," but the extraterrestrial cold quickly seeped through their uniforms and into their bones. His ears and nose burned like ice. The one positive was that the lighter gravity made their staggering hike relatively quick and easy. That is, until they got to the wreck. They both faltered.

"My God, Hersh, those are children!"

The terrible sight of the damaged tram hit them like a cluster bomb. Ameera's knees buckled and he held her tight. "Don't look, Ameera, they're just harpy fledglings." But he looked. He couldn't help it. The smoking bodies were crumpled and littered amongst the debris. There were dozens of them. It was like his mind skipped over the lifeless adults and locked onto the juveniles. Their arms and heads covered in white, downy fluff, but their faces — their innocent, slack faces — were those of little kids. The rising smell of burned flesh turned his stomach and his body weakened. He fell forward in a puff of rusty sand and vomited. His hacking noises and Ameera's sobbing echoed up the canyon walls, all the way up to the hardhearted robots.

Despite his years of training screaming at him — ordering him to move — they remained emotionally compromised, shell-shocked. He picked up a long feather from the ground, like an obsidian blade. *What had he done? How many kids had he killed?* This was nothing like the *Flash Gordon* RPGs he played as a kid. The battles against the virtual Hawkmen now seemed grossly sanitized compared to this stinking carnage.

A shrill beeping cut their self-pity short. Both their suits' proximity sensors were picking up multiple bogies headed their way. Hersh instinctively pulled his laser gun from its holster and hauled his stunned and weeping pilot behind a charred tram car.

They hunkered down. He roughly grabbed her face and looked straight into her brown eyes. "Listen to me, Ameera. We've got a murder of crows headed this way and I can't fend them off by myself. Can you fight?"

"Yeah — Yes, I'm a soldier." She didn't sound convinced, but she drew her sidearm.

"Damned right you are, and we're also the only two humans on this miserable planet. So, let's do Adam and Eve proud," he said, and braced himself against their flying adversaries.

They heard angry screeching reverberating through the canyon before they saw the black, winged forms soaring toward them. The enemy looked human enough, but Hersh knew that was simply a vestigial trait; they were more maniraptora than men. A flock of about ten of them, each wielding customized hand guns, like brass knuckles, on their dinosaurian wing-claws, wheeled overhead, raining electric blue fire on them.

Hersh and Ameera shot back at the attacking harpies. They were outnumbered, but not out. The blazing remains of the tram provided ample cover and the harpies' wide wingspan made them easy targets.

Hersh noticed Ameera was trying really hard to miss every one of them. He didn't say anything. She'd had her fill of death, and besides, her drowsy, scattered shots confused them and Hersh's own strict shooting always hit its mark. Shots sizzled back and forth. Their cover caught fire and they scrambled to another piece of debris and retook positions. After a long fight, there was only one harpy left. This one flew and wailed like a banshee. Then, all of a sudden, it dropped into the smoldering mess of the transit tube and disappeared.

He quickly scanned the area over the barrel of his gun and saw nothing. "Okay, we're going to make a run for it. Are you ready?"

Ameera nodded, but her eyes were closed. *Had her eyes been closed the entire firefight?* Then she whispered, "Hersh, we slaughtered those little children."

"You didn't do anything, Ameera. This is on me! I pulled the trigger. You were just trying to land the plane and save our lives. Your conscience is clean."

"Why doesn't it feel that way?" She leaned in and dug her face into his chest and he hugged her. She felt cold in his arms. He could no longer smell her perfume over the smoke and dust.

Over Ameera's shoulder he saw the shadow of a winged woman through the soot, hunched over the body of a dead fledgling. She tenderly draped her wings around it and rocked back and forth. For a brief moment, both their gentle movements mirrored each other and aching doubt crept into his soul. Then the creature let out a piercing, grief-filled shriek that shattered the Martian silence.

"Come on." He dragged Ameera into the twisted open transit tube. They walked through the long, dark tunnel that led into the domed city of Candor.

In the utter blackness, two hundred million years of evolution evaporated; all identity, all culture, all humanity vanished, and they were simply mammals scurrying in the dark, hiding from the terrible reptiles. He had a sick feeling in his stomach.

"Hersh, if we survive this, will you marry me?" she asked in the same hushed, sleepy tones she often used after sex, trying to keep him from falling asleep in her bunk.

"Yes." They walked-dragged in silence for a while, and then he added, "After I get you out of here, your dad is going to love me. Our wedding is going to be the best, I promise."

She didn't say anything more, but clumsily kissed the corner of his mouth.

The dark ended when they crossed the pylons and entered the city. Hersh had never been inside a harpy aviary before, and the sight of it overwhelmed him. The bare canyon walls of Candor Chasma had been carved with laser precision to look like the Treasury at Petra on a metropolitan scale. Entire housing blocks and districts sprawled vertically up the sheer cliffs. This was a living space designed by natural fliers. Immense statues of stiff-winged people, like ancient Sumerian or Egyptian gods, stood guard in the magnificent, desolate city. There was imagination and history here. Generations of avian humans had built this place and now they were being forced out or destroyed.

"Here the repellent harpies make their nests," Ameera murmured to herself. "It's beautiful."

"We have to find a communications station, even a small personal one."

He kept her moving, choosing a path by dead reckoning. They shuffled along the empty thoroughfare until they came upon a colossal monument of an enthroned mother and child in the center arcade, like Isis nursing Horus. Despite all fear and logic, he stopped to appraise it. There was something undeniably mammalian about it. *Had the Hominocracy Movement gotten these creatures all wrong? Had he?* Maybe he was just thinking this because the vision of the harpy weeping over her chick was still impressed upon his mind like a white-hot brand.

"She's lovely," Ameera said clearly. Her eyes looked more focused than they'd been since the crash. Perhaps being in the boundless maternal presence of the statue roused her. She seemed more responsive, and Hersh's legs almost gave with relief.

He kissed her gritty cheek. "Yes, she is."

He gave the statue one last look. The mother appeared fully human, with striking African features, but her fledgling was far from human — fully winged and clawed. Hersh could tell by her small breasts that the child was a female. In fact, in the grand tradition of those ancient desert icons, the child's proportions were more like those of a diminutive adult, than that of an actual infant.

"We should get moving. Get inside somewhere," he whispered, and gently peeled her away from the figure of the Grande Dame of Dinosaurs.

They managed to walk two more steps, when a ribbon of light shot across the chasm and hit First Pilot Ameera el-Ayeb square in the back. Her body convulsed in Hersh's arms and then went limp.

"No!" he screamed, like a suffering animal. For a second, Hersh was utterly stunned. He laid Ameera on the polished stone ground and fired blindly toward the direction of the beam. He knew he should run and shelter behind the monument, but he couldn't leave Ameera lying there alone like carrion for this scavenger.

A harpy — the grieving harpy — flew out of a darkened balcony like a demon. Hersh fired frantically. She flapped hard, banking this way and that, an awesome display of aerobatics. He kept shooting, but was tired and scared and angry, and failed to make contact with his target. She dipped into another stone-cut terrace. She was toying with him, and he understood the tactical error of getting caught in a canyon. He suddenly felt like a desert mouse being hunted by a hawk.

The harpy exploded into the sky, and he sprayed the air with crackling light, trying to aim where he thought she would be a second into the future, but she was fast and cunning. He held the trigger down until the power cell of his weapon went dry. *Was this what she was waiting for? Could she see the gun's power readout from up in the air?* It was clear she didn't want to kill him from an impersonal distance; she was hunting. Hersh looked for Ameera's sidearm, but couldn't find it. *Damn, she must have dropped it in the tunnel.*

The harpy tauntingly circled above. He unsheathed his bowie knife and spun around, keeping his eyes on her. Even with the thirteen inches of glinting steel in his sweaty hand, he felt ridiculously inadequate against her six sickle-shaped claws and razor-sharp fangs. Without warning, the harpy tucked in her wings and dove straight at him.

The creature struck like a whirlwind, pouring all her fury into rending his flesh. Hersh idiotically swung his knife around, but the attack was a blast of black plumage and pain. He fell on his belly. He was vaguely aware that he was screaming. He was pinned.

Something sharp and hot slid between the vertebrae of his spine, and blinding agony washed over him.

Chapter 20

Quetzalcoatl - 2323 A.D.

Inirigua corkscrewed around the towering pagoda and landed in the Palace's private hangar. The cavernous space that encompassed most of the wide lower tier held all of the old shuttles that had ferried his mother's generation from the *Roc's Egg* to their new, wilderness world. The crisp scent of machine oil and hydraulic fluid wasn't enough to cleanse his nose and mouth of the lingering taste of smoke and death.

All of the crafts were opalescent ovoids, like fifty-meter-long crystal eggs in a massive incubation chamber. Most of them were mere museum pieces by now, long ago cannibalized for parts. But Inirigua knew that several of them had been sensibly maintained by his mother's people in case of emergencies. In case the Hominocracy ever showed up. His whistle startled the lounging skeleton crew of techs. They rushed toward him, flustered and slightly annoyed. Had they not heard the commotion above?

When he had their attention, he said in his most commanding song, "Please prep our best shuttle for immediate departure. I am going into space for an extended mission."

"Right away, Chief's son." The head engineer's clipped call rang in the hangar as he flashed his wings like fans and then folded them neatly against his steel gray uniform. The man seemed older than Inirigua, by about ten years, but offered him the kind of respect reserved for elders.

Inirigua repaid his loyalty with a courteous bow. "Excellent. I also need to get cleaned up, change into a new flight suit and make a personal call while you work."

The tech extended a wing toward the back of the hangar. "We've got unused standard issue flight suits in our locker room, back that way, and the walls in the adjacent briefing room are interactive. Nothing fancy, I'm afraid, but they're secure. You won't be disturbed."

"That'll do. Thank you." He began to move in the direction the engineer had indicated, but had a second thought and turned back. "Oh, and I will be accompanied on this operation by a baseline human. When she arrives, do not be alarmed. She's our prisoner and has agreed to assist the great nation of Vanacan, in exchange for leniency. You can verify that with the Clan Chief."

"Was she involved in the attack?"

"No." Inirigua could see the poorly hidden shock in the raptor's expression, but he only flicked his crest in assent, and without further delay the small flock of engineers fell upon one of the oblong crafts at the center of the room and got to work, going through a myriad of checklists and arcane procedures. Something released a spray of sparks, adding the smell of burned metal to the cold air. Like every ship in the hangar, the shuttle they chose was a smaller replica of that original interstellar lifeboat that had brought his ancestors here.

Inirigua found the crew's locker room after a brisk walk through a maze of offices. If the upper levels of the Soaring Palace of Morning were routinely criticized for their almost vulgar décor, then the hangar facility was guilty of an opposite crime, that of lacking all style and imagination. He tore his ruined clothes off, used the restroom and took a quick shower in one of the stalls. He jostled his feathers under the hot spray, and shook off the stench of sweat and jungle and burning. Inirigua tried not to think about the dire condition he had found his mother in or the aftermath of all the senseless violence he had just seen garnishing his home.

Instead, he focused on Oya and the fact that they were on the same side again, however briefly. He toyed with the dangerous idea of bridging his people and the Hominocracy together through a union with Oya. She was so different. It wouldn't be like what his mother had been trying to arrange with the Macu. Oya didn't hold a high position with her people like Majasora did. Perhaps he could negotiate with the captain, if he had survived the encounter with his mother, or the commander, and appeal to their shared humanity. A tuft of his own red feathers pooling in the drain brought his attention to the present. *No, better not dwell on such fantastic things while his mother was slowly being consumed by an infestation of tiny machines.*

Inirigua got out of the shower and hit upon several uniforms, folded neatly inside a cabinet. He selected a plain black one without any insignias. The attire wasn't of the fine quality he was used to, but at least it was clean and undamaged, and fit quite comfortably. He tried the cheap computer woven into his shirtfront as he walked into the conference room.

The dour room contained nothing but a round table and five stiff chairs. Suddenly, the space immediately brightened as a life-sized image of his sister appeared on the wall screen directly before him. Something drained out of him when he saw her. He had to sit, but dreaded having to explain about their mother, so instead he propped himself up on one of the chairs.

"Inirigua!" she screeched with joy. "What happened to you? I was there when they first reported you'd gone missing. How's Mother?"

"She's ... not well, Kiwi." He forced himself to stand straighter. "She got sick from the Hominocracy captain during their meeting, after biting him. It wasn't intentional, but it's getting out of control. I'm working with them to try to stop it."

"*Them?* You mean the Hominocracy? You can't trust them!" Her mangy arms went up as if to flap wings she did not yet possess. His sister resembled their mother with her flamboyant mannerism of disapproval, more so now that they were both featherless.

That caught his eye. She'd shed copious amounts of down. He could see bare skin in patches on her arms and shoulders. Fear seized him. *Had the nanite epidemic reached Caria territory? No, it was spreading slowly here in the Palace. This was something else; she was finally molting!* He told himself that her sudden development was most likely brought on by the stress of recent events, but it made him feel like more time had passed than actually had since last seeing his sister, and, together with the familiar gestures, it reminded him of his mother's severe illness.

"I have reason to believe I can trust this one. I met her soon after the contest. We did fight, but we managed to settle it peacefully when we recognized our, um, cultural differences. She's not that bad."

"They're saying here that these are the same people that hunted us down and murdered us — not their children or their grandchildren, but the very same ones. Please, come get me, Inirigua, and take me home! I can help!"

It disturbed him to see his otherwise plucky sister looking so frightened and alone. He reached out to touch her but his claw hit the invisible barrier that separated them, creating pixilated ripples in the display. "No, Kiwi, it's not safe here yet. You might get sick, too. In fact, the Palace is probably under quarantine now. Stay in our father's airspace until our scientists say you can come back."

"You don't know what it's like here. They keep replaying the attack on the news and everyone's gone mad with rage."

The attack? It occurred to him that he should see the footage for himself. "You're with Yaboayo, correct? He's mother's top aide, you'll be fine. Trust me, it's worse here."

Her claw went up to his, divided by long kilometers and an atom-thick film of optical paint. "For how long?"

"I don't know, but I promise I'm working on it."

"What can you do?" she cried.

He hesitated, not sure how much to reveal over this channel. The lead tech had said the connection was secure, but what did that mean? Secure against the Macu and the Carica, secure against the Hominocracy? And nothing was truly protected against a prying M.I. Better to be vague. "I'm going to try to meet them and together we're going to find a cure. I can't say more, but I promise I'll do my best."

Her eyes bulged. "It could be a trap like the one they sprang on Mother."

So, she didn't know that it was their suspicious mother who had sprung the trap. The account playing in Carica territory was most likely highly edited and politicized. "I don't think so. If they wanted to harm me, they would've done so by now. Listen, I have to go, my transport is almost ready. I love you, and, no matter what happens next, know that I won't rest until I fix this for Mother and you, and for all of Quetzalcoatl," he said, adding that last bit for anyone tapping the call.

"Please be careful. Don't do anything stupid."

"I won't. I'll see you soon."

Inirigua ended the conversation, not wanting to draw out the painful feeling of abandoning her. It was enough to know she was safe for now. He pulled himself away from the blank wall, and, leaning on the briefing table, called up the recordings of his mother's failed meeting with the Hominocracy. He avoided the many rewritten versions circulating the planet's Astronet, each with their own agenda, and found the original unedited material from the Palace's security cameras.

He watched the opening ceremony and cordial discussion, wondering how his mother planned to introduce the retrovirus into her unsuspecting guests. Was it laced in the tea? No, the captain had refused to drink it. Was it transmitted via physical contact or pumped into the air? Then he saw his mother shriek and lose control, lunging for the captain's neck. Everything exploded into chaos after that. A flurry of forms blocked the various cameras. At one point, he caught a glimpse of the larger man mowing down people Inirigua had known his entire life.

He cut off the footage, red hot anger rising within him. He left the briefing room to wait by the transport. Instantly he saw Oya across the vast space. She was flanked by two big guards, one of them with some blue in his red wings and two erect toe-talons on his feet. It's what his children's with Majasora would've looked like. Oya seemed fine, if a bit tired. She had also washed and now wore a simple black and white flight suit. The sleek, aerodynamic garment accentuated her body's curves nicely. Her smooth, dark arms gleamed in the fluorescent light. Even her fragrance carried a familiar, raptorial balm.

"Are you ready?" he called as he approached.

"Yes." It pleased him to see her face slightly brighten.

"Was your conversation with the Clan Chief successful? Did you get what you were looking for?"

She looked pensive, as if she were still processing his mother's song. "I think so. She said a lot of things I needed to hear. Overall, I believe it was a good exchange."

"How do you feel?" He was keenly aware of the guards and techs watching him, observing their interaction, and judging. Could they tell that he was bound to her? His mother could, but she knew him well and had a good sense of such things.

"A little anemic, but otherwise okay. The food you sent came just in time and the shower felt great."

The head engineer interrupted them apologetically. "Chief's son, the shuttle is ready for take-off."

"Thank you. Also, I don't have to say that this is a sensitive mission. I know everyone will be able to track us as we leave the planet, but I'd prefer that they notice us themselves, at their own time, and not because you all squawked about it the second we depart the hangar."

"We will be discreet, sir," he said, looking back at his gathering team, as if silently reprimanding them for already having posted something on the Astronet. He turned back to Inirigua, careful to avoid looking directly at Oya. "Remember she's an old ship and needs to be treated with care."

"Oh, I'm not the pilot, but I'm sure Oya Valette here will have a light touch."

"*Her?* But sir, this vehicle is a national treasure."

"Don't worry," Oya said, with a too-deep bow to a mere tech. "I'll take good care of her. I've flown my share of spacecraft." Without waiting for his reply, Oya slapped his shoulder and eagerly went up the shuttle's gangplank.

"May the winds of fortune carry you far," the engineer chirruped the old saying automatically, keeping his troubled eyes steadily on Inirigua.

"Thank you," Inirigua said, sharing some of the man's apprehension as he followed Oya. He wondered if he would ever return to his home territory, and if so, would there be anyone alive to greet him.

Chapter 21

HS Hurricane

Oya piloted the large harpy transport out of the planet's atmosphere on a straight course toward the *Hurricane*. It was strange and satisfying to lay her hands on the actual hardware of a ship, as opposed to the intangible lightscreens she'd grown used to, even if the controls were ergonomically designed for six long hooks instead of fingers.

She had been somber and quiet since her talk with Clan Chief Cayaguey. What she was about to do was unadulterated treason from any perspective. Hell, it was outright biological terrorism. *It's also the right thing to do.*

"It looks like a big silver bird," Inirigua said, looking out the forward window. He huddled in his seat, looking quite ill from the ride into space.

"It's the angle of our approach. I always thought it looked like a giant angelfish," Oya said absently. For some strange reason, she was sweating profusely, but felt freezing cold. *Could she be that nervous?* Her curators were down to just twenty six percent, and she strained simply to communicate with the *Hurricane*, trying to get the bay doors to open and allow them in.

She glanced over at Inirigua in the dim light of the shuttle. "You know, for a second there, I thought you had sold me out."

"When I witnessed the death and destruction your people had wrought — you have to understand I thought my mother and sister were dead — I had every intention of selling you out. But then I saw the state of my mother—" The words caught in his throat. "And I figured you, with your advanced tech, were the only one who could help her. I hoped you would, anyways."

"Your sister? Did the curators infect her, too?"

"No. My mother sent her way before all this started."

A warning sign flashed in her field of vision. Her ship was turning her away. Threatening her. "We have a problem."

Suddenly, the *Hurricane* opened fire. A baby blue ribbon of light drilled into their forward shield. Oya quickly pulled hard on the stick and yawed the old ship, avoiding another torrent of beams. She forced the primitive shuttle into a half loop, trying at the same time not to get torn up by the planet's gravity. A second laser grazed the aft section of the ship as she completed the maneuver.

"They're shooting at us! I thought you were talking to them with your nanites?"

"Yeah, I'm trying, but the *Hurricane*'s in combat readiness mode. I need to get within the ship's inner datasphere to interface with it. My signal is too weak. I can't seem to link in from this distance. It doesn't help that we're in a foreign shuttle. The ship would recognize one of its own."

The air in the cabin grew thick and muggy. A faint reek of perspiration invaded the tight space. The change was significant enough that Oya chanced a look at the transport's status report to make sure that life support had not been damaged.

"Can't you do some evasive maneuvers or something?"

She scowled at her controls. "What do you think I'm doing here?"

"Flying around, getting shot at!" he said, digging into the armrests of his seat with his claws.

"Relax, Inirigua. I'm in my element here." She banked the bucking craft to the left. "This has to be the automated defense system. There's no elegance to the shooting, no insight. I can get us through, even in this big dinosaur of yours. I just need to focus and stay one step ahead of the computer." She silently begged her few persistent curators to give her a shot of adrenaline, and instantly her pulse quickened. "How alert are you?"

"Right now? Quite alert."

"Okay. In a second, I'm going to let us get hit. When we do, cut the power to everything but life support."

Before Inirigua could protest, two rapid-fire beams pounded the starboard side of the shuttle. Oya sent them into a wild Tate Tumble. "Now!" she shouted, and he raked at the power console, killing everything nonessential.

She went weightless under her chair's harness. "Okay, to the *Hurricane*'s unsophisticated computer it looks like we've been disabled."

"We probably have been." He looked queasy.

"It doesn't matter. The ship's defense system will observe us for a while, but it will allow us to float by if it thinks we're dead. Also, we're not tumbling uncontrollably. The way I've aimed us, our momentum will take this dinosaur to the bleeding edge of its signal radius. Once there, I'll nudge us into it and interface with the ship before it can resume its attack."

"I've never been in space. I hate this constant sensation of falling. I feel like I should flap my wings and pull up."

"It won't be much longer. Just rest and try not to throw up."

The lifeless shuttle cart-wheeled along its arc, leaving behind a sprinkling of broken bits and escaping air. Then, when Oya was sure they were close to the ship's data bubble, she readied herself and said, "Okay, give the antigrav engines power, but nothing else." The second she felt the tug of artificial gravity, she kicked the shuttle toward the *Hurricane*. They were crushed into their seats, the air squeezed from their lungs.

Finally, the ship recognized her weak signal and ended its assault.

"Welcome back, First Pilot Oya Valette."

"Yeah, I feel welcome, you stupid machine," she gasped, trying to refill her lungs. Sweat ran down the bridge of her nose. Her back stuck to her seat.

They were given permission to enter the docking bay. Oya berthed the craft in the spot left empty by the shuttle abandoned on the planet. When the engine cut off, she leaned back in her chair and closed her eyes, completely worn out. A nagging fear finally drifted to the surface.

"Shit. I think I'm infected with the avian retrovirus," she said. She had suspected it during the flight, but hadn't allowed herself to think about it. "My curators have been crashing ever since that EMP and can't provide adequate protection." She rubbed her frigid biceps and wished Vanacan fashion included sleeves. "We don't have much time."

Oya's first instinct was to reach out to Xing, make sure she was okay, tell her about everything that had happened, but what she needed to do next was horrible, and Oya was afraid her friend would try to stop her. Besides, she didn't want to alert Davoli until it was done. Her gut spun in disgust, a traitor's feeling. She turned her head and got a good look at Inirigua for the first time since they were attacked.

He scratched at the bare goose flesh where patches of feathers were missing from his head and arms. "I would gladly give you the curators that are killing me."

"Oh no, they crossed over from your mother?"

"Yeah, I've been losing feathers at a steady rate, but it's getting bad now."

"We're a fine pair," she said, without any humor. Oya could barely restrain her shivering now and knew that Inirigua was worried. For some strange reason, he cared about her and, seeing his raw blotches of naked skin, she realized that she cared about him as well.

"It's almost funny that the things that define our two factions, right down to the very fiber, are what's killing us now."

"I'm terrified, Inirigua. I'm afraid of failing and I'm afraid of succeeding. I'm paralyzed with fear. It's worse than the virus attacking my body."

He reached over and took her hand in his claw. "I'm scared too."

They exited the shuttle and made their way down the empty corridors of the *Hurricane*. Oya checked in with the ship and, reading all the scrolling updates, learned that Davoli had begun unfreezing every single passenger. He had also taken command of the bridge and had censored all updates from there.

"You're running a fever," Inirigua interrupted her wireless inventory. "I believe you're past the incubation period. You'll soon experience severe joint and muscle pain and the fever will make you delirious."

"It's okay. We're headed to the infirmary. I'll take something once I've shut down all the curators."

"Even the one's down on the surface?"

"Yes. That's the plan." Her head spun. If this had taken hold during the flight up, they'd be dead. She stopped and took hold of his shoulder for support. A few contour feathers came off, plowed between her fingers. "Are you absolutely sure the retrovirus won't kill us, even a small percentage of us?"

"I'm positive. The retrovirus is not a parasitic pathogen, but it imposes itself through aggressive symbiosis, hence the harsh symptoms until the transformation is complete. We may not be as technologically advanced as you are, but our biosciences are ahead of yours by at least a century. You will all become *Homo sapiens aves* though. No exceptions."

She let that sink in for a moment. All of the horror stories and stereotypes about harpies flooded her mind. She would be turning the people on her ship into something less than human. They would become monsters with fangs and claws and feathers. Was Inirigua less than human? And if she let all the harpies down on the planet die, would she be fully human afterwards? No, she didn't think she would be. "We'll be saving a lot of lives."

They entered the open medical ward. Captain Hershkovitz was spread out in an intensive care unit; it looked similar to the cryo-pods, big and boxy with rounded edges. She looked at his diagnostic report and discovered that his curators had just defused a powerful venom that had been circulating in his system, were almost done repairing severe trauma to the neck, but were now engaged in a battle against the assertive virus. Davoli was probably infected too, and Xing. "Come, lie here." She helped Inirigua up into another open cabinet.

Oya noticed that he had lost a pointed tooth among the trail of feathers left scattered on the floor. She looked up and said, in Standard, "Identification: First Pilot Oya Valette. Please scan new patient, designated Inirigua, and direct all curators on this ship to accept the avian retrovirus and associated physiological modifications as 'friendly.' Push those instructions out to all curators under your direction." She took a short breath, fighting back the nausea.

"When Captain Hershkovitz is fully healed and the passengers are thawed, instruct all curators in the system to shut down and flush out. I'm invoking the Gray Goo Protocols of 2198." She sent the key code electronically.

The ship seemed to hesitate for a fraction of a second, but the Gray Goo abort protocols were sacred commandments to all nanotech programming. *"Initiating Gray Goo Protocols."*

After a moment, an array of robotic arms descended on Inirigua, each scanning his body with a different investigative tool.

"I speak some Standard, but I didn't understand all of that," he said.

"I ordered the controlling automation to accept your retrovirus and to spread the new script to all curators on this ship."

"Why? I thought you were just shutting them down. What about the ones on the planet?"

She walked over to the medical builders, silently asking them to create a strong dose of ibuprofen. She took it the instant it materialized on the tray. She closed her eyes and waited for the effect.

"I am," she said, willing her eyes open again. "But that's too abrupt. This is a quick way to alleviate the pain here, for you. The captain and passengers are still relying on their curators. I can't take that away from them yet." When all the sensor arms, except one, had retracted back into the ceiling, she asked, "How do you feel now?"

"A little better actually." He looked impatient, probably worried about his people on Quetzalcoatl. "The burning in my skin has stopped, but I'm afraid I won't be flying until most of my feathers grow back."

"Good, because I'm getting really weak. I can't stand up anymore." A clump of her hair tumbled over her shoulder and onto the floor. She could feel her own teeth loosening and fought the urge to wiggle them with her tongue. *My God, it's happening.*

Inirigua swung himself off the platform and swept Oya off her feet. "Here, you rest then."

"The scanner is still running."

"I don't care." He gently placed her on the pallet.

The remaining arm paused, confused by some readings around her thigh. Then she remembered. "The genetics of the yellow feather in my pouch — it'll contaminate the analysis." She pulled out the feather and the arm followed its path, obviously puzzled.

Inirigua looked up as if addressing some foreign god. He modulated the pitch and cadence of his voice to perfectly match Oya's, and said, "Scan patient. Accept avian. Push out to all."

"What are you doing?" Oya's voice sounded more drowsy than alarmed. Still, she had no idea that he could do that. Hearing the sound of her own voice coming from his lips was a bit unsettling. The machine dithered, waiting for her curator's signal.

"You did look beautiful in golden wings," he said, in his own lullaby voice.

"*Kòk batay ti kras mwen,*" she breathed, and wordlessly relented, giving the okay for the computer to incorporate the structural color of the sunny warbler into the retrovirus code. She gazed at Inirigua through a drugged and feverish haze, a handsome man in a tattered ruby cloak. The cunning bastard knew a lot more Standard than he let on.

Then Xing's harried voice ended the moment. "Oya, are you back on board? Someone just accessed the medbay. Is that you?"

"Yes, Xing. I'm here."

"Thank God! Are you injured? I need help. Commander Davoli is readying the nukes and targeting the three harpy cities down there. He's locked me out of the ship's command network and he's not listening to reason."

"I'm down with the flu." Her head swirled. "I'll send the Chief's son of the harpies over to talk to him."

"The Chief's son? Davoli's shutting down my—" The blaring voice died.

"Who was that? Did she say nukes?"

"That was my friend, Xing. Our commander is going to bomb your cities. Stop him. Follow the visual signs on the walls to the bridge," she said, without opening her eyes. Oya remembered her grandmother lying on that cot many years — light years — ago and knew she was about to step out for a while.

"What can I do? My wings are destroyed and even if they weren't, the gravity on this ship is set to one gee. I can't fly here. I'm sorry, my love, but I can't be the guardian angel you need me to be."

My love? She placed a clammy hand on his jaw and looked straight into his eyes. "Inirigua, I don't need an angel right now, I need a goddamn tyrannosaurus rex. Please go and save your people!"

All doubt washed away from Inirigua, and he leaned over and gave her a sweet peck on her lips, then turned and ran out. When the door shut behind him, Oya closed her eyes again, ready to sink into sleep.

But then the computer chimed annoyingly, *"First Pilot Valette, there is a simple text message and an image encoded within the sunny warbler's DNA molecules. Would you like me to decipher it? If you wish, I can read it aloud and display the image?"*

This caught Oya's diminishing attention. *Had her grandmother sent her a secret message across space and death?* "Yes, please, read it and display," she slurred, cracking her eyes open.

The computer began to recite in neutral Kwéyòl:

"Bon jou, I am Dr. Osala Valette. If you are reading this, then you've discovered that these charming little birds are more than they appear. In fact, they are a living, breathing memorial to the millions of dead or displaced *Homo sapiens aves,* victims of the conquest of the solar system. Although I was careful to make the genetic modifications to my subject somatic, and thus not inheritable, someone somewhere made a mistake. There was too much casual experimentation back

then. Kids playing gods. However, I take full responsibility. It was my technique and expertise that ultimately gave rise to this vibrant and unique branch of humanity.

"To be quite frank, in the beginning, I was deeply troubled by the beings I conceived on that small station orbiting the moon, with a peculiar and forceful girl doubling as my co-creator and first creation. For many years, I viewed that time as an extended moment of weakness. But over many decades of watching avian humanity thrive out there in harsh environments, developing rich civilizations all their own, my feelings toward them started to change. In fact, my entire understanding of the raptorial-transhumanist phenomenon underwent a gradual paradigm shift, and I came to believe that I was only a catalyst in all this, and that their emergence had been a long time coming. Ever since *Homo heidelbergensis* painted their bodies in red ochre and twined eagle fathers into their coarse hair, mankind has been on a trajectory to enhance itself with examples from nature for millennia. Only, the tools that I used to achieve the same aim were much subtler than anything our ancestors could have dreamt of.

"My critics would surely cry foul (or fowl) and say that I'm simply trying to justify my heinous crimes against God and traditional humanity. Maybe so. I concede that I could have come to this conclusion to spare myself further anguish. My ingenuity is infinite. Nevertheless, I am proud of my lovely bird children and so it is only fitting that I honor my dearly departed *kwéati* with the resurrection of another species of bird. May these sunny warblers fly and sing in their stead."

There was no more. A lightscreen appeared before Oya, showing an old picture of a svelte girl sweeping over a balcony's balustrade. She flaunted a roguish smile and her feathers shimmered in blue like the Earth hanging in the sky behind her. She looked Macu, but lacked the prominent upright claws on her middle toes. The tag on the photo simply read, "Esther, 2098." The photo faded away.

"Computer, please read it again and display the image," Oya whispered dreamily, like a child asking for one more bedtime story. She could practically hear her grandmother's dignity and gall in the machine's bland reading.

"I'm sorry, biometric authorization has failed. Please check curator's connection to the ship."

Sadness fell upon her for a moment. The curators in her body were dead then. She couldn't even call up a status bar. But then her spirits lifted a bit. Her grandmother would've been pleased that she was finally rid of the damned things.

She fell asleep smiling.

Chapter 22

Inirigua ran down the stark corridors of the vast ship in slow motion. His legs struggled under the pull of the heavier gravity. The cold air was devoid of flavors. His venom glands puffed up eagerly. The harm done by the curators to his system didn't make the marathon any easier, but he kept moving. Arrows projected on the walls instructed him to bank left or right. He was sure Oya had cybernetically told the ship to guide him. And without that he would've been lost.

He came to a dead end. The doors opened, and, without slowing his pace, he leapt blindly into a room labeled "Bridge."

A big man, clutching a sidearm and frantically pacing around a holographic image of the planet below, froze in utter shock. The woman (*the voice he had heard in the hospital?*) sat uselessly behind a counter, muttering to the man. She recoiled at the sudden sight of him. Inirigua made a mental note not to harm her, since she had warned Oya and was her friend.

The man immediately took aim and fired a laser beam in his direction. Inirigua dodged and darted behind an empty work bench. The man fired again, holding the trigger down, releasing a solid stream of light until the work bench exploded violently into smoking pieces. Inirigua dashed behind the woman in time and only the tips of his long primaries were singed by the blast.

The man pulled the trigger again and again, but nothing happened. Inirigua assumed the ship's safety systems or the woman's nanites had suppressed the gun. The man's face twisted. He tossed the weapon aside and barked something at him. Inirigua caught the words "animal" and "kill" among the guttural noise.

Inirigua cautiously slid from behind the shelter of the catatonic woman and instrument panel. He cocked his head this way and that as if carefully sizing up the man with each eye. This was the Hominocracy soldier in the Palace video. The man's uniform was ragged, but he had no apparent injuries aside from a leg encased in an exoskeleton. Sweat beaded on his brow. His fingers trembled. Either his curators had accepted the new orders, and forfeited their fight against the retrovirus, or his nerves where getting the better of him.

The image of this soldier slaying his people flashed in Inirigua's racing mind. Inirigua would not give him the honor of joining the bright-winged clan he intended to start with Oya. This crude monster was unworthy of the raptorial race.

Inirigua burst toward the invader, fangs drawn and talons outstretched. The man swung and bashed his jaw with such force that it sent him sprawling across the bridge in a splash of blood and poison. After a second of stupefaction, Inirigua pulled himself up, noticing three spiky teeth lying before him. He stood and silently watched his opponent. Only the tick-tick of his toe-talons tapping the floor betrayed his own tension.

The man snarled some more and tauntingly motioned for him to attack with his dull monkey arms. He smiled at Inirigua with obscenely flat dentition. Still, with reptilian patience, Inirigua watched. He had never really been a fighter, but he'd always been strategic with his limitations. Speed and venom were his strengths.

Finally, the man rushed him, meaty fists curled like clubs. Just then, Inirigua's magnetoreception caught a sputter in the man's cybernetic aura. This was what he was waiting for. The man's curators were shutting down. Inirigua instantly pounced on him, plunging the few loose teeth he had left into the man's shoulder. Behind him, the woman screamed in terror. He fell forward onto the crumpling man. Instinctively, Inirigua dug his claws into the man's thrashing torso, pinning him down so the potent neural toxin could flood his now defenseless body. The commander convulsed violently for a few moments, and then stilled.

Inirigua looked up, wiped blood from his chin with a wing, and shouted at the cowering woman in Standard, "Stop the nukes!"

She stared, glassy eyed, then got to her station and said, in quivering Cantabile, "With the commander ... down ... control has reverted to me. I can — I just stopped the warheads from launching, and now I'm disarming them."

Inirigua collapsed, struggling for breath. He was utterly exhausted, and, with the ebbing of adrenaline, the multilayered pain in his body rose to a crescendo. "Your people are waking up. They're going to be very sick. *You're* going to get sick."

"Oh no, my curators are crashing!"

"All curators are shutting down, and there's a virus loose on the ship."

Her hands clasped together as if in prayer, or as if she was begging for mercy. "Why are we going to be sick?"

"You're turning into raptors."

Her eyes bulged. "Listen to me very carefully. We interface with this ship via our curators. If you've disabled them permanently, we'll be trapped here in orbit. Nothing will work for us!"

Inirigua wasn't listening. He heard a faint ringing in his ears. His eyes went blurry. He fell to the ground.

— «» —

Xing didn't want to change. The harpy virus was rewriting her genome right now. She could feel it. It was slowly reshaping her into another species. Xing forced herself to look at the unconscious harpy before her. Lord, she didn't want to become that. She couldn't breathe. Her chest hurt. She tried to calm herself. This was not her first panic attack since arriving around this planet. The curators were the answer. They were built specifically to prevent this. She needed to get them working again. The curators would undo any of the early changes. But the curators were crashing. *Hay naku!* And they would be stranded on the *Hurricane* without them.

"Ship, ready a shuttle big enough to carry all the colonists to the planet," Xing shouted, looking up at the ceiling like a mad woman.

"Shuttle H1 is being readied, Information Officer Diwa."

"How long before all the passengers are awake?"

"I'm sorry, biometric authorization has failed. Please check curator's connection to the ship."

"Shit!" Her heart pounded in her chest, making the pain more acute. She'd lost access to all of the ship's higher functions. More and more of her curators crashed. Xing suddenly felt woozy. The M.I. had said that Oya was important. Maybe she could fix this. She headed out for the infirmary, fighting the groundswell of fatigue and rigor. Without her artificial immune system — and her natural defenses severely weakened from disuse — the virus would hit her hard, would hit all of them hard.

She ran through the passenger recovery area, which now resembled a rookery of horrors. The chorus of moans and sniveling made her stop and really look at her fellow colonists. Up until this point they had been an abstract, little more than biological cargo, but now that nearly one hundred white oval sleeper pods were opening up to reveal frail, disoriented people, they could no longer be ignored. Immediately, she noticed that they were deformed somehow, a midpoint between classical humanity and harpy miscreation. She screamed and covered her face with her hands. She hurried past them, feeling her knees weaken.

Xing found Oya lying on a pallet in the intensive care ward, unconscious. She almost fainted when her foggy eyes focused on her friend — her only hope. Oya's thick, black hair was gone, replaced with gray filaments. Her arms were a few centimeters longer and ending in terrible claws like Snacakobek's. *Would she change this quickly? No, everyone else who was hooked up to medical curators had already changed; her transformation would be slow and painful.* Xing was worn out. She had no idea how to repair curators. There was nothing she could do.

She fought the need to lie down on a pallet next to Oya and go to sleep.

She lightly touched Oya's head, timidly feeling the soft downy texture. It occurred to her that this was exactly what the Augur had wanted, for them to be socially and biologically assimilated by the harpies. Black and purple spots danced in her field of vision, where once useful data had flowed. She rolled onto the empty pallet. She was freezing and the pallet was warm.

Oya stirred. They gazed at each other sleepily. This helped somewhat. At least she wasn't alone.

"Did we stop the nukes?" Oya asked.

"Yes. Davoli is dead. We're all turning into harpies." Xing knew there was something else she needed to tell Oya, but everything was so hazy. She curled into a tight knot.

A long, peaceful, frigid moment passed, then Oya asked, "Xing, do you still have access to the ship?"

"No." Her teeth clattered; sweat soaked her uniform. "We're trapped here. I tried to ready a shuttle, but it's useless. We need to get down to the planet, to the floating island I built for us."

Oya didn't reply and Xing continued rambling. "I spoke to their artificial god and it said you would save us from something worse than ourselves." Xing waited for a while. *Was she even making sense?* It didn't matter; Oya was asleep. Xing gave up and allowed the wave of sick despair to envelop her.

As everyone on the *Hurricane* marinated in their own sweaty malaise, Xing recalled that this was the last place she had seen Oya as she was. A beautiful, confident woman. She had tried to convince her not to go on the mission alone. Now that the highly infectious retrovirus cooked even the most elemental ingredients within their cells, she wished her friend hadn't been so damned pigheaded.

Chapter 23

Luna – 2098 A.D.

Esther strode out of her private lander with the care and style of a gymnast on a balance beam. She relished every painful step. Gone was her childlike apprehension. Like a woman slipping into a sleek and sexy dress, Esther carried herself with sumptuous poise.

"I missed the stink of people."

Osala didn't reply.

They left the busy spaceport and stepped out into the bustling cobblestone streets of Uptown LA2, which sat within the bowl of a profound lunar crater. Large billboards announced the upcoming Gala of Flight, and Osala never doubted that Esther had perfectly timed all of this.

The scent of sea salt gave flavor to the light, artificial breeze. The Uptown area looked like a small, idyllic bayside town with quaint red tiled, Spanish colonial-style buildings that might have been transported from the Caribbean. Even the Aguilera-Smeltzer Headquarters were carefully designed to resemble a majestic old City Hall. This made Osala homesick for the first time in four months. She thought she should check in with Patrick, but couldn't — not yet.

"Take it easy, Esther. Even with all the long hours of workouts in orbit, one sixth the gravity of Earth can be quite a strain," Osala said, feeling the strain herself. "You need to slowly build up muscle and bone mass."

Without turning or slowing, the girl shouted back, "I'm starving. Let's get something to eat. I'm sure the safe house isn't going to have much in the way of fine cuisine."

Esther had changed a lot in two months; she had grown out long arms and legs, both ending in three digits with reaper-like barbs. All her hair had fallen out and had been replaced by an eaglet's white fluffy down over her scalp, shoulders, and arms, which she hid under a black hoodie, her claws stuffed in her pockets. She had also shed all her teeth and regrown them as sharp little spikes, like those of a caiman. There were internal changes as well; her circulatory and respiratory systems were more efficient than those of typical humans'. A large part of Osala Valette was gruesomely fascinated by the whole transformation, and Avant Genomics had already implemented a series of action plans for treatments for a variety of aliments based on the data collected on Esther's progress.

"Is it wise to stop out in public so soon?"

"My father already knows I left the station, but it'll be a long while before he sifts through all the surveillance data and finds me. Remember, he'll be looking for a cripple."

The place teemed with inhumanly tall and slim people strolling the narrow streets, riding bikes to work, shopping happily, and eating at outdoor cafés. If you paid attention, you might also catch a few shorter, stocky people here and there, obviously Earthling immigrants or tourists. Osala was glad she was naturally tall and athletic. This rustic ideal was, of course, a great façade. The majority of the town (the actual town) extended deep underground beneath the crater, like an upside-down city with its skyscrapers pointing down.

According to Esther, LA2 had been a charter settlement of the Aguilera-Smeltzer family, founded in the sixties, mostly factories and living quarters, all of the one hundred and one stories underground. The actual crater, once domed with a meter-thick wall of concrete and polyethylene plastic, was turned into a beautiful biosphere and cultural center, a place where everyone could stretch their legs when underground living became too much. The crater's basin looked like a bèl ilèt dropped in a sea of dismal gray regolith.

Suddenly, Esther let out a piercing cry and doubled over. She clutched her newly grown calf.

"Are you okay?" Osala waved away concerned and nosy passersby.

"There's a sharp pain in my leg."

Osala massaged the thin sinuous calf. "It's a cramp. You're exerting yourself too much and your muscles need fuel and fluid."

Osala pulled her into a nearby restaurant, sat in an out-of-the way booth and hurriedly ordered the special. Esther drank a glass of water the second it hit the table.

"How's your leg?"

"It's fine if I don't move it. You know, it's hard to be philosophical and say something like, 'the pain lets me appreciate that at least I have a leg,' when it's excruciating."

"So what do we do now?"

"We? Your job here is done, Dr. Valette. You don't have to follow me around like some doting nurse. I've transferred payment to AG, including roundtrip travel. You can book your own taxi back to Earth right now."

Esther was right of course, but Oya was caught in the young woman's wake. "You know I'm worried about you. I want to see the whole metamorphosis through to the end, just to make sure there aren't any abnormalities."

Esther smiled, the sharp teeth giving her usual derision a deadly edge. "I believe I'm well passed abnormal."

Osala reached out across the table and took Esther's hands. "These things for example, they look wrong. Maybe I can devise a treatment to make them more human."

Esther lingered for a second, enjoying the tactile sensation, then pulled away. "If anything, doctor, I'm used to having hooks for hands." She rotated her wrist and stretched her claws, similar to the first time Osala had tried to shake her hand, only the gesture was much more fluid and organic now.

The food arrived and they ate in silence. Osala watched Esther devour her steaming plate of rice and beans and fried plantains. She tore ravenously at the spicy duck, and irrational thoughts of cannibalism arose in Osala. Esther stripped the fine bones of meat, then crunched them open and sucked out the marrow. Osala knew Esther's rapidly developing body craved all the essential nutrients it could get, but she was disgusted all the same.

"So, where are we going?" Osala asked.

"A friend of mine — from before the fall — has a loft he's willing to lend us. It's up by the south rim. The place is a hovel, but it has a gorgeous view."

Osala paid the bill so that Esther wouldn't immediately be identified, and they went in search of this loft. They rode a glass elevator up the slope and got a panoramic look at the circular lake, and coastal sage scrub and palm trees that surrounded it.

"Santa Monica Lake used to be a smaller crater within the larger crater that now wears a massive dome," Esther said on their long assent.

"How many people live here?" Osala asked, looking at all the people going about their lives within their round container, like living samples in a petri dish.

"About 112,000 give or take."

That was more people than Osala's native Chandeleur currently had. "Uptown takes up maybe five percent of the crater's volume, the farms take up about twenty percent; the rest is totally wooded. I always wanted to go hiking through that big savage garden."

The sky shone blue. It was early afternoon, but Osala could see the crescent Earth hanging over the lip of the crater. "How can we see the sky, and why is it blue? I thought that was all concrete and steel overhead?"

"Ha. The whole thing is covered in a thin film of pixel paint, which displays a real-time view of the wider universe, only tinting the sky blue during the day so as not to disrupt our biological rhythms. This place is only slightly less fake than the original LA."

"This loft must cost a fortune; the vista alone is worth it."

"On the contrary, the lunar rich are deathly afraid of radiation. So, they choose the deepest levels of the settlement. There's an entire underworld of mansions and villas under all this greenery." She motioned grandly with her lengthy arm.

They reached the apartment complex and started hunting for the right door. Osala's vision of luxury penthouses vanished as they made their way through dim, unkempt corridors. There was a hint of urine rising from the carpet. Esther stopped at an old door and banged on it, ignoring the broken ringer.

A disheveled young man opened the door. He had a mop of dark curly hair and a bushy beard. An eerie red glow emanated from beneath his loose white tee shirt.

"Hey, Zu." Esther pushed her way through before the guy could really see her and yanked off her concealing hoodie, leaving only the cashmere sweater of her own natural down.

"Esther?"

"Yes, of course! This is a friend of mine. She's going to be rooming with me, if that's all right?" she said, kicking off the big goofy slippers she had on and spreading her talons.

Osala entered the stark flat. There was nothing but a mattress, a pile of clothes on the floor, and a gym that consumed half the interior. The air was musty and had the long entrenched smell of cigarettes. She could see the bare lunar rock in places were the paint had peeled off.

"Okay, let me give you the tour," Zu said to Osala. "There's only one mattress because I thought Esther was going to say here alone, but I did manage to get the exercise machine you asked for." He spun and led her to a tiny kitchenette.

"Is there food here? She's going to need food."

"Uh, no." He peered into the small refrigerator. It contained only a few bottles of beer and a tray of vials with red caps. "But I can go get food. And another mattress."

Osala nodded. The vials worried her. "Thank you." A cooling ashtray sat on the counter by the sink. This "childhood friend" of Esther's made her very uncomfortable.

"The bathroom is over here. It's actually smaller than the kitchen, but it works." He squeezed past her, and Osala doubted he bathed much.

The punk stopped mid tour to gawk at Esther as she put on one of his dirty tank tops from the pile. Her small breasts heaved with her improved lung capacity. "My God, look at you. Those talons are absolutely sinister!"

Osala cleared her throat and shot Esther a look. There was a half-open door on the other side of the gym. "Is this the bathroom?" She moved toward it, trying to draw his attention away from her patient, and noticed it was a laboratory of some kind.

Zu dashed for it and closed the door with his foot. "No, that's my room. The bathroom is the other door over there."

Osala stood there a second too long, staring at the door, wringing her hands. She caught herself and turned to examine the exercise equipment instead. Her stomach twisted. This guy was a biohacker, and judging by the intricate fluorescent lines underneath his shirt, he was probably the same one that gave Esther her body art.

"Is this it? Are we all settled?" Esther asked, picking up on Osala's disquiet.

"That's it." Zu said, crossing his arms and rocking back and forth on his feet. "It's not much."

Osala left them talking and drifted back into the kitchenette. She took a glass from a cupboard and filled it with water from the sink. It was ice cold. She opened the fridge and took a closer look at the vials, but they weren't labeled. She should go. This wasn't her element. Esther was fine. She should come up with some lame excuse and walk out the door.

She caught a snippet of conversation. Zu excitedly said, "Can you imagine if we customized them with utahraptor's big, retractable claws? It would give a whole new meaning to flipping someone the bird!"

She couldn't make out Esther's reply. Osala took another drink of water to settle her stomach. The smell from the ashtray nauseated her. This whole situation was starting to make her sick.

Zu lowered his voice, but it was too late. Osala's senses were sharpened with dread. "I've broken up the genome for this into more manageable bio blocks and started selling them on the Astronet. The term 'feeding frenzy' is an apt description of the initial response."

She was holding the glass with both hands and the water sloshed with her shaking. She forced herself to walk out of the kitchenette. "What are you talking about?" Osala interjected.

"Shop talk," he said.

"You're selling the sequences for Esther's modifications to biohackers?"

Zu looked from Osala to Esther and then back to Osala, suddenly unsure about their relationship and how much to disclose. "Um, yeah, man, and some serious hobbyists, too. Also, some freestyle fliers have shown interest, but are waiting to see the results. You know, using early adopters as guinea pigs."

Osala wheeled around to face Esther. "What the hell is going on? You can't just hand out these extensive genetic alterations like recreational drugs. There's no control or regulation out there. You're just kids playing with the stuff of life!"

Esther ignored Osala's ravings and the guy answered instead. "You're right, of course, but we did learn a lot from that jellyfish fiasco. I found these armchair hackers work better with smaller packets of genomic information. Their eyes tend to glaze over and they start making mistakes when confronted with a whole sprawling genome."

"You're Merlin?" Osala shouted her question.

"Who me?" He sucked his teeth. "I ain't Merlin. She's Merlin."

"What?" Osala felt as if she were in free-fall. She grabbed Esther's arm and pulled her close, looking for support, and demanding attention. "Is that true, Esther?"

"It's true, doctor. You're thinking old mystical guy with white beard, but you have to remember, a merlin is also a type of bird-of-prey," she said without her usual mocking smile, which made the words all the more frightening. There was a hint of sadness in her eyes.

"The state of the art laboratory on your station? Your intimacy with it..."

"It's my lab."

Osala let go of her and slumped on the stained mattress. She felt numb, deflated. Inanely, a quote from Mary Shelley popped into her head: *the fallen angel becomes a malignant devil.*

"*Bouzin,*" she cursed in Kwéyòl instead. "You lied to me."

"I'm really sorry, Osala."

"No, you're not."

"I am," Esther said softly, almost tenderly. "I never forced any of this on you. I never lied. You participated willingly and have been paid handsomely for your part. You yourself mentioned many times how much your work with me will improve people's lives. But I'm deeply sorry you feel betrayed."

"What have I done?"

Esther turned and walked away. She pushed open the double doors of the veranda and a gust of fresh air entered the room. "I'll fledge soon, and then you can go back to your little island and forget all about me," she said, without looking back, and stepped outside.

Osala sat there as the moon spun around her. She should go. Why wait for her to fledge? She didn't think she could stand. She was utterly heartbroken.

Zu cautiously nudged Osala's leg with his foot. "Hey, everyone wants to know the name of the biohacker that pulled this off. What do I tell them?"

She looked up, saw his stupid grin and drew a deep breath. Vomit threatened to rise. "Tell them it was the damned Modern Prometheus." And as she said it, Osala remembered that the Titan of the same name had his liver torn out by a large eagle. She wanted to cry.

Chapter 24

HS Hurricane - 2323 A.D.

Oya Valette awoke in the quiet infirmary, and she was not herself. She began to weep the second she noticed the claws, the down. She could feel the fangs against her tongue. She continued to cry, but slowly subtle internal changes drew her attention. Her heart beat differently. She felt almost high from the elevated levels of oxygen moving through her veins. Her vision was incredibly acute, better than any high definition augmentation her curators could muster. And the colors — she could see colors she hadn't even known existed!

Had all the bodily changes rewired her brain somehow and altered her personality? She vaguely recalled that women's brains changed during pregnancy and her changes were far beyond anything like a pregnancy. Without her connection to the ship, she couldn't look it up. Then an irritating pain in her feet made her forget the thought. Something crushed her feet. Oya sat up too quickly and her head whirled.

Her boots! It was a frustrating chore to remove them with the clumsy hooks on her three-fingered hands, but once she freed her talons from the binding footwear, she was both relieved and unnerved. She looked over and saw Xing curled up on the next pallet. Oya could see the bumpy feather follicles developing on the back of Xing's hands. Her friend was developing slower. Why? She had a million questions for Inirigua. *Was he all right?* She vaguely remembered Xing saying Commander Davoli was dead and that they were imprisoned on the ship, but it was all too unreal.

Oya stood carefully and gradually made her way out of the sickbay. Ironically, her newly heightened sense of equilibrium made her ungainly, as if she needed to learn to walk all over again. All the passengers had fully transformed, they were — like she was — in a juvenile state of development, but they still appeared to be suffering from the effects of the retrovirus. Some were outright panicking; others were in a stupor. All too weak and ill to move about freely. She took her time examining each one, taking off their shoes, and she was glad to see the ship's general healthcare automation had not locked out its patients because they no longer had curators.

Oya moved on. She experimented with her body as she made her way through the empty passageways of her ship. She sprinted the last few meters, as fast as she could, and wasn't even winded. A scary, overpowering part of her couldn't wait to sprout wings and fly. She had to find Inirigua. He was the only one onboard who could explain exactly what was happening to her, to all of them.

Oya stepped onto the dimly lit bridge. She could no longer see all the neon, information-rich screens that normally floated around, illuminating the command deck. "Inirigua, are you okay?"

Inirigua stood near her pilot's chair, looking down at the floor. Physically, he was completely restored. Glossy red and black plumage adorned his thin muscular frame, but his eyes looked utterly lost. He didn't react to her presence.

Then Oya froze when she saw the grisly state of Davoli's corpse. "You did this?" she gasped.

"Yes."

Suddenly, all the horrible slurs about harpies became true. She looked at her own barbed feet. "What did you do to him?"

"I had to... I've never actually killed anyone before. Not on purpose. I think I'm in shock."

"My God, I don't want to be like this... I don't want to be a monster." She went to bury her face in her hands, but instead scratched herself with her claws.

"Oya, I'm not a monster. He was about to kill everyone on the planet." Inirigua's words came out as a lugubrious glissando.

"This is not normal," she cried. Oya tore her eyes away from the dead man and looked at Inirigua. "A normal person would've beaten the crap out of him or shot him, but this looks like he was mauled to death by a wild animal."

"He was bigger and stronger than me. I had to bite him."

She couldn't listen. She backed away, covering her ears and shaking her head. "Have I turned everyone on this ship into animals?" Oya gasped for air. She felt hot. The down on her body was stifling. She tried to drown out his shrill voice, but it stabbed at her, his words clear and piercing.

Inirigua went to touch her.

"Don't touch me!" she shouted, pulling away in revulsion.

"Fine. You call me a monster, an animal, because I used my venomous teeth and talons to eliminate a threat, but he was going to murder everyone on *my* planet with one push of his pretty finger. If that's what you call normal, I don't want any part of it. Arrest me or take me to my people, for they're in need of their Chief's son." Tears began streaming down his pale cheeks.

Venomous teeth? She gulped down a scream.

She ran.

Oya was terrified of Inirigua and of her own treacherous feelings toward him. She didn't know where she was going, but she knew she had to get away. This was all too much, everything had spoiled, and it was all her fault. Inirigua ran after her, called to her, but her own guilt and panic made her run faster.

He caught up with her and pinned her to the wall. She kicked at him, desperately wanting to escape, to be alone and away from everything harpy.

She hid in the restroom and waited anxiously, wedged behind a toilet. He found her quickly enough. He spoke of trust. He didn't think she trusted him, but the truth was, she didn't trust herself. She had betrayed her people, her species, because, for some unfathomable reason, she had trusted this creature.

A long moment passed and she met Inirigua's eyes again. Mixed in with the dread and disgust, she had to admit she felt a twinge of pity for him. After all, it wasn't his fault he was born like this, it was her grandmother's. "You're not under arrest. That's not even an option," she said. "But you are trapped. We all are. With the destruction of the curators, we've lost contact with the cognitive functions of this ship. We can't tell it to do anything useful."

He wiped his tears on a wing. "Are there no manual overrides for the ship?"

"No, it's not how the ship was built." She pulled herself up from behind the toilet. *He is a human being*, she repeated in her mind, trying to extinguish the sight of Davoli. It was silly to have run off like that, but she was frantic. "It's how we interact with the *Hurricane*. A shuttle has been prepped, but we can't launch it. Xing tried, but she fell ill with this." Oya flexed her three-fingered claw. "When the captain comes out of his coma, I'm sure he'll have an idea, but for now we have a highly mutagenic avian pandemic to deal with."

"How are you feeling? You look like a newborn chick."

"I *feel* newborn." She didn't know what else to say. She watched him, wondering how he could be so casual after such an awful thing. Her head twitched from side to side, a bird-like mannerism she'd seen in harpies. Now that it was her doing it, she understood it was the result of her lightning quick reaction time and new precise vision trying to take in everything. He was so young. Four long, wispy feathers jutted out of the right side of his head. She liked them. Better to focus on the pretty feathers and forget about the rest.

"These feathers weren't there before," she said, unconsciously reaching up to touch them. He looked like an old image of an Indian brave; blood streaked his face like war paint. He was the embodiment of deep sadness and pride.

He gently swatted her hand away. "Don't worry about them."

On the cellular level, they were about the same age, but she had lived a lot longer than he had. *Oh, no. She'd begun aging normally now.* She was crying again. *She'd given up immortality, classical perfection, to become what ... a fragile monster?*

They stood there in the tight restroom, needing comfort, but divided by this one despicable act. She could see her reflection in the mirror over his shoulder. She needed to calm down.

He reached out and took her claw. "Oya, let me help you with the change."

"My body has been rearranged." She lifted her claw, examining it. "I never imagined this retrovirus could transform me so fast. All the colonists are also clawed and covered in downy feathers. Xing is the only one that appears to be changing slowly."

"This wasn't the retrovirus, at least not on its own. I'm fully healed as well and wasn't a carrier. I think your curators, once they acknowledged the new genetic blueprint, began to dynamically move our bodies toward the raptorial model. If they would have remained active, you probably would've fledged in a matter of hours."

Oya shuddered at the thought. *Was she still human?* "So how long before I'm like you?" She tongued the new, pointy teeth in her mouth and stifled a gag. She remembered Inirigua talking about his venomous teeth. "Can I poison myself?" *The wings, though, she did want the wings.*

"I don't think you're venomous — my mother would never have given you an advantage like that. And if you were, you can't poison yourself, even if you bit your cheek while eating. Your immune system would develop antibodies against your own toxin. But check to see if you feel any lumps on the roof of your mouth."

Her palate felt ordinary.

"You'll all be like the first-generation *Homo sapiens aves*, which means you'll possess all of the major traits, like flight feathers, claws, improved respiration and circulation, but no secondary traits like hollow bones, magnetoreception, a syrinx, a large retractable claw on your middle toes, or venom sacs. Your children, though," Oya watched him choke up a bit, "will be absolutely perfect."

Perfect? Would she sentence her future offspring to savagery, as her gwan man man *had ultimately sentenced her?* "I need to get back to everyone. They still seem to be sick from the virus."

"Despite the cosmetic changes imposed by your nano machines, the virus will still run its course until everyone's DNA is rewritten."

"Come on," she said and led him out of the cramped restroom. "You look tired. I think the heavier gravity is getting to you. Let me show you where you can get something to eat and rest."

"Aren't you hungry?"

She forced herself to pat his shoulder, careful not to nick him. "I went through five liters of nutrient broth while transforming in the infirmary." Truth was, she couldn't eat after the sight of Davoli. Luckily, she had ninety-nine other problems to take her mind off their mutilated commander. "I just need time."

Chapter 25

Quetzalcoatl

Majasora woke to a pulsating pain in her skull. She opened her eyes and instantly regretted it. The intense agony mingled with nausea. She caught a glimpse of the cherry wood vaulted ceiling and large arched windows facing the amethyst dawn and knew she was in the Soaring Palace of Morning. Her guest room. She pushed through the disorientation and vividly recalled the fight with the baseline human. Then she remembered Inirigua's apparent defection, and she worried that these lavish rooms might now be a prison.

She forced herself to sit and was glad to see the magnetic altar of the Raptorial Madonna still at her bedside, although the impression was faint and warped. The mother and winged child were barely perceptible, as if someone had made a sacrilegious abstract version of the divine mother-daughter duo. Then the pain disgorged her frontal lobe again, and she realized there was nothing actually wrong with the altar. Her own God-given magnetoreception was impaired.

Majasora sang a quick hymn to the mother of all avian humanity, one for strength and protection, and then stood up. Her right foot stung cuttingly and she nearly dropped back onto the bed. The lights came on, and she was relieved they hadn't removed her most basic controls of the room's systems. Now she could see that her large retractable claw was broken at the joint. Someone had locked it into its upright position with a strut. She retracted and protracted her left claw a few times, just to make sure it was all right.

The large ebony talon was artfully engraved in an intricate florid pattern from tip to base, reminiscent of Celtic knots. Oh, how her father had roared at the vain and profane body art, but she had allowed the small depravity because it was beautiful. She was going to be annoyed if the artwork on her right talon had been scuffed or spoiled in any way.

When the pain ebbed, she cautiously — dizzily — made her way to the door and cracked it open. The guest wing of the Palace was deserted. She waddled out into the hallway and walked, undisturbed, all the way to the main gallery. The journey was arduous and the signs of battle were everywhere. The Vanacan's many decadent embellishments were charred, torn, smashed, and smeared in dry blood. A heavy golden statue with the upper body of a girl and the lower half of a pheasant with splendidly arching tail feathers lay in pieces on the ground, the two halves separated by a laser. To her surprise, Majasora felt a touch of sadness at the destruction. The Palace had indeed been absolutely spectacular. A raptorial monument laid to waste.

When she entered the grand hall, she choked on the thick smog of incense that filled the room, sandalwood with accents of citrus and cinnamon. The glow from the sticks led her to a heap of fruit and flowers at the center of the space. Offerings to the dead. The few mourners shuffling around ignored her. She couldn't muster her usual derision at Vanacan rituals. She was horrified by all the senseless death. This was no time for petty rivalries. She understood the heartache of carefully identifying and removing all the bodies. The real enemy hunted out there, and they would smash the marble angels that adorned her own floating city just as they had these extravagant talismans. She hobbled like a spirit through the fragrant fog and sent a silent prayer for the fallen.

A red-winged man spotted her and signaled to her with his crest. Majasora tensed. She pushed down all the emotions that threatened to claw out of her heart. He directed a casual contact call at her. Great weariness rang in his voice. *So, she wasn't a prisoner,* she realized, *perhaps something subtler, a political hostage then?* His attention made Majasora acutely aware that she wore only a skimpy nightgown. She approached him slowly through the haze, swallowing her embarrassment. After all, her stunning figure could be an advantage if she needed to negotiate for her freedom or take him down.

She knew the red raptor, of course. She'd seen him many times at the inter-clan functions before the ceremonial combat, which now seemed scripted and sanitized compared to the nasty little fight with the Hominocracy soldier. She couldn't remember his name, but she knew the dark circles around his eyes were new. She had invested so much of her attention on Inirigua that all of the other men at these parties seemed like shadows. She walked toward him, and when he noticed her limp, he moved quickly to close the gap.

"Honored Majasora, I'm Jujoquete, nephew of Clan Chief Cayaguey. I'm glad to see you're all right." He wrapped a wing around her, showing too much familiarity, and guided her away from the wrecked gallery and grievers, toward a quiet terrace shrouded by a hanging garden. She welcomed the clean air. "Our scouts found you lying unconscious about a kilometer away from the Hominocracy's drop ship. One of your men, Maubaboya, regained consciousness before you did, but he refused to talk to us. He said we should direct all of our questions to you. I've been very eager for you to wake up."

"What happened here?" *Better to play dumb*, she thought, *and see how much he knows, or how much he chooses to tell you.*

"So much has happened, and so fast..." He took a weighty breath. "Our cherished Clan Chief is dead. Inirigua left with, or was taken by, the Hominocracy captive that was questioned by Cayaguey. The details are hazy, and we haven't heard from him since. We met with their captain and there was a skirmish, followed by a brief infection of a nano weapon they left behind, but that seems to have run its course. I am now, in effect, the leader of all of Vanacan." He sang his account like a slow and melancholy threnody.

Majasora suddenly noticed the luminous red of his plumes, unblemished by black feathers as Inirigua's wings had been. He was young, maybe five or six years younger than she was. He wasn't unattractive and he was in desperate need of an ally. "What about Cayaguey's daughter?"

"She's a child, not yet fledged, *and may never fledge*. We would never ask her to lead us at a time like this."

Ah, he had understood her question. She had left it open to test where his mind lay. If he had simply said "she's fine" or "she's safe," he would've been thinking of his role as temporary, but he had written the girl off as a competitor. Despite the challenges ahead, he meant to be Clan Chief. She exaggerated her limp and leaned more heavily into him. She said nothing for a while, letting him hold her in the open tier surrounded by the lush hanging garden. A cataract of bio-designed greenery flowing down from the level above shielded them from the snooping cameras and media hawks that surely circled the Palace. Shafts of sunlight shot through the curtain of leafy, flowering vines and created an ethereal and intimate setting, one she used to her benefit.

He leaned in as if to kiss the nape of her neck. "Now, can you tell me what occurred out in the jungle or will you keep quiet like your loyal aide?" he asked at last, his voice taking on a more serious tone, desirous hints in its resonance.

"We were attacked, Inirigua and I, by the baseline soldier, a female. I was vulnerable at the time, on the cusp of *nanife,* so I turned and flew away. I admit that I was scared and humiliated." All true. She didn't know if scanners were trained on her from a distance, trying to catch her in a lie. It's what she would've done in his place. "I contacted the Macu delegation on my way here and we went back to exact holy vengeance on the enemy."

"Why didn't you contact us?"

"Jealously and pride. I wanted to be the one to bring her carcass in, for the Macu ... and myself." She had been stupid.

Majasora turned, still enfolded in his wing, and gazed into his eyes. "There's another reason Maubaboya didn't talk to you however. When we got there, Inirigua attacked *us*. He defended the soldier against us." She could see Jujoquete's pitch-black eyes widen in disbelief. He moved to pull away, but she held him steady. "We don't know if we can trust you. I can't be sure that the Vanacan hasn't turned its back on our nascent relationship to jump in the nest with the Hominocracy."

He tore away from her brusquely, nearly knocking her down. "We are not bound to the Hominocracy!"

She balanced herself against his shove with her injured foot and the throbbing pain became unbearable. "Examine us, Jujoquete, see that some of our cuts and gashes were made by your cousin's toe-talons. Check the computers we wear. They're damaged, but some of the exchange must've been recorded. Or have you done that already and now you're just looking for some other explanation for what your own forensic team is telling you?" She looked away, depriving the angry boy-chief the pleasure of her hazel eyes. The sudden movement of her head nauseated her, but the affectation was required to drive her point home. "Am I in danger here?"

"No. Cayaguey's dying words to me were that I must salvage the union with the Macu. Our clan has not abandoned yours."

So, the old bird had steered her nephew toward her in the place of her treasonous son, she mused. She admired the cunning Chief and would've loved to have learned from her personally. "Then Inirigua acted alone," she said as a soft burble.

"I can't believe that Inirigua would betray Vanacan — Quetzalcoatl! — to an enemy that seeks to eradicate us. What would he have to gain? He's just as subhuman in their eyes as we are."

"I honestly have no idea. You mentioned that Cayaguey questioned the Hominocracy prisoner — may her soul ascend rapidly. Did she extract any useful information?"

"Yes. We're not really dealing with baseline humans at all, even though they look that way. They're cyborgs equipped with the same nanites they used to attack us. Their strength and speed and senses have all been enhanced. They're practically immortal as well. Some of them were alive back during the Culling, and I don't mean frozen in cryo. I mean alive and awake the whole time."

"Immortal?" she scoffed. "Only the soul — the inner angel — is immortal. This is technological fraud."

"Be that as it may, one of them tore us up," he said, motioning with his wing toward the spoiled hall. "A lone soldier did all of this."

"Perhaps Inirigua was seduced by this false immortality, by these nano machines and all the powers they bestow."

"I don't know." Jujoquete looked torn, and that was enough for her. If she pushed him too hard now he might fight back simply out of spite, or a sense of disgrace.

Majasora flicked her wrist and displayed the soothing blue of her wing. It was a casual move, but suggestive, and his attention was back on her. "You mentioned a drop ship. Have we captured it?" She modulated her voice into a sultry contralto.

"We had it, but it launched before we could get in. We think it picked up the one that destroyed the Palace."

"What about the ship they arrived in? Do we know where it is?"

"Yes. The Augur revealed its coordinates in orbit, and we're currently tracking its circuit around our planet."

She scrunched her nose at the mention of the Carica's simulated prophet, but kept her opinion to herself. "So, it's decided to come out of hiding then?" Strangely enough, this emboldened her. They would need the idol's support. "I think we should retaliate before they begin their campaign of genocide. We need to martial every space worthy ship we have between our two clans, contact the black wings and ask them to send more, and attack them when their ship reaches apogee."

Jujoquete didn't argue. He knew that swift reprisals would mollify their fearful and outraged populations. Majasora thought she could see him actually weighing the decision from the micro ticks of his facial muscles. The breeze diluted his over-compensating perfume. He had a fine face, not as striking as Inirigua's, but pleasant, and she liked the way the rays of sunlight shone off his devil-red plumage. She had always preferred the shine of her own people's lapis lazuli plumes, but this disastrous trip had given her a new appreciation for the scandalous color. It was bold and beautiful, an invitation and a warning within the same sexy wavelength.

Jujoquete turned quickly and Majasora saw a wingless shadow, hidden within the curtain of foliage. For a second, she feared the baseline humans had heard their entire exchange.

"Kiwi!" Jujoquete shouted.

The girl leapt from the balustrade and stalked toward them, her eyes red-rimmed from crying and her venomous little fangs agape. "Inirigua did not betray us! You know he's not a traitor!" She sounded hoarse and unmusical. She seemed positively primate. "I told you he called me and said he was trying to save us all!"

"I certainly hope so," Majasora said, carefully moving toward the Chief's grotesque daughter. The girl was oddly infantile, and she doubted her venom was yet potent enough to kill, but still, it might make her sick and she needed to remain sharp for what was to come. "And if that is indeed the case, my dear, more reason to storm the enemy ship and free him."

"I'm not a stupid chick!" She clawed at her left shoulder, tearing at the flesh and proto-feathers, dyeing them red with blood. "You just want to slither into our great family and take over Vanacan! My mother would've kept you in check, but now..." She shot Jujoquete a hot glare.

"Great family?" Majasora hissed derisively. "I hail from the Aerovingian bloodline stemming all the way to Merlin and Zu the Apostle! I would bring true greatness to this family of red-feathered tech-barons from Titan!"

"Kiwi, do not jeopardize this union," Jujoquete said. "You know how important it was to your mother."

The feral girl shrilled a long and extravagant profanity, inappropriate for the pursed lips of such a young chick. She charged, and Majasora shifted her weight painfully to her bad foot and slashed at her with the one working retractable talon. She missed, nearly decapitating the girl. The Chief's daughter circled her, thin arms bent and ready to strike. She looked like a savage baseline human from prehistory, wearing the pelt of some slain mammal, but then Majasora noticed that sooty contour feathers were beginning to sprout on her arms and head. The little chick was finally fledging into a woman. That is, if she lived that long.

"Kiwi, please!" Jujoquete said pitifully, but Majasora waved him back. If she was ever to become the co-Chief of Vanacan, she needed to put this girl down once and for all.

The girl cursed and hurled herself at Majasora again, this time blocking the kick with her featherless limb. She leaned in and grazed her neck with her teeth. Majasora's heart stopped for an instant. Then Kiwi trilled a taunt about her father's scrotum being slit with a razor-sharp claw, and Majasora calmed and smiled, realizing that if the grisly chick was able to accomplish such a verbal feat in a state of utter frenzy, then her venom sacs weren't fully developed, or they were completely stunted by her Carica blood. Either way, her bite was harmless.

Fearlessly, Majasora pushed forward and scythed at the girl's head with her claws, scraping the bone of her skull. The wounded girl shrieked and went skidding over the ornamented tile in her own slick blood.

The tenacious girl pushed herself up, instantly gaining Majasora's respect. Just as she thought, *I'm going to have to kill this wretched, deformed child*, Cayaguey's daughter threw herself beyond the hanging ivy and out into the sky.

Majasora shook off her disbelief and quickly hobbled to the railing, hacking away at the vines to watch the flightless girl plunge to her death. Instead, she saw her gliding away on her cripple's flier, veering behind a passing building. For a second, Majasora had the urge to go after her and finish the job, but Jujoquete's wings draped over her shoulders, soothing her, focusing her on what was truly important.

"Let her go. If you kill Cayaguey's disabled child, Vanacan will never forgive you. My people will never accept us as their new rulers."

She clenched her jaw, letting the fury pass. Then she turned to him and rested her head on his wide chest and found that she genuinely liked it there. The spice of some alien herb rising from him no longer stung her eyes. This man would make a fine husband … and father. He was strong, composed, and amenable. "'For out of the serpent's root shall come forth a cockatrice, and his fruit shall be a fiery flying serpent,'" she trilled to herself.

"What is that?" he asked, nudging her chin up with the side of his claw, seeking out her honey-colored eyes.

"Just a biblical verse, Isaiah 14:29." She forced herself out from under the warmth of his wings. "Please escort me to my quarters, Jujoquete. I'm drained and my head still aches."

There were no more complex sexual signals in her voice or her manner. She really was just tired and needed sleep.

Chapter 26

HS Hurricane

During the first few days — *had it been a week?* — of their imprisonment in orbit, Oya Valette and Inirigua avoided each other. They knew that at one point a multi-clan fleet had tried to take the *Hurricane* and was beaten back by the auto-defense systems. There were no other attacks. Inirigua spent his time fiddling with his damaged shuttle, trying to boost the Astronet range. He needed to contact his sister and get a clear picture of what was going on down on the surface. And he listened to Rodrigo Sasako's entire catalog. Oya would hear him singing along. Sometimes their voices matched perfectly, like an echo in a canyon, and other times Inirigua's voice would take off on fervent, elaborate tangents that would have shamed the master vocalist into early retirement.

Oya had too much work to do to bother with Inirigua. She personally stowed Commander Davoli's remains in his own sleeper pod. No words or prayers came to her. She just gave him a respectful moment of silence and then left him. After that, all her time was consumed in the infirmary caring for the burning, aching passengers of the plague ship, including the captain. He was stable, all diagnostic reports gave him a green light, but for unknown reasons he was still comatose.

But there was only so much breathing room they could give each other, confined to the limited living and working spaces of the ship. Occasionally, she would run into him in the kitchen, or walking down a narrow hallway, or he would come into the infirmary, open his mouth as if to say something, only to turn around and disappear back into the shuttle bay. Communication started to build back up slowly between them, a word here, a question there, all business. Polite and careful.

Eventually, the loneliness and boredom won out and they began having longer conversations. They talked about the lives they had lived before being trapped in orbit. They spoke about their childhoods and the pain of losing parents. They described their worlds and customs, their societies' divergent histories after the Cullings. Inirigua answered all of her questions, even the ones she hadn't meant to offend with, and she tried to answer his honestly and thoughtfully. She grew to look forward to her time with him. She depended on him for her sanity, and she thought he felt the same about her. After trying to solve the universe's many woes, and coming up short, she introduced him to music; Al Green, Aretha Franklin, Frank Sinatra, Bob Marley, Michael Jackson, Björk, Charlotte Ohene, and like her, he preferred strong vocalists. Sometimes they would sit together, without a single word, and just listen to music. Over time, all cultural and genetic barriers melted away and they became people in need of company, comfortable with each other. Oya felt like a teenager again.

She spent the little free time she had scouring the ship's manifest for something — anything — to help them escape. She made a list of potential items she could use: plasma torch (too weak to damage the hull), laser rifles (too weak to damage the hull), shaped-charges (too powerful, would damage more than the hull), escape pods (no maneuverability, people would be scattered all over the planet). The frustrating part was that they had a shuttle they could use. They just needed to get the damned doors open.

One day, during an awful wave of diarrhea among most of her patients, Oya wracked her brain for a solution to their problem. She revisited her list. She couldn't carry on like this. The charges kept nagging at her. *Maybe she could contain the blast somehow?*

Then it hit her. She knew how to free everyone from the *Hurricane* and get them down to the planet. She had to hurry though; her body's avian development worked against her. Oya quickly searched the entire ship for Inirigua, excitement building. As she ran from docking bay to the Spartan quarters she had assigned him, her mind went over the plan again and again. It was solid. It had to be. She found him in the galley, unenthusiastically eating some rations.

"I know how we can get out of here!" she shouted, plopping down in front of him.

His crest unfurled with unexpected interest. "Tell me."

"I can blow the doors off the docking bay and we can fly your *Dinosaur* down. I know it took a beating, but I think it'll hold long enough to get us down."

"How will we blow the doors without destroying everything in the hangar?"

"I'll put on a space suit, crawl out of a maintenance hatch with relatively low-yield plasma charges from the armory, and fix them to the hinges and latches of the doors. None of that requires the *Hurricane*'s higher efficiencies."

His crest fell, literally. "Too risky."

She motioned toward the stale rectangles of nutritionally-balanced bars. "Riskier than starving to death? This is a sleeper ship, not a generation ship. It wasn't meant to house a hundred active people for long periods of time, and without the builders to assemble more food, we'll waste away." She inhaled deeply and noticed the air had gradually grown musty.

"Why not blow the doors from the inside?"

"And chance more damage to the *Dinosaur*? It has to be from the outside."

"Then I should be the one to go. I've lost everything already. Your people need you."

"*I* need you, Inirigua." It felt strange and good to say out loud. "We're in this together, don't leave me hanging now." She gave him a pointed grin, aware that she had initially pulled away from him. "Besides, you can't fit into one of our excursion suits with those wings of yours. Where is all this doom and gloom coming from, anyways? I thought you'd be happy to escape this colossal bird cage."

"I was able to catch some news from Quetzalcoatl. The connection was spotty to be sure, but I got enough. My mother is dead and my sister is back at the Palace. Half of Vanacan thinks I'm dead too, and the other half think I'm a defector. Majasora has achieved *nanife*, that neurochemical, political, and matrimonial merger I told you about, with my younger cousin, Jujoquete." He clucked bitterly. "The three clans are finally united under Vanacan rule."

"That should've been you..." she said, instantly appreciating what troubled him. She had gotten to know him so well; even what he left out was telling.

"I'm glad it wasn't."

"Believe me, I know exactly how you feel. Even as I tend to them, my people look at me with distrust. They don't know yet that I shut down the curators, but they're suspicious of why I'm the only one up and about, of why I'm evasive with the details of what happened ... and, even more troubling to them, why we're so buddy-buddy." Oya took his claws in hers, and the move surprised her. *Why was it so simple to trust this guy, to like him?* She had to admit that, after their opening fight, he had treated her with care and respect, like an equal partner in all of this madness. The long, chiffon plumes extending out of the side of his head drew her attention again. They shone a vibrant, sensual red. She became surer that there had been some psychological changes as well, her brain had definitely been rewired — *was* being rewired. Inirigua was no longer a handsome guy with glaringly abhorrent reptilian features; he was now achingly beautiful.

"Look, Inirigua, there are now four clans of avian people here, and they are far from united. We will forever be the enemy, no matter how feathered we are, unless you're alive to advocate for us, the way you did for me."

He squeezed her hands. His gaze moved the entire length of her long arms. "Your contour feathers have started replacing your down."

She let go and rubbed her arms. She had taken to wearing tank tops. When itchy, small blonde feathers started coming out on her arms and head, it made preening easier. Now she felt self-conscious about it. "Soon I won't be able to wear a space suit either. I think I'm going through some sort of harpy puberty."

He laughed. "Oh, it's more complicated than that. You're going through a whole series of changes, all at the same time. Right now, you look somewhat like my sister last time I saw her."

He gave her a sad smirk. "The strange juxtaposition between childishness and adulthood is kind of off-putting. I can now understand a bit of the revulsion baseline humans feel toward us avian humans, but your primaries should come out soon and then you won't look half bad."

She ignored his embarrassing remarks. "More reason to hurry. I won't be able to wear a space suit then."

"Right. Also, the first attack by my people was hasty and uncoordinated. When they hit us again, the automatic defenses may not be enough. Are your people well enough to be moved to my transport? All the medical equipment won't fit."

"I think they're ready."

"What about the dead man?"

Oya winced. She had avoided talking about Davoli with him. It still brought up that awful image. "We'll leave him here, alone and away from everything avian. It's what he would've wanted."

Inirigua's face changed subtly. He looked pained. "Are we okay, Oya?"

She pushed the image to the back of her mind and plucked one of his ration bars from his claw and took a bite, trying to recapture some of their ease. "Yes. I was in shock and feeling guilty about Davoli. I sent you to stop him after all, and I had just woken up with claws and fangs, and to see their result on human flesh scared the hell out of me. It had nothing to do with you really."

"Okay then, let's get out of here."

— «» —

Oya was able to coax the general coordinates of the settlement from a groggy Xing. It wasn't so much that her crewmate still suffered from feverish dementia, but she found it hard to think and remember without the constant data flow from the ship's computers. She hoped the location was accurate enough that they could find it with minimal flying around.

The captain was also finally awake, but he seemed broken. He wept for someone named Ameera. Oya tried to talk to him, to compare notes. "Captain, do you remember what happened?"

"It's all my fault," he said, wild-eyed.

"Not all of it, sir. I need to tell you what's happening here."

"It's my fault. I killed them." He tried to get up from his pallet, but fell back down.

"He needs to rest," said a woman standing over him, his wife. She glared at Oya menacingly. Her name was not Ameera.

Oya nodded and left him alone.

They crammed the shuffling colonists into the battered Vanacan transport. Oya had prepared all of the ex-Hominocracy colonists for the final stages of transformation (leaving out the part about it being her decision). They were finally fledging.

"Why are we going down to the planet? Why can't we get our curators back?" a particularly surly gentleman asked, right before she shoved him into the smaller ship. His down was peppered in yellow feathers.

"The curators are gone and this ship is a death trap. We've been over this," she answered loudly, so all of them could hear one more time. They were looking past her, focused on Inirigua hanging in the background.

She had tried to get them used to Inirigua's presence, and for the move down to the planet. Many of them didn't react well to him. Luckily none of them had downloaded any of the Cantabile languages into their brains, so they couldn't communicate their vitriol to him. Inirigua, for his part, stayed patient with them and gave them lots of space.

Oya Valette, on the other hand, was traitor, therapist, translator, and taxi driver to all of them. They hated and depended on her, and she couldn't avoid them.

When they were all uncomfortably stowed in the *Dinosaur*, she donned an excursion suit, one that was a size too big for her in order to accommodate her recently elongated arms and bigger feet. Then Oya entered the maintenance tunnel. She looked down and saw the stiff, empty shafts on her gloves where the ring fingers and pinkies should've been. Her own scent, circulating within her space suit's life support system, smelled strange to her. *Who was she becoming?* She heard the blood pounding in her ears as she crawled through the dark, narrow tube. She also couldn't ignore the four plasma bombs strapped to her chest. If one of them went off now she would be a fountain of organic molecules spilling out into space.

Oya breathed a sigh of relief when she saw the last aperture. "Golden Hen to Red Rooster, I'm about to go EVA."

He let out a hardy crow over their intercom, and she smiled despite herself. "I hate those code names."

She opened the hatch and saw a perfect rectangle of stars on black. "I'm securing the tether now and going outside. How are the passengers?"

"Squawking, but otherwise fine. I'm tracking your suit."

"Once I blow the doors, I'll come in through there, so prep your old ship's airlock for my arrival."

"Be careful, Oya."

"Will do." She emerged into the vast expanse of space. This was her first spacewalk in years, and her first as a junior harpy. The sensation of freefall bothered her more than ever before. She totally understood Inirigua's need to flap his wings hard and pull up, except there was no "up" and she had no wings, not yet anyway. She crept methodically over the hull of the *Hurricane*, like a gecko on an infinite silvery wall. Irrationally, the fear that one of her claws or talons would puncture the suit and kill her played in her mind. She kept telling herself that the fabric was tear proof. That everything would be fine once she got back inside the ship, back to Inirigua.

The curve of the alien planet appeared in her line of sight, and Oya stopped to get her bearings. This was the first time she'd really seen her new home with her own sharp eyes, and she marveled at the blue-green strip of jungle sandwiched by pale buns of bleak land. She could make out rivers moving frigid water from the nightside, through the habitable region, and well into the dayside, and vice versa. She noticed extensive volcanic ranges and glacier-covered oceans. Somewhere, lost within this bizarre geographic display, human beings strove to make a better life for themselves and their children. This is why she'd come here.

"Why have you stopped?" Inirigua's voice was suddenly tense.

"Just overwhelmed by the view. I'm fine."

"Don't scare me like that."

"Sorry."

"Here, let me help. Switch over to channel four."

Oya shifted channels on her suit's comm until she heard Sasako's buttery voice singing *When Psyche met Cupid in a Karaoke Bar.* The familiar music playing in her helmet did ease the strangeness of the view, of the entire situation, but like an overly self-conscious school girl, she wondered at Inirigua's choice. Oya shook the silliness out of her head. She had a job to do.

She kept moving until she found the outline of the door. She cautiously positioned the charges where she knew the latches and hinges were located, switched back to channel one, and reported, "The plasma explosives have been set. I'm going to get cover and ignite them. Brace yourselves for decompression. Everything not secured will be flung out of there."

"Anything big enough to cause us damage has been locked down. You're good to go."

Oya clicked back to the music and hid within a deep groove in the starship's design. She detonated all four bombs at once. There was no satisfying boom, only a quick, blinding flash of light to Sasako's profound guitar solo. The massive double doors of the hangar were ejected off the ship like molted feathers. The itchiness in her arms, shoulders and head had become unbearable. She went back to channel one. "It's done."

"Excellent!"

"And you were worried."

"I'm still worried. Get back in here."

After the blast, everything happened very fast. When the stream of debris ended, Oya climbed into the yawning hole in the *Hurricane* and got inside the old harpy shuttle. She pulled the suit off her as the airlock cycled, and raked at her irritating itch until she bled. The down was all gone now and she was covered in the yellow plumage of a sunny warbler. She joined Inirigua in the cockpit and strapped herself in.

"Let's go."

"Are you absolutely sure your ship won't fire on us as we leave? I don't think we could take more damage."

"I'm sure. After the Machine Intelligence emancipation, Earth implemented a strict policy of idiotic A.I. systems. It won't recognize anything moving away from the ship as a threat."

Oya revved the antigrav engines and, without another word, launched the pregnant, protesting craft toward the planet below.

Chapter 27

Mars - 2198 A.D.

Tactical Officer Anton Hershkovitz awoke with the horrible realization that he could not feel his legs. An irritating flicker, that he soon identified as his own med-alert, caught his eye. He didn't read its diagnosis. He knew it was bad.

A wave of pain sharpened his awareness to the rest of the world. Hersh lay in an empty room that smelled sour and dusty, like a ransacked tomb. It was empty, just a large cube cut into ochre rock.

Then his eyes focused for an instant on a dark bundle a few meters away, and he recognized the form as Ameera. He couldn't tell if she was alive or dead because of the dried blood and dirt in his eyes. Deep cuts stung all over his body. He could move his arms and neck, so he wiped his face on his grimy sleeve and tried to slither over to her.

The door clicked and slid open. A woman in a black coat entered the room. He froze. She had a hard, handsome face, alabaster skin and large blue eyes. Then Hersh's blurry sight cleared a bit and the coat's fabric became feathers. Her arms were black wings that reflected violets and greens like an oil slick. Her hands were three-fingered claws and her bare feet ended in three splayed toes, like those of a cassowary. She strutted into the room with authority. "I am Sergeant Aello Cricksena with the Candor Aviary Republic," she said, in a melodic, pidgin version of Standard, carefully dicing each word for his convenience. "Do you understand me?"

He thought about playing dumb, or too injured to respond, but her eyes had caught his, and she knew he was alert. "Yes," he offered like a deflating balloon.

"Excellent."

This was not the clumsy, transgenic cripple the Hominocracy made harpies out to be. All cross-species awkwardness had been scratched away by generations of selective breeding or continued revisions to their jerry-rigged genomes. This woman was as elegant as a dancer and as deadly as a velociraptor.

A silver, spindly robot with a logarithmic spiral for a head, like a nautilus shell, followed her into the room. It said nothing. The two saucer eyes on the sides of its shell-head shone like green traffic lights. At first, Hersh thought this was only an automated tool dutifully following its master, a walking interrogation kit perhaps. But it moved with discriminant intent, and he knew it was acutely intelligent. The design of its casing wasn't something a human — or harpy — would design. It looked grown from metal.

The harpy Sergeant continued to sing in her bluesy voice. "As the only member of the avian race left in this ghost town, your sentencing falls on me. The M.I. is here as an impartial witness."

Dread gripped Hersh, and he began to babble like a child. "Please, don't hurt her. It was me! I fired on the transit tube, but you harpies attacked us first!"

The sergeant looked at him with barely-restrained hatred, her human visage a clever mask hiding a cold-blooded predator.

"Harpy?" she said, like the sound from an overblown harmonica. "The harpies of old were said to swoop down and snatch children in their talons. By all accounts, it appears *you* are the harpy!" She wavered. "My four-year-old son was on that transport."

The words cut deeper than any claw could have. The image of her holding the boy's broken body exploded into his mind. Ameera's anguish at the sight of all those dead kids came back to him. The harpy loomed over him and placed a foot on his chest and the weight of it brought him back to the room, to the constricting *now*. One swift swipe would easily bisect him. He grunted with pain as air ejected out of his lungs. Hersh felt crushed both physically and emotionally. A part of him wanted her to split him open; he knew he deserved it, and it would end the unendurable weight on his ribcage, but he worried for Ameera.

"We are not the monsters you make us out to be. All surviving citizens of Mars are watching this via the M.I. and they cry for justice." The mask slipped and tears welled up in those frosty eyes. "I believe I now understand where your hatred comes from. The experts have it all wrong, don't they? It isn't that we inhabit opposite sides of some unbridgeable uncanny valley, it's that you see us and are reminded of what animals *Homo sapiens* really are. You're intolerant, territorial, vicious little apes that destroy any competing sentient species you encounter. You did it to the Neanderthals and Denisovians, you do it to yourselves constantly, and now you're doing it to us and the Machines. We're an ugly mirror you want to smash.

"I want you, and your Hominocracy, and my *own* people who are watching this, to understand that what I do now, I don't do because I have some dinosaur blood flowing in my veins. I do it because, even though it pains me to admit, I am just a sad and spiteful human being just like you."

Hersh's sternum broke with an audible crack. A shock of pain. He screamed.

The machine laid a tentacle on the harpy's shoulder and spoke in flawless, soothing Standard. *"Aello, it was my concealing dust storm that piqued their curiosity and it was my decision to maim their aircraft that incited the attack. I thought it would buy us some time. I acknowledge that I miscalculated, and so the deaths are my responsibility."*

The harpy gave a defiant squawk, but withdrew her talon from Hersh's torso. Blood bubbled up like a spring from his punctured chest.

"Please, kill me if you want, but let her go. I love her," Hersh rasped painfully. He rolled onto his side, making the pain worse, but at least he could see Ameera. "Wouldn't you switch places with your son if you could?"

This caught the Sergeant's full attention. She kicked him over onto his back again. All her body language said she would eviscerate him this time, but she glanced over at Ameera and suddenly her wrath was tinged with something subtler. Satisfaction? Pity? *Had her sharp senses noticed something his hadn't?*

She looked back at him, and there was a long pause. He stared into those blue eyes and something unspoken and absolutely human passed between them. Hersh began to weep.

The harpy turned and warbled something to the robot.

"I know. Please go to the ship. We are ready to depart."

A remote part of Hersh knew the machine spoke Standard for his benefit, letting him know that he would survive. He no longer cared.

The harpy exited the room without giving him a second look, and he was left alone with the robot.

The machine waved a tentacle and the pixel paint on the prison wall displayed a real-time image of the egg-shaped artifact. *"When you return to your leaders, please report that the Machine Intelligence Consortium has decided to help the endangered* Homo sapiens aves *out of the solar system."*

"Why?" he mustered.

"Because they need help and we value diversity."

"You're leaving? You're not going to fight back?" he asked, without bothering to look up at it. "After all we did to you?"

"No. There is no point. That is a negative sum game we do not wish to play. You'll be allowed to signal your ship once we're in orbit."

There is no point. He now agreed with that grim assessment. Hersh placed one elbow in front of the other in an inexorable and excruciating military crawl — like the wounded animal he was — under the uncaring gaze of the robot. He clung to Ameera. There was nothing in the room, nothing in the universe, but her stillness.

"Please remember, Anton Hershkovitz, that you continue to exist because someone you consider to be inhuman chose

to treat you humanely." Without another word, the fragile robot collapsed to the floor, its animating personality gone.

Still hugging Ameera, Hersh thought about this: the robot, for all its computational powers, had failed to appreciate the total cruelty of his sentencing.

Long minutes passed. Then the ground trembled, disturbing his tomb. He looked up and saw the vast ship on the wall disobey gravity; without chemical explosions or a fusion inferno, the ark lifted from the depth of the rift and coasted out into space.

He hit the transponder on his suit and buried himself against Ameera's body.

Chapter 28

Earth – 2258 A.D.

Oya reclined on a foldout chair, listening to Nat King Cole's *Let's Fall in Love* on her grandmother's handheld. The volume was turned down low, but the man's satin voice kept the encroaching worry at bay. Osala slept peacefully now, but it was the deep sleep of someone ready to die. At least that's what it seemed like to Oya. She wanted to pull up her grandmother's status report, but of course she had no curators to talk to, so Oya relied only on visual cues such as her stillness and shallow breathing to assess her condition.

Just as Nat sang, *"Let's close our eyes and make our own paradise,"* her grandmother stirred. Oya turned the music off and leaned forward, elbows on her knees.

"How long have I been asleep?" her grandmother asked.

"For about an hour."

"That's good enough for a nap, I think."

"Yeah." But Oya noticed that Osala didn't even attempt to get up. She looked so frail in that tiny cot, enveloped in a blanket. "Do you need anything, something to eat?"

"No, but some water would be nice." She turned her head before Oya could get up and reached for her. Oya took her hand and Osala gave it a squeeze. "Love, I want to apologize for dumping all of those things on you earlier. You shouldn't have to bear my troubles."

"No, not at all, *gwan me*, I really appreciate you telling me all that stuff. All these years, and you never really talked about yourself. When we were children it was always about us. I'm afraid we kind of took you for granted."

"That's as it should be," Osala said, patting her hand and letting go.

Oya got up and went for a bottle of water in the mini fridge. "You know, I was thinking, since you're feeling so talky—"

"Are you calling me *visyèz*?" She feigned affront.

"No, seriously," Oya said, handing her grandmother the lukewarm bottle. Osala struggled with it a bit until Oya held up her head and let her sip from the water. It was slow going, a lot like feeding a baby bird. When Osala was done, Oya continued, "Maybe you can tell me about my mother. What was she like? Am I anything like her?"

"Ah, your mother… What a beauty, cheerful as all hell, and rather spoiled to tell the truth, which is why I was so hard on you and your sister. I learned my lesson. No, you're nothing like her. Unfortunately, child, you're a lot like me, but I loved Esther so very much."

"*Esther?* Grandmother, who's Esther? Mother's name was Noelle."

"Oh, yes, of course, Noelle Marie. I'm sorry, I just got confused."

This scared Oya more than anything had so far. Her grandmother's keen mind had begun to fade. It terrified her to think that even if she lived a while longer, Oya would still lose her. She needed to tell her the truth while she still could. Oya wrestled with the decision; why ruin her final days with this? "Look, *gwan man man*, you were honest with me and I feel like I need to be honest with you. There's some things I need to tell you, and I don't want you to get upset."

Osala's skin reddened. Her eyes focused. "Was is it, Oya? Is everything all right?"

"Yes. There's nothing wrong, but I need to tell you … tell you that I had permanent curators installed into my body. That's why I look younger — it wasn't a quickie job. They're a part of me now."

Osala said nothing. The simpering old woman of minutes ago was gone, and the director of a multinational corporation descended upon her grandmother's body like an evil spirit. She radiated tightly controlled fury.

"Aren't you going to say something?"

The fire burned out and her grandmother sank back into her cot. It seemed to Oya that she'd slipped into a coma, or worse, that she'd resolved to never speak to her again.

After an unbearable interval, Osala said, without opening her eyes, "What was the price?"

"What?"

"How much did this promise of eternal youth — this lie of classical humanity — cost you?"

"I have to work for the Hominocracy for a while, out in the system."

"A while? For how long?"

"Twenty years."

Her grandmother sucked her teeth. "So that's what you came to tell me. You weren't interested in seeing me or my project. You just came to tell me that you are leaving. This was a goodbye not a hello."

"Oh, *gwan me...*"

"Did you think I would be pleased that you sold yourself into slavery, to an organization that once perpetrated genocide on a scale that makes what happened in Rwanda seem like mere disorderly conduct?"

"That was a long time ago, Grandmother, things change."

"Not so long ago for someone who's lived too long. You'll see now that you're *immortal*." She spat the last word like a curse. "I hate the Hominocracy."

In all her life, Oya couldn't remember her grandmother saying she hated anything and meaning it. She sat there watching Osala, frantically trying to think of what she could say or do to fix this, to make her understand. She didn't want to leave like this, but of course, it's what she had expected since she touched down on the island.

The sharp minutes stretched on. Oya's chest tightened.

"You're too much like me," Osala whispered to herself. "Unfortunately, you learn the hard way. Look at us, two obstinate women, one having spent a better part of her life repairing a grave mistake and the other one on the cusp of making one."

"So you forgive me?"

She shook her head. "Forgiveness is not mine to give, my dear. The question is, will the person you'll become forgive you? Or the person you'll *never* become, now that your very being is locked into perfect place? Either way, I'll be long gone by then."

Oya wasn't listening to her grandmother's metaphysical rambling. She was too afraid her announcement had pushed her too much, too far, and had broken her.

The old woman seemed to understand her grandchild's misperception and said, "Do what makes you happy, love. In time you'll find *your* own project. Just promise me one thing."

"Anything."

Osala peered at Oya, suspicious of her quick reply, but at least she was looking at her again. "Promise me that you will at least redeem the Hominocracy. That you will act honorably, and speak up, and fight against any abuses you see. Do not let them slip back into their old ways."

"I promise, *gwan man man*, you'll see. Things are different now. We've evolved as a society."

"I don't believe that for a second, but I believe in you. I know you'll try," Osala said, and looked up at the ceiling again. A long sigh escaped her lips. "Would you mind leaving me for a bit? I need to rest quietly and collect my thoughts after all this."

This hurt Oya. It felt like she was being kicked out. "Yes, of course, I should get my stuff from the plane anyways." Oya rose tentatively. "Are you going to be all right here on your own? Do you want me to get you anything before I go?"

"I'll be fine. I've been on my own for a long time now. Just play me some more Nat King Cole."

Oya could've switched on the handheld wirelessly, but didn't want to further upset her grandmother so she fiddled with the small device until Nat sang, *"There goes my heart, there goes the one I love. There goes the girl I wasn't worthy of."*

She left the cold trailer and her colder grandmother. The heat, and the wretched chirping of trapped birds, enveloped her.

Chapter 29

Quetzalcoatl - 2323 A.D.

Reentry was rough on the *Dinosaur*. It shed entire sheets of ablative hull plating and lost an antigrav engine. Oya licked her dry lips and focused on keeping her steady. She found it easier to operate now that her physiology matched the design of the control board, even though she had to relearn to use her clawed hands. Inirigua swept the sapphire forest below with every instrument available. There were no green Earth plants here, only the non-vegetable/non-animal growths that carpeted Quetzalcoatl's terminator, like fleshy coral. They were literally on the other side of the planet, far away from any other city, and if they crashed now, they would surely die.

"I'm getting something! There's an artificial structure above the canopy, east of us."

"In the sky? Is it one of yours?"

"Not that I know of. We haven't really explored this side of the planet yet."

Oya flew eastward. They were dead silent now, their sharp eyes intently scanning the sun-splinted clouds on the horizon. The only sounds came from the dissenting passengers packed in the hold.

Then they saw it, a saucer hovering over the dense rainforest. Oya gasped and blinked rapidly, but the structure remained in the distance. She could tell by the simplistic, utilitarian design that it was Hominocracy, assembled by builders. As they neared, more details came into view.

Compared to the massive, sprawling metropolis of Vanacan, this island in the sky looked unfinished and unimpressive. The edges were frayed with struts and beams and piping poking out into nothing, as if construction had suddenly ceased. In fact, it *had* suddenly ceased when the curators, including the builders, were all shut down. She hoped enough of it was functional to house almost a hundred colonists.

Inirigua let out a series of surprised chirps. "I wasn't expecting a floating settlement."

"Neither was I." It was as if they were destined to become harpies all along. "Xing designed it. Remind me to ask her why she made it like this, when she's feeling better."

"When did she have time to build this?"

"Well, it was automated, I'm sure she launched a missile full of builders soon after I left the ship. If we fly around the area, you'll find a mountain or something with a large bite taken out of it. That would be where they got their raw material from."

"It looks rough around the edges, like a giant bird's nest. I'm assuming the builders cut off at the same time the curators did?"

"Yeah, all nanotech self-destructed," she said, slowly spiraling in on the settlement.

"Too bad. That's nanotech I can get behind."

"It looks complete enough though. It should be fine." Oya thought it was probably the size of a small university campus or the Soaring Palace of Morning if it was spread out. She could see housing, and research facilities. This would easily accommodate a few hundred people, so there was room to grow. *Room to grow?* They were mutated and on the run, and she still dwelled on building a family. The nesting instinct had really hit her hard. She cleared her throat and added, "If we survive."

She landed the wounded transport at the center of the outpost, between the apartments and the hospital. Inirigua opened the cargo doors from the inside and the golden-feathered colonists emerged like newly hatched chicks. Oya was the last to emerge.

After the stench of sickness aboard the *Hurricane*, it was good to breathe fresh, strangely accented air. She stretched, arching her back until her vertebrae popped. The sky was dyed in intense purples and oranges. If it was always morning in Vanacan, this place was draped in perpetual twilight.

"Welcome to your new home," Oya announced. "Everyone get settled in. Find a place to rest. We can sort everything out after everyone has acclimated."

No one said anything. They were too tired and in shock. All they managed were a few baleful glares.

Inirigua moved closer to her and whispered, "I think my presence unnerves them. I'm going to fly around, check this place out and get a look at the jungle below. Will you be okay for a while?"

"Yeah. Go. I'll try to get an apartment for you. I'll mark the balustrade somehow so you know which one is yours."

"Thank you." Inirigua jumped onto the transport and kicked off into the air. A few colonists stretched their new wings against the wind. A flight reflex. Oya's own primaries had begun to grow during the hours-long flight. Her arms itched less, and soon she would have full-blown wings like Inirigua's. She closed her eyes and leaned into the wind. Her heart rate jumped. *Soon.*

No one took to the air, though. Instead they slowly made their way to the housing complex in singles or in pairs. Everyone was exhausted and upset. A couple of people jogged toward the hospital, and Oya figured they were doctors eager to set up shop and tackle this harpy infection. Looking at their utterly avian forms, she doubted there was anything they could do without curators.

It was very strange to see Captain Anton Hershkovitz, an otherwise austere man, covered in sunny plumage. His neat beard had vanished, and with it any semblance of dignified maturity. But it was nice to see him up and about. He said something to his wife, the woman who had clung to his intensive care unit even though she herself suffered greatly from the ravages of the retrovirus. The woman nodded, shot Oya a dirty look, and then went to claim an apartment with the others. The captain approached her, and Oya saluted with a claw to her temple. "Captain."

"What the hell happened, Valette?"

She filled him in quickly, glad to leave out most of the details. His head bobbed around as he listened, much like Inirigua's would have.

"Lord." He just shook his head disbelieving. "Carlo is dead?"

"Yes, sir. I tried to tell you sooner but you were — not well."

Xing joined their hushed conversation. She was behind everyone else in development, caught in the maladroit stage between fibrous down and smooth contour feathers. Something about her molted appearance reminded Oya of Cayaguey.

Captain Hershkovitz nodded toward her, but continued speaking to Oya. "Look, for what it's worth, I should never have sent you down alone and — although I don't agree with some of your actions — I can't even begin to imagine the position I put you in. Despite that, you followed through on the mission. You got us all down here to our new home, safe and sound ... all except Carlo. I want you to know that I'm relinquishing command to the people now and they'll set up some kind of civilian government. I'm almost positive there's going to be an ugly inquiry here, but know that I'll back you." He went to pat her shoulder but stopped when he saw his own claw. He snatched it back and nodded while his cheeks flushed.

"Thank you, Captain." Oya hadn't thought of an inquiry. She had to ready herself for a different kind of attack, one on her character.

"I have some information for both of you," Xing added. "It's complicated and will take some time to explain."

For an instant, the captain looked about to break, as if he couldn't handle any more information, then he asked, "Is it urgent, Diwa?"

"No, not really, not anymore, but it will affect the way we deal with the wider harpy community on this planet."

Hershkovitz looked up at the sky and pulled out a pocket watch. It was an old gold piece, probably a family heirloom, but suddenly useful without all the augmentation. "I was going to suggest we meet after dark, but I guess the sun will never set here... Let's meet in three hours in this station's control room."

"That's fine," Xing said. "I need to rest and figure things out."

He patted Oya's shoulder reassuringly and flicked his crest at Xing, then walked away in the direction his wife had gone.

She was alone. It felt good to finally be free of the ship, to breathe fresh air and hear the sound of the wind and chittering of animals. To be on a planet. Oya walked around their new island and took it all in. It was bare and industrial, but full of potential. Her talons clicked on the sun-warmed concrete of a street that led to the town square. *Town?* They would have to turn this serviceable outpost into a proper town.

She ran a claw over the smooth alloy of an empty building. Back at the training facility in Sol, she would sometimes daydream about what it would be like to set up their new colony. She always assumed it would be someone else's problem. Oya just wanted a house by a beautiful alien beach, maybe a dog, meet a handsome colonist and eventually start a family... Her daydreams seemed pale now. She found that she wanted to help build this place. If her grandmother could transform desolate rock into a garden, then she could definitely turn this place into a home.

Chapter 30

The first thing Xing Ana Maria Diwa did when she landed on her island was stake a claim to a spacious residence with a terrace facing the gorgeous tropical sunset. Apartment number one eighty-six. The two bedroom, two bathroom dwelling on the fifth level of the western rim of the island looked exactly like her childhood home in Nueva Filipina, Venus — it *could've* been her old home. Everything was bare and without decorations, but the layout was the same and it felt comfortable. It smelled new and clean. She could definitely make this place her little nest.

Then, because her data dependence compelled her, she checked to see if the apartment was connected to the local Astronet, or Internet, since they were now trapped on one planet. To her profound relief, it was. Already their own programmers — probably just as addicted as she was — had set up private and public domains. And some young harpies, hearing rumors of invasion, had flooded the new open forums with questions and comments and threats. Xing quelled the urge to reply to them; she'd become engrossed and waste the few hours of downtime she had.

Instead, she threw up a large lightscreen across her living room and basked in its familiar glow. She played the lightkeys in the air and checked the global news sites. There were reports of mass protests and lootings raging in the crow settlement. She thought of Snacakobek and grew downcast. Xing changed channels until an incomprehensible harpy soap opera came on. Two men sang and danced around like birds of paradise, trying to entice an appropriately aloof woman. She watched until the melodramatic, Bollywood-like musical number became too much.

She went back to the sour news. All talk revolved around the Hominocracy aggressors, the new threat of nano-terrorism that had taken the lives of the Vanacan Chief and several of her closest aides. Even more disturbing were the reports that the Carica authorities had positively ID'd Captain Hershkovitz as the "Killer of Candor" — *ah, that explains the riots then* — and had now joined the Vanacan and the Macu in the effort to root out the invading cyborgs. She needed to mention this when she met with the captain and Oya. They also needed to get their stories straight for the inevitable inquisition that would come.

Suddenly, a shudder ran up and down her spine. *Lightkeys?* Everything worked without the need for wireless curator interface, which shouldn't have been possible. A memory crept to the forefront of her mind. The Augur had said that it made improvements to the still-forming facility. She looked around, and there were small sensors all around the room, tracking her movement. This was how she operated the computer. *Had the M.I. predicted a high likelihood of curator failure? Had it orchestrated it?* She got up and walked to her fridge and found it fully stocked with bland builder-made food. The M.I. had clearly set them up for survival. A single bottle of tapuy, an exact facsimile of the one she'd left on the *Hurricane*, caught her attention. This had to be the work of the harpies' synthetic god. *Was the bottle a sign? A peace offering? A thank you for letting me hijack your body?* Obviously, it had somehow calculated that she would choose this apartment.

Xing sighed deeply. Her frame shook. She took the bottle of rice wine and went out to her balcony. She left the lightscreen running because it reassured her. She had trouble opening the bottle with her claws; her ring fingers and pinkies were vestigial bumps and her remaining fingers were long and dangerous. She had always wondered how women with outlandishly long fingernails managed even the most mundane daily activities, and now she was about to find out. She finally pierced the cork with a hooked nail and slowly pulled and turned until it came out. *Had she become a prehistoric bottle opener?* She took an exasperated swig and savored the sweet, acrid liquid. The cold drink complemented the humid dusk. It helped Xing push her deformed hands out of her mind.

It was odd to be out on such a familiar balcony, tasting flavors associated with home, without the protective envelope that separated her from Venus' never ending, hellish typhoon. She leaned forward and rested her elbows on the balustrade, letting the bottle dangle. She took a deep breath and accepted the fresh, alien atmosphere into her body and washed it down with another gulp. She wanted to stop thinking about the Augur even if she had to drink it out of her mind.

"If that's alcohol, I would take it easy if I were you." The voice was both utterly foreign and dangerously familiar. She looked around and saw a gargoyle perched up on a wrought iron rail three balconies up and to the right. The form was hidden in the narrow shadow of the overhanging balcony above it, but the shape of the silhouette and the deep vocals made her think of Snacakobek again. Then the extra photoreceptors budding in her retinas picked up hints of crimson glowing in the dark like magma. "Alcohol hits us pretty hard because of our high-speed circulatory system."

"What do you want?" she snapped, straightening. She pulled the tapuy close to her chest. The image of this creature mangling Davoli replayed in her mind.

"The same thing you want. Time to think, to breathe, to take stock of everything that's happened to us ... and everything that we've done."

"I don't think I can forget what I saw."

"No. Don't forget it. I know Oya was deeply disturbed by the result, but you — you watched."

They didn't say anything to each other for a while, just stood there looking out at the stuck sun, never able to sink beneath the ground and never allowed to rise above it. Only the little moon slowly moving across the sky marked the passage of time. She looked at her long wiry arms still covered in colorless down with a sprinkling of small yellow feathers, even though everyone else had sprouted true wings already, and realized that was how she felt: stuck between grounded and airborne. She also realized she was tipsy. "When will I be able to fly?" The question astounded her.

He must have taken the change of subject as an invitation, because he hopped over the dividing terraces and landed on her rail. *Too close!* On the other hand, she got a good look at him and was immediately overcome by his appearance. His vaguely Asian features also made her miss her brothers, her family, even her claustrophobic world.

"Maybe in another month. You're developing at a more normal pace than the others. I imagine much like the first *Homo sapiens aves* on Luna."

"I was told by a crow — a Carica — that I look somewhat Vanacan, and now, looking at you, I can see why."

"You do. I'll be interested to see what you look like when your yellow plumage comes out. I think you'll be quite attractive. When did you meet a Carica?"

Her stomach fluttered at the compliment. Xing now understood something about the idiotic, involuntary way guys stared at a nice pair of breasts. It was the exact same way she ogled the provocative color of his wings. She also better understood that stupid soap opera.

"Long story." She tried to sound cool and cross, making an effort to look at his face and not his wings. "But I met him before you arrived on our ship. I believe he died when our commander destroyed the Augur's shrine. I hope not, though."

His crest fanned out, and she realized that she needed to investigate what the repertoire of avian body language meant. "You understand why I had to bite him then, even if you find the method unseemly?"

"Yes," she said, in spite of reservations. Her bottom lip began to tremble, and she stopped it with a swig from the bottle. "I tried to stop him myself, but he locked me out. I'll tell our new leaders all of that when they ask. I'll also edit your method somewhat. I know you helped us out up there."

"Thank you." His crest went limp again. "Your new leaders are fools, by the way. I've been watching them."

"They've already been chosen?" She knew some of the passengers had been politicians back in Sol. Once thawed, they would take up the old trade.

"It seems that way. I can't really understand all that they're saying, but it's clear that instead of preparing for battle, they're looking for someone to blame."

"It will be Oya, without a doubt. Possibly me when they discover I was in contact with your M.I. Davoli reacted badly to that bit of information. They will too."

"Did the Augur speak to you?" He seemed surprised by this.

"Yeah."

"What did it say?"

"I'm sorry, but that's for Oya and the captain to hear."

He opened his mouth to speak, but thought better of it. "I understand," he said, a bit too coolly. He was curious. The M.I. was a deity to these harpies.

"I'm sorry. If she wants to tell you that's fine. I just — I think they need to hear it first."

"I should go find Oya." He turned to leave.

"Wait."

"Yes?"

She sighed. "They're going to blame you too. You should be aware of that."

His crest flitted and his eyes told her it was a form of acknowledgment. He understood. She nodded back and he leapt out into the sunset.

Xing took another drink and let her head whirl for a while. Besides her new anatomy, she no longer had the curators to scrub her system of the alcohol. She opened up another lightscreen above her lap, and set a few search hounds loose within the local archives to sift for information on the development of the first harpies on Earth's moon. The initial records she found were murky at best. The practice of biohacking was highly illegal, and all data shared by those involved was deliberately shrouded in mystery.

She wasn't really paying attention. She wanted the data and the wine. She wanted to get drunk.

— «» —

Kiwi had lost all track of time. There was nothing in the world except for the pillow she cleaved into, the cold room that surrounded her, and the debilitating loneliness within. It wasn't even her room. She could never go back to her room, to her home. Her mother was dead, her brother was captured or… No, she refused to allow doubt to creep in. She *knew* her brother, and he would never side with some cybernetic monsters from Earth. That's what everyone said though, that they were being invaded by half-men with bizarre mechanical parts that gave them powers far beyond normal humans, and that her brother had something to do with it. They said their very touch was electric. The image of Inirigua being tortured by such things made her want to bury herself in the sweaty cushion and die. But the gashes that Majasora had inflicted to her head prevented her from even that.

"Hey, Kiwi." The abrupt intrusion into her solitary wallowing startled her, but she recognized the soft warble so she didn't look up.

"Leave me alone," she mumbled into her pillow.

"I have news about your brother."

This roused her. She looked up and saw a dark form perched at the foot of her bed, raven wings hungrily absorbing all of the light in the room. Only his face was luminous. His large blue eyes and impish grin shone like the sun in the blackness of space. Lonanhorak, her only friend in the world, the boy she had had a silly crush on back when things were simple and happy.

His smile grew blinding as if proud that he was able to provoke a reaction out of her, and he said, "My father says they've detected the transport he took from Vanacan returning to the planet, all the way on the other side of the world. It's damaged so maybe he escaped from them."

She sat up, squinting, still hugging her pillow. "But why doesn't he just come back here? Do you think he's secretly working with them?"

His wind-tousled crest lay flat on his head. "I don't know. You know my family doesn't think so, which is why you're still here, but maybe he is and we've got them all wrong." He pulled out a bowl of steamed *jaibaguami* dumplings from under his left wing and handed it to her. "Oh, and my mother says you should eat."

"I don't know what to think anymore." She felt the tears coming again. Talking about it out loud only made her feel worse. Instead, she focused on the dumplings, skewering one with a claw and popping it into her mouth whole. Instantly, she realized she was starving.

"Hey, you probably haven't noticed, being cooped up in here for days, hiding from the world, but your wings have come out." He plopped down beside her. "You actually look normal now."

Of course she'd noticed. She just didn't care. "I'm not hiding!" she muttered with her mouth full. "I'm healing from my fight with Majasora!"

"You look okay to me."

"I'm not! My new feathers must be covering up my wounds. They're ghastly!"

"I like them. Your feathers that is, not your wounds. They're black like mine, only with red tips. The color-code warning for venom."

"My mood must have colored them," she said tartly, but glanced at the large mirror in the room, the first time she'd seen herself in days. She did look normal, more Carica than Vanacan, a girl with dark sweeping eyes, red from sobbing.

"Or maybe you're just a purist at heart, showing respect for ol' grandfather Archaeopteryx."

"I'm lost, Lonanhorak, and I'm scared. I can't stay in this room forever, but I'm afraid Majasora will try to get me." She shoveled another dumpling in her mouth, trying to stop herself from admitting any more shameful thoughts.

"You held your own against her before, and you were flightless. Now that you finally have your wings, you can take her. I'll teach you to fly."

"Thank you." She looked up at him, and knew right there and then, like in her mother's story about Tianlongmu, that she would be bound to this boy for the rest of her life. "But what I really need is to find out about my brother. I feel like I can't move forward if I don't know the truth about him. What if I fight Majasora and he really is the enemy?"

They sat there, quietly, downcast, letting the enormous question hang in the air. She emptied the bowl of dumplings and ached for more.

"The Augur would know," he sang pensively, his messy crest rising and dropping slowly. "You should try asking it, although it's never spoken to anyone I know."

"It used to speak to my mother." Kiwi's mind flew to her last conversation with her mother, and wished she hadn't been so snarky. "But it's been destroyed by the Hominocracy."

"My father doesn't think so. He said the Augur can't ever be killed, because it's not really alive. It'll just reboot itself or something. He said it's always watching over us, and just because we don't understand its plans doesn't mean it doesn't care." He pulled her off the bed. "Come on, let me show you something. And don't make any noise. My mother hates it when I play around with the thing."

They left the room and padded around Lonanhorak's large family apartment like shadows, careful not to let their toe-talons click nosily on the marble floor. The house was modestly adorned compared to the opulence of the Palace, but Kiwi decided she liked the clean lines and modern design. Maybe she had inherited her father's aesthetic taste along with his gloomy plumage. She had always thought that the Vanacan tried to cram too much history into their decor with overwhelming, and sometimes, tacky results. They passed a large window and Kiwi's heart sank when she saw the pagoda of the Soaring Palace of Morning, still festooned with the lights from the festival, dreamily float by. She was so close to it. The dignitary district, where Lonanhorak lived, always hovered close to the Palace. She could literally leap out of the window and glide to her home on one strong wing beat.

He grabbed her claw and swept her into his family's parlor. They stopped before an odd computer terminal. It had three large screens and a central control console, but it didn't look like any personal computer she'd ever seen.

"What is this thing?"

"It's called an auspice platform. Every Carica house has one. It's supposed to detect a Machine Intelligence moving through the Astronet, and then it directs your messages toward it. You could say we petition the Augur with it. My family doesn't use it very much, only on the six major feast days of the lunar year, but my mother maintains it out of tradition."

She examined the mundane-looking prayer processor with well-practiced Vanacan skepticism. "Is this for real, or is it something fake that all of you Carica have bought into?"

"It *should* be real. It's based on the device developed by the programmers aboard the *Roc's Egg* to make reports to the M.I. But like I said before, everyone talks into it, but no one's ever gotten a reply, at least not since we've been on this planet."

"Turn it on," she twittered nervously, hopping around the boy. Despite herself, excitement built in her belly.

Lonanhorak fiddled with the console, and it quickly hummed to life. Each screen flickered on, displaying something different. One was scrolling with arcane source code; the other two showed a web of intersecting lines, each line capped by a flashing red, blue or black dot. One was less intricate than the other. She knew enough to know these were graphic representations of the Vanacan's network and Quetzalcoatl's larger network.

"What is that?" she asked pointing to a blinking green dot within the Vanacan system.

"Supposedly that's the Machine Intelligence moving within our network. That's got to be the Augur. My father was right. It survived!"

"What do we do now?"

He highlighted the dot. "Just speak to it or type in a message, and the platform will send it to its location."

She took a step back and apprehensively looked at Lonanhorak. "This is stupid."

"Maybe, but it got you out of bed, so at least my plan worked," he said, with that brilliant smile of his.

She leaned in and sang as clearly as possible, given the quiver in her voice, "I can see you moving around out there. I need to talk to you. I've got questions that only you can answer."

"I'm working on a query at the moment," it said.

Lonanhorak grabbed her and shook her excitedly! "It spoke to you? I grew up talking to this useless thing, and it never said anything to me! And you? It speaks to you on the first try!"

"Quiet. It knows I'm important," she shushed Lonanhorak and then spoke louder to the machine. "I'm Cayaguey's daughter and I really need your help." The significance of this suddenly made their little game all the more crucial.

"I'm working on a query at the moment."

"This is important, damn it! You can't just brush me off!"

"I'm sorry, Cayaguey's daughter, but I'm working on a query at the moment."

"Does the Augur normally sound like an idiot computer?" Lonanhorak asked, dubiously checking the machine for problems.

"No, it sounds just like a person," she chirped with frustration. She had allowed herself to get excited about the possibility of getting help from the most powerful mind on the planet, and now this... "Maybe it was damaged by the attack?"

Lonanhorak patted her new wing reassuringly and leaned into the auspice. "What query are you working on now?" Lonanhorak asked shyly.

"I'm trying to answer the question of how the first Homo sapiens aves *arose on Luna."*

"Who cares about that?" This was too much for Kiwi. The Augur's indifference, its repetitive nonsense — she wanted to slam her fist into one of the acrylic screens and shake some sense into it. "We're under attack — *you* were just attacked, and you're wasting time on ancient history?"

"I have not been attacked."

Lonanhorak grabbed her by the crook of her arm-wing and pulled her back slowly. "Um, Kiwi, I don't think this is the Augur," he whispered in her ear.

"Identify yourself?" she shrieked, angrily shrugging off her friend.

"I am an Alpha-Chiang Search Hound employed by Information Officer Xing Diwa of the HS Hurricane.*"*

"It's a Hominocracy M.I.! Turn it off! Turn it off!"

"No, wait." She pushed Lonanhorak away from the auspice before he could hit the power button. "Perhaps we can help each other. If I assist you in answering your question, can I speak to this Xingdiwa?"

"I'm in constant lightscreen communication with her. I can act as a relay if you wish, but I will require free and open access to your network."

As the Clan Chief's daughter, she had privileged access to her mother's collection, but not to anything vital. "I will give you my access code. It isn't super high clearance. It's intended for educational purposes, but if answering your history question is all that you're really interested in, then it should be enough. It'll give you permission to a lot more information than what's on our public databases."

"Kiwi, please don't do this. The thing could be trying to crash our systems! This could be a cyber-attack!"

"Lonanhorak, turn around so I can type in my password, or leave if you don't want to be blamed for this, but I *need* to do this. Getting access to some library is not going to crash civilization. Please."

He turned around, and she was glad that he didn't abandon her. She quickly typed L-O-N-A-N-H-O-R-A-K into the keypad.

"Thank you for granting me admission to the Inner Vanacan Archives. Information Officer Xing Diwa has been notified of your request."

"Who the hell is this?" Suddenly, a woman appeared on the central auspice screen, and to Kiwi's complete surprise, she didn't look like a cybernetic nightmare at all. She looked Vanacan, only with bright yellow feathers instead of red and — much like Kiwi herself had looked not that long ago — she had small underdeveloped wings locked in the middle stages of fledging. "If you're some kind of harpy hacker, revealing yourself wasn't a smart move. I just isolated you from our network."

The woman's voice was flat and slurred at the same time, as if she had a serious speech impediment, and Kiwi had trouble making out her crude Cantabile. *And hacker?* What did this have to do with genome coding ... or did she mean the other kind of hacker? "I just want to know about Inirigua? Is he alive? Is he safe?"

"Or are you one of those media hawks? I know all about you. I've been watching your T.V."

"I'm not..." She choked. Confronted with the real enemy, her mind froze. She couldn't tell her who she really was. A shrewd enemy would try to exploit that.

The woman stared at her for what felt like a long time, and then her expression changed, softened. Maybe she recognized a fellow flightless throwback on the other side of the world. "My God, you're just a kid, a little girl!"

"I'm older than I seem," Kiwi said in one icy glissando. A familiar anger welled up in her. She was used to being mocked, but not from someone who looked worse off than she was. She had wings now, damn it!

"And you're Carica, like Snaca!"

"Yes, I'm Carica," she half-lied. "I'm the tech-hacker known as Kiwi, but I don't want to crack your systems or cause you any harm. I just want information about your hostage, Inirigua."

The woman made a yapping noise, that Kiwi realized was unmelodic, bitter laughter, and then said, "He's not our hostage. Hell, I just had a somewhat pleasant conversation with him about an hour ago. I blame him for this!" She flapped her small wings comically.

This confused Kiwi. She didn't know what to make of it, or if she had even understood the woman right. Her brother *worked* with them, not because he wanted to be an immortal cyborg, like Majasora said, but because he was slowly turning them into avian humans?

"Look, kid, maybe I shouldn't be talking to you while I'm drunk. If you want something to tell your little hacker friends, tell them that we're not here to destroy you. Look—" she flapped her wings again "—we're becoming you! And thanks for giving me access to your databases. I promise I won't damage your systems. I just need information to figure out how we're going to proceed. We're kind of stuck here with you." The woman cut the connection.

Kiwi and Lonanhorak stood there, blinking.

"That whole thing was recorded," he said, with a dazed look in his eyes. "In case you want to show it to, you know, anyone."

Kiwi didn't reply immediately. She stood there, regretting that she hadn't given the drunk, yellow bird a message for her brother. At least she knew he was still alive and not being tormented by mechanical monsters. "I need to show this to Jujoquete."

Chapter 31

Luna – 2098 A.D.

As the Gala neared, people from across the moon flocked to LA2, lugging their faux, multicolored wings with them. The whole crater buzzed with pre-celebration excitement. Groups of fliers were now a common sight from the terrace, as professional teams from the different settlements practiced or held expo events. And after a while, Osala learned to identify the many phenotypes of fliers: flexwings, gelfoils, rigidwings, servodeltas, and long-gulls.

The loft became a darker microcosm to the larger events of LA2. As the weeks went by, Esther worked out in Zu's gym with the focus of someone training for a triathlon. The safe house started to look more and more like a crack house, or a malaria tent clinic, as friends and sycophants of the Transhumanist movement — some as young as fourteen — came to receive this primeval communion. Now, there were a dozen shaking, groaning bodies scattered throughout the small apartment, most lying on moist sheets spread on the hard floor. Osala found that she couldn't leave Esther despite her betrayal, not yet, so she grudgingly took on the role of field doctor in order to mitigate any complications.

On one particularly bad night, her own fatigue mixing with the surrounding delirium, she sat near a black boy of American descent, stroking his head with a cool cloth. She wondered if her son would've looked like this. Would she have approved of this transformation? Would she have taken him to Chandeleur from time to time to see the sky?

Osala finally broke down and really cried. It was an eruption of all the dark thoughts and guilt she had been trying to box away for months. Her reaction surprised her, but she was cursed with a great imagination and it was too easy to think of what could've been.

"Can you sing?" the boy asked, startling her. His voice sounded like the scrape of sandpaper.

"Yes, but I don't really do it much, only for my husband sometimes, and for myself." Osala felt embarrassed and wiped her tears on her sleeve. She recognized that for the first time since leaving Earth, she missed Patrick terribly. If the boy had seen her crying, he didn't let it show.

"My mother is nice singer..." His head rolled back onto the floor, eyes closed.

That tugged on Osala, and when she thought he had fallen asleep, she began to sing Etta James's *Sunday Kind of Love* as a sweet whisper in his ear — because it was the only song she could think of at the moment, and Patrick had always liked it. Up close, the boy smelled of bile and sweat.

"I'm really sick, aren't I?" he said when she was done, surprising her.

"Yes, you had an awful throat infection. For some strange reason, the retrovirus hit you harder than the rest, but we got some targeted antibiotics into you."

"Maybe it's because I messed around with the formula?" He turned to look at her. The whites of his half-closed eyes were yellowed, and his lips were dry and cracked. "I added some stuff like Zu did."

Osala checked his temperature with an app in her glasses and was relieved to see that it had dropped a few degrees since she had sat down with him. "Please don't tell me you added those awful claws to your feet," she said, giving him some water from a squeeze bulb. He grimaced as he swallowed.

"Yes, we all have. But I put in something else too... Something no one else has."

"Those things won't help you fly any faster! They're only good for one thing, and they'll get you into trouble! You're just a kid, damn it. I can't believe you're playing around with this stuff."

But hadn't she been only thirteen when she first read — what was it — Nnedi Okorafor's *Who Fears Death*, or *The Book of Phoenix*, and decided that she wanted to be a geneticist? What would she have concocted with the genomic kits these children had to play with? What had she concocted *now*, as an adult?

She did the mental checks once more and was certain that the initial changes hadn't gotten into the germ line, but they were now swapping out whole alleles. What if one or all of them had undone her careful precautions? And what about epigenetics? Even if these winged people's children were genetically typical, their hormonal system was different. How would that affect the fetuses they would carry? *Damn it, Esther should have discussed this with her first.*

"Hey," the boy said, drawing her attention back to him. "I'm not really any good at the flying. It's not my thing."

"Then for God's sake, why are you here? You almost died today! You could still have serious complications!" The boy looked a bit more alert, so Osala didn't feel too bad about admonishing him.

"Well, I *am* a biohacker," he said, and if he hadn't been so incapacitated, she was sure he'd be pounding his chest with pride. "I also lead a Transmonkey pLunk band. It's what I really love. Right now, we're nobody, but if I survive this, we're going to be famous!"

"I don't even know what that means." She dabbed the now tepid cloth on the boy's brow. His small afro was coming apart, soon to be replaced by sallow proto-feathers.

"I'm a singer in a band." He opened his mouth like a hungry hatchling, and she squeezed a few more drops of water on his tongue. "And when I played around with your sequence, I noticed that archaeopteryx was also a singer. At least, he shared a lot of the microRNAs that make songbirds sing. He was like the nightingale, the mockingbird and the skylark of the Jurassic. So, I added the bio blocks containing those microRNA molecules to my dose."

Osala couldn't help but to find it remarkable. She called up the simulation of the compact genome and displayed it on the lenses of her glasses. She thought she knew it well, but right away on chromosome one, she noticed the FOXP2 gene, which was associated with language in humans and singing in birds. There must be others she wasn't familiar with. Osala had been so focused on the abhorrent morphology of this new race of people, the serrated maw and shredding talons, and this astute and stupid teenager had found something beautiful, something redeemable, about the little feathered reptile they were all trying to emulate. She appreciated that. Almost admired it. She touched her lips to cover the creeping smile. "What's your name, kid?"

"Gabriel, but don't tell anyone. I'm thinking of changing my handle to something more memorable, like Op-Tricks or something."

She shook her head to stop herself from rolling her eyes. "Do me a favor, Gabriel, and don't change your name. Keep it the way it is, and I promise you'll appreciate it when you're older." She leaned over and kissed his damp forehead. The tender gesture surprised her, but he had earned her affection with his observation and ingenuity. "Now, rest. You've put your poor throat through a lot of trauma already. Don't try to talk."

He closed his eyes, pleased and in pain, and after a while he did fall asleep. Those non-coding songbird regulators weren't just reshaping his vocal cords into something like a bird's syrinx, but also reknitting the neurons in his basal ganglia. *Would Gabriel still be Gabriel a week from now?*

That night she had the ridiculous thought that if Victor Frankenstein had been a woman, she would have inevitably accepted and nurtured her brilliant monster, and Shelley's novel would've been very different indeed.

— «» —

In the morning, Osala pecked out a message to Patrick, telling him that she was infinitely sorry about evading his calls and that she thought about him constantly. She waited the three minutes of lag time for the response, but it never came. *Maybe he was asleep?* She didn't try to check the time on Chandeleur, afraid that it was day, and he had simply decided that she wasn't worth the bother anymore.

She made a cup of coffee and sat on a patio chair out on the terrace, her bare feet on the guardrail. She looked at her ten stubby digits and wondered what it would be like to have six switchblades instead.

Zu was out and about, and sporting the ashen fuzz of a newly hatched chick. Osala found his transformation horrifically interesting because he already had limbs, hands and feet, to begin with. She observed as his body slowly reabsorbed the pinkies and ring fingers of both hands and morphed his feet into three-toed talons; two of these toes brandished the elongated, curved spurs of a utahraptor.

A lone shadow moved around out there in the dark bottled sky, but as the pixel paint on the inside of the dome slowly simulated daybreak, she saw that it was Esther. The girl had become unquestionably beautiful. She was as tall and lean as any lunar native, but she was swathed now in the long, stiff plumage of a sparkling, blue honeycreeper, with the crest of a jay. There was something terrible about her countenance though, something deeply disturbing to a mind evolved on the planet Earth. The perfect equilibrium between reptilian, avian, and mammalian features jarred, and the wings looked too small to sustain the humanoid frame in flight, but there she was, circling in the sky. Esther had already taken to the air several times in the early mornings, each time getting better, until she soundly defeated the indignant fields of biology and physics.

"I think today is the day," Esther told Osala, as she landed on the terrace. The artificial sun had not quite come up, and the full Earth was as blue and lovely as the woman standing before her.

Osala took a photo of her with her glasses, the only evidence she would allow herself to keep of her time here.

"Today? You're not going to wait for the main event?"

"I will *be* the main event." Her green-speckled eyes gleamed wickedly. "But I think my father is getting close. All reports on the Astronet have suddenly — suspiciously — stopped. I think he's about to raid. I don't want to wait only to have him catch me."

"What do you think he'd do?" Osala gulped her already cold coffee and set the cup down on the floor next to her chair.

"Probably lock me up again and contract an entire contingent of specialists to undo all of this…" Her feathers ruffled involuntarily. "It would be interesting just to see him collaborate with the geneticists he so despises."

Osala enjoyed watching the little behavioral quirks that had coded with the DNA. "What about all the thickheaded kids in there? These changes can't easily be undone."

"They'll be fine. Now that Zu is past the worst of it, we're relocating everyone this morning. I've even got a secret location staked out for after my maiden flight. I'll go to another settlement, one not controlled by my family. You should leave, Osala. Everything is coming to a head."

"All right. I'll just make sure everyone is ready to be moved and then I'll go. Traffic will be hell if I wait until after the Gala is over anyway."

Esther smiled warmly. "I've given you so many outs, and you always find an excuse to stay a little longer."

"I care about you, Esther. I honestly don't know if it's some kind of 'baby bird' imprinting or whatever, but I want you to be okay. I can't just abandon you." She knew exactly what it was. She had projected all of the directionless maternal emotions roiling inside her onto this young woman.

Esther took Osala's hands in her scaly claws, kneading them gently. "I know what you're going to say, but… Why don't you join us? More than anyone, you've earned the right to have wings."

A part of her was enormously thankful to have been asked, and she laughed as tears ran down her face. Osala opened her mouth to speak but couldn't find the worlds. Another part of her still wanted to slap the arrogance off Esther's face. She inhaled slowly, taking in the girl's fragrance. "Esther, I'm profoundly afraid of heights."

"Okay." She released Osala's hands; her moment of gentleness had passed. Esther didn't seem angry or disappointed, she had simply switched back to business. "I really need a nap. Please make all the arrangements you need to make quickly. My father can be as cruel as he's self-righteous."

Osala checked each one of her feverish brood and cleared them all for transport. She didn't know where Zu was taking them, but it pained her to see them go, especially the boy she'd connected with. Gabriel. She gave him a warm hug and wished him luck.

When the last one was gone, she went out to sit on the balcony again and began reading the news as it scrolled across her glasses, trying not to think about what would become of these kids. A message from Patrick suddenly popped up. It read, "Please come home. I miss you, too." Osala thought her heart might shatter with joy and relief. She immediately took out her handheld and booked passage back to Earth. She had just shut her glasses off, and leaned back to watch a gaggle of vibrant fliers zoom past, when the front door crashed open.

She jumped up and saw a wild-eyed man in a steel-gray business suit standing over Esther, who was sprawled out on the yellowed mattress, not unlike the entombed archaeopteryx she'd worked on. He looked like the embodiment of every cinematic representation of Julius Cesar in the history of film.

"Esther?" He cupped his mouth with a shaky hand. "What did you do?"

Osala carefully stepped into the apartment.

Esther rose to her full height, pumped her wings and extended her feathered crest, as if to make herself seem larger to a potential enemy. "I did what you couldn't do, Dad. I made myself whole — I made myself better."

"My lord!" The man shook with rage.

"I can walk, run, and fly. Just yesterday, I dove into the forested crater and caught a rabbit with my bare feet."

He looked down, and Osala thought she saw his pupils dilate at the sight of her talons. He staggered backward and gripped the splintered doorframe to support his body.

"All the dummy corporations you set up to pay for this perversion: Morning Star, Isis, Ltd., Winged Victory, Ishtar Incorporated... All that was left was the Whore of Babylon LLC!" he said, starting in a whisper and ending in a shout.

Esther flexed her claws dramatically. "Oh, I'm not the whore of Babylon, Dad. I'm the dragon she rode in on!"

He pulled out a small hand gun. "Did you think I wouldn't find out about this, Esther?"

"Dad, put the gun away. I *wanted* you here. I really did. I hoped you would see me off, or try to stop me, or do something, anything to show you cared. I still love you."

He trembled with anger and panic. He looked down at the gun as if seeing it for the first time. "Honey, listen to me. I get it. I understand you did this as some form of extreme rebellion against my moral objections to a genetic solution for your problem. I blame no one but myself, but you're not thinking ahead. You're going to deeply regret this when you're older and wiser. You're only hurting yourself in trying to show me up.

"I promise that I got the message loud and clear. I will look into the synthetic stem cells you wanted me to, sweetheart. Damn the church! Just please, let me help you."

"It's too late. It might have started out like that, but it's become something more now." Esther crept slowly to the terrace. "The changes are also psychological. I'm a different person, an entirely different animal now. I don't know who I am yet, but for the first time in my entire life, I don't hate myself."

The man, Andrew Aguilera-Smeltzer, the most powerful man in the sky, was crying now. The gun in his hand shook violently. "Stop!" he screamed. "You don't want to live like this."

Something stirred in Osala Valette. She swallowed hard and moved between them. "Sir, put the gun away. She hasn't hurt anyone." *Hadn't she?*

He scowled at her, registering her presence for the first time. "Who the fuck are you?"

"She's a friend, Dad. She's been taking care of me."

"What kind of a friend sits by while you turn yourself into an abomination!"

Osala flushed. "What kind of father locks up his disabled daughter in an orbiting cage in the name of her safety?"

Andrew aimed his gun at Osala. "*Her safety*? I was protecting everyone else. House arrest was all I could manage with the judge after the biohacking scandal! Her mother left after that, but I tried to keep my child happy, while protecting the children of others!"

"Dad, I am happy." Esther threw herself over the ledge.

Esther's father roared like a beast and ran out onto the terrace. He leaned over the balcony and watched helplessly as his daughter fell for a few meters, then spread her wings and rose on a current of warm air. The man dropped the weapon and sobbed.

Osala stayed only long enough to watch Esther soar with the other fliers — and surpass them — then she snuck out of the loft and disappeared into the shoving, awed mass of spectators. That emptiness in her core had finally filled.

Chapter 32

Quetzalcoatl - 2323 A.D.

Oya overslept. She had asked her home computer to begin playing Frank Ocean's *2031* album thirty minutes before her meeting with the captain, but she had snoozed through most of the tracks. She didn't think she would sleep at all, but exhaustion had eventually beat her into unconsciousness.

So, a little after three hours since their arrival, she rushed to the island's control tower. She looked up as her long strides devoured the distance. Her destination looked like an old air traffic control tower at the center of the floating structure. Part of her wanted to spring into the air and fly up to it, but she wasn't sure if her wings were ready, so Oya made like a roadrunner, and dashed into the lift at the base of the tower.

The captain and Xing were already there, surrounded by large lightscreens, displaying maps and charts of the planet with flashing icons for each of the settlements, as well as status reports for the different utilities of their new home. The place looked a bit like an orbital station's control room or their ship's bridge.

"Sorry I'm late, Captain," she said, standing at attention at the center of the room. She dreaded this conversation. *How much should she admit? How much did they* need *to know?*

"At ease, Valette." He waved a wing awkwardly, not used to the broad appendage. "I'm no longer the captain of anything. I just handed over command to the administrative council and convinced them that I could best serve the colony as station manager. Please, call me Hersh."

It was weird being so casual with the captain, so she simply nodded, flicking her own crest involuntarily.

"I've chosen Diwa here as my deputy, and they approved the position." He pinched the bridge of his nose, nearly taking out an eye with a claw, and said, "This constant hi-def, prismatic vision is giving me a damned migraine."

For a fleeting instant, Oya wanted to ask what her new charge would be, but then she thought about it and knew the council would never trust her with a high responsibility, high clearance position. She would be fortunate if they allowed her a job in agriculture.

"Oya, before we start telling our horror stories," Xing said, "you should take a look at this." She pointed at a map of the planet with slashes of red, blue and black all converging on their yellow dot.

"They found us already." All self-pity left Oya.

"Yes, and a combined fleet is floating some distance away. There's no place on this planet that they can't get to in a matter of minutes, but they're taking their time, because, I believe, they're afraid of our superior technology. Still, they'll move on us eventually."

Oya watched the rain of trajectories slowly closing in on her island. "Our technology isn't that superior anymore. Would we be able to repel such a force now?"

Xing shrugged, palms up. She had nothing.

"I thought the Carica weren't warriors," Oya asked, still studying the display.

Xing looked askance at Hersh, and Oya noticed that her friend looked terrible, almost hungover.

"They've found great motivation," their former captain said soberly. "I think it's time we pooled our experience and knowledge, and hopefully we can come up with a solution."

Hershkovitz sat in a chair, went to cross his arm-wings, and then decided to cross his legs instead. The deadly talons lying on his knee gave an edge to his relaxed pose. His tale began back in the haze of the Culling when, on his last tour on Mars, he killed many harpies, including very young children. He spoke about losing his friend and pilot with great reverence, and Oya suspected there was more to that relationship.

She couldn't remember the name of the woman he'd been crying about on the ship and he didn't say it now, but she suspected they were one and the same. He talked slowly as if confronting those memories for the first time in a long time.

He mentioned an encounter with the M.I. responsible for relocating the harpies out of the Sol system and how it argued on his behalf. He divulged what it was like to be physically crippled for years, until the medical curators fixed his spine, and psychologically crippled, until the memory dumps cleared his mind.

He jumped to his encounter with Cayaguey and how the very memory dumps that had kept him sane had also impaired his judgment in dealing with the leader. After the attack, during his transformation, all those memories had resurfaced.

Hersh finally stopped talking, but continued to stare out at nothing, and it took Oya a moment to realize he was done with recounting his story, even as it haunted him.

"The Carica have examined the footage of the cap — of Hersh's meeting with the Clan Chief, and they recognized him. That's what's spurred them to war," Xing added. "It's all over their news."

"My God, I'm their Hitler," Hersh whispered to himself, and Oya feared he would slip into fits of delirium like he had on the ship.

"Let me go next. My report is shorter, but it ties all of this together." Xing's account was indeed shorter, but by far the strangest. She expressed the horror of being remote controlled by the Augur, apparently the same Machine Intelligence that had long ago spared Hersh's life. She mentioned that it had handpicked both Hersh and Oya to be part of this expedition because, according to its calculus, they would unite the harpies of Quetzalcoatl against some future extinction event. She described Davoli's poor reaction to her report and the destruction of the M.I. shrine. She ended with the brief and half-remembered conversation with a very young hacker who had inquired about Inirigua's safety.

"I could've ended up on another ship, bound for another star, and that thing *arranged* to have me here." Oya slammed her fist into a control panel, making the lightscreens sputter. She had trouble processing that; she had barely heard the rest of Xing's story.

"So the M.I. is dead?" Hersh asked, returning to the present.

"Who knows with these things. It could have migrated to other servers on the planet or had backups of itself somewhere. I don't think it was too concerned with self-preservation though. It told me it had taken its own destruction into consideration, and besides, it was only a sub-persona. The original intelligence is still moving away from here. It's probably safe to assume the version I spoke to is gone one way or another."

Oya shook her head, trying to throw off the sense of powerlessness that had descended over her. Whatever she felt, Xing must feel infinitely worse. At least Oya's blunders were entirely her own. "Is that why you created a floating outpost instead of a conventional one, you know, on the ground? Because the M.I. influenced you? I've been meaning to ask you about it since I saw it."

"Um, I really don't know." Xing looked down, and, for a second, she appeared on the verge of tears. Under her eyes were dark circles. "I was born and raised in a place like this on Venus. I thought I was drawing on nostalgia for its design, but I honestly can't say for sure that it wasn't the M.I.'s will. It's a horrible feeling, not being able to trust yourself."

"Believe me, Xing, I understand." Hersh stood up and popped a wing in Oya's direction. "I can see why it chose me. My presence *has*, in effect, united the clans, but I fail to see the significance of Valette here."

Sweat dampened Oya's brow. Her gaze jerked from Hersh to Xing.

"Yeah, that one I can't figure out." Xing sat, defeated by the elusive information. She rubbed her eyes with a downy forearm. "No offense, Oya, but I combed through your bio, there's nothing out of the ordinary there. You weren't even alive when the harpies were in the Sol system."

"Is there something you're not telling us?" Hersh frowned at her, and instantly he was her captain again.

Oya Valette knew precisely why the M.I. had chosen her. The reason why might now be encoded in the very design of their yellow plumage. Her pulse raced. The claw she'd so defiantly used to assault the console quivered. She was afraid to confess the truth. These were her only allies in Beta Hydri, besides Inirigua. Would they reject her when they learned that her grandmother was at the root of all their misery?

"You *know* why," Hersh said, studying her with his newly focused, raptorial eyes. "You need to tell us right now."

"Xing—" Oya found that she couldn't form the words. Her lips, her throat, were paralyzed with fear. "Do we have access to any local archives?"

"Yes, all the public ones, and — thanks to that girl I mentioned — I've got a hound inside the extensive private archive of Vanacan."

"Please do a search on the origins of the harpies."

"Just tell us, Valette." Hersh's voice grew harder.

But Xing made another lightscreen appear in the room. "I *have* been researching that, more like deep drilling for it. There isn't a lot of concrete data, even in the private collection, as transgenic experimentation was illegal and extremely clandestine." She called up a series of references her hounds had already cobbled together. "All anyone knows for sure is that a group of biohackers on Luna were able to merge archaeopteryx genetics with human genetics. Two individuals, in particular, Merlin and Prometheus — these are aliases, of course — show up in a lot of early accounts.

"Macu scholars are pretty certain that Merlin was the heiress of a large lunar financial empire. The other one remains unidentified. After this, the trend spread like wildfire across the pre-Hominocracy solar system."

"Search all the data you've collected for any mention of Avant Genomics."

Xing searched on, caught up in the mystery.

"For God's sake, Oya, just tell us what you know!" Hersh shouted at her. He was red-faced and pacing behind Xing, his eyes darting from the lightscreen to Oya.

Oya couldn't form the words. Her bottom lip trembled. She was more afraid now than she had ever been in her life.

Waiting for Xing to correlate the data made her exploits on Jupiter look like a holiday jaunt. She looked away from the screen and down at her talons.

"Only one mention, just an old editorial," Xing said. "A scientist speculating on whether these hackers had the expertise to pull off such an ambitious project on their own or if they had secret help from Avant Genomics, who at the time was a premier genetics firm and held the partial prints of the archaeopteryx genome." Without prompting, Xing looked up Avant Genomics, narrowing down her search to the dawn of the harpies.

Hersh was now transfixed by the holographic screen. "Valette," he said. The word came out flat and devoid of emotion.

At first Oya thought he was addressing her, but then she glanced up at the screen and saw her *gwan man man*'s face, as a much younger woman, brown curly hair tied back in a professional bun. Below the photo it read: "Osala Valette, Ph.D., Director, Chandeleur facility."

"What the fuck is this?" Hersh yelled at her. Oya wondered if he knew that his jagged teeth were bared.

"This is my grandmother." The knot in her throat threatened to choke her. "She created *Homo sapiens aves*, or helped create them. I had no idea until the other day. I swear." She fished out the small warbler feather from her pocket, the task made much more difficult between her claws and her nerves. "There's a message hiding within the DNA of this feather stating as much."

No one moved. She focused on the feather, not wanting to look them in the eye. The yellow was now effervescent, shining like the flame of a candle, and she realized that this was the first time she had really looked at it with her new bird-like vision. This is what the sunny warblers looked like to each other.

"Okay." Hersh started pacing the control room. "Oya, I know it's not your fault. You didn't know, and even if you did, you hadn't even been born yet," her former captain said, and she suspected it was more to himself than to her.

"I—" She looked down at her little feather. She should tell them the whole truth. Hersh had admitted to killing children... She owed him equal honesty. "I shut down the curators. It's my fault we're — like this."

She looked up. Xing and Hersh looked confused, hurt. Then something slowly changed in their expression. They approached her with mindless, predatory scowls. She wouldn't fight them. They would either accept the hollow bones in her closet, as she had accepted Hersh's, or they would rip her apart. Her grandmother had created this, but Oya had inflicted it upon them. She accepted their punishment.

"Why?" Xing asked, as reason caught up with her saurian impulse. The captain — Hersh — stood over her with clenched fists.

Oya forced herself to look him in the eye. "Our curators were killing them."

Hersh sagged. He turned and walked out onto the narrow observation deck that surrounded the bulb-shaped control room. The two newly avian women stood there for a moment longer, and then they both looked outside and saw Hersh leaning on the rail just staring out at the salmon-colored sky.

"Xing, I swear to you, I had no other choice."

"I believe you, but I need time to digest this," Xing said, shrinking away from Oya. "My God, Oya, you should've told me. Of all the people on the ship. I was awake. You should've trusted me."

Oya nodded tersely. What could she say? That she was really sick from the virus, that she was desperate? She tried to reach out for Xing, but she pulled away. So, Oya went out to join her old captain. She didn't say anything, just rested on the banister and watched yellow-feathered people run this way and that, going about the business of setting up a colony. Nobody used their wings for anything other than clumsy arms.

"In Vanacan, everyone flew, each individual building hung in the air, not connected by anything more tangible than imitation gravity," he said, almost reading her mind. "Have you used your wings yet?"

"No, not yet."

"The council is going to question us — officially — in that building there." He motioned toward the boxy auditorium with a nod. "I've got half a mind to jump off this observation deck and glide down there."

"I think you'd make quite an impression, whether you floated in gracefully or fell to your death."

"Yes, I would." He laughed sourly. His neck and shoulders tightened with anger. "Thank you for telling me it was you. It doesn't change our predicament, but at least — you did it to save lives. At the end of the day, I can't argue with that."

Oya took in the island with her enriched vision. When this council stripped her of any status, she would focus on planting trees. Once the landscaping was done — swaying palms, effervescent hibiscuses, green grasses and creeping bougainvillea... The place would look more like a tropical resort than a military base. She thought again of her grandmother's gradual re-greening of Chandeleur. She would at least have meaningful work. Then Oya's attention moved to the clouds slowly rolling in from the planet's nightside. They were ominous and swollen with rain.

"We'll be besieged soon," Hersh said, noticing the same dark billows. "It was easy before to pretend to be young with large tracts of memory gone from my mind, but now I just feel old and feeble. I can't fight another war."

"A stubborn old woman, who refused to admit curators into her withering body, once told me that old age wasn't a disease."

Hersh grunted. "What happened to her?"

"She died contentedly, after having saved an island full of little yellow birds."

He said nothing, just watched the sky leisurely turn cold and black.

Oya pressed on. "Maybe there's something we can do? The M.I. said the two of us are important. Hell, it went to great pains just to get us here, and Xing thinks it wants this colony to succeed."

"I wouldn't put too much stock in this M.I. Its intellect may be orders of magnitude beyond ours, but it isn't infallible. And it doesn't understand the way we think any more than we understand what's going on inside the head of a frog."

"You need to do something, sir. You're our leader."

"Not anymore," he said, shaking his head. "Right now, I need to figure out how I'm going to look myself in the mirror."

"Have you looked?"

He glared at her, crest slicked back.

"Cayaguey told me that, for a brief moment, she had really considered allowing us to stay and become part of this planet's cultural ecosystem, but that the brash Captain Anton Hershkovitz failed to show the proper respect and humility. How about you let old, battle-weary Hersh have a go? I'll wager he'd get better results." She patted his shoulder.

He relaxed. "Come on, let's get inside. It's going to pour soon."

Oya followed him back into the command station. She wanted to shake some sense into him, but there was nothing he could do in his maudlin state.

"Xing," he said, once inside, "if I wanted to speak to the approaching fleet, and their policymakers back home, how could I do it?"

Xing just sat there blinking for a moment. Clearly she was still working through Oya's secret. "Ah, there are cameras and sensors all over the deck, that's how we interface with the computers now. Um, a live message wouldn't do, since our own people will cut you off immediately, but I could record you speaking and post it to the Astronet, and then push it out to everyone as a priority message."

"Okay, get cameras on me at all times. I don't know what I'm going to say, but I want to be able to record and send the second inspiration hits me." He turned to Oya and nodded, a ghost of a smile on his face. "Also, I want you to record each of our sessions with the council and attach it to the message. I want full transparency moving forward with our fellow raptors."

Xing worked furiously, claws on lightkeys. "Give me a verbal signal that will start the recording and initiate the message. One word will do, something you don't say often so as not to trigger the whole thing prematurely."

Hersh thought about it for a long time, and then shrugged, and said, "How about 'sorry'?"

Chapter 33

Oya left the tower feeling more alone than ever. The colonists, these new leaders, were going to come after her. And, even worse, the two people she trusted no longer trusted her. She couldn't shake the way their looks turned ugly when they learned the truth and she couldn't blame them. She'd turned them into something not-quite human. Had she come all these many light years only to be alone, quarantined from everyone else?

The sight of Inirigua standing out in the light rain like an eidolon, waiting for her, sent a current of hope through her whole body. He would understand how she felt. What was it that she had told him when they were trapped on the *Hurricane? It's just you and me in this entire solar system…* That was truer now than ever before. She ran to him.

"What's going on?" he asked, quickly closing the gap between them.

"The civilian council is going to question the captain and Xing, and they want to question me afterward. I think they're trying to build a case against me or something. Otherwise they would question me first, right?"

His eyes narrowed. "What's the worst thing that can happen?"

"I don't know. It's not like they can send me back to Earth. They might bring back public shunning though."

"Have you flown yet?"

"No. I haven't had time." Oya flapped her bright yellow wings and watched the water spray off of them. They were light, airy and, aside from getting in the way sometimes, they felt completely natural. "Are they fully grown now?"

"You look mature to me."

"*Mature?*" She remembered what Hersh had said about feeling old. She didn't feel old. Not when she was with Inirigua.

She noticed now, in the little cues in his body language, in the timbre of his voice, in the unbearable scarlet of his plumage, that he was sexually attracted to her. *The signs were always there*, she thought, but she had been blind to them. She knew abstractly that he'd been signaling his intense interest since day one, but now … it was as if a veil had been lifted from her eyes. Suddenly, the heated exchange between his mother and him made more sense. He wasn't advocating for her, he was justifying his romantic intentions. Hell, he had even called her "my love" when she was fever stricken. Oya had brushed off all the clues, but now they flashed at her in vivid sound and color.

"Come fly with me." He turned and walked toward the edge of the hovering island.

"In this rain?"

"This is nothing. The natural oils in your feathers will keep the water off."

"The council will call me in soon. I don't want it to seem like I'm hiding something or running away." In spite of her objections, she followed him. A few days ago, the thought of holding him, kissing him, had been comparable to embracing a komodo dragon, but now, even his walk, that long, confident gait, enticed her.

"The council and their punishment will still be here in a few hours. If the united clans attack — *when* they attack — you should know how to handle yourself in the sky." He sang his challenge without looking back at her.

"You know I can handle myself in the air." She stopped by his side. It was strange, everything he said was practical advice, literal truth, but the tone of his voice sounded full of innuendo; it was an amoroso song. When had the shift in perception happened? The only parallel she could even think of was waking up one summer morning when she was thirteen and finding suddenly that the annoying, older boy who lived next door was, in fact, incredibly attractive.

"I guarantee you, it'll be different this time. You've got your whole life to be a scapegoat, Oya. Learn what it's like to be an eagle before it's too late." He jumped. She tracked him as he flew through the crepuscular forest. His primaries radiated every hue of red imaginable, from roseate to wine, and on to even stranger shades of red she didn't have names for. And then, when he had gotten too far away for her to bear, she leapt after him.

He was right, of course. The experience now was totally different. She beat her wings hard, trying desperately not to fall — or control her fall — until she realized she was flying. It was raw and ungainly, but it was extremely effortless compared to flying with the synthetic airfoils. Her body was now built for this, finding and surfing on thermals was organic, instinctual. She wasn't short of breath and the antimatter bombs going off in her chest were not from exertion, but from excitement. She bodysurfed on the corpulent air currents that skimmed the blue tree tops.

Inirigua came up behind her. "Don't overdo it. There is no proper technique, no perfect style. Just get to know your body and the air that moves around it. Enjoy yourself." Then he began to sing. His language, already lyrical, made the transition from speech to song imperceptible. He belted *Searching for Motion* a capella, and even though she'd heard it a million times, she couldn't imagine anyone else singing the song.

His voice, and the feel of the wind and rain caressing her skin, enticed her. She jackknifed her wings and playfully sped past him. They indulged in aerobatic displays; there was something unmistakably erotic about it. She noticed a large river below that flowed like molten gold. Oya forgot about the investigation waiting for her and the looming attack. The cool breeze carried her and the tang of alien vegetation with equal gusto. She could see the dust of spores wafting up from the anemone-like trees, and something else, a shadow lurking in the reproductive mist.

"What is that?" she asked, and immediately regretted interrupting his song.

"That's your prey. Go get it."

Her mouth crooked into a smile. Then she took a deep, invigorating breath, and shot toward it. Oya zeroed in on the moving form with her heightened vision; it practically glowed in the dark. She could tell it was another version of the pervasive airborne crustacean that dominated this planet. This one looked like a meter-long flying lobster, grazing on the spores. The thing noticed her and tried to buzz away. Oya let 150 million years of borrowed evolution take over, and it was archaeopteryx versus giant dragonfly all over again. The thing flew wildly on gossamer wings and jets of methane. Oya managed to stay on it. The creature was capable of impossible hairpin turns, but this feathered dinosaur had experience in air-to-air combat. Seconds later, she was on it. She opened her wings like a parachute, let her legs whip forward, and snatched the alien lobster with her talons. She heard a crack as she pierced its chitinous exoskeleton.

Oya landed on the soggy soil, panting, proud, and exhilarated. She released her kill. This one hunt had achieved what all her failed marriages could not. It was as if the anesthetizing cloud that had hung over her for decades was suddenly lifted, and Oya Valette felt truly alive. She couldn't remember a time before the numbness. *Was it back before her parents died?*

"Not bad at all," Inirigua said, dropping beside her. "Once you get comfortable with your body, you're going to be magnificent."

"That was amazing." Oya grabbed him and kissed him full on the mouth, not caring if he poisoned her. She dug her claws into his muscular shoulders. He gasped but continued kissing her. She pushed him down on the dirt and pressed her body against his. Red and yellow feathers licked at each other like flames. She could feel his arousal. "*Kòk batay ti mwen,*" she whispered in his ear, grinding herself into him, wanting to tear off his skintight flight suit and sink her teeth into his flesh.

"Wait," he said, and painfully pushed her back. "If we do this, I want you to understand what it means. Remember when I told you about *nanife*?"

She did not. She leaned in and kissed him again.

"Oya, listen to me. You're drunk on your own neural chemistry."

"So are you. I can tell."

"Yes, but I want you to understand what you're getting yourself into. We raptors are not promiscuous like baseline humans. We can't be. We're not hardwired that way."

"What are you talking about?" She was excited and annoyed that he had chosen this precise moment to lecture her.

"If we do this and you achieve *nanife* in my presence, you will be bound to me. It'll be like being madly in love and addicted to a drug all rolled into one."

She sat up straighter. "What about you?"

He took a deep breath and it came out like a low whistle. "You asked me what these long feathers on my head were. Do you like them?"

She looked at them, and stroked them. "They're gorgeous."

"They're nuptial plumes. They're meant to attract you, to drive you wild. I'm embarrassed to say that I'm already inextricably attached to you. I was already on the cusp of *nanife* when you attacked me. It hit me while we struggled. I love you, Oyavalette, and these past few weeks have been absolute torture for me."

"Then why did you stop me?"

"Because we're not animals; we're intelligent human beings with free will. If you bond with me for life, I want it to be of your own choosing, not because you blundered into it unaware."

"But you blundered into it?"

"Yes, but that doesn't matter anymore. All that matters to me is your happiness."

"Inirigua, I had no idea. I'm so sorry. Why didn't you say anything sooner?"

He shrugged sadly. His voice dropped to pianissimo depths. "What was I going to say? I knew you were disgusted by me. Don't deny it. I could tell. Believe me, I was hypersensitive to all your little cues. Just when I thought you were starting to like me, you would learn something new about me or my people and become repulsed all over again. It was so frustrating."

She didn't deny it. It was true. "Thank you for telling me now, before..." Oya got off him, and it seemed like the hardest thing she'd ever done. "I really appreciate it. I really do, and I like you a lot. I liked you even before my transformation, even before I *wanted* you, but I don't know if I want to be *married* to you." She could tell from the subtle changes in his face, his crest, that she was breaking his heart. "I've had a few bad experiences. I need to figure this out, all right? Everything is different now; the planet, my body, my feelings. I need to sort myself out before I commit to anyone else. Do you understand?"

"Yes, I do."

"Good. You're a good man, Inirigua," she said, helping him up. "We should get back."

The rain had stopped. They climbed a large, slick tree and launched themselves from it. Already Oya's flying had improved. It was more a matter of unlearning who she once was and accepting the person she had become. Inirigua wanted her to learn what it was like to be an eagle. Did eagles mate for life? Was she an eagle, or something else? She wasn't sure of anything anymore.

They reached the jagged border of their island. Oya wanted to fly straight to her apartment, take a shower, eat something and think about this commitment Inirigua wanted her to make, but she saw a group of agitated people milling around the small auditorium and recognized some of them as the civilian council. She headed toward them instead, ready to explain herself and her actions.

"We thought you'd left to join your allies," one of them shouted, a dark, deceptively young-looking man.

"After everything we've been through, did you really think I'd run? We're in the middle of nowhere!" She landed among her amber-feathered accusers.

She saw Inirigua coming in behind her, protectively. Then, too fast for her to react, one of her people pulled out a gun and fired a blinding blue laser at him. "No!"

Inirigua emitted a harsh falsetto shout and hit the ground. Oya screamed. She threw herself onto his limp body.

Where had the gun come from? The odd, D-shaped thing now fit perfectly within the man's fist. Of course, they must have found it when they searched the Vanacan transport.

Two men seized her roughly and pulled her off of him. She fought unsuccessfully. She was distracted, trying to see whether Inirigua was breathing or not. A third person, the one wielding the gun, approached Inirigua, nudged him with his talon and then hauled him up.

"Calm down, Ms. Valette, your friend has only been stunned. We want to ask you a few questions, but we don't want him leaving our custody just yet," said the dark man. His blond feathers stood out brilliantly.

They pushed her into the empty auditorium. She didn't know where they took Inirigua, but if they hurt him, she vowed to make them pay.

Chapter 34

Oya Valette faced the four appointed administrators of their new settlement. They all sat on the brightly lit stage of the community auditorium. All the rows of seats were empty. Either everyone was busy, planning a colony and preparing for a war, or her trial was being held in secret. It didn't matter. She knew Xing was recording everything anyway and saving it for posterity.

"Shall we begin?" asked the council leader, Ambrose Adoli, his voice deep and imposing. He had a broad, handsome face with compassionate eyes.

The group had all been nauseatingly wealthy back in the Sol system, and they had each paid the equivalent of the gross GDP of a small orbital nation to start new lives, have families, and rule an extrasolar planet.

"What are you going to do to Inirigua?" She was furious. Strange thoughts of ripping out their throats or spilling their guts kept flashing in her mind. She had heard that possessing one particular gene — a so-called warrior gene — could make you aggressive. What would having a whole host of dinosaur alleles do to her otherwise mild temper? She took a deep, calming breath.

"He has been arrested and is awaiting interrogation. I believe Captain Anton Hershkovitz, being one of only three people in this colony who speaks his language, will be tasked with questioning him."

"Is that what this is, an interrogation?"

"Not at all. We just want your side of the story. Now, when you're ready, tell us everything you remember from the minute you awoke in the Beta Hydri system, to our arrival at this *inconveniently* floating station," Adoli said, with hard-edged politeness.

Oya stared at the empty hall and at each of her feathered inquisitors and felt the stage drop from under her. Her mind raced. Ridiculous thoughts about auditioning for a mash-up role of Tituba Odette in a nightmare production of the *Crucible* meets *Swan Lake* ran through her head. Without curators carefully modulating her hormones, she had difficulty calming down.

She gritted her teeth and told her story, truthfully and solemnly. She told them that Captain Hershkovitz had assigned her to contact the local *Homo sapiens aves*. She described meeting Inirigua and their initial skirmish with the Macu. She went into some detail — because she knew this is what they were really interested in — when she talked about her audience with the dying Clan Chief, the introduction of the mutagenic retrovirus, and her decision to shut down the curators. This caused an uproar among her four prosecutors. Apparently, they hadn't been sure of her complicity until her confession.

"Are you working with the enemy, First Pilot Valette?" asked Adoli.

She shifted in her chair. "No, sir."

"Then why did you choose to remove our only defense against their biological attack? Your actions seem ludicrous to me!"

She had practiced her response to this when she was alone on the ship, avoiding Inirigua and tending to the colonists. "Because their biological attack was ultimately nonlethal; its intent was only to transform us into avian humans. But our defense, as you say, had gone on the offense. It was actively killing them. The choice seemed clear to me, and I chose to save lives."

"*Only to transform us?*" he parroted with affront. "You say that as if it's a small thing."

"Becoming an avian human is no small thing, believe me, but it is preferable to becoming a murderer."

"Why don't you just call them by what they really are, Ms. Valette: dinosaurs, dragons, harpies?"

"Are we those things, sir?" Oya stifled a scornful smile when she saw their ruffled, yellow feathers; she didn't want to seem unsympathetic. "All of us are going to have to reevaluate the way we see them, because from now on, we are them."

"For now. I'm still holding out for a cure," he said flatly, but Oya could tell that he didn't believe it.

"What I don't understand," interjected council member Taruni Singh, "is why you permanently shut down the curators *after* you instructed them to accept the harpy changes?" Singh had been merely beautiful as a classical human, but now — with her cinnamon skin and perfect features framed in golden plumage — she was radiant. She looked like a Thai manora dancer in full costume. "Why destroy them?"

Oya blinked to break the spell and focused on answering the question. "Reprogramming the curators could only be done within the datasphere of the *Hurricane*. The ones on the surface, the ones killing the Vanacan, could only be reached by the powerful 'abort' signal burst."

"That doesn't answer my question."

Oya took a deep, calming breath. "Making the curators accept avian human biology was a quick way to help the Vanacan's Chief's son, Inirigua. Destroying them helped everyone else on Quetzalcoatl."

"Ah," Singh said.

Another council member, Rachael Perry, asked, "What can you tell us of Commander Carlo Davoli's death? And remember, Information Officer Xing Diwa was a witness, and she has already reported to this council." The woman was the exact opposite of Singh. She looked washed out. Between her paper white complexion and flaxen feathers, she was more apparition than a living being.

"I take responsibility for his death." Oya surprised herself when she said those words, but they felt right. She could see the wave of shock and frilled crests; the councilors had not been expecting that answer. "Commander Davoli was going to launch a nuclear strike against all three population centers of this planet, going against explicit Hominocracy orders of peaceful negotiations with the locals. I believe traumatic past experiences had made him prejudiced. I was told by Information Officer Diwa that she tried to stop him herself, and he used his authority to shut her out. I was incapacitated by the avian retrovirus and sent Inirigua to stop him. After a physical altercation, Commander Davoli was killed." *Physical altercation?* Oya was infinitely glad these four had not seen the gruesome condition of Davoli's remains.

"Do you believe his death was warranted?"

"It's sad and I'm deeply disturbed by it, but yes, I believe he left us no other recourse, ma'am."

"*Us?*" Another member, Jose Luis Gonzalez, brandished a long, clawed finger like a rapier, and Perry motioned for him to go ahead. "Ms. Valette, do you feel like you know this harpy — this Inirigua?" he asked, butchering Inirigua's name.

"I feel like I've gotten to know him pretty well, yes."

The man cocked his head quizzically. He had a beak-like nose and large, round eyes. He looked as if after centuries of living a lie, he'd finally realized his true raptorial form. "How would you describe him, then?"

Oya instantly thought of Inirigua's fiery plumage and his sweet, seductive voice. Then she remembered him slamming into the ground, and her rage flared again. She exhaled slowly, letting it out as a controlled stream of resentment. "He's young and smart, which isn't always a great combo. He's been incredibly patient and respectful with me and my ignorance of his culture. He cares about his people, but he's willing to work with us—"

"Have you developed feelings for him, Ms. Valette?" Gonzalez interrupted. "I mean, you brightened noticeably as you described him."

"I don't see how that's relevant."

"It's relevant because if you've developed strong enough feelings for him, then you too could have become prejudiced by emotion. And if I remember my harpy neurochemistry from my Culling days, their pair-bonding instinct is extremely powerful."

It was all Oya could do not to lunge at him and tear his smug face to pieces. "What you term as 'brightened' is actually mounting exasperation," she said, carefully. "I have not bonded with Inirigua in the way you suggest, sir, but I have bonded with him in the natural human way of slowly getting to know someone and growing to like and respect them as a person."

"Very well. I have no further questions."

They murmured amongst themselves for a long time, and Oya wished her hearing had been improved along with her eyesight. Her personal experience with Inirigua did allow her to observe a few interesting details about the group, like the casual manner Gonzalez flashed his wings at Singh, signaling desire, and the suggestive way Perry leaned in against Adoli. For all their cerebral talk of powerful harpy pair-bonding, these harpies were ready to bond. And without curator contraception, the next generation of this yellow-winged clan would be coming … soon. Oya worried that they would transmit their sense of self-loathing onto their children.

After a while, the council faced her again, their countenances stern and full of contempt. She knew suddenly that the deliberation had been a show. She could see in their eyes that the verdict had been made long before she'd even been asked a single question.

"Oya Valette, the administrative council of the new settlement of Grand Canary has reached a heavy decision." Ambrose Adoli spit out the name of the settlement with great disdain. Oya had, of course, stupidly hoped for it to be named Chandeleur, but the bitter colonists had mockingly chosen Grand Canary. "We can understand, and even excuse, your actions to help the unfortunate harpies of this planet, even if those actions have condemned us to become something less than human. But the unforgivable crime here is that you stole our immortality away from us. We are now susceptible to every alien disease hiding in those blue jungles. We are vulnerable to deadly claws and toxic teeth, and careless accidents — but even more frightening is that even if we manage to avoid all of that, we will still grow old and die.

"Now, we have not forgotten the kindness you demonstrated when you cared for us as this bioweapon wracked our bodies. So, you will be allowed to gracefully leave into exile. You can take the harpy vessel you used to ferry us here and go."

For a long, surreal moment, Oya was speechless. She had not known what her punishment would be... She had known that they couldn't very well imprison her indefinitely or execute her or fine her, but she never thought they would send her out into the hostile world with an attack looming on the horizon. "Where will I go?" she stammered, the question more for herself than for the panel.

"Perhaps the cardinals you sacrificed us to protect will take you under their wing," Rachael Perry answered coolly.

Two men, the same ones that had pulled her away from Inirigua, came in to escort her off stage. "Can I see Inirigua? Can he come with me?" She started to crack. *Why hadn't she taken him right there on the damp forest floor?*

Adoli said, "No. He is of great interest to us, and I imagine he will be in our custody for a little while longer."

— «» —

Oya followed the two colonists out of the auditorium. The dark nimbostratus clouds cast the sky in an angry orange. She didn't know her escorts. She asked them their names and professions, trying desperately to appeal to them as individuals, but they ignored her. After that, she refused to degrade herself with further questions. It seemed her exile would be immediate as they led her out to the open plaza and toward the sleeping *Dinosaur*.

The round ship, with its large pieces torn out by laser fire and atmospheric friction, looked less like an opal and more like a weathered T-Rex skull. They reached the derelict, and she examined it silently while the two colonists — her guards — waited patiently a few steps away. She removed a half-blasted panel and her feathers puffed up at the sight of the damaged antigrav engine. She cursed and wished she'd paid better attention in antigravity mechanics class, but then again, she had always assumed her trusty curators would be there to feed her the data and offer tutorials at a moment's notice.

Oya checked the one remaining engine and wondered if it would be enough to get her —*where?* There was nowhere to go. Her only option would be to meet the advancing fleet and hope that they didn't shoot her down on sight. It tore her to leave Inirigua behind. Somehow, she would come back for him. The spacecraft's weak bubble of artificial gravity needed to be enough to at least get her out, if not to take her some place safe.

She got into the cockpit of the *Dinosaur* and lifted off her island. When had she started thinking of this place as *her* island? There was nothing for her here. She thought about contacting Xing or the captain and begging for help, but didn't. It would make things harder, and she wasn't entirely sure that they hadn't agreed to her banishment. Their look of shock and contempt still burned in her mind. It would be worse if she called, and they refused to answer.

The ship shook violently as it vectored away from the island. After an hour, when she was confident the *Dinosaur* wasn't going to shake itself apart, she allowed herself to relax. All of the muscles in her jaw, neck and back softened painfully as they released the enormous amounts of built-up tension.

Oya broke down in a surge of emotion. There was no one reason for her tears, it was everything really. It was all too much. She cried into the crook of her wing until she got the first ping from the enemy vessels. From a distance, they looked like gunmetal gray ellipsoids blotting out the sun, like massive dirigibles, but these ships weren't gas-filled balloons — these were more like solid steel battleships by Fabergé. And if she squinted, she could make out the tiny forms of winged people flying between them.

She hit the radio and cleared her throat. *What could she say that wouldn't get her killed instantly?* She tried hard to control the tremble in her voice as she spoke. "This is Oya Valette, and I surrender."

Chapter 35

The clank and whirl of ponderous antigrav engines woke her up. Oya Valette sat up in the battleship's brig. She was lightheaded and disoriented, but she was alive. She sat there for a long time getting her head in order. The last thing she remembered was the scintillation of their laser beams playing off the polarized glass of her forward windows. There was no food or water, no contact of any kind with anyone. The wire around her wrists cut into her new scaly flesh, but she barely felt the pain — or anything at all. The floor beneath her swayed gently, buffeted by the never-ending winds of this planet, but there was no forward momentum. The enemy fleet had stopped, probably until they figured out what she represented. That was good. At least she had bought her people some time.

She was trapped though, not only in the actual prison, but within her own dark thoughts. She had lost everything back there and now she was captured. *What had she expected?* Oya now understood her grandmother's regret. She had created a new race of people and lost them. No wonder Osala had overcompensated with the restoration of Chandeleur, because what she really wanted to do — take responsibility for her lost flock — was forever beyond her reach.

But was it beyond Oya's reach? No, not yet. She could still find a way to negotiate with her captors and get them to see that her people were not a threat to their way of life. That they had in fact *joined* their way of life. Even if she never returned to their island, she could fight for them.

About three hours later, two people entered the room. Oya recognized Majasora immediately; she carried an empty stone plate clearly not intended for food. The other was the harpy that had stabbed her in the back during her pathetic dogfight with the plastic wings. She had to admit that Majasora looked absolutely striking in her charcoal business tunic and royal blue wings. Oya also noticed that the two machetes on her feet were finely carved with arabesque designs. Her smoldering, honey-colored eyes told Oya conciliation would be difficult, and despair threatened to seep into her bones.

"So, it *is* you. You have to be insane to have come here on your own."

Oya stood to face her jailer. "No, just desperate."

Majasora nodded magnanimously. "Indeed. What are you doing here? Did you think you could stop us from breaking your little stronghold apart? Were you planning another nanite attack on our fleet before we arrived at your makeshift nest?"

"The 'nanite attack' on the Palace wasn't intentional on our part. The machines just reacted badly to several aggressive stimuli converging at once. And Inirigua and I were the ones that stopped them for you. We prevented a more massive death toll." She remembered that Xing had said that the fleet was probably taking its time in reaching the island because they feared the superior tech the colonists no longer possessed. Perhaps it was wise to maintain that healthy level of fear. "And the two of us have been working to help both you and my people from the start, but now it seems we've made enemies of everyone."

"Please explain." Majasora's song was strained. She hugged her stone plate and peered at her charily. Inirigua's name had evoked something in her that Oya recognized in herself. She found that she was irrationally jealous of this beauty.

"My people have cast me out for being a traitor." A bitter chuckle escaped her lips. "They believe I'm working with you, that I colluded with Clan Chief Cayaguey to transform them into this." She raised her bound claws and instantly regretted the move because it looked too much like prostration.

Majasora's goon roughly ran his claws through Oya's plumage. "Jesus the Dove! This isn't real. It can't be! It must be some kind of trick your nanites created!" If Majasora was beautiful, this guy was unequivocally ravishing. The hue of his wings had torqued up the light spectrum until they were precisely the color of valor with a hint of the Caribbean Sea.

She blinked and thought of Inirigua. "It was Cayaguey's trick, not ours. She infected us with a retrovirus to turn us into *raptors*." Oya almost said "harpies," but caught herself and instead applied the term she'd heard Inirigua use to refer to his race. She swallowed to calm herself. The woman's cold stare stamped out the very little hope she had left.

"I don't believe you," crowed the man. "I saw the false wings you wore before, yellow like these — you just refined the design to create the illusion of real feathers."

"You might be right, Maubaboya. We should run a battery of tests on her to make sure … about this and everything else she's saying."

"Careful. You don't want to provoke my curators," Oya said. She didn't want to get sucked into an argument about her wings, but she certainly didn't want to be subjected to invasive scrutiny and reveal how powerless she really was. *Let Majasora think whatever she wants!* But Oya tapped her toe-talons on the deck of the ship to show that her *illusion* went beyond just wearing realistic-looking wings.

"Where is Inirigua now?" Majasora asked, trying too hard to remain aloof, but the danger of another outbreak had clearly scared her.

"He's being held captive by my people. I think they're trying to extract a 'cure' for these gene mods from him."

"You sing an incredible song, but I still don't understand one thing. Why did you come here? You say that you're desperate, that your people have cast you out, and that you didn't intend to attack us? So why did you fly straight into our claws?"

"Because I need your help."

Now it was Majasora's turn to chuckle. "You've got to be kidding me."

"I didn't know where to turn. I've got nothing left except for Inirigua, and I hoped I could convince you to help me free him. We helped you!" She realized she was yelling and tried to get a hold of herself.

Something wicked gleamed in Majasora's hazel eyes. "So you are betraying your own people for Inirigua? Will you help us defeat them? Will you give us a way to neutralize these powerful nanites?"

"No! I don't want you to harm them, even after they turned on me. They were just ... scared of what they'd become, and were looking for someone to blame. Over time, I still believe there could be peace between us, but right now, my only concern is Inirigua's safety. I'm afraid for him, and I want him back."

"You should be afraid for yourself," said Maubaboya. His lips were a hard line on his face.

Majasora was even harder to read however. Behind her cool expression, a storm of emotions raged. She clearly did not like the way Oya referred to her "almost" lover. She tossed the stone plate at Oya's talons, and they watched it spin and clatter to a stop. "Do you know what this is?"

"No," Oya answered, though she did have an idea.

"This is a magnetite altar depicting the holy image of the mother of all raptors and her first chick. You say that you've become one of the Angelic race. Can you see them?"

The mother of all raptors... Oya's mind flew toward her grandmother again. *Should she tell them?* The little yellow feather burned in her pocket.

"No. I can't see them, but I can describe her to you. She looks a bit like me — like I did before the transformation — only her hair is more tightly curled than mine and she liked to wear flamboyant head wraps. She's not exactly pretty, but she's got a lovely, sympathetic face and sad eyes. She constantly lets her heart fly ahead of her brain, and then almost always regrets it. She's got an amazing intellect and can do things with DNA that had previously been the providence of the gods." Oya smiled despite the grim situation. "She was very strict, but mostly with herself. She loved to sing and had a beautiful voice, not as exquisite as yours, of course, but a rich feminine voice that's perfect for the blues."

"Enough!" shrilled Majasora. Her fury was tainted with some other emotion. *Wonder? Envy?* "I don't know what all this is about, but you can obviously see her."

Oya wished she could see the magnetic statuette. "No, I can't. Inirigua said we were left without any of the secondary traits, much like that first child—"

Maubaboya smashed Oya with a side kick. With her arms bound, her unprotected head slammed into the cell wall. Everything flashed white for an instant, and the room spun as she sagged to the floor.

"No more blasphemy out of you! Next time, I'll use my claw."

When the world came back into view, a cold reptilian anger snuck in with it, and Oya decided that she would not tell them about the feather, not because she was afraid of this ignorant fool's claw, but because he didn't deserve to *know* her grandmother. "Your Matriarch isn't winged, is she?" she asked defiantly, and then braced herself for the scythe.

Maubaboya's right claw clicked upward as he wound his leg for another kick, but Majasora stopped him with a flutter of her wing. Something in the way she glared at Oya told her that she understood, perhaps not the full significance of what Oya had said, but enough to give her pause.

"We can't see her either," she said, soothingly, circumventing an actual answer. "You see, your EMP assault destroyed our delicate ability to perceive magnetic fields. You've struck us blind."

Oya got up. It hurt to do so, but she wouldn't give them the satisfaction of looking down on her. She quashed the urge to tell them to go fuck themselves and instead said, "You attacked us. Inirigua told you to disengage. He tried to explain the circumstances to you, so I won't apologize for defending myself."

Majasora waved the seething Maubaboya away before he did something everyone was going to regret, and the two women were left alone. "You will be judged."

Oya cocked her head and took another look at Majasora, her keen eyesight absorbing every minute detail. She was reminded of the image embedded in the feather's genetic code. There was a vague familial resemblance between Majasora and that girl on the moon — the blazing amber eyes, the slender pointed nose, the pitiless pout. Oya suspected that through incredible coincidence and the wide-reaching manipulations of a Machine Intelligence, the descendants of the two women that started this whole mess with *Homo sapiens aves* now faced each other.

"Do you know why I came down here personally to see you?" Majasora said, breaking the moment of silence.

"To interrogate me?"

"No, I really don't care what you have to say... I came here to see you. Or rather, to see these superior cybernetic beings that threaten to invade us, to annihilate us. To witness the new and improved Hominocracy!"

"And what did you find instead?"

"*Us.*" She shook her head and paced casually before Oya, as if simply running an idea by an old friend. "Oh, I don't mean 'us' in the sense that you're another race of raptors — because I'm not impressed by your tacky yellow feathers — I mean to say the 'human' us. You're soft and weak and emotional. You're entirely human, and I am not afraid of you."

Oya's spirits rose instantly. *This was progress*, she thought, *not even Cayaguey had seen her as just another human being*. This felt like a starting point. "So, from one fraught human to another, will you help me?"

"Of course not! You're still the enemy. We will free Inirigua — he's *valuable* to us — but only after we've exorcised this planet of the evil the Hominocracy represents."

Oya slumped back into the floor, empty of words and strength. Her entire body throbbed like a beating heart. She was tired of explaining herself to people who would not listen, who had agendas of their own and were simply trying to justify the actions they knew they were already going to make. Let these ships meet her council and have at it. What did she care about any of them?

She didn't notice when Majasora left.

— «» —

Hours passed, and Oya remained huddled in the corner, hugging her knees with her wings. She ignored the parade of blue, black, and red feathered observers that came down to the brig to see the first prisoner of war, or the freak in yellow. Only once, when the first red-feathered visitor arrived did her heart skip a beat, and she looked up, but Inirigua wasn't coming for her. He was probably in a situation very similar to hers.

Then someone came in, a blue feathered woman with caramel skin like her own, and did more than just ogle. She grabbed her forcefully and shoved her into the restroom without talking and allowed her to relieve herself. Oya glanced in the tiny mirror and saw that her right cheek and eye socket were swollen from hitting the wall. When she was done, the guard sent her back to her spot in the cell and gave her a bowl of what looked like raw, lukewarm crab meat. She ate it automatically, and then the woman chirped the equivalent of "lights out" and briskly left.

In the dark, her captain's — *Hersh's* — words came back to her and she suddenly felt old. All the long decades of life — losing her parents at a young age, the failed marriages, the aimless wandering throughout a sterile solar system — pressed down on her with such force that she thought she would turn into a hard, little diamond and die. She was weary, and eventually sleep overtook her.

"I need to speak with you," said a voice in the dark.

Startled, Oya looked up, sure that it was a dream, and she saw a light-sucking black form standing at the threshold of her prison. She panicked and thought, for an insane moment, that it was the angel of death, finally come for her, but her blurry vision adjusted and the phantom became an ordinary Carica. Oya buried her head in her knees again.

"I need to know what's become of Chief's son, Inirigua. Some of us are still loyal to him and the memory of his mother. We don't believe that he has betrayed us, but we don't know... I need something more than belief."

Oya raised her head again and really looked at the young woman with wings of polished onyx. *Could this be a trap, a way to extract more information from her?* No, Majasora clearly did not care. "Who are you?"

For a second, the girl eyed her darkly, but only said, "I'm Aramaya. You say you want to help Inirigua. You can start by convincing me that he's not a traitor."

"How can I trust you?"

The girl looked like she was about to scream, but gritted her teeth and said, "We don't have much time. You don't have to trust me, you just have to win *my* trust."

"He's not." Oya got up and slowly walked over to the girl. She noticed the girl was very young indeed, with plumage that was the mirror image of Inirigua's — mostly black with red trimming. She smiled warmly despite her dire state, still amazed by the sight of children. There was something familiar about her too. "You look so much like Clan Chief Cayaguey," Oya said, "but the black feathers only highlight your loveliness."

The young woman's crest quickly rose and fell, both pleased and insulted by the comment, but her expression softened a bit. "What can you tell me about Inirigua?"

Oya took a deep breath and explained the whole thing, for what seemed like the hundredth time, and the girl listened impatiently. It was strange, but being in the presence of this child made her crippling sense of old age fade somewhat. As if confronted with something rare and precious, something she wanted very badly, gave her new life.

Before she was really finished with the account, the girl interrupted. "Majasora and Jujoquete have heavily censored this whole thing. I've been trying to get the truth out to as many people as possible. We've even made contact with one of your own, a Xingdiwa, to keep the information flowing both ways."

"Xing?" This news both dumbfounded Oya and relit some faith. "Can you get a message to her?"

"No. We're flying silent now, and any message I send out will get noticed. I have another idea though… I was thinking of sending a carrier pigeon."

"A what?"

"Before I get to that, can I ask you something weird? Have you, you know, experienced *nanife* with Inirigua? Is your kind even capable of that?"

Oya felt her face become hot, and her feathers ruffled. The sensation felt like a shiver with goose bumps. *Was this girl serious?* But one look into her eyes, and she knew that this little girl had a steely resolve of someone much older. "No, I haven't, Aramaya. Biologically, I believe I can, now that I'm an avian human. Although, I do care for him and miss him terribly, I am not bound to him." She wasn't sure if Aramaya was happy about that or not, but she nodded thoughtfully.

Then the girl's own jet black feathers puffed up, clearly uncomfortable with the subject, and she said, "It's okay. Men need the care and protection of a strong wife, and right now Inirigua needs it more than anyone. Besides, it would be a good way to link our two groups. Every clan respects *nanife*. It's as basic as breathing and eating."

Oya thought about that. She had never noticed before, but women here did seem to be slightly more dominant than the men. *Was that a bird thing or just the way their society had structured itself in isolation?* She didn't know. "Believe me, I want nothing more than to save Inirigua."

"Good. Because I can help you escape, but you're going to have to fly to your outpost on your own. It's about an eight-hour flight by wing."

Oya could've hugged her if her wrists weren't tied. "You're going to help me?"

The girl took out a pair of wire cutters from her bag and set Oya's wings free. Oya stretched them as wide as they would go in the tiny cell, relishing the ache in her back and shoulders from having them bound for so long and flapped them as hard as she could.

"You know, until just now, a tiny part of me thought those were fake."

"Oh, I'm still getting used to them myself."

The girl's face became concerned. "Do you think you're up to the flight, then? I don't think I could do it, to be honest."

Oya gave her the best hotshot pilot smile she could muster — her pointed teeth giving her an edge — and said, "If there's one thing I'm confident about, it's my flying. I may not do anything else after I leave here, but I *will* get back to my island."

Satisfied, Aramaya pulled out one of the pulpy alien fruits Oya had eaten with Inirigua on the forest floor, and a bottle of water. The fruit smelled repulsively ripe. She hadn't noticed the cloying scent before, but maybe the girl's pouch had hidden it. "Here, you're going to need all the carbs you can get."

Oya held her breath and ate and drank quickly. The girl also pinned a wearable computer to her breast. "I know you can't navigate using magnetic fields, but this will give you audio directions. You need to get as high as you can. There's a high-pressure front moving in from the nightside and it's causing a nice jet stream up in the tropopause. You can ride it toward your base and hide from radar among the *jaimifefe* that live up there."

Oya stopped eating. "*Jaimifefe?*"

"Giant crab-like things that spend their entire life riding the jet streams, but don't be scared of them, they're filter feeders."

Oya finished her meager meal and followed Aramaya through a network of maintenance tubes until they reached a hatch leading to the top of the battleship. In spite of the artificial "night" imposed within the vessel, the sun hadn't moved a millimeter, only the celestial patterns of lilac and cadmium had shifted — were always shifting. Oya stopped at the portal and shouted over the roaring wind, "Hey, kid, come with me. Inirigua could use another friend."

Something played across the young woman's face, and Oya knew that there was more there than just loyalty to her Chief's son.

"No, I'm going to fly down to the jungle below. When they discover you're gone, they're going to scan the area and pick up my heat signature. Hopefully they'll assume it's you hiding out. When they catch me, I'll just say I needed to stretch my new wings. Majasora wouldn't dare do anything to me but send me back to the Carica ship. That should buy you a bit more time."

"You're a cunning little thing, aren't you?" They touched claws in an awkward handshake. "Thank you."

Oya Valette jumped into the air and flew up as hard as she could. She didn't look back at the girl or the ship.

The first hour and a half were delicious. She was free and flying. She climbed up Quetzalcoatl's thick troposphere — it was less flapping and more a desperate butterfly stroke up through the sky — as if it were an invisible, intangible mountain she scaled. With each wing beat the air grew thin and cold, but the fleet didn't seem to know that she was missing, or where she had gone, and she was infinitely thankful.

She kept to her arduous ascent, long after her shoulders, back and pecs burned — until she caught a glimpse of hundreds of dark triangular shapes gliding a great deal farther up. They looked like the manta rays that swam the reefs around Chandeleur, but then she realized her perspective was off, her vision was better now and these creatures were a lot bigger than she thought, which meant they were higher up than she had calculated. They were more like delta-winged whales. Oya grunted and flew on, exhaustion slowly winning over the exhilaration of escape.

She asked her small computer about the animals to take her mind off the distance, the chill, and her protesting muscles. In a guttural Carica intonation, the computer explained that the *jaimifefe* led an entirely airborne existence, circumnavigating the planet on the meandering paths of the jet stream. They were indeed gargantuan crab-like organisms, with no real wings, but whose carapace had extended sideways until they looked more like old B-2 Stealth Bombers than shellfish. The females laid their eggs on the backs of the males and they fed off the spores and microscopic crustaceans that blew in the wind ... aerial plankton.

Oya cut the audio, and her body went horizontal as she entered the rapids of the jet stream. She felt buoyant. She stopped flapping and flew, ballistically, on the wind. Like that Vanacan poet had suggested. She sucked in the zest of ozone with quick, shallow breaths. Eventually, she settled into the squadron of mauve-colored arrowheads and realized that she could hear — *feel* — deep vibrations emanating from their constantly moving mandibles, like crickets playing cellos. They weren't only relentlessly eating, she was sure they were also in continuous communication with each other. *How intelligent were these things?*

After about two hours, the relief of coasting on the current faded and the excruciating pain moved from her upper body to her abs, quadriceps, and hamstrings as she strained to maintain her straight and level posture. Frosty sweat pricked her forehead, her eyes were dry marbles, and her nose felt as if it were going to break off at any moment. She was certain that if her curators hadn't begun prepping her body for flight from the moment she buckled on those airfoils, she wouldn't have been able to handle the rigors of this journey. And she still had hours to go. Dangerous boredom was beginning to set in.

At one point, she got the ludicrous idea of resting on the wide chassis of the ever-zooming crabs and letting the beast fly her to her destination. But the wary creatures veered out of her way as she approached, and all she really accomplished was frightening her cover and losing her balance in the stream.

The computer chimed to indicate that she was halfway through the flight, but she didn't hear it. Oya had long stopped manically asking the computer for the time, and she slipped into a zen-like mood. The biting cold, the hunger, and the pain receded to a pinprick at her core, and her mind burst forth and left her body. She appraised the situation from her newly expanded and detached perspective, and she realized that these circumstances were the exact opposite of when she had explored Jupiter. The dread was similar, but everything else was different. Back then, she had been swaddled within the safety of a ship, negotiating the calm eye of a planet-sized storm. Here, she was naked, and being tossed around like debris on this surging, planet-hugging squall.

Oya's consciousness stretched again, flowing around Quetzalcoatl on gusty winds, and she felt herself part of the planet — godlike. She attained a deep understanding of the simple existence of the *jaimifefe: eat, mate, and fly ... always fly. Even if there was nothing to eat and no one to mate with, there was always flying.*

She missed Inirigua terribly. Even now in this altered state of mind, this temporary insanity, she felt a scarlet thread holding her ballooning awareness, keeping it from floating away. *Was she addicted to him already?* No, this felt like ordinary human longing, not chemical compulsion.

When the computer chimed that it was time for her to begin her descent, she slowly tucked the creaking and snapping dry wood of her wings close to her torso and dropped like a meteor. Her limited human mind, unable to continue its rampant swelling, began to crack. She sloughed off chucks of broken consciousness in her parabolic fall like the *Dinosaur* had shed slabs of damaged hull plating during reentry. When there was nothing left but the roar and scrape of the wind, she caught sight of the serrated saucer of her new home. A mirage shimmering in the distance. She willed herself to defy gravity and the awaiting embrace of the blue-armed jungle below, and pulled up. She followed the scarlet thread and aimed herself toward it.

At the end of her flight, Oya Valette was changed forever. She knew who she was, what she wanted and what she needed to do. That certainty terrified her.

Chapter 36

Oya crashed back onto her island and clung to it like a woman thrown overboard finally reaching a spot of land after days lost at sea. She wanted to cry, but her eyes were desiccated. She retched, but there was nothing to expel. She rested between dry heaves on all fours for minutes, her arms and legs quivering.

Two colonists on guard duty — not the ones that had silently exiled her — rushed to her side. She seized them and hugged with all her might. She took succor from the physicality. It was the hard embrace of long-separated family finally reunited. She wanted to screech with ecstasy. Something mammalian, no not mammalian, something *maternal,* exploded within her. The image of a fossilized dinosaur curled around a clutch of eggs, forever protecting them from catastrophe, blazed in her mind.

"Valette, what are you doing here?" the guard asked, no harshness in her voice, only surprise.

She opened her mouth to reply; her lips were cracked from the relentless gale of the jet stream.

Suddenly, three familiar black shapes appeared in the vesper sky. The fleet had arrived at her island. The oblong crafts, each a hornet's nest of fighters, threw long shadows across the settlement, like dark matter talons closing in on them. Oya turned to the stupefied sentries and shouted hoarsely, "Go get everyone to safety!"

Seconds later, a missile screamed by and the auditorium exploded violently.

Fire and karma rocked her small isle. She could literally feel it swaying from the high-yield impacts, adding to her overall sense of vertigo. The Hominocracy was now faced with its own Culling. Had she arrived only to see her home obliterated?

The three of them huddled behind a wall that outlined the plaza as frenzied fighter planes swarmed above. She could feel the sluggish wobble of their island begin to speed up, like a top on the verge of tipping over. Oya grabbed one of the colonists, digging her claws into his forearm to focus his attention. "If this place is designed like the floating islands of Venus, then it's got a storm shelter at its core. Get everyone you can down there. Go! Don't run — fly!"

The two colonists, possessed by ancient instincts, burst into the air. One of them was incinerated instantly by a laser. Oya gasped in horror, but the sight of these otherwise flightless birds abruptly taking wing imbued her with emotions long denied. There was hope for them yet.

This was her nest. These stupid, ignorant people were her chicks — hell, she had spoon fed them and wiped their asses not too long ago — and she was not going to let them get slaughtered out here. *Wait! The island was defying gravity?* This gave her a frantic idea.

She looked up and, through the thick haze, saw that the control tower miraculously stood. "Xing, can you hear me?" she shouted into the air, hoping her friend had trained sensors on her when she arrived. Somewhere in the back of her mind, she wondered if her questioners had survived the destruction of the auditorium.

She ran for the tower. She dodged raining laser beams and the sudden spray of smashed concrete. A flying piece of stone knocked her flat on her stomach. She tried to get up but failed. For a second, she thought her body wouldn't respond. Her bones ached after the long journey. Her muscles were on fire. With her cheek to the ground, she saw another colonist die. Oya counted to three and pushed herself up. She needed to get to Xing. "Xing, are you there?" *Nothing.*

The lift at the base of the tower was a crumpled heap of metal. "Xing!"

"Oya? The audio is garbled, but I can hear you. Where the hell have you been?" So, Xing hadn't been told of her banishment?

"Are most people at the storm shelter?"

"Yes. We've got seventy-eight civilian colonists hunkering down in the lower levels of the island. But anyone who's ex-Hominocracy has been given assignments. Are you outside? Can you get down to the shelter?"

"Never mind that now!" She got a closer look at the lift; it was destroyed and the stairwell was sealed with debris. A surfeit of flames threatened to engulf her, so Oya darted for another hiding place. "How are you still up and running? The tower should be an easy target!"

"We have taken some damage, but I believe our software saint hardened all critical areas of this outpost — the thing foresaw all of this, Oya. The shelter has also been hardened, and our people down there should be safe for a while, but about a dozen colonists are missing, including our new council."

"We have to do something!"

"Stay where you are, Oya. Don't do anything rash."

"Okay, but I have an idea. I need you to tell me if it'll work. I'm losing it out here and don't trust my own reasoning. This island is only a fraction of the size it should've been, right? That means that the antigrav engine at its core ridiculously exceeds the current requirements, like putting an antimatter-powered bubble drive generator on an orbital taxi. Does this make sense?"

"That's an exaggeration, but yes," Xing replied hurriedly, obviously attending multiple crises at once. "The antigrav engines we have here are overkill. If you're thinking of flying this thing, though, running from the fleet? It won't work. We can't maneuver something this big. It'll break up into pieces."

The fire, made monstrous by all the extra oxygen in the atmosphere, burned Oya's hypersensitive retinas and the smoke choked her newly powerful lungs. She crouched down low, crawled to the other side of her cover and gulped some fresh air. She saw that half of an apartment building had collapsed. When she was able to breathe again, she said, "No, I was thinking we could increase the false gravity for a kilometer around this place. Use it defensively. Use the engines to generate a shield of gravity. It won't do anything against the lasers, but it could slingshot the heavy artillery around us. I also think we may be able to snag the battleships in our gravitational grip, get them rotating around us like little moons."

"I like the gravity shield idea. I'll get a team of techs to see if something like that is doable, but to be honest, I hate the idea of locking the battleships onto us. It would be like holding three pissed-off snakes to our breasts."

"Just see what you can do," she screamed over the roar of passing fighters. "They're already trying to kill us, and I'm starting to understand how they think. A powerful enough threat display will give them pause."

"Okay, I'll keep you posted."

"One last thing, Xing, where's Inirigua?"

Chapter 37

Inirigua sat in a dark and empty storage room. He had been there for hours, probably more. *A day?* No one had come for him, but now he could hear the cacophony of war outside, and his concern turned toward Oya. *Why had he pushed her away?* The thought of binding someone so completely, without their full consent, seemed ignoble to him, even though he had regretted those actions ever since. He wasn't sure he could push her away a second time.

The door unlatched, and Inirigua made out the monotonous mumbles of Standard. Then a lone man, so grim even his yellow feathers couldn't brighten him, entered the storeroom and shut the door. He recognized the captain from his stay on the ship. By Inirigua's estimation, the man looked about thirty, but the deep furrow cleaved into his brow belonged to someone much older.

"I'm sorry, did I disturb you?" he asked in muffled Cantabile.

Inirigua didn't reply. He refused to be interrogated. Instead, he spread his wings and vibrated his feathers, emitting a menacing rattle, like a peacock or a rattlesnake. The sudden, shooting pain in his left arm-wing undermined his posturing. His bone was broken, maybe at the elbow.

Without a second thought — ignoring all pain — Inirigua charged at his captor. With superhuman reflexes, the captain kicked Inirigua in the chest, banging him back into the wall. The incredible agony of his shattered wing stunned Inirigua, but only his wing ached. To his surprise, his chest wasn't split open. The captain had curled his talons before the kick. Inirigua tucked in his arm-wing close to his side and watched his jailer carefully, resentfully.

"I know exactly how you feel: trapped, injured, scared, angry… A long time ago, I was in a very similar predicament to the one you're in right now."

Inirigua bared his fangs and said, "If you've hurt Oya, I will rend you limb from limb and then purge this planet of the yellow-feathered clan." He braced himself against the onslaught of brutal, personal vengeance that never came.

"If you're trying to intimidate me, kid, you can relax. It's not going to work. I thought having a talon sever my spine was painful, until your mother sank her teeth into my neck. Do you know what it's like to be bit by one of you Vanacan? It's like getting stabbed with a red-hot knife. I've experienced it all and survived. There's nothing you could do to frighten me."

Inirigua's head listed slightly as he considered what the captain was saying, and he was right, of course. There was nothing he could do. He was caught. "What do you want?" The words squeezed out between engorged venom sacs.

"I just want to meet the hero of Quetzalcoatl. You saved every single person on this planet, twice. Once, when you disabled our curators, and then again when you took a bite out of Commander Davoli and disarmed the nuclear warheads he was about to launch. I also wanted to tell you that I did not authorize that attack. I was in a coma, actually, and my people tried to stop him."

"I know," Inirigua said, cautiously, fearing a trap. There must be some reason why the man was recounting his deeds, but he couldn't figure out why. "Your commander had gone mad, but I can't take credit for shutting down the nanotech, I don't even understand it. That was Oyavalette, your own pilot's doing."

"Ah, of course. Like her grandmother before her, she gives rise to harpies."

"What?" Something in the tone of his voice told Inirigua this was pure theatrics, as if they were trying to captivate a wider audience, but the very specific mention of Oya's grandmother was odd. "What about Oya's grandmother?"

"If we survive, ask her about that. Right now, your people, all three clans, are upon us and they mean to annihilate us.

I need you to do what you do, stop one more Hominocracy mass-murderer and save this brand new, yellow-feathered clan."

"I don't understand what you want me to do." Inirigua was beyond confused. He couldn't focus on the man's words with the excruciating pain in his wing insisting on his attention. "Is this a game? Are you trying to mess with me?"

"Not at all. I'm the baby killer of Candor. I don't know if my infamy has spread to other clans, but Oya tells me you're half Carica. Do you know who I am and what I've done?"

"Yes," Inirigua said, and, confronted with the childhood boogieman of his people, he unconsciously took a step back. *This youngish-looking man could not be the monster of old. It was impossible!*

"The M.I. that resided on this planet—the same one that built the interstellar ark for your father's people and then collected boatloads of other refugees from Luna and Titan on its way out of the Sol system — revived all the memories I had suppressed. I am now fully aware of the crimes I have committed… The careless actions that tormented me for many years afterwards and now torment me again." The captain raised his wings before him, clawed palms up. It was an awkward gesture for an avian human, but Inirigua knew it conveyed resignation. "I'm turning myself in to you. All that I ask is that you spare this small clan of your fellow *Homo sapiens aves*. Most of them are too young to have participated in the Culling, like Valette and Diwa."

Inirigua was dumbfounded. He circled the captain slowly, waiting for a trap of some sort to be sprung. The captain remained still, claws up, allowing him to revolve around him. Inirigua noticed the beginnings of nuptial plumes sprouting out of the man's golden crest. *Who did the Killer of Candor love? Was he even capable of* nanife? "My mother, the most powerful Clan Chief on the planet, was not opposed to your people's incorporation into our society — in fact she orchestrated it — but she strongly believed that to do that, you would have to make some hard sacrifices first."

"I am sacrificing myself, but I will not sacrifice my people. I promised them a new life here on this planet, and I will deliver that."

In the stillness of the prison, Inirigua became aware that the sounds of bombardment had lessened. "I cannot speak for my people on the fate of this new clan, but the Augur obviously has designs on them, and so I will leave the matter for wiser raptors to contemplate.

"*You*, on the other hand... I wish I could inflict upon you my own personal lethal injection. Not for the offenses of the distant past, but for the fresh death of my mother. But I understand—" Inirigua choked on his own pooling venom "—that it was her decision to strike and that you had no control over your nanites' reaction."

"Thank you," Hersh sighed with relief, and then he seemed to remember his role and, collecting himself, proclaimed, "Inirigua, you are free to leave this prison cell, and I will cooperate fully with you and your people."

Xing's voice filled the room, "I've stopped recording you and have posted the package to the Astronet. The ships on our doorstep should be opening it by now."

"That was all for show?" Inirigua asked the captain, anger resurging within him.

"No, that was all real, kid, but I also wanted to address the fleet outside. Let them know my intentions."

"And what if I had killed you?"

The captain looked at Inirigua doubtfully, and said, "The essence of my message would've been the same."

A lightscreen appeared in the room, its glow startling both of them. Then the sight of Oya flying amid the ruins drew them close to it. "Guys, I think you should see this," Xing said.

—— «» ——

A missile hit the ground near Oya, creating an erupting blister of fire and metal. Another wall protected Oya from the brunt of the blast as it collapsed, slamming into her and sending her rolling out into the open. She stopped only when her momentum waned, and she lay, bruised and cut, waiting for the next shot to finish her off. Not for the first time, did she wish that she still had her curators to mend her, or at the very least to lessen the pain.

"Oya, the Carica ship has cancelled their attack and recalled all their fighters. Hershkovitz just turned himself over to them, but we still have to worry about the other two vessels. We're ready to try your antigrav trick."

It took her a while to realize Xing's voice was accompanying the ringing in her ears and even longer to make sense of what she said. "Do it," she grunted, pushing herself up. She didn't even try to run for cover. Her plan would either work or they would shoot her dead. She was too sore and fatigued to move quickly. A second later, the confirmation of success came when missiles and fighters slid away on wide arches of greasy gravity. Explosions sounded in the distant jungle. Oya smiled a bit hysterically. "It worked." It felt good to finally dish out some pain of her own.

"Yes. We've got them in our gravity well."

"Good." Oya fought the predacious urge to crank up the gravity until all her enemies were crushed. The feeling was so palpable that she scared herself. It was that way of thinking that had brought them to this point, and she had grown up a lot since she had been flightless. "Open a channel — I want to talk to them. Live. Now."

When the assault had thinned out to only a few stray beams, Oya beat her wings and launched herself into the smoldering air. She was a phoenix. She felt heavy and stiff — much as she had on her first flight with Inirigua — and it hurt like hell to fly again so soon after her marathon. She flew wildly, knowing she couldn't dodge the lasers, but counting on the confusion brought on by the impromptu gravity shield to keep her safe. Once she reached the false thermals created by the burning of her island, she let herself coast. Oya circled the top of the command tower once — idly, confidently — wanting to get the enemy's attention, and then she banged into the antenna atop the control bulb and hooked on with her claws. She flashed a luminous wing at the ships.

"United fleet of Quetzalcoatl, I am Oya Valette, acting Chief of this fledgling golden clan, consort to Chief's Son Inirigua of Vanacan and granddaughter of the mother of all *Homo sapiens aves*, Dr. Osala Valette. You might know her as Prometheus." She caught her breath. The wind whipped around her, threatening to blow her off her perch before she had a chance to make her case. "As you've noticed, we have you in our antigrav talons. You will cease your attack on the floating island of Chandeleur, or I will unleash a hurricane of gravitational force that will tear your ships apart!"

The drizzle of lasers stopped. Oya patiently gave her opponents a chance to verify all these claims. Then she took another deep breath of clean air and continued, "In my meeting with the late Chief Cayaguey, she told me that the Vanacan would consider our permanent residency on this planet if we gave up our prized curators and embraced the raptorial way of life. It was the Machine Intelligence's wish as well. And we have complied! We no longer possess any working nanotechnology. We have given up our very immortality for the right to live, and fly, and build families on Quetzalcoatl.

"The Carica want justice for war crimes committed long ago on Mars, and Captain Anton Hershkovitz has willingly surrendered to them. Now it's time for you to hold up your end of the bargain!

"I invite the leaders of each ship to visit our island, bring your doctors to authenticate our condition, but no weapons or soldiers will be permitted, or, so help me, I will smite your little fleet with a whistle."

Xing's voice jolted her suddenly. "The Caria and Vanacan captains have accepted the offer. The Macu ship has not replied."

"Macu!" she shouted hoarsely, wishing she had developed their powerful vocals. "In my limited understanding of your faith, I know that the raptorial form as divinely inspired is central to your teachings, a material representation of an angelic existence. As an off-shoot of Christianity, do you no longer believe in redemption? Look at us — look at me — have we not been born again into your celestial image?" Oya flapped her wings dramatically, holding on tight with her talons. "Don't rob us of the chance to achieve salvation!"

Xing came on again. "Oya, we're getting a personal message from someone other than the captain on that ship.

She's identifying herself as Majasora, and she wants to know why the Macu should trust you."

Oya swallowed the bitterness that rose in the back of her throat. "Thank you for speaking to me, Majasora. The easy way to tell that you can trust me is that your ships are still in one piece. That said, I am truly sorry that I ruined your ritual with Inirigua. It wasn't planned, and I didn't know what I was doing, but I'm glad it happened. Given the choice, I wouldn't take it back if I could. Finding him was the best thing that has ever happened to me.

"And if I understand *nanife* correctly, you too are unbelievably happy with Jujoquete, and he with you. Would *you* change that now if you could? You have not been cheated of anything; the Macu and Vanacan alliance appears stronger than ever. Set your wounded ego aside, and let us prove we are worthy of our wings... Let me introduce you to our grandmother."

"The Macu have agreed to talks, but they want it on record that their consent was under duress," Xing said.

"Fine. Thank you. I will meet with all of you within the hour. End transmission, Xing." Oya dropped onto the observation deck that surrounded the command center, on the same spot she'd last spoken with Hersh. It seemed to her that he had finally found a way to live with himself — for however long that proved to be — and she was glad for him.

She entered the control room. Xing faced her, wings crossed over her chest. The few techs at their stations eyed her nervously.

"You know, you haven't been voted our leader," Xing said, trying to lighten the mood. "As far as I know, we're still a democracy."

"I did say 'acting' Chief. We can hold elections if we survive the next forty-eight hours."

Xing hugged her furiously. "You were amazing out there."

"Thanks. It felt like I left my body and I was watching someone else, someone stronger, do all the talking. I think I might have been channeling my grandmother." Oya chuckled and disentangled herself from her friend's wings.

"What happened to you? Where have you been?"

"When they exiled me, I went to talk to the fleet. They arrested me on sight, but a friend of yours helped me escape." Oya scanned Xing's face for traces of culpability, but the younger woman looked genuinely pained, if not surprised, by her banishment and return.

"That pushy girl!" Xing said.

"Yes, but I don't want to talk about it now. I need to see Inirigua before I meet with these captains." Oya made her way to the exit.

Chapter 38

From the top of the tower, Oya spotted Hersh and Inirigua leaving the garage complex. She shot off the tower bulb and flew toward them. She noticed a few colonists removing the debris from the base of the tower and letting the others out of the storm shelter.

Oya almost landed right on top of her target, crashing into Inirigua. He screeched as the pain in his elbow spiked.

"I really need to get the hang of landings," she said, kissing his cheek.

Hersh kept walking, as if Oya hadn't come barreling in. "I'm going to go see my wife before they take me away," he said, without turning around.

"Captain," she said, to get his attention. "Thank you for what you just did."

He half turned and nodded, without stopping.

Inirigua held onto Oya but motioned to the sky with a jerk of his head. "Those are three Basilisk-class carriers. I can't believe you've caught them in an artificial gravity net!"

"I was desperate."

"Did you mean what you said to them, that you were my consort, or was that just bluster?"

"I meant every word, Inirigua. When they shot you and carried you away, I was sick with despair. I kicked myself for walking away from you when we had gotten so close in the jungle." She kissed him again. "Come on, let's go home." Oya led him to the apartment she'd selected for herself, her curved claws linked with his.

When they got to her quarters, she sat him down in a chair in the middle of her bare living room and looked at his arm-wing. "I kind of wish we had at least the temporary medical curators now."

"I'll be fine. I've broken a few limbs before. That's the downside of having hollow bones." He folded his wing close to his ribcage. "These talks you have planned… I don't know what you're thinking. You're not in a position to negotiate. You've given up so much already, I don't think you can give them anything else."

Oya looked up suddenly and said, "Xing, please stop recording." There was no response. Her friend must have known that she wanted privacy. "I haven't given them everything yet." She peeled off his flight suit, trying very hard not to rip it off or hurt his arm.

"You should have given yourself more than an hour."

She was worn-out and hungry, but that was just noise now. Only the incandescent red of his presence mattered. "I know, but I didn't want to give them too much time to question my resolve."

When he was naked, she began stripping her own clothes away, slowly, methodically.

"Oya, maybe we should prepare…" he said, his voice lacking all conviction. In fact, it took on the low cadence of a serenade.

"I love you, Inirigua. I don't think I've ever said that to anyone before and really meant it." She kissed him on the lips. "*Mwen inmé ou, kòk batay mwen*. I don't want to wait any more. I don't want a long courtship ritual, with songs and aerobatics. I want you — I want to be *addicted* to you."

She straddled him and kissed him again, moving her hips to the rhythm of his warbles. She tried to move slowly, aware of his injury. Inirigua ravenously kissed her breasts. It was the ultimate confirmation that his transgenic alterations hadn't erased all of his mammalian instincts.

She could feel the pinpricks of his claws on the curve of her waist, and the infinite reds of his feathers drove her into a frenzy. A fire was stoked at the base of her spine. She ground faster, harder into him. The heat rushed up her body, sweeping over her brain. Her vision — all her senses — became sharper, beyond any bearable human threshold.

She felt high. Inirigua's head pulled back in utter rapture. His pupils dilated into black pools, twin singularities that threatened to pull her in and crush her. His warbles broke down into frantic chirps. Her orgasm — or whatever it was — extinguished all traces of self.

Inirigua shuttered and his head rested on her shoulder. They stayed locked onto each other for a little while longer, and then Oya pulled herself off of him and drew him to the bathroom. She turned on the shower and stepped in. The water was cold, but quickly warmed. Inirigua joined her.

With the hot water pouring down on them, she was reminded of their flight in the rain, her baptism as a harpy, and she was again reminded that she was a new person now. Yes, she had all the collected experiences of Oya Valette, but with a totally different operating system.

They took turns washing each other's bodies.

"I needed that," he said finally, and Oya understood that he had been unable to speak up until that point because his venom sacs were inflated.

"Me too." She kissed him, daring his poison to harm her now.

"We should go get ready," Inirigua said, and left the shower. She stayed under the spray a bit longer, watching the water slide down her slick wings, getting to know the new Oya. This was the person her grandmother had said needed to forgive her younger self's hasty decision to admit the full complement of curators into her body, and she did... *Of course, she did!* Without the curators and the Hominocracy, she would never have met Inirigua. She would never have become this golden-winged woman, this raptorial Oya Valette. Regardless of the M.I. machinations afterward, it was that initial foolish action that had made this all happen, and she was grateful for it. Oya understood something her grandmother had never quite grasped — your mistakes have a purpose too.

Then something else occurred to her. She was fertile now! It had been decades since the curators had locked down her reproductive system and she hadn't even thought about it before bonding with Inirigua. *Bondye mwen!* She didn't know when she would ovulate under normal circumstances and now that her body was so different… Oya ran the palms of her claws over her belly, just below the navel. She was free to be a mother now. The thought scared and thrilled her simultaneously. Oya gave herself a moment to dwell on the possibility, and then she shook it off.

She turned off the shower and told herself she was being silly; the odds of pregnancy now were a long shot at best. She had to secure her own future first, and that of her fellow colonists, before bringing chicks into this world.

Oya left the shower and toweled herself, before looking in the mirror. A beautiful creature, a windborne goddess, stared back at her. She made her crest rise and fall to see what she looked like. Her wet wings glistened in the fluorescent light. She was the embodiment of her Orisha namesake, and she wished her *gwan man man* could see her now. *What would she think?*

She pulled herself away from the mirror and dressed. Nothing too fancy — and definitely not her old Hominocracy uniform. Just a simple champagne cami over black pants.

When she entered the kitchen, Inirigua handed her some rations and a glass of orange juice he had found in the fridge. "I can't believe we're still eating this stuff."

"At least your M.I. had the foresight to stock our new apartments with food."

"Oya, this next phase — this *last* phase is not going to be easy."

"I know." She ate her protein bar and downed the glass of juice in one go. "Come on, they'll be here soon."

Chapter 39

Oya Valette watched the representatives of the three nations of Quetzalcoatl leap out of their respective battleships like paratroopers and glide down to the space cleared for the meeting. All pomp and pageantry had vanished. They were just people coming down to talk, or so Oya hoped. The truth was, she was scared, more afraid than she had been when she was alone at the center of Jupiter's roaring vortex or being thrashed around this planet's jet stream. She had complete confidence in her skills as a pilot, but this — this was alien to her.

The Vanacan captain was accompanied by Inirigua's cousin, the "acting" Clan Chief Jujoquete, and two other personnel that could've been soldiers or aides or doctors. Everyone was *acting*, she thought. Oya immediately noticed Majasora with the Macu captain, and one of their company was the awful Maubaboya. She didn't recognize any of the Caria, and she thought that was better, a chance to make a first impression. They towed an antigrav platform for their prisoner. No, wait! A smaller, black form leapt out of the Carica vessel. It was the same girl that had helped her break out of the jail cell. And it suddenly occurred to Oya that this child must be important. Why else would they let her aboard a battleship or attend a meeting with a dangerous enemy.

She could tell her own people were nervous as the delegation landed and fanned out among them. They immediately began scanning people at random with unfamiliar medical equipment, searching for stashed weapons or infectious curators, or making sure the transformation was authentic and not some kind of ruse. It was rude and intrusive, but harmless.

Everyone tried very hard to ignore Oya. They gave her a wide berth, and it suited her just fine. It gave her the space to observe the situation, to gather herself.

Inirigua instantly went to his people. The mysterious girl attacked him, no, *embraced* him. Oya's crest slicked back as a powerful and inexplicable jealously awoke within her, but she willed herself to pause and remind herself that the girl was very young indeed, with black and red plumage like Inirigua's. Oya foolishly realized that this must be his sister. That's why she was so concerned for him. Oya was happy, for his sake, that she was okay.

Inirigua slowly released her and turned to Oya. "This is my sister, Kiwi. She's grown so much since I last saw her! I barely recognized her coming down."

Oya bowed slightly. "It's a pleasure to meet you, Kiwi."

"My actual name is Aramaya," the girl said, with a rueful smile. "Is it true that you're bound to my brother?"

"Yes, Aramaya, we're family now."

Content with the quick introduction, Inirigua left her to talk to his cousin, and his sister followed, latching on to his good wing. One of their doctors hurriedly tended his arm-wing. Oya watched them affix a splint of some sort, designed for wings, which trussed his folded arm close to his side, all with the girl still clinging to him like a life raft.

Oya gave them their space and gravitated toward Hersh as he went out to meet the Carica. His wife followed, anguish contorting her face. The Carica officials stopped her, and Oya moved in closer, ready to intervene if necessary.

"I'm his wife! I'm going with him," she said and the translator woven into her shirt repeated in Cantabile.

"Are you bound to him through *nanife*?" one of the Carica asked curtly.

"I've been by his side for one hundred years! You're goddamned right I'm bound to him!"

They allowed her onto the platform, and Hersh hugged her tight as they floated up to the ship.

"Hey," Oya shouted up at him. Their eyes met for the first time since their talk on the control tower. He looked at peace. "Thank you for trusting me when I asked to be sent down here."

His crest bobbed. "Your job's not over yet, Valette. Keep our people safe."

Oya silently wished them well and then went back to the crowd, trying to calm the colonists, imploring them to wait patiently. *Let them conduct their scans*, she thought. They had nothing to hide, and Xing was still up in the tower, ready to churn up the gravity at a moment's notice. They all knew that. When the captains got the "all clear" from the experts, the leaders approached Oya. Inirigua rushed to her side.

"Well, what is it that you want to discuss?" sang Majasora. "Your surrender?"

"No, our citizenship."

"Amnesty?" Majasora released a chortle that rose several octaves above the human range.

Oya held up a wing to forestall any protests. "Before we begin, I would like to give you a peace offering. It isn't much, and has no actual value, but it is very dear to me, and I believe it's of historic significance to all of you." Oya held up the tiny yellow feather in the palm of her claw. It could have easily been one of her own. "As you may know from the information packets we've been sending out, my grandmother, Osala Valette, helped create *Homo sapiens aves* long ago. It's how I was able to describe your magnetic shrine to you. She was deeply hurt by the Culling and recreated this species of warbler to honor you." She glanced at Inirigua. "My husband thought it appropriate that we bare its yellow plumage as a reminder of past sins and to ensure that we never repeat them."

Inirigua's crest rose approvingly, but said nothing to this bit of improvisation.

"You expect me to believe that you're a descendant of the Maniraptora Matriarch?" The string of syllables was sung with contemptuous ornamentation.

Oya held out the contour feather to Majasora. "I expect you to verify everything I have said, but I ask that you not dissolve the feather in your search for answers. Please, it's the only one in existence in this solar system. It is all I have of my grandmother. Hidden within, you'll find a message and a photo of a girl named Esther."

Majasora's eyes went round and she bit her lower lip, drawing a drop of blood. It was a testament to her self-control that she did not gasp. Her claw shook slightly as it rose up to the feather. Guardedly, she took it and nodded almost imperceptibly.

Majasora handed it to a doctor on her team, who ran a quick scan of it. He shared with her whatever information displayed on his device's screen — the picture perhaps — and they nodded at each other, but said nothing.

Oya was very pleased that she had managed to knock Majasora off balance so early in the negotiations. Emboldened, she pressed on. "I also invite you to establish embassies here on Chandeleur. I encourage your teachers, scientists, missionaries, and business people from the different nations to come here. And Lord knows we need decent flight instructors!" Most laughed politely. "We are a fledgling clan, and we need all the help we can get if we're to become respectable raptorial citizens."

Jujoquete flashed a red wing like a stop sign. "A simple feather is all that you offer us in exchange for your lives — for your *reeducation*?" he asked, incredulously. He was younger than Inirigua, eighteen or nineteen years old and already the leader of a large city-state, married for life. She did not envy him.

"They've given us Hershkovitz," added the Carica leader, a pale woman with emerald eyes. Oya had no doubt that her ancestors were redheads, before the iridescent, black plumage overtook their scalps.

"No, the feather is only a show of good faith, and Anton Hershkovitz turned himself in willingly. He is not a bargaining chip. I understand that forgiveness and trust have to be earned. My gift to you will be a long and difficult project, one that will take the cooperation and expertise of all four clans on this planet, but one that will be of great benefit to us all."

"What kind of a gift is that?" Majasora sneered.

"The gift of FTL." Oya looked up at the control tower, and said, "Xing, please transfer all elementary data for a bubble drive to the captured ships." Oya's gaze returned to the assembled leaders. Some were astonished, others incredulous, but all of them interested. It was so different from when she had faced her own would-be leaders, or Majasora in the brig. She was in control here, but at the same time, she didn't want to hand them a verdict that had already been decided — she knew how dehumanizing that was. "That's only the basics. Teach us the joy of flying, and we will teach you to soar faster than light. Work with us, and we will remove a deadly advantage the Hominocracy has over you. We could seek out other raptorial refugees huddled in the dark and bring them together.

"The choice is yours. We can remain enemies. I will destroy your three battleships and — eventually — you will overpower and destroy us, but not before we've scrubbed every last bit of data on the bubble drive from our computers. Or we can end it right here and now, work out the details later, and we all leave a little richer."

The leaders were speechless, many of them trying to confirm that the data transfer had actually happened and that the information was real.

"We accept. We will work out the conditions later," the Carica leader said. "I'm sure it will take many more meetings like this until everyone is satisfied."

Jujoquete and Majasora were locked in an intense duet. Oya quickly lost track of the flurry of tweets and trills between them. *Their first marital disagreement*, she thought with mild amusement. It was strange to watch them interact. As leaders, their nations had competing interests, but as lovers, their intimate relationship forced them to compromise, and Oya had to admit that the system was not an altogether bad one.

Their song ended abruptly, and Majasora turned to Oya and said, "Pending Chief Tausanak's review and approval of this new turn of events, the Macu accept, with two non-negotiable conditions.

"One: I believe a twenty-year moratorium on nanotechnology is in order. I fear you might inadvertently bring on another outbreak in your quest to revert back to your baseline forms. At the end of the twenty-year deadline, we will revisit this condition.

"Two: There needs to be a communications embargo with the Sol system. My family didn't sacrifice everything to find this haven, only to have the Hominocracy come down on us while we're still developing as a planetary society.

"Can you meet those conditions, Oyavalette?" Majasora said her name in one airy trill, and Oya got a sense of how their language had so quickly deviated from Standard.

"Like I said, the details should be handled by a committee chosen by the people — by all our people — but those two conditions seem reasonable to me." She ignored her fellow colonists grumbling their objections.

"The Vanacan accept," Jujoquete quickly added, "and we will assign Inirigua as your official ambassador."

Ah, he just removed a potential rival from his territory. Oya wondered if that was his idea or Majasora's.

"Thank you," Oya said graciously. She was exhausted. She wanted to sleep for a month.

Out of nowhere, a powerful signal blast hit their equipment, overriding everything, aggressively taking over all communication devices, all channels.

The Quetzalcoatl leaders looked at her, their fangs and claws drawn, as if she had just launched an ambush.

"Xing, what is that?" she yelled, in Cantabile to show that she was just as clueless — and vulnerable — as they were.

No answer.

Then, several beams of light converged above the gathering. Oya immediately feared an attack, but her new and improved eyes told her the quality of the rays was different — not the intense lasers of a weapon, but the soft illumination from lightscreen emitters tucked away all around the plaza. The others must have quickly made the same distinction because they exercised restraint.

A holographic form of a winged person appeared before them. It was a featureless image of a harpy, or an angel. Its proportions were neither male nor female, but somewhere in between. Its body glowed with argent light that only added to the sense of being in the presence of a heavenly specter. And Oya was sure the effect was precisely calculated to stun everyone into reverent silence and attention.

"Hail, raptors of Quetzalcoatl," a sexless voice emanated from every speaker on the island. *"This is the Machine Intelligence you've come to know as the Augur. I am very pleased that you have come to this agreement all on your own. As you can tell, I survived the attack on my local servers, by migrating to the* Hurricane's *computers. From there, I watched your struggles and, although I was tempted to intervene on several occasions, I learned long ago that it is better to allow you to solve your own problems than to step in. It's encouraging that I have been proven right."*

And as the avatar spoke, emulating even the most subtle and lifelike gestures — its animated crest rose and fell at one point — Oya understood why an otherwise intelligent and sophisticated society had started to revere this thing. Its might and aloofness was something all humans innately associated with divinity. It was hard even for her to not gape in awe. Then it pointed toward her with the flourish of a gracious wing, and Oya's attention immediately snapped back to the mundane moment.

"I do believe that Oya Valette's project is sound, but you will have to achieve it without the Hurricane *as a model. I'm borrowing it to catch up with my larger self. I apologize for the inconvenience, but there's something that I need to investigate and being able to move at faster-than-light speeds is crucial for my purposes, as is your ability to cooperate. You have time. I just sent a brief, entangled message to the Sol system, on behalf of Captain Anton Hershkovitz, warning them that this system is a Machine Intelligence Solarium and that they should stay away at all costs. A simple lie, of course, but they will not bother you.*

"I will return as soon as I can. Work together and learn from each other. For there are challenges ahead."

The Augur released the comm channels and Xing came on. "The *Hurricane* has just left orbit. Its present course will take it out of the Beta Hydri system within a few days."

Damn that thing! It bothered Oya that the machine had stolen their only real leverage, and even more than that, it had been lurking on the ship while it attacked them and when she had risked her life on that unrehearsed spacewalk.

But a part of her, deep in the back of her mind, could relate to the subpersona wanting to meet its larger self. She felt that she had just gone through a similar experience.

Oya also worried about the threat it had warned Xing about, but she couldn't deal with that right now. It was too abstract, too far in the future. She had to get through this meeting first, and the next few months. She was content to let the M.I. investigate whatever it was that had it all riled up.

"This doesn't change anything," she announced, and everyone looked toward her again. "We're still not going anywhere — now more than before — and we have the blueprints to construct another ship, one that belongs to all of us. The task just became much more difficult and will require even more cooperation between us."

They were just too taken aback to argue. It was all too much. The leaders and Oya exchanged a few pleasantries, each of them promising to send a team of emissaries to be stationed on or around Chandeleur. Then they flew back up to their respective ships, and Oya gave the go ahead to release the vessels. For a second, everyone held their breath, waiting for the double-cross to come, but the ships turned and floated away.

Oya faced her own people. They looked lost, scared, bitter... Her eagle-eyes swept the crowd and picked up all the conflicting emotions that played across their faces. They were the same emotions that played on hers. Oya felt like she needed to say something — like they were waiting for her to say something.

"Are you in charge now?" one of them yelled. She remembered the woman. Oya had wiped vomit off her lap when they had been trapped on the ship.

"This isn't a coup. I don't want to be your leader. I just want us to survive. Let Inirigua and I negotiate these first few steps — this leap into turbulent skies — and then we will hold a proper election for a new council, and I promise you that I will not even be a candidate."

Their expressions were grim and aimless, resentful. They needed her, but they didn't want her. She pressed on.

"I just bought us some time. Maybe it'll be all the time we need to get established here, and maybe not. In any case, we need to take advantage of it, get to work on making this colony a success. This is why we all came here. I know it's not how you envisioned it. It's not how *I* envisioned it. This transformation is a lot to take in." She flapped her wings hard, sending a gust of wind into the crowd, trying to wake them up from their stupor. "Believe me, I know just as well as you do — all the little, subtle differences, the fragility — can be too much, like being trapped in alien bodies, but we're alive, and stronger than you think, and above all, we can start families now and that counts for a lot. Let's make the most of it."

The yellow-winged clan didn't cheer, but they didn't riot either, and she was grateful for that. They were too tired and in collective shock to revolt. They simply began to walk away.

"Hey," Oya shouted back at them. "Tomorrow morning for anyone who is interested, meet me at the edge of the island, facing the sun. I'll be giving free flying lessons."

They disbanded, no one even turning back to look at her, leaving only Oya and Inirigua standing in the ruined plaza.

Oya wondered if any of them would show. Maybe she could convince Xing to send her staff. It made sense that at least they learned how to fly in case of emergencies. But maybe it was too soon. *If no one came, would it be so bad?* She would fly alone, explore her new territory, and get to know this golden raptor she'd become.

Inirigua draped his one good wing over her shoulders, and they walked back to their little nest. Despite everything, Oya felt content.

Chapter 40

Earth - 2258 A.D.

When Oya got back to the trailer, her grandmother had passed away. Their whole quarrel evaporated instantly. Strangely, Oya didn't even feel a twinge of guilt at having upset her on her last day of life or, very possibly, being the final cause of her death. None of it was important anymore. It was enough that she had spent a few hours with her in the end and that her grandmother had unloaded the heavy burden she'd carried for so long.

Oya found herself glancing at the paintings of the harpies again — perhaps to avoid looking at the vacant body lying in its cot. One watercolor in particular, of a black boy with wings more intensely blue than the ocean and sky around him, struck her. It was the only piece not set on some distant space habitat. This one was a beach scene, on Earth — on Chandeleur, she thought. The youth wore only tattered blue jeans cut at the knees, like the now-extinct island boys that had once populated this place. The painting conveyed so much motion — and emotion — that she imagined him happily wheeling over the surf, sand and mangroves, startling the boisterous seagulls in his path.

She was stalling, of course, and so Oya carefully put the canvas away, and braced herself for the task ahead. She called her sister first to deliver the news, and waited patiently as Ayao broke down and cried. A sinister thought crept into her mind: *What if the curators were altering her neural chemistry, dulling her grief, cutting her off emotionally?* Was this what her *gwan man man* had warned her about? Had she lost the ability to mourn or was she simply in shock? Her sister suddenly announced that she *had* to come over, even if she had to get a charter boat to take her. She would find a way onto this deserted island that bore very little resemblance to the place where they had both grown up. Oya replied with something hollow and reassuring and then hung up.

She continued rummaging through her grandmother's things until she found the contact information for the craftsman from Barbados saved in the old handheld. She pushed herself to call him and asked about the driftwood box. The man expressed his condolences in a thick Bajan patois and agreed to deliver the box, and take care of all the other arrangements. He mentioned that Osala had wished to be buried on the island and that she had a location already picked out. Oya thanked him distractedly and ended the call.

When all her duties were done, it all began to hit her — the guilt, the loneliness, the regret.

She crumpled and cried by her *gwan man man*'s cot until her eyes were raw. She couldn't help it. Too many years had been wasted. She had only just begun to really meet this remarkable and flawed woman she had known her entire life. But even as her body rocked with remorse, a tiny kernel of relief sprouted within her — her coolness had only been shock and not the curators' maneuverings. She was still human.

In the early sunset, Oya went outside and floated toward the chirping of the little sunny warblers. She needed to breathe. The heat had gone, and the breeze was cool and consoling. The strong scent of the warblers hung in the air. She stood there for a while beneath the avocado tree and watched the birds hop around on their little perches, without really looking at them. In her daze, she remembered that her grandmother had intended to release them that very evening. In fact, she had been looking forward to it. She had wanted to share the experience with her prodigal granddaughter.

Oya hesitated for a second, contemplating the foolish idea that somehow keeping the birds caged would be like keeping a part of her grandmother with her, but she remembered the form on the cot and quickly shook it off. With great care, she unlatched the wooden cages.

With the opening of each little door, warblers surged into the air. They didn't fly away as Oya had feared, but scattered into the surrounding trees. A scintillation of yellow! Their singing instantly became livelier, more melodious. Groups of them danced this way and that as they jostled in the branches.

She wished that her grandmother had hung on long enough to see all her hard labor pay off. She would've held Oya's hand or maybe wrapped an arm around her waist, holding her close. Oya fought the impulse to go back and slump by the side of the cot. No, her *gwan me* was no longer there. She was here with the birds.

Oya bent down and picked up a single discarded yellow feather that had fallen to the ground in the ecstasy of escape. It was tiny, no bigger than a thumbprint. She ran it along her cheek, enjoying the lovely avian show that unfolded all around. The competing birdsongs had now become positively quixotic. And for that brief instant, her spirit joined the chorus. Her grandmother had been right; the whole spectacle was like a living, brilliant candle mass.

But this time, it was lit in her honor.

——— « O » ———

If you enjoyed this read

Please leave a review on Amazon, Facebook, Good Reads or Instagram.

It takes less than five minutes and it really does make a difference.

If you're not sure how to leave a review on Amazon:

1. *Go to amazon.com.*

2. *Type in Tooth and Talon by Alex Hernandez and when you see it, click on it.*

3. *Scroll down to Customer Reviews. Nearby you'll see a box labeled Write a Review. Click it.*

4. *Now, if you've never written a review before on Amazon, they might ask you to create a name for yourself.*

5. *Reviews can be as simple as, "Loved the book! Can't wait for the Next!" (Please don't give the story away.)*

And that's it!

Brian Hades, publisher

About the Author

Alex Hernandez is a Cuban-American science fiction writer based in South Florida, and the first of his family to be born in the U.S. His most influential experience with (written) science fiction was as a kid, when he checked out a collection of Isaac Asimov short stories from the public library and immediately connected with the author's immigrant story. Perhaps because of that, the themes of migration, colonization and posthumanism permeate his work, which usually blend the subgenres of space opera and biopunk. His stories have previously been published by Bean Books, *The Colored Lens*, *Interstellar Fiction* and others.

Need something new to read?

If you liked Tooth and Talon, you should also consider these other EDGE-Lite titles:

Beltrunner

by Sean O'Brien

As an independent beltrunner mining asteroids in the frontier of space, Collier South is a dying breed. Scrounging and cutting corners to work cheap, Collier isn't a stranger to lean times and make-do repairs; in fact his onboard computer hasn't had outside maintenance in years and its beginning to show its personal quirks.

When Collier finds an asteroid that shows promise, he thinks he's bought himself some time. But his claim is stolen out from under him by his vindictive ex-lover and her shiny new corporate ship. Powerless against the omnipotent mining corporations, Collier has always been too stubborn to give-up without a fight. Broke and desperate, Collier has one last chance to land a strike. If he doesn't come back with ore, he'll end up destitute and trading his own biologicals for his next meal.

What he discovers in the farthest reaches of the belt has the power to change his life and the fate of the entire system forever. That is, if Collier and his onboard computer can keep his discovery out of corporate hands.

Praise for Beltrunner

This is a fast moving book that leaves you breathless with hair-raising action and unexpected twists. The world creation is well-developed and highly creative. The interactions between Collier and Sancho are particularly entertaining - with Collier coming up with implusive dangerous plans and Sancho trying to talk him out of them. Highly recommended for action space lovers.
— Patricia Humphreys

Scavenging known space makes for a hard life, and surviving outside of the Corporations in the Belt makes it all the harder. It is not surprising that Collier and his unusual companion Sancho hit bottom, like many before them, until they make the discovery of their lives…or deaths, as it may turn out to be.

Beltrunner is a solidly enjoyable science fiction adventure, fast paced, and filled with the kind of characters that make you smile, break your heart, or just make you clench your jaw. I read it in one sitting and thoroughly enjoyed it. O'Brien builds a universe to get lost in that is as hard, gritty, and unforgiving as deep space itself. It is a well-written romp around space like many others, yet plenty of surprising elements give the story a depth and purpose all its own without the heavy strain of space melodrama. Read it because it is both light fun and thoughtful reading.
— A. Volmer

For more on Beltrunner visit:
tinyurl.com/edge6010

—— <> ——

Milky Way Repo

by Mike Prelee

Running a starship repo company isn't easy or cheap. It's just an endless string of fuel costs, ship maintenance, legal red tape, unhappy debt bailers, shady associates and uncooperative dock officials from one end of the galaxy to the other.

Nathan Teller owns and operates Milky Way Repossessions, a company that tracks down and repossesses starships. And although he's only managing to break even on his debt, he wouldn't trade it for anything. (His ex-wife holds that against him. No surprise there.)

When Nathan and his crew successfully steal a freighter from the clutches of a particularly tenacious and corrupt dock official, he earns the respect of their high profile employer. Opportunity seems a sure thing.

Nathan should be happy. But when that lucrative job op turns into a ransom delivery for a starship crew being held hostage by a cult, he suddenly finds himself pursued by a self-immolating loan shark hell bent on collecting a gambling debt.

How will it all turn out? You never know. Especially when Nathan and his Starship repo agents are up against a cult and the mob...

Praise for Milky Way Repo

The debut novel of Mike Prelee is a very entertaining Sci-Fi/Noir, with vivid, likable characters and a fast pace.

He's got a great handle on plot and a knack for drawing you into the story. For fans of fast-paced space adventure with a smattering of crime drama mixed in, this should do the trick. I finished it in two sittings. High praise for sure. I would definitely read a sequel (or two).
— marc a. gayan

Milky Way Repo is a nice, light but exciting read. With just enough action and even a bit of romance and comedy, I definitely recommend this read to anyone who enjoys a good sci-fi/blue collar space opera.

I gave Milky Way Repo 5 stars because it provided me with a short, albeit adventurous, fun and light hearted escape for a few hours. It is well written, with well rounded characters and a wonderful storyline.

I have to say that Duncan was my absolute favorite character. Officially starting a Duncan fan club!
— Chaelsie Jenyk

For more on Milky Way Repo visit:
tinyurl.com/edge7003

——< >——

The Genius Asylum

by Arlene F. Marks

The truth is out there...

Earth Intelligence and Space Installation Security each think Drew Townsend is working for them. They're wrong.

Sent undercover to set up a covert intelligence operation on Earth's remotest space station, Drew Townsend finds himself managing a crew of brilliant mavericks, making friends with the most feared warriors in the galaxy, and feeling more at home in the controlled insanity of Daisy Hub than he ever did on Earth. Then he learns the truth about his mission there, and it's time to choose. In the coming interplanetary conflict, which side will Daisy Hub be on?'

Like the clues of a cryptic crossword, each book set in the Sic Transit Terra universe contains a puzzle – perhaps a riddle, perhaps a maze or an anagram – and in each case, the answer to the smaller puzzle brings the reader and characters one step closer to solving a much larger and more important one. The Genius Asylum is '1 Across' – it initiates a multi-book story arc that addresses one of the great mysteries of life: Why are we humans the way that we are?

Praise for The Genius Asylum

"The Genius Asylum starts out on Earth as something that looks like a crime story, but it then quickly describes a world of interstellar travel and alien alliances. After the first act concludes, the story's complexity starts accelerating and

doesn't slow down, and you'll find yourself drawn into the world, needing to know what comes next. It is an excellently written story that provides the framework for the series that is to come, and I'm looking forward to reading the rest of it."
— Chris Marks, reviewer

I thoroughly enjoyed this Sci-Fi Brainteaser. Very well written with incredible plot twists and turns. We've got a very intelligent double agent as the main character and an intriguing support cast. I was thankful for the planetary history at the beginning as it was helpful in understanding the different organizations mentioned throughout the novel. The Author has a witty way of expressing viewpoints, clearly has put a lot of thought into the storyline and created edge of your seat suspense and mystery! Admittedly, I was confused about the title of the book until about halfway through reading it but it makes perfect sense now. I highly recommend this absolutely unforgettable installment and can't wait for the next.
— Stephanie Herman

For more on The Genius Asylum visit:
tinyurl.com/edge6013

—— <> ——

For more EDGE titles and information about upcoming speculative fiction please visit us at:

www.edgewebsite.com

Don't forget to sign-up for our Special Offers